Best

Kept

Secrets

A Novel by

P.J. HOWELL

Also by P.J. Howell

Jorja Matthews Mystery Series
No Mother of Mine
Best Kept Secrets
Ties That Bind
Cross My Heart
Price of Betrayal

Short Stories
1313 Psycho Path
11:11 Anna's Awakening

NonFiction
Note to My Author Self

Best

Kept

Secrets

A
Jorja Matthews
Mystery

Volume 2

Best Kept Secrets
2nd Edition
Copyright © 2019 Paula J. Howell
All rights reserved

This is a work of fiction. Names, characters, businesses, places,
events and incidents are either the products of the author's
imagination or used in a fictitious manner. Any resemblance to
actual persons, living or dead, or actual events is purely
coincidental.

ISBN-13: 978-1097651498

DEDICATION

For the men in my life:
Carl, Jordan & Conner
With their love and support I can do anything.

And to my entire family:
The unfailing love and support I receive,
as I continue to live out my
dream, means everything to me.

~PROLOGUE~

The slight drizzle on the windshield matched her mood as she drove down the driveway to the house. She mechanically went through the motions while she pushed the button on the garage door opener, drove into the garage and parked her car just short of the tennis ball hanging from the ceiling. She sat inside the car for a few minutes, running the day through her head. She had hoped to come up with an idea to solve her dilemma other than what she had finally decided she had to do. The past few months had been so difficult, the most emotionally draining she had ever been through. After admitting to herself that no further rationalization could alter her decision, she finally grabbed her purse and coat, climbed out of the car and headed into the house. On a normal day she would turn on the television and listen to the news while going through the mail. The girls would already be home from school, having been latch key kids due to her work schedule, and they would excitedly tell her about their day. They would eat dinner, work on whatever homework was due the next day and then they would sit together to watch their favorite evening shows.

Today, however, was not a normal day. The girls were not at the house, the news held no interest for her and the mail was thrown on the table to be left unopened. Instead, she kicked off her pumps, dropped her purse and coat on the table and went straight to the fridge. She pulled a wine bottle from the fridge and placed it on the counter. She chose a wine glass from the cupboard, placed it on the counter and then stood on her tip toes to reach for a paper bag on the highest shelf. Carefully, she removed a glass from the bag and poured a small amount of wine in the glass before pouring her own separate glass of wine. Leaving the half-filled glass behind on the counter, she carried her glass as she slowly walked through the empty house back to the master bedroom.

Scanning the bedroom as she entered, her eyes did not focus on any item other than the bedside table. She opened the drawer to her nightstand and felt her heart flutter when she reached inside to pull out an envelope and a journal. Wishing to hold them no longer than necessary, she tossed them onto the bed before closing the drawer and moving into the attached bathroom.

The bathroom was clean and tidy, as she expected it would be. Her housekeeper, Mrs. Cavanaugh, was an elderly woman who actually enjoyed the very act of cleaning. She herself did not enjoy the chore so did not mind paying someone else who did. She sat the glass of wine on the side of the tub and ran the water, playing with the nozzle until she found the right temperature. She then added her favorite bath gel of vanilla and lavender for soaking bubbles. She took off her jacket and skirt and placed them neatly on the counter after folding them. She then removed her blouse and underclothes which she tossed in the laundry basket. When the water was at the right level, she turned off the nozzle before taking one last glance at her body in the mirror. She had worked so hard at taking care of herself; now she wondered why she had bothered. Shaking her head to keep her thoughts in check, she opened a drawer to remove a plastic baggy she had hoped never to use. She opened the baggy, poured the crushed pills contained in the baggy into her wine glass and flushed the baggy down the toilet. Once she was sure the baggy had disappeared down the pipes, she took a few big gulps of wine before she could change her mind.

She placed the glass on the side of the tub again and gingerly placed her feet in the water. She sat down and then lay back to completely submerge her body in the hot water, enjoying the pleasurable feeling as the hot soapy water surrounded her. It was, she was certain, the blissful comfort babies must feel while they are in the womb. She let her mind drift off as she enjoyed the comfort of the water until it began to lose its warmth and she felt the pills taking effect. With final resignation, she decided it was time. She took one last large gulp from her wine glass and reached for the razor blade lying on the side of the tub. With determination she used her left hand to cut deeply into her right wrist. She was shocked at how much blood immediately flowed freely from the cut. She knew she could not waste time so she moved the razor to her right hand and cut as deeply as she could into her left wrist. Her right hand was already weakening. While she still had some strength, she dipped her right index finger into the blood on her left wrist. She then used her finger to write on the wall in blood…

MICHAEL DID THIS TO ME

Tears ran down her cheeks as she thought of her daughters and she prayed she could be forgiven for her sin. Laying her head back against the side of the tub she closed her eyes and whispered to herself, "God, please forgive me." As she began to weaken and felt her soul slowly dim away, her last realization was how awful the sight in the bathroom would be for Mrs. Cavanaugh when the elderly lady arrived to clean the house the next day.

CHAPTER 1

"I did *not* kill my wife!" Michael Stafford shouted from his chair in Jorja's office. His face had turned red and his knuckles were white from gripping the arms of the chair. After the outburst he quickly lost steam as he leaned back in the chair, ran his hand through his brown, wavy hair and closed his eyes while he attempted to calm himself.

Jorja waited. She could understand the level of his outburst if he was innocent. However, if he was not, she knew it was all just an act. She was trying to figure out for herself what the truth might be.

Michael finally opened his eyes to look at her. "I apologize. I didn't mean to shout. You just can't imagine what it's like to have people believe you killed your own wife. That I killed the *mother* of my children."

She accepted his outburst, but she wasn't yet sure if she trusted his truthfulness. "That's okay. I guess I can understand that, but we need to talk about your case and what you want me to know before I investigate. I'd like to do that without you getting upset whenever I point out anything in the reports that might make you look bad. Your attorney has filled me in on your defense and what he would like me to do, but I also want to hear from you and what you expect. We have to go through the evidence the prosecutor has against you and what a jury might hear if this goes to trial."

Sitting up straight, he replied, "But everything the prosecutor says about me isn't true. The jury is only going to hear lies and based on those lies they might actually convict me!"

Jorja picked up a pen and glanced down at the reports the attorney had provided to her. "Michael, I understand why you're upset. Let's just get through the reports so you can tell me what you want me to know and what I should look into further. Okay?"

He ran his hand through his hair again, took a deep breath and leaned back in his chair. "Okay."

"Good. Now, let's start with your alibi. Where were you on the night they say your wife died?"

"I was home. Alone. And, no, I don't have anyone who can account for my whereabouts. Of course, the police had no interest in believing me."

Jorja made a note on her note pad. She then looked at Michael and asked, "What about your children? Do you have one or two? The reports weren't clear on that fact."

"My ten year old, Tabitha, was at her grandparents. I thought it was best for her to stay there where she'd be less likely to cry herself to sleep after she learned she'd no longer be living with her mother."

She nodded. "And it was that same day you were in court with your wife and you gained full custody of Tabitha?"

"Yes. Obviously my wife didn't take the news well." He reached over to a side table where he had placed his coffee and he took a sip as he waited for Jorja to ask another question.

"And your other daughter? What about her?"

Michael hung his head slightly and stared at his cup. He took a moment to respond before he finally said, "Liz passed away six months ago."

Jorja felt her face flush. The attorney who hired her had neglected to inform her of that fact. She felt terrible going on but she had to continue to gain information from him. "I'm really sorry. I know this must be difficult, but can you tell me what happened? How old was she?"

He took a deep breath as he continued to stare at his cup. "She was 14 years old. She fell in with a bad bunch of kids and began drinking. One night she was out doing God knows what and I got a phone call from the police to tell me she'd been in an accident. It was the worst night of my life."

"Did they tell you what happened? Whose fault it was?"

Michael finally looked at her. His eyes were teary and bright with a madness only a parent who knew the loss of a child too soon could feel. "Oh yeah, they told me. One of her little friends who was old enough to drive thought it would be great fun to drink and drive. He killed not only my Liz, but himself and one other girl. I hope he's rotting in Hell."

She felt a shiver run down her back. Whether it was his anger or the idea of a child dying so horribly, she wasn't sure. She decided to let the subject drop. Going any further was not going to be productive at this point.

"I can only imagine what you and your wife went through afterwards. We don't have to talk about the accident or Liz any longer if you'd prefer. Let's move on through the report, okay?"

He nodded in agreement and seemed to relax so she moved on to the next subject. "You say you didn't do what the police and the State allege. What do you think happened?"

"What do I think happened? She killed herself!"

Jorja began to realize Michael's anger appeared to turn on and off like a faucet. She wondered if it was the circumstances or his personality.

"Okay, you believe she killed herself. But why did she write on the wall that you did it to her?"

"I don't know. She was crazy. Why would anyone kill themselves so they can blame another person? That's just insane, don't you think?"

She made a few notes while she pondered his question. Why would anyone take their own life only to blame it on another? Was it because Michael's wife couldn't bear losing custody of her youngest to him after already having lost the oldest to a tragedy?

"We really don't know what your wife was thinking. Do you have any knowledge of her mental state beforehand or during your marriage? Is there any proof that she may have been unstable?" As she waited for him to respond, she made more notes to remind herself to ask the attorney about obtaining medical records and any other information relating to Michael's wife's mental history.

"Well...not really. I mean, I never noticed anything that bad. We had our problems and that's why we split up a year ago, but I can't say she was off her rocker until she came up with the horrible idea of committing suicide. I just have no idea what she was thinking. It's not like she was never going to see Tabitha again. She was going to have visits on a regular basis. It was extremely selfish of her to do what she did. She has no idea what she did to our daughter."

Jorja nodded, thinking how terrible the loss must have been for the youngest daughter after already losing her sister.

Michael continued, "Besides what her state of mind was at the time, if you believe what the prosecutor says, they think I killed her and set it up to look like a suicide. Why would I do that? I got custody of my daughter. Why would I want to kill her mother? It just doesn't make sense. They can't prove I had any motive."

"Well, they found her journal where she wrote how afraid she was of you. She claims there was some domestic violence between the two of you. Apparently the police were even called out to the house at least once. Is that true?"

He sniffed loudly in disdain. "That detective was useless. Yes, she called the police, but it wasn't a big deal. She was just mad at me because I yelled at her about letting Liz get out of control. She was lying to cover for Liz when she didn't come home at night and I was tired of the lies. I had very little faith in that detective when I realized he seemed to believe her story that I slapped her. Eventually he saw the light when she wasn't able to show him any obvious injury."

"Do you remember the detective's name?" she asked, waiting to write down a name.

"It's a cop who's also working on this sham of a case the State's trying to build against me. His name was Reynolds."

Jorja's brow furrowed. "Officer Reynolds?"

"Yeah, well, I mean, no. He was a detective, technically. Not an officer. It was the county sheriff because we're outside city limits."

She made another note to ask Officer Reynolds with the Tenino Police Department whether he knew of a Detective Reynolds with the county sheriff. Jorja then looked at Michael, hesitant to ask her next question. Finally, she said, "Your wife made allegations against you about a certain kind of behavior. Something that came out during the custody case, correct?"

His face turned red. "That was a complete lie! I can't believe she'd say I'd ever *touch* our daughter in that way. It's disgusting…" His voice faltered and he shook his head with a distraught look on his face.

"She was talking about your oldest daughter, Liz?"

"Yes, but she made the whole thing up in an attempt to gain custody of Tabitha. The Guardian ad Litem obviously believed she was lying or he wouldn't have recommended to the court that I be given custody of Tabitha."

She made a few more notes to speak to the Guardian ad Litem and to obtain a list of any witnesses he spoke to in order to make his recommendation to the court.

"Your attorney informed me that there was evidence obtained at the scene which the State plans to use against you in court. How would you explain the wine glass with your fingerprints and the sleeping pills in her wine glass?"

Michael placed his mug on the nearby table. "Man, I went over this with my attorney. It doesn't make sense, but I'm telling you what I told him. I don't know how that wine glass got there. It's probably a glass I used before I moved out of the house. Wouldn't it still have my prints on it? And the pills? So what if they're the same kind of pills I use. I don't know how they got there."

"Well, I'm sure your attorney told you that the police found no pill bottle and no evidence to indicate where the pills may have come from."

He could only shrug. "Again, I have no clue. I don't know what to say about it."

Jorja finished with a few more notes before sitting back in her chair. She stared at Michael briefly, trying to size him up. She knew he wasn't heartbroken over the loss of his soon-to-be ex-wife, but she was having a hard time with his cool behavior about the death of the mother of his children.

"Your attorney asked me to help you with your defense on this case. I'll speak to the detective and the Guardian ad Litem. I'll interview the housekeeper and I guess I should speak to your wife's sister..." Glancing at her notes, she continued, "Gail, correct? Is there anyone else you think I should speak with?"

Michael shook his head. "I don't know right now. I don't have family to speak of and my attorney told me I probably won't be able to use character witnesses in court. Just do whatever it is you do and help me out. My attorney told me you're good so I expect good things from you. He told me about that cold case murder you solved. That's really impressive."

"Thanks. I'll certainly do my best. If you decide you have other witnesses you want me to speak to, let me know. I'll be checking in with your attorney regarding my progress, so I expect we'll be meeting again next time at his office to go over the information I'm able to obtain."

Michael stood and Jorja followed suit. "Sounds good." He reached out to shake her hand before moving toward the staircase in order to leave the loft she used as her office. "I'll look forward to hearing from you. Thanks again."

He turned away from her to take the stairs down to the lower level where the book store was located. She watched him until his head disappeared before she sat back down in her chair. She glanced over the notes she took during the meeting, made a few more notes to clarify a few things and then gathered them along with the police report she had reviewed with Michael. She placed them in a file folder and set it to the side of her desk. She was anxious to get started on the case, but she had other obligations to take care of first. While she had obtained her private investigator license and was glad to be able to put her skills to work, she still had a book store to run. She decided to check in with her best friend, Taylor Bishop, who helped her run the bookstore and managed the coffee stand.

Jorja went downstairs to the lobby where she found Taylor helping a customer at the cash register. She waited patiently, watching Taylor at work. Her best decision had been to ask Taylor to move back to her home town with her after Jorja lost her aunt, inherited the family home and decided to open the bookstore. She couldn't imagine what she would have done without her friend's support after she discovered her deceased aunt had actually been her mother. It was a secret that had almost cost Jorja her life.

She was brought away from her memories when Taylor moved close to her. "Hey there, how did your meeting go?"

"Oh, it went fine. He's in a world of hurt if the prosecutor believes he killed his wife, but I'm going to help his attorney discover if there's any truth to his claim that he didn't do it."

Taylor raised one eyebrow. "Do you think he did?"

Jorja shrugged. "I really can't say. He seems to be a hothead, but I don't see yet what his motive would've been, unless he's just a psychopath. Anyway, I'm going to work on that later. Have you received your licensing paperwork in the mail yet? With my agency license, you shouldn't have a problem gaining an individual private investigator license as my employee. That's if you're still interested in helping me out."

Taylor grinned. "Are you kidding? I love the thought of working together as a female detective team. I know I have a lot to learn, but I'll just do whatever you need help with since we have a lot going on here at the bookstore too. We should have a team name so you can blog about our experiences. How about Team Coffee Bean? Isn't that catchy? It would make sense too since we're a detective agency in a bookstore called Books 'N Brew. I think it's perfect."

"Uh, well, it's a catchy name, but I think I might stick with the agency name of Matthews Investigations." Jorja didn't want to burst Taylor's excitable bubble, but she wanted to be taken seriously.

Taylor laughed. "Don't look so serious. I'm not going to ruin your newly acquired reputation. I just thought it would be a fun name to use during our book club meetings. You know the girls will be dying to ask questions about what you do as an investigator. I know you'll be limited on what you can say, but letting them feel like they're part of a team will keep them coming back for more. Don't you think?"

Jorja enjoyed the way Taylor came up with ideas to help with the business. She had to admit, using the book club meetings to give the members tidbits of what it was like to work as a female investigator would draw interest. She smiled. "You remind me every day why it was such a good idea to bring you in as a business partner. You're right. It's a fun idea."

"Good. If you didn't agree with me now, I was just going to work on you harder to change your mind so I'm glad you made it easier on yourself." Taylor laughed when Jorja rolled her eyes in resignation.

The bell over the door rang and they both turned to see seventeen year old Kathleen Myers, who worked at the store after school.

"Hey, Kat, how was your day?" Jorja asked. She felt a certain sense of ownership over Kat's well-being and treated her more like a younger sister. Kat had first approached Jorja just before the bookstore opened, asking for help in locating her mother who had run away when Kat was only five years old. After Kat's father passed away, she hoped to find her mother and form a relationship, but once Jorja began to investigate, she discovered something much worse than a mother who had abandoned her child. Instead, the investigation led to the discovery that Kat's mother had actually been murdered by a local police officer. Jorja could never forget that police officer, since he was the one who had almost taken her own life.

Kat threw her backpack on the floor and shook off her jacket. "It was good. I got a new teacher today who's subbing for Mrs. Fuller in my history class. I guess her back is worse than they thought so they had to bring in a replacement until the end of the year. Can you imagine? It's only January and I heard she'll be laid up for about five months!"

Taylor couldn't hold her tongue. "Well, she better not blame the horse. You can't go riding a horse if you don't know what you're doing. Especially on a wet, muddy trail during a lightning storm. Not really the best decision I've ever seen a well-educated person make."

Jorja tried to hide her grin. It was an awful accident, but she couldn't fault Taylor's quick assessment. From what she had heard, the teacher only rode the horse in an attempt to show off skills she had never acquired.

Turning to Kat, Jorja asked, "So what's your new teacher like? Do you like her?"

Kat nodded. "Yes, I like *him*. His name's Mr. Carter and he's cool, for an older guy. He made the class really fun. Don't tell anyone, but I won't really miss Mrs. Fuller because she just never made class any fun."

Kat continued to describe her first day with the new teacher, but Jorja felt her attention shift from the conversation back to the details about her new case with Michael Stafford. If she was going to get any work done, she knew she'd have to stay busy in order to keep herself distracted. But as Jorja stood by the register to go over the list of items to be completed that day, it didn't take long to realize how difficult it would be to stay focused on books when, instead, she was ready to move on with the investigation involving Michael's wife's death.

CHAPTER 2

Mrs. Edith Cavanaugh reached over to take the business card Jorja held in her hand over the coffee table. The housekeeper grabbed the card with her left hand while she used her right hand to lift the glasses hanging around her neck in order to read the card. Even with the glasses, Jorja noticed how the housekeeper had to squint to read the print, making her wonder if she should reprint some business cards with a larger font.

Mrs. Cavanaugh lowered her head to peek at Jorja over the rims of her glasses. "I've never seen that spelling of your name before. You say it like Georgia with a 'G' correct? How did your parents come up with the spelling of your name?"

Jorja began to speak, but suddenly realized she wasn't quite sure how to answer that question. As far as she knew, her biological mother had chosen the name for her and the parents who raised her hadn't changed it. She really didn't know where Gloria had come up with the spelling of her name except that Gloria may have liked the spelling of Jorja, which matched her twin brother's given name of Jacob better than Georgia did.

She finally gave the only answer she could come up with. "My mother was young when she gave birth to me and I guess she just wanted to give me a name that was different than the usual spelling."

Mrs. Cavanaugh gave a curt nod. "Well, it certainly is different. But, I like it. I always thought my name was old sounding, especially when I was a young woman, but back in my day, you were usually given a family name and my parents would not allow me to go by any sort of nickname."

The housekeeper placed the business card on the coffee table as she removed her glasses to let them hang from the chain around her neck. She gave Jorja a steady stare. "I guess we should get on with it. What sort of questions would you like to ask me?"

Jorja fidgeted on the couch the housekeeper had asked her to sit on as she adjusted her legs to allow a flatter surface to write on the tablet on her lap. "Well, how long did you work for Mr. and Mrs. Stafford?"

"For twenty-five years. Before they were married, I was employed by Miss Cynthia's family and when she married Mr. Stafford, her parents asked that I continue on with Miss Cynthia in her new home."

"Miss Cynthia? Is that what you called Mrs. Stafford?"

Mrs. Cavanaugh nodded. "I've known her since she was a small child and after she was married to Mr. Stafford, Miss Cynthia told me I could continue to address her how I've always addressed her. I think it made her feel less homesick."

Jorja tucked a loose strand of her auburn hair behind her ear as she looked down to make a few notes. The housekeeper patiently waited until Jorja raised her head and asked, "What was her relationship like with Mr. Stafford? Was it a good relationship?"

The housekeeper glanced away to break eye contact. Jorja felt a warning bell go off. "I suppose they had a good relationship. I really cannot say. He worked a lot and when he was home, it was usually after I had already retired for the evening."

"Did he treat her well? Or did you see anything that may have caused you any concern?" Jorja waited, pen poised over her notepad.

The housekeeper cleared her throat before answering. "I didn't really *see* anything. It's more like what I perceived from Miss Cynthia's moods. She just appeared to be unhappy, but I cannot say for a fact why. I could only guess and that would not be sensible."

Jorja nodded. She felt there was more here, but she would let it go for now. "Since the police have released the house back to Mr. Stafford, do you plan to stay on with him? Do you know his intentions for this house?"

Mrs. Cavanaugh shivered involuntarily. "I will not work in this house except to help prepare it for sale. The spirit of Miss Cynthia needs to move on and I believe she will not move on if she feels my presence here for too long. As for Mr. Stafford, no, I do not intend to continue working for him. I would if only for sweet Tabitha, but he has made it clear he does not need my services."

Jorja tried to stop herself from wondering if the spirit of Cynthia Stafford really was in the house, clinging to this world until she was satisfied with the results of the message she communicated before she died.

Jorja placed her notepad and pen on the coffee table and stood up. "I understand you probably don't wish to be here, but I would like you to take me through the house to show me what you saw that day. Can you do that for me?"

The housekeeper took a deep breath as she nodded. "Yes, I can do that. I already showed the police and I understand you need to hear it too."

Mrs. Cavanaugh slowly stood, bracing herself with the armrest as she stood. "Oh, dear, my knees sure do give me a hard time these days. I'm not able to clean like I used to because of the pain."

The housekeeper then moved around the coffee table toward the front door. "I let myself in the front door with my key that morning, as I always do every Monday, Wednesday and Friday. I didn't expect Miss Cynthia to be home because she would have already left by the time I arrived at ten o'clock. I walked through this hallway into the kitchen and placed my purse and some new cleaning supplies I had purchased on the kitchen counter. That was when I spotted the wine glass and just assumed Miss Cynthia had herself a drink before going to bed. I poured the wine from the glass down the drain and then placed the glass in the sink before I turned on the television to one of those satellite radio channels. It was the week before Christmas so I was listening to holiday music as I began to dust the living room. I like to work on the living room, bedrooms and bathrooms first before finishing with the kitchen. After I dusted and vacuumed the living room I was going to begin on the master bedroom when I realized Miss Cynthia's jacket and purse were sitting on the dining room table."

Mrs. Cavanaugh pointed at the table as she continued to move into the master bedroom with Jorja right on her heels.

"I became concerned at that point. I was worried Miss Cynthia was sick and home in bed for the day so I quietly called her name, not wishing to wake her if she were still sleeping. Of course, I had already vacuumed and I doubt she would have slept through it, but I wasn't thinking that clearly. I was just concerned. When she didn't respond, I pulled back the window curtain to allow some light and I saw the bed was empty. I then moved around the bed and entered the bathroom where I saw the worst sight I have ever seen in my entire life."

Mrs. Cavanaugh then began to cry. She tried to utter more words, but her voice cracked and she held her hands over her face as she continued to cry. Jorja put a hand on the housekeeper's shoulder. "I'm so sorry for your loss and I know how difficult this is. Do you want to go back to the living room for awhile to take a break?"

Shaking her head, the housekeeper sniffed loudly and wiped her face with a handkerchief she pulled from her pocket. "No, I'm fine. I just miss the poor girl so much and I wish I could have been here to help her. I don't know what happened, but she did *not* deserve to die that way, by her hand or anyone else's."

Jorja stepped back to give the woman some space. "I understand she meant very much to you. I wouldn't be asking you these questions if it weren't important. You understand that, don't you?"

Mrs. Cavanaugh nodded. "I understand. But if that man did anything to harm her, I hope you aren't trying to keep him out of jail. If he had a hand in her death, he deserves nothing less than to take responsibility for his crime."

The housekeeper sniffed again and used the handkerchief for one more good wipe before continuing. "I saw her there, in the tub and I had absolutely no idea what to do. I knew she was gone, but I wanted to remove her from the water. I wanted to wrap her up and hide her nakedness from the strangers I knew would soon be imposing in order to investigate once I called 911. I just wanted to save her, bring her back, try to understand what happened. Many, many emotions flooded me as I just stood there and stared at her. I finally realized I had to get help and I called the police. I finally saw the words she wrote on the wall and that scared me terribly. I can't say I know Mr. Stafford very well, but I would not have thought him capable of such a heinous act."

Mrs. Cavanaugh took a deep breath. Jorja worried the stress might be too much for the older woman, but she knew she had to continue with her questions. "Can you tell me what else you saw? Did you move anything while you waited for the police?"

The housekeeper shook her head. "No, I wanted to move her and cover her up, but I knew that would be wrong. I surely didn't want to get into trouble. What I saw in here was blood. Just blood. The tub was dirty looking from the blood and I saw the dried blood on her wrists and on the wall. I really don't recall anything else in here. It was later, when I left the room and while I waited for the police that I walked around the house. I just couldn't stay in the bathroom any longer."

"What did you see when you walked around the house?"

Mrs. Cavanaugh walked around Jorja to leave the bathroom. She pointed at the bed. "I saw a book lying here. I guess it was her journal. I also saw an envelope and out of curiosity, I'll admit I did look inside. I found plane tickets and a notepad with a to-do list she had made out to prepare for the trip she had planned to take Tabitha on after Christmas." She began to choke up again as she continued, "She was taking Tabitha to Disneyland. I sure hope that baby's last memories about her mother aren't that her mother never took her to Disneyland like she promised."

Jorja jotted down a quick note on her notepad. Why would Cynthia kill herself if she planned to take her daughter to Disneyland? Did losing custody of Tabitha really cause her to go over the deep end?

Hoping to avoid making the housekeeper cry again, Jorja tried to move her along with another question. "Did you see anything else in the room that the police found interesting or anything you have thought of since?"

Shaking her head, Mrs. Cavanaugh said, "No, not anything important. I moved from the bedroom back to the dining room and kitchen. I saw the mail Miss Cynthia left on the table along with her jacket and purse. There was really nothing out of place other than the items being thrown on the table. But then I looked at the wine glass in the sink. It was as I was thinking about how Miss Cynthia must have had a glass before taking a bath that I realized I had actually seen another wine glass on the side of the tub. I didn't want to enter the bathroom again, but I had to make sure I was right. What I saw was a second wine glass on the side of the tub. So I began to wonder...who would she have had wine with that evening? And why would she invite anyone over for a glass of wine after losing Tabitha to her husband? Especially if it was her plan to kill herself?"

Jorja was jotting down the questions posed by Mrs. Cavanaugh as quickly as she could. She looked up from her notepad and asked, "What about a friend? Would she have invited a friend over to talk about the custody case and for a shoulder to cry on?"

The housekeeper huffed loudly in disdain. "Miss Cynthia hasn't had any friends for quite awhile now. Mr. Stafford kept her busy with his demands and they did not include get-togethers with female friends. He was very jealous if she ever went anywhere without him. Even after they separated, I think she had been without a good friend for so long, she just didn't know how to reach out to anyone. That's why I feel so terrible. I should have been here for her."

Jorja worried Mrs. Cavanaugh was going to cry again, but instead, the woman puffed up her chest as she straightened her back. "No, Miss Cynthia did not have friends because of him. So the real question is who was here before she died? Will you do your best to find out? I know the police are working on it too. They believe Mr. Stafford killed her and if he did, then I hope they build a strong case against him. I'm sorry you're working for him because if he is a killer, you're working for a very bad man."

Jorja appreciated the fact that Mrs. Cavanaugh did not use her role as a defense investigator against her. Regardless of what anyone thought about her role in the case, Jorja would not allow anything to weaken her desire to discover the truth, even if the truth might not set Mr. Stafford free.

CHAPTER 3

"So how did your interview with the housekeeper go?" Taylor asked as she sat beside Jorja on the couch in the bookstore.

"It was sad, really. The housekeeper has known Cynthia Stafford ever since she was a child and finding her like that was very difficult. I think she's taking some of the blame, believing she could have done something." Jorja leaned forward to place her coffee on the old steamer trunk acting as a coffee table.

Taylor shook her head, causing her brunette bangs to flutter. "That's awful. I can't imagine."

Jorja filled Taylor in on what Mrs. Cavanaugh shared with her as they enjoyed a few moments of peace now that the bookstore was empty of customers. They were preparing for their evening book club meeting so it was likely the only time they'd be able to catch up before they could head home.

They heard the bell chime when the door opened and both turned to see Kat enter the store, her arms full of baked goods she picked up at the local bakery, Dylan's Sweet Delights.

As Kat placed the boxes of treats for the book club meeting on a nearby table she said, "Wow, Dylan really set us up for tonight. We have donuts and tea cookies, shortbread and coffee cake. It all looks so good!"

Jorja and Taylor helped Kat decorate the table with the snacks along with napkins and small paper plates. Taylor enjoyed decorating for any occasion so she had already prepped the table with a winter-themed table cloth and trinkets.

Jorja stepped back to survey their work. "Okay, looks good. Kat, would you get the apple cider from the fridge and bring it out here?"

Kat's long blond pony tail bobbed as she nodded. "Sure, be right back."

When Kat headed to the break room in the back of the store, Taylor took a deep breath before approaching Jorja about a sticky subject. "Hey, did Kat happen to mention anything to you about the meeting tonight?"

Jorja's eyebrows rose in question. "No, why? What does she need to tell me?"

"Well...maybe she didn't think to mention it, but I thought you should know, um...well-"

"Okay, spit it out. What should I know?" Jorja crossed her arms, waiting for what she realized may not be good news.

Taylor cleared her throat and finally blurted, "Lydia will be at the meeting tonight."

"What? Why?" Having not had much contact with Lydia Myers since the night involving the attack by Officer Cooper, Jorja was immediately on guard. She wasn't yet sure she forgave Lydia, who eavesdropped on a conversation Jorja had with Lydia's boss and then later shared that information with Officer Cooper which ultimately led to his attack on Jorja.

Taylor continued, "You know how Kat has been trying to strengthen her relationship with Lydia, especially since Lydia is the only family she has left. You can't blame her for wanting to include her aunt in what she's interested in, can you?"

Jorja reluctantly sighed in resignation. "I guess. It's just difficult, that's all. It's not like Lydia and I had a great relationship before the incident with Cooper, but the fact that because of her I could have been killed is really difficult to forget."

Taylor smiled at her friend. She knew that as long as Lydia made an effort, Jorja's forgiving nature would lead to a mended relationship. She just hoped Lydia would push aside her own animosity toward Jorja due to their past so that the mending could begin.

"With Kat working here, you're going to have some contact with Lydia and at some point, you need to bury the hatchet with her. Or at least try."

"I know, I know. But she's the one who held a grudge from high school first. That's certainly not as good a reason as mine for being upset with her." Jorja sat down on a nearby chair. She was beginning to feel anxious about having any type of conversation with Lydia, who was the most difficult person she knew. She never understood Lydia's need to hold a grudge from high school, where Lydia presumed to believe Jorja stole a boyfriend from her when in fact, the boy had chosen her over Lydia. It didn't make matters any better that the boy from high school now also lived in their hometown. And then Jorja made matters worse when she went against Lydia's wishes by agreeing to help Kat find her mother. She was actually surprised Lydia would come to the book club meeting and she wondered why Lydia couldn't keep her distance due to at least some guilt at putting Jorja in harm's way.

She came out of her reverie to look at Taylor, who was patiently waiting while Jorja ran thoughts through her head.

"Well? Are you and Lydia going to be able to be in the same room together or not?" Taylor smiled, knowing full well Jorja wouldn't cause a scene. Even so, she enjoyed putting Jorja on the spot.

"Yes, Taylor, we can behave ourselves. Well, I guess I shouldn't speak for Lydia, but I'll be good. I promise."

"Good. Let's finish getting ready. Everyone will be here soon."

Jorja tried to smile as she mentally prepared herself for the evening. She would be prepared for whatever attitude Lydia might walk in the door with.

Kat brought a pitcher filled with cider back to the table and asked, "Do you mind if I have one of these cookies?" Kat pointed to a cookie with chocolate swirls.

"Sure, go ahead. Do you want a peppermint mocha to go with it?" Taylor asked.

"Oh, that's sounds good. Thanks, Taylor."

The doorbell chimed when the first group of book club members entered the store. Jorja was immediately pleased to see her friend Ruth and quickly noticed Ruth had a new guest with her. She smiled at Ruth as they made eye contact, but her smile faded when she noticed Lydia standing in the doorway. She and Lydia made eye contact briefly before Lydia looked away.

Jorja brushed away the perturbed feelings that threatened to take over and took a few steps toward Ruth. "Hello Ruth, it's good to see you." She gave Ruth a hug before turning to her guest. She quickly noted the woman's small stature and shy demeanor, especially when the woman's eye contact didn't even last as long as Lydia's. "Hello, my name is Jorja." She reached out her hand to the young woman, who awkwardly shook it.

Ruth spoke when the woman did not. "Jorja, this is Bailey Maxwell. She's a new member to our church. She lives just out of town and recently moved here from Colorado."

Bailey gave Jorja a shy smile. "It's nice to meet you."

"Welcome to the club, Bailey. I hope you enjoy yourself. There's coffee and cider as well as some cookies and cake over there on the table. Go ahead and find yourselves a seat. Everyone will be here shortly and then we'll get started."

As Ruth and Bailey moved toward the coffee stand, Jorja turned to find Lydia standing in her path.

"Did Kat tell you I was coming?"

"No, but Taylor did. I'm glad you and Kat are finding things to do that you're both interested in." Jorja thought small talk was likely impossible and she was right.

"Well, if you don't want me here, just tell me. I didn't want to turn Kat down since she asked me to come, but if you tell me to leave I'll just tell her you didn't want me to join the club."

Jorja sighed. "There's no reason you can't be part of the group, Lydia. I'm sure you and I can be civil to each other, can't we? At least for Kat's sake?"

Lydia stared at Jorja for a moment without responding. Jorja had the impression Lydia wanted to say something more but was having difficulty finding the words. She wondered if it was an apology, but doubted she'd ever hear Lydia mutter one even when pigs did fly.

Finally, Lydia shrugged. "Sure, for Kat's sake. I can deal with that."

Lydia suddenly pivoted and quickly walked away to sit by Ruth. Jorja didn't know whether to laugh or take seriously the fact that she had to figure out how she could mend a relationship that had never been able to form beyond unstable. She had a feeling it was going to be a long and strained evening.

CHAPTER 4

The drive home was a short one, and after such a full day, Jorja was thankful to finally be home. After parking her Jeep in the driveway, she took a few moments to sit in silence as she ran the day through her head because she knew she wouldn't get any peace and quiet as soon as she entered the house. It was during the quiet moments she took for herself now and then when she would wonder where she would be right now if she had stayed in Vancouver. She wondered where she would be if she hadn't decided to move back into her childhood home in Tenino after it had been willed to her by her Aunt Gloria. How blissful her ignorance might have been if she had never discovered the secret that her aunt had really been her mother and that Gloria spent two decades in a mental hospital after attempting to take Jorja's life and that of her twin brother after their birth.

The fact that her life was completely changed by all these events did not alter the reality that Jorja felt better off now than when she first made the decision to move back to Hillcrest. She had discovered that her twin brother, who her family thought had perished due to Gloria's actions, was alive and had unknowingly been brought up as the child of another couple. After meeting her brother, who was now known as Ryan rather than his given name of Jacob, she wasn't expecting any more surprises until she met Ryan's son, Nicholas. Jorja had never entertained the thought of being an aunt, but she adored Nicholas more than she could have imagined possible. She had never lived with a child before, but after the attack by Officer Cooper where she and Ryan were almost killed, Jorja hadn't second-guessed herself when she asked Ryan and Nicholas to move into Hillcrest with her and Taylor.

As much as she loved them, though, there were days like today when she enjoyed the complete silence in the Jeep before heading inside. Eventually, Jorja began to feel the chill through her jacket and she knew she had better head inside before Ryan came looking for her. She opened the door and stepped out of the Jeep, grabbed her purse and headed toward the porch of the old Victorian. As she climbed the steps of the porch, she could hear yips and excited growls coming from Piper, the lab-mix she rescued after finding her hurt on the side of the road. Jorja would often take Piper to the bookstore to hang out with her as she worked, but she had known today was going to be a long day and had decided to let Piper stay home. She doubted Piper would let her forget it.

She stood in front of the door and was about to open it when the door suddenly swung open.

"Aunt Jorja! Finally, you're here. We've been waiting for you for *hours* and *hours!*" Nicholas stood as tall as his five-year-old frame would allow as he looked up at her. Her exhaustion from the day was little match for his big brown eyes. He raised his arms and waited, which was all Jorja needed. She immediately reached down to pick him up and gave him a hug. His arms wrapped around her neck and he squeezed her with all the might his little arms could muster.

"Nicholas, I've missed you so much. Did you have a good day today?"

She bent over to place Nicholas back on the floor so she could remove her jacket.

Nicholas clapped his hands together and grinned. "I had a really good day today, Aunt Jorja. I get to be in a play. In school. Do you know what I get to be?"

After hanging her jacket in the nearby closet, she left her purse on the hall bench before moving into the living room to the left of the foyer.

"No, Nicholas, what do you get to be?" She smiled at Ryan as he entered the living room from the informal dining room off the kitchen.

"I get to be a bear! We all get to be an animal and I get to be the bear." Nicholas skipped around Jorja as she tried to sit down on the couch. When she was finally able to sit, Nicholas stood in front of her and placed both of his hands on either side of her face to make her look at him. "Will you come and watch the play Aunt Jorja? My teacher said you can help with the play too, if you want."

She raised her eyes to look at Ryan. "Well, I think your dad might want to help you with the play, isn't that right, Ryan?"

"Of course I'm going to help. We could always use the extra help though, in case not a lot of parents volunteer." Ryan said as he also took a seat on the couch.

Jorja looked at Nicholas again, who was staring at her with anticipation. She knew there was absolutely no way she could deny him. With his hands still holding her face, she nodded. "Of course, I would love to help you with your play."

Nicholas released her face and began to hop up and down as he said, "In a cave in the woods sleeps a great brown bear. In a cave in the woods sleeps a great brown bear!" He suddenly sprinted across the room to pick up one of Piper's toys. "Come on Piper, let's play!" Nicholas threw the toy down the hall in the foyer and giggled as Piper clumsily ran around the corner to chase the toy.

Jorja smiled as she marveled at the energy level of a child. She turned to Ryan and asked, "So what play is he in? He's playing a bear?"

Ryan nodded. "Yeah, it's based on that book called *Bear Snores On*. I've been reading the bear books to him I bought from your store and he loves them. I guess the teacher thought a play about animals that hibernate in the winter would be a good way to teach them while they have fun and she chose the *Bear Snores On*. I don't know what she was thinking when she came up with the idea to have Nicholas play the bear. He can't lay still long enough to pretend to be a hibernating bear." Ryan chuckled at the thought as he stood up. "Come on. I have dinner ready for you if you're hungry. I hope you didn't snack too much at the book club meeting."

Jorja's stomach growled on point. She really hadn't had much chance to eat at the meeting. "No, I'm starving actually. Whatever it is, it smells great." She followed Ryan into the country kitchen and helped him place plates and silverware on the table.

"We're having stew and biscuits. Best meal to have on a chilly day. Is Taylor going to come home in time to eat?"

Jorja shook her head. "No, she was going to lock up and then head over to Dylan's bakery. They have plans for dinner tonight."

"Nicholas, come sit at the table. Still talking about their wedding plans, huh?" Ryan asked Jorja as he sat down at the table.

Jorja watched as Nicholas ran into the room before climbing onto the chair to her left. After he was settled on the chair, he turned to Jorja and grinned.

She grinned back.

She then turned back to Ryan on her right. "Yes, they are still talking wedding plans. The wedding isn't for another eight months, but you know how fast that's going to sneak up on us. I have a lot to do to prepare myself since I'm the Maid of Honor. I have to read the bride books at the bookstore just to figure out everything I'm supposed to do and from what I've read so far, it's quite a lot."

Ryan used a ladle to serve the stew. He grabbed a biscuit for himself and then a second one for Nicholas. Jorja grabbed her own biscuit and tore off a piece to dip it in the juice of the stew. "Oh, yum. Very good. Every time you cook for me, you make me glad I asked you to move in." She grinned as she tried a spoonful of stew.

"It's the least I can do, especially since I'm here most of the day working anyway. That's the best thing about my job as a book editor; I can do it where ever I happen to be."

Jorja couldn't argue with that. The next best thing to working from home, in her opinion, was running your own business and enjoying what you do. For her, the bookstore was something she knew she would enjoy. To make money, she added the coffee stand and then later, after solving the cold case murder involving Kat's mom, she had decided to become a licensed private investigator in order to actually make money on something she discovered she had a knack for. The trick was to find the work and begin establishing a reputation. So far she was working on both. She just hoped this time the case she was working on didn't end up risking her life.

CHAPTER 5

"Hi, Betsy, how's your day going?" Jorja asked the city police clerk as she entered the office of the Tenino Police Department.

Betsy placed some papers she'd been looking through on the corner of the desk and she moved toward Jorja. "I'm doing very well, thanks. What can I do for you today?"

"I was just curious if you know where Officer Fritz and Reynolds are this afternoon. I actually have a question for Officer Reynolds."

Betsy held up a finger to indicate she'd be a minute before she opened an interior door and stepped around to the other side. "Hey Stan, can you come out here for a minute?"

Jorja was surprised at the lack of formality and her surprise was apparent on her face when Betsy walked back into the office. Betsy quickly raised a hand in dismissal at Jorja's look. "Oh, the Chief and I lost all sense of properness years ago. We've both been working here for so long, we're more like family. He probably won't like that I didn't call him Chief in front of you, but what's he going to do? Fire me? I don't think so." Betsy grinned. "I could answer your question for you, but he needs to get off his duff now and then so it'll be good for him to come out here to help you."

Before Jorja could reply, the outer door to the lobby opened and Chief Douglas walked through. While Betsy had always been helpful and friendly and very approachable, the Chief was a different matter. Jorja would describe him as an old bear with a constant thorn in his side. She wasn't even sure she'd ever seen him smile.

"Hello, Chief Douglas. How are you?" she asked, hoping to start the conversation on a positive note.

"Good, but busy. What can I do for you?" He stood in the doorway holding the door open with every intention of keeping the conversation short.

"Uh, well, I was just wondering if you happened to know where Officer Reynolds and Officer Fritz might be this afternoon. I just needed to chat with them, but wasn't sure how I could get word to them."

Jorja saw the Chief glance quickly at Betsy, although she was sure it was more of a glare. "They're both out on patrol. That's what police officers do in this town when there are no crimes to solve. Is it important? Do you have a crime to report?"

Good grief! Jorja thought to herself as she wondered whether she'd ever get on the good side of the Chief. She didn't know if it was her or if he acted this way with everyone.

"No, I don't have a crime to report. I'd just like to speak with them. Is there any way you can get a message to them so they can stop by the bookstore when they're patrolling through town? I'd really appreciate it."

The Chief lowered his head a bit to see her more clearly over his reading glasses. He held her eye contact long enough to make her uncomfortable before he finally said, "We'll get word to them for you and I'm sure when they aren't busy working, they can find the time to stop by. Is that it?"

"Well, yes. Thank you." She waited for him to say 'you're welcome,' but instead he turned to let the door slam behind him as he walked back to his office.

Jorja let out a breath. Every time she dealt with him she felt like she was straining against a negative energy. She turned to Betsy. "Is it me or is he always that way? I never seem to catch him on a good day."

Betsy frowned slightly as she replied, "Honey, that man hasn't had a good day in thirty years."

That piqued Jorja's interest immediately. "Why, what happened thirty years ago?"

Betsy quickly glanced behind her to make sure the inner door to her office was shut. "I guess you wouldn't know. His wife died around thirty years ago and then his nephew, the only other family he had, ran away and was never seen or heard from again. He was a wreck. I wasn't working here then. I was serving school lunches for the elementary kids. They're so cute at that age. Anyway, Stan had been a cop for a few years, but once his wife and nephew were gone he just couldn't pull himself together. He turned in his badge and left. No one saw him for about five years and then suddenly one day he was back. I was working here then, having been hired by the previous chief. When Stan came back looking for a job, it wasn't long before he was hired back on the force. He worked his way up from patrol and he's been the acting chief for the past ten years, but he's been a straight no-nonsense shooter ever since he returned." Betsy frowned as she continued, "I've tried to bring him out of his shell but he's a tough one. He just doesn't *want* to be happy. I wish it weren't so, but he just can't seem to let go of his past."

Jorja was surprised by the story involving the chief. She was sad for him and knew it made some sense about his attitude, but she didn't appreciate that he used it as an excuse to be rude.

"It's too bad he can't get past the past, but I wish he didn't have to make me feel like he'd rather kick me to the curb as much as talk to me. Well, I have to get back to the store. Take care and I'll chat with you more next time."

Betsy nodded. "I agree with you, the treatment is not warranted, but I just hope you understand a little bit more about why the Chief might act the way he does. You have a nice afternoon and don't wait too long to stop back by to say hello."

Jorja waved before she shut the door and walked outside. She understood what Betsy was trying to do in her attempt to defend the chief's actions, but Jorja also saw more than that. She thought she saw a woman in love with a man who had absolutely no idea how to love again.

CHAPTER 6

Paperwork was going to be the death of her, she was sure. Jorja felt buried behind her desk as she stared at various piles of paper for the bookstore receipts, bills and inventory, police reports and notes regarding the case she was investigating for Michael Stafford and notes and other items related to the book club and the bookstore blog. She was beginning to feel overwhelmed in her attempt to concentrate on only one thing so she was happy for the interruption when Taylor buzzed her on the phone.

"Hey Jorja. You want to come down here for a minute? You have some company."

"Sure." She didn't care who the company was as long as she could give her eyes a break for awhile. She stood to walk around the desk to take a peek over the railing. She let her gaze roam the store until she spotted her visitors...Officer Reynolds and Officer Fritz. Both had been dispatched to her house on the fateful day when she and Ryan were attacked by Officer Cooper. She later learned the two had taken a large role in proving Cooper's involvement in two murders once they determined what Jorja had discovered about him wasn't as crazy as it sounded.

As Jorja moved down the staircase, she watched both men intently. They were quietly chatting with Taylor, who was rearranging books around a new display. Fritz appeared half interested while Reynolds was asking questions about a new action adventure for teens his son was reading.

When Jorja reached the bottom of the staircase, Fritz caught her gaze and he immediately straightened. He then smiled at her as he watched her move toward him. She began to feel self-conscious about his stare so she broke eye contact to glance at Taylor, who was grinning like the cat that ate the canary as she watched Fritz watch Jorja. Giving Taylor a hard stare only caused Taylor to giggle in delight before turning her attention back to the books. She knew Taylor was amused with Fritz's apparent newfound interest in her ever since the first night they met. While Jorja would admit she had some interest in Fritz, she resisted the idea of diving head first into a relationship.

"Hi, Jorja, how are you?" Fritz asked her as he closed the distance between them with a few steps. "We had a few minutes so we thought we'd stop by. Chief said you were looking for us."

Reynolds moved toward them so that he stood beside Fritz. The two of them were quite a pair, if Jorja had to describe them. Fritz was at least six foot with dark features and a muscular body, visible through his uniform. Reynolds was taller; she thought possibly four inches taller than Fritz, leaner, and with his Native American skin had even darker features than Fritz. Taylor had commented to Jorja more than once that the city could easily earn some extra cash by selling a calendar with the two officers posing each month. Jorja could never think of a reason to argue against the idea.

Feeling her cheeks begin to flush as she tried to push away the thought of how the two might look posing for the month of July, she forced her attention to the reason she needed to speak to them. "I was or, actually, I was looking for Officer Reynolds." She tried to ignore the fleeting crushed look on Fritz's face.

Reynolds pointed to himself as he asked, "Me? What can I do for you?"

"Well, I was just wondering if you happened to know a Detective Reynolds, with the county sheriff's office. Is it a coincidence or are you related?"

"You're talking about Tom Reynolds? That's my brother, actually. Why?"

Jorja leaned against a nearby bookshelf. "His name came up because he worked a possible murder case last month and I may have to speak to him about it."

Fritz became interested at this piece of information. "Why would you need to talk to him about a case? What do you mean *possible* murder case? Someone was either murdered or they weren't. I hope you aren't digging into something that could put you in danger again."

His concern was evident, but Jorja didn't appreciate being told what to do. She crossed her arms. "Maybe I am. I'll be careful. I've been hired by an attorney on a case and I need to investigate, which means speaking to the officers involved and it just so happens that he's related to Officer Reynolds. Whether the deceased was murdered or not remains to be seen."

Fritz's dark brown eyes narrowed as he realized what she was saying. "You mean you're working for the guy who was charged with her murder? I thought once you got your P.I. license you were just going to use it to locate people. Why would you get involved with defending criminals? And working for defense attorneys? All they do is work at putting the criminals back out on the street so they can commit more crimes."

Jorja uncrossed her arms and held up a hand to stop Fritz's rant. "Okay, okay. I know how you feel. But I have my license, the attorney really wanted to hire me and I really want to do it. I've been taking it easy by working on simple stuff for almost two months while I've recovered from the attack, but criminal law is interesting. As a cop you have to agree this field of work is interesting."

Fritz frowned as he shook his head at her. "No, my field of work is dangerous. And I don't like the idea of you working for the dangerous types we're working our hardest to keep behind bars." He then turned to Reynolds. "We need to get going. I told the Chief we'd try to make contact with that witness about the domestic violence case from last night." Fritz then gave Jorja a passing look before he turned to Taylor. "You girls have a good night. Come on, Tim, let's go."

Fritz turned to leave the store, leaving Reynolds to say his goodbyes. Reynolds gave Jorja an apologetic look before turning to catch up with his partner.

Once they were gone, Taylor blew out a breath. "Man, does he have it bad for you."

Jorja huffed in frustration. "I don't know what he has, but he doesn't have the right to tell me what I can and can't do. He's just a typical cop. Probably believes everyone who's arrested is guilty just because they were arrested. Well, I learned otherwise working in the legal field and I will always give others the benefit of the doubt, no matter what they've been accused of."

Taylor didn't argue. She knew Jorja would do whatever she wanted to do, no question, but Taylor had been watching Fritz and she saw his growing interest in Jorja while he continued to remain a friendly distance. She was willing to bet she might get to watch some real fireworks between the two of them if Fritz wasn't willing to admit his arguments about Jorja's safety were a disguise for his true feelings about her.

CHAPTER 7

"Good morning, Detective Reynolds, thanks so much for meeting with me today." Jorja said as she shook his hand before sitting down at the table.

"No problem, Miss Matthews. I have about a half hour before I need to leave for a meeting. What can I do for you?" Detective Reynolds sat down across from her, his long lean body and coloring a striking resemblance to his brother.

"Please, you can call me Jorja. I just had a few questions about a case you investigated in December. The case involving Cynthia Stafford." She placed a notepad in front of her on the table and grabbed a pen out of her messenger bag. She had decided to treat herself to a new messenger bag for her investigative work, rather than a formal briefcase. The bag cost more than what she would normally spend, but she decided she wanted something nice that would also last.

Detective Reynolds nodded. "Yes, I was the lead detective on that case. What would you like to know?"

"Well, I've read over the reports, but I wondered if you could verify a few things for me. First, did you believe at first that the case was a murder? Is there anything that may have led you to believe it was actually a suicide?"

"I realize your client is trying to say he didn't kill his wife and that she committed suicide. I get that. But it wasn't just what she wrote on the wall that led us to believe he had something to do with her death. If you've read the reports, you must realize that."

Jorja nodded. "Yes, I realize you discovered evidence which led you to eventually arrest Mr. Stafford. Let's start with the wine glass. He used to reside in the house with his wife. Wouldn't you expect to find his fingerprints still evident on a glass that might not have been used since he moved from the home? She had a number of wine glasses hanging above the wine rack, from what I remember. It's likely she may have used the same glass repeatedly."

"Maybe. But the glass was on the counter with wine in it. As if he had been there and hadn't been able to finish the drink before leaving."

"Okay, but why do you think she would have invited him over for a glass of wine on the same day she lost custody of her child to him? It's not as if they had anything to toast about. I would dare to guess she probably didn't want to be in the same room with him. Does it make sense to you that she would invite him over for a drink?"

Detective Reynolds straightened in his chair, if that was even possible because Jorja thought he was sitting ramrod straight as it was.

"Have you read her journal yet? Your attorney should have provided it to you if he hasn't already. She wrote about her fear of his increasing anger toward her. He thought she was getting in the way of the new life he was trying to establish since their separation. She believed he had a new girlfriend and was tired of waiting for her to get out of his life so he could move on and marry again. While there is no record of any real domestic violence between them, there is at least one time when the police were contacted by her in relation to an apparent threat or possible physical assault."

He held up his hand to stop her questions. "No, nothing came of that because there was no obvious injury. However, she wrote about an increasing fear she had in her husband. She thought he was capable of more and once he gained custody, he would have the power to do more to hurt her. She was determined to talk it out and somehow find a middle ground they could agree on for the sake of their daughter, Tabitha. That's why she invited him over and her last journal entry included her thoughts about what she would say to him when he arrived that evening. She wanted to work things out so that they could have a somewhat normal relationship. She appeared to fear what might happen to Tabitha if the two of them couldn't work things out. She was very fearful of losing Tabitha like she did her eldest daughter. You know about that, right?"

Jorja nodded as she finished writing notes. She then looked up to find him staring at her, waiting for her to answer his question.

"Well, yes, I was informed the oldest daughter died in an accident. I feel for any parent who has lost a child. How do you know Cynthia wasn't so depressed about not only the death of her daughter, but also the final straw of losing custody of her youngest to her husband that she didn't decide to take her own life?"

Detective Reynolds raised his brows in question. "And set her husband up for murder? Why?"

"I don't know what she was thinking or what her mental state was, but she went through the separation with her husband, the death of her daughter and then the custody battle. That would be enough to put anyone over the edge who wasn't already fragile. Do you know what her mental state was before her death?"

Detective Reynolds curtly shook his head. "No, I don't. That's not for me to say. If the prosecutor or the defense attorney wants to get into her head, that's their job. Mine was to investigate a scene and determine to the best of my ability what happened. It's my opinion based on the evidence that she did not commit suicide."

"What else makes you believe that?" Jorja asked, pen at the ready to take more notes.

"Suicide victims don't usually spend a lot of money making plans for the future if they know they won't be around. She had purchased airline tickets and had prepaid a hefty down payment on a trip she had planned for her and her daughter to Disneyland after Christmas. Does that sound like someone who was planning to kill themselves?"

Jorja had to agree, to herself, it did not.

Detective Reynolds continued, "And then there were the drugs. She had sleeping pills in her system. The pills had been in her wine. While some people do take pills to either commit suicide or make sure they don't have the ability to later change their mind, it's certainly not possible for a person to commit suicide while leaving behind absolutely no evidence of where the pills came from. There was no pill bottle. In fact, there was no prescription for that type of medication in her name. However, your client had a prescription for the exact kind of sleeping pill the doc found in her system. How can your client explain that one?"

Jorja scribbled quickly to keep up with what the detective said and then glanced at him as she replied, "I really can't say since what he tells me is covered by attorney-client privilege."

She immediately regretted her statement when she realized he might consider her answer flippant, even if it was true. She was relieved when he showed no attitude toward her as he said, "Fair enough. But you get my point, don't you? She had the pills, but where did she get them?

Why was there no evidence of how the pills were even in her possession? You don't just have a handful of sleeping pills lying around just in case. They weren't prescribed to her, but she got them from somewhere. It was just one more thing about the case that didn't make sense."

Jorja looked down at her notes and then glanced at notes she had taken while reviewing the police report earlier. "So, you found Mr. Stafford's prints on the glass, but no prints other than Cynthia's on the razor, correct? Does that make sense to you? Why would he cover his tracks with the razor, but then leave the glass behind when it could tie him to the scene?"

Detective Reynolds shrugged. "You tell me how you would react after slitting the wrists of your spouse. I'm only assuming he's never killed someone before and the sight of the blood or the sight of her dying affected him more than he realized it would. He probably panicked and got the hell out of there, completely forgetting about the wine glass."

"Okay, but you're guessing. Other than the fingerprints on the glass, which could have been there from when he still lived in the house, what do you really have to tie him to the scene?"

Jorja felt his mood shift at that point. He placed his elbows on the table as he held up both hands, using one index finger to point to the pinky finger of the other. "Well, let's see. First, we have the glass with his prints. If it had been a glass he had used months in the past when he still lived in the house, why was it sitting on the counter, with wine in it, as if he had just set it down?"

He pointed to his ring finger. "We have the evidence of sleeping pills in her wine glass and in her system with nothing to indicate where they came from, if she actually obtained them, while at the same time we have proof they are the exact type of pills prescribed to your client. There's that and the fact that it isn't as likely she would use both means to commit suicide while pills are often used by murderers to make their victims less resistant."

He moved onto his middle finger. "Three, we have the journal with her notes about her fear of him, but regardless of her fear, it was her intention to speak with him that evening."

Next was the index finger. "Four, she bought airline tickets and paid for a trip to Disneyland she planned to take with her daughter after Christmas. People who plan to commit suicide don't plan ahead when it comes to anything beyond the suicide. And five," he continued as he moved on to his thumb, "your client had the means, the motive and the opportunity and on top of that he also has absolutely no alibi."

Jorja was thankful for the fact that she was able to use her own form of shorthand while taking notes. With it, she was able to keep up with his long list of what he considered an open and shut case.

She decided not to further discuss the issue of Michael's alibi. She knew some suspects might make sure to create or make up an alibi if they knew they could later be questioned about a crime, but it was hardly a defense to say a defendant must be innocent since he didn't know any better than to create an alibi for himself.

Once she finished with the last of her notes, Jorja closed her notebook. "Well, Detective, you've given me a lot to think about and I appreciate the fact that you were willing to meet with me. I have no additional questions at this time, but I hope you won't mind if I contact you again later if anything else comes up."

Detective Reynolds stood up and pushed his chair back in place in front of the table. "It's not a problem. But as we go deeper into this case, if it looks like we're going to trial, I may have the prosecutor sit in on any additional meetings. Just a fair warning to you."

Jorja smiled. "Sure, I understand. I appreciate your time and it was very nice meeting you." She held her hand out to shake his.

As he shook her hand he said, "Nice meeting you too. Here, I'll walk you out."

As Detective Reynolds escorted her out of the sheriff's office, her thoughts were racing while she made a mental list of other witnesses she needed to speak with regarding the case. She was determined to discover whether Michael Stafford was telling her the truth about his innocence and if his statements turned out to be true, she was even more determined to discover why Cynthia would go to such terrible lengths to label her husband a murderer.

CHAPTER 8

Helen Matthews breezed into the bookstore to find Jorja looking over paperwork at the cash register. "Good morning, dear. How is your day starting out so far?"

Jorja looked at her mother and smiled. "Hi, Mom. It's a good day so far. We had our usual morning crowd and we're getting ready for one of the elementary classes to arrive for a book reading. How are you?"

Helen gave Jorja a hug before removing her coat and gloves. As she draped her coat over her arm and placed her gloves in her purse, she eyed her daughter with concern. "Honey, you look tired. Are you taking on too much or just not getting enough sleep?"

Jorja averted her mother's perceptive stare by glancing back down at the paperwork on the counter. "I'm fine, Mom. I may not be sleeping as well as I should, but I'm okay. I guess I need to get to bed earlier."

"Why aren't you sleeping well? It's because you have too much on your plate, isn't it?"

"Maybe. But it's more than that…it's just that – I'm just having a hard time getting a good night's sleep."

Helen wouldn't let the matter drop. "Why? Is it that you can't get to sleep or can't stay asleep?"

Jorja shuffled the paperwork around in an attempt to delay her answer.

"Jorja? Can you tell me what's wrong?" Helen reached down to grab Jorja's hands to stop her from fidgeting with the paperwork.

She finally looked at her mother. "It's nothing, really. I'm just having a lot of dreams lately and when I wake up it takes me awhile to get back to sleep."

"Why? What kind of dreams are you having? Do you mean nightmares? Are you dreaming again about that night? Come here." Helen pulled on Jorja's hands to force her around the counter and to the couch where they could both sit down.

Jorja took a deep breath as she prepared to answer her mother's questions. "Yes, I'm having dreams about that night. But it's different this time. Before, I dreamed Ryan actually died because I wasn't able to save him. Now, I still dream he dies, but I've been having another dream as well."

Jorja quickly glanced at Taylor who bounced down the staircase toward them.

"Hi, Helen. How are you?" Taylor asked as she stood by the couch to look down at Helen and Jorja.

"I'm well, Taylor, and you?"

"I'm doing great. You're staying over for the weekend, right?"

Helen quickly glanced at Jorja. If she'd had any inclination to head home to Edmonds, she would have already changed her mind after her brief conversation with Jorja. "Yes, I plan to stay over, at least for tonight."

Taylor gave a quick nod. "Good. Then I'll have more time to visit with you later. I need to take care of putting together a book display so I'll let you get back to what you were talking about."

Jorja didn't miss the sly glance Taylor gave her before she slipped away. Taylor was very perceptive and while Jorja knew she'd love to be a part of the conversation, if not out of sheer curiosity, she also knew to give Jorja and her mother their space.

Helen was quick to get back to the conversation. "What are you dreaming about now?"

Jorja hesitated. This was a touchy subject. It had been hard enough on her mother to finally admit she wasn't Jorja's biological mother, after Jorja discovered her Aunt Gloria had actually given birth to her and Ryan. She didn't want to bring up the subject of her biological father, but in the case of her dreams, she really had no control.

"Well...I'm dreaming Ryan survives, but not because of what I do for him. I've been dreaming about someone else who steps in to save both of us."

"Oh? Who?" Helen's curiosity turned to apprehension as her brows furrowed and she swallowed a lump that suddenly formed in her throat.

"Mom, don't be upset. It doesn't mean anything, but you know I'll always wonder...you know it's only natural for me to wonder-"

"Who your real father is." Helen finished.

This time Jorja swallowed hard. "Yes. I can't help it. These dreams make me think about him more often. I've been dreaming that he's there, just before Cooper shoots Ryan. When Cooper pulls the trigger he doesn't shoot Ryan, he shoots our father who suddenly jumps in between them to save Ryan's life. But before I can get to him to try to save him or to finally see who he is, I wake up. Every time. And each time, I wake to the sickening thought that it's possible he really has died and we'll never know who he is or why he left Aunt Gloria when she was pregnant. We'll never know if he had a good reason or if he was just some big jerk who hated the thought of having kids."

Helen leaned over to give her another hug. "Oh honey, I know this is hard for you." She pulled back to look at Jorja as she held her shoulders. "I'm sorry I can't give you the answers you need. Maybe it's a good thing you don't know. Wouldn't it be better to imagine he had a good reason for leaving rather than find out the truth is ugly and heartless?"

Jorja shook her head. "No, Mom. I'd rather know the truth. Look at what happened to Kat once I helped her discover the truth about her mom? She thought her own mother abandoned her. She never understood why and she wanted answers, even if those answers were heartless. It's not knowing that's worse. And even though I discovered her mother had been murdered, she's somehow dealt with that much better than I thought possible. I've asked her about it and you know what she told me?"

Helen shook her head and waited.

Jorja continued, "She told me that it saddens her to know her mother's life ended the way it did, but it helped her to understand her mother didn't willingly abandon her as a small child. Everyone wants to feel wanted and if you believe your own parents don't want you, it's a very hard reality to accept."

Helen removed her hands from Jorja's shoulders and leaned back with a heavy sigh. "Which is exactly why I never wanted you to know the truth about Gloria. Imagine growing up with that knowledge as a child. God only knows how Kat turned out to be such a great kid after having that knowledge, even though it wasn't the truth. It's a true testament to how her father raised her. I'm glad you never knew as a child. See how it's affecting you now? At least as an adult you can deal with it much differently than while you were growing up. I'm sorry, Jorja, really I am. But you can't let the 'what if's' and the 'if only's' take over life. Please, don't let it affect you so that you lose sleep or make yourself sick. I'm here for you, both your dad and I are, but we can't change the truth about your past and we don't have the answers you need. I know it's an important fact about your past, but please don't let this one unknown truth take over your life."

"You'd tell me if you did know, wouldn't you?"

Helen's mouth opened slightly in surprise. "Of course I'd tell you," she said, holding a hand to her chest. "You can't really believe I'd keep it from you, do you?"

Jorja closed her eyes in resignation. She knew there was no going further about this subject with her mother, who would rather the past remain buried just like she attempted to do when it came to the truth about Gloria. For now, Jorja would tell her mother what she wanted to hear, but she felt a defiance she couldn't shake.

"No, Mom, I know you'd tell me. Thanks for listening though. These dreams have shaken me up a bit, but maybe talking about them will help me get past them."

Helen nodded in agreement. "Yes, it's good you told me. I'm sure if you just realize there are some things in life we will never be privy to, you may finally get a good night's sleep. Now, I should probably get to work. I have a hair appointment with Sandra at twelve-thirty so I want to get as much done as I can in the next few hours." Helen patted Jorja's hand before standing up. "Do you feel better?"

Jorja nodded as she also stood. "Yes, I do. Thanks. I should also get to work myself to prepare for the kids who will be here soon. I'll be busy with them for awhile so the desk is yours."

She watched as her mother grabbed her belongings and moved up the staircase toward the office. As much as she faulted her mother's inability to take part in discovering the truth about Jorja's past, she was grateful to her mother for always being there for her.

Jorja's thoughts were interrupted as the doorbell chimed and Kat entered the store. Her long blond hair was tucked under a pink stocking cap and scarf and her nose was bright red. She wrapped her arms around herself and visibly shivered as she caught Jorja's stare. "Hi, Jorja. Boy, it's cold out there! I decided to walk over from school and the walk didn't help warm me up at all."

"Hi, Kat." Nodding toward Taylor who was now at the coffee stand, she said, "Go over there and get yourself a hot chocolate or something. The second grade class won't be here for another fifteen minutes or so. That should give you time to warm yourself up so you're prepared when they get here."

As Kat moved to ask Taylor for a hot drink, Jorja smiled. She enjoyed having Kat work at the store and she would never forget the first day they met, when Kat had asked her to find her mother. Jorja had immediately felt a need to assist Kat and take her under her wing by giving her a job. It was a decision she had never regretted. Kat was like the little sister she never had. The only sticky part of the situation was the fact that Lydia was Kat's aunt; something Jorja couldn't hold against Kat.

Jorja finished organizing the paperwork she'd been going through before her mother arrived and then moved around the counter toward Kat and Taylor.

"So you get credit for class by coming here to read to the kids? That's great. I wish we had fun projects like that when I was in high school." Taylor said. "Jorja, did you get fun projects like this when you were in high school? I know I didn't."

Jorja shook her head. "No, I don't remember having to earn community service hours each grade like they do now. We just took our classes and worked odd jobs to make extra money after school. What about you?"

Taylor laughed. "Nope. The most fun I had as a volunteer had nothing to do with school. I was a life guard at the local pool during the summers."She winked at Kat. "It was a great way to meet cute guys."

Kat grinned at Taylor as she took a sip of cocoa.

"So are we all set for the kids? Do we have enough cups and cocoa for them?" Jorja peeked over the counter to see what Taylor had put together for the grade school kids. She saw cocoa packets and some boxes of cookies. "Did you get these from Dylan for today? When did he stop by?"

Taylor nodded as she smiled. "Yeah, he made some cute cut-outs for the kids. Each is either a snowman, a snowflake, a mitten or a penguin. Aren't they cute? I stopped by there on my way this morning."

Jorja opened a box to take a better look at the cookies. Dylan had outdone himself again. "They're adorable. The kids will absolutely love them. So we're all set then?"

"Yep. All set. With cocoa, cookies and the bookmarks, the kids are in for a real treat. Kat, we thought we'd give each of the kids their own bookmark. Just let them pick their favorite from the box Jorja will give you."

Kat smiled as she unwound the scarf from her neck and finally took her hat off. "That's a great idea. It'll be fun handing them out to the kids. Whew! I'm finally beginning to feel warm again." Kat placed her hat, scarf and gloves on a nearby chair so she could remove her jacket. "I'll take these back to the break room."

After Kat left them to walk to the back of the store, Jorja and Taylor heard the doorbell chime. The store was suddenly filled with twenty five students, all talking excitedly over each other as the grade school teacher filed in behind them. Mrs. Gibson gave Jorja and Taylor a smile before she turned to her grade school class and held her hand above her head. She then pointed her index finger up at the ceiling while remaining completely quiet. Jorja and Taylor watched as the children continued to talk excitedly to one another until one student saw the teacher's stance, told his friend and then another student noticed the upraised finger and told her friend. Before Jorja and Taylor could count to ten, the whole group of children had all become aware of the raised finger and had quieted down.

Mrs. Gibson lowered her hand and smiled at her students. "Great job, class. Now, we're at the bookstore today for a special treat. We're going to spend some time here to look at books, have some cocoa and cookies and one of the high school students will be reading one of her favorite books to you. So let's get in two lines, boys and girls, here in front of this coffee stand. You each get a cup of cocoa, pick out a cookie and then go over to the children's section there to wait for the book reading. Come on, two lines. There, great job." Mrs. Gibson turned back to Jorja and Taylor. "They're all yours."

Taylor moved around to the coffee stand just as Kat also returned to help. Jorja stood closer to Mrs. Gibson. "We have another treat for the kids today too. We have a box of bookmarks for them to pick from before they leave."

Mrs. Gibson clapped her hands together. "Oh, that's splendid! What a great idea, Jorja. All the children will love it."

"If you would like a cup of coffee after we get all the children settled, just let Taylor know and she can get that for you. No charge."

Mrs. Gibson smiled. "Well, thank you. A nice Carmel Macchiato sure would hit the spot right now."

"Then that's what we'll get you." Jorja felt a hand tap her lower back and she turned to find a couple of students who already had their hot chocolate and cookies. One of the taller boys spoke first. "Where do you want us to sit?"

"Oh, it's just around the corner there. Do you want to follow me?" Jorja worked her way to the children's section with a few of the students following right behind her. She pointed to the chairs and pillows where they could sit and told them the reading would begin once everyone was ready.

Taylor and Kat finished serving the rest of the class and before long the children were comfortable on their chairs, pillows and floor mats as they waited for Kat to sit in the reading chair positioned in the corner of the room.

Once Kat was settled, Jorja moved next to Kat to address the room first. "Hello, everyone. My name is Jorja and I want to welcome you to Books 'N Brew. I'm so glad your teacher, Mrs. Gibson, brought you here to meet us today and I hope you enjoy your visit. While you drink your cocoa and eat your cookies, we're going to listen as Kat reads us a book. After the reading, you can all look around the store and enjoy some of the games we have set aside for you to play. Each of you will be receiving a bookmark as a gift from us so make sure you pick a bookmark before you head back to school. Kat?" Jorja turned toward Kat before sitting on a nearby chair.

Kat stood up, holding a book in her hands. "Hi, my name is Kat and I'm a senior at the high school. The book I'm going to read to you today is called *Stellaluna* by Janell Cannon. It was one of my favorite books when I was little and my dad used to read it to me. It's a very special story and it helped me when I was young and had a hard time understanding why my life was different from my other friends because they had a mother and I did not. This book helped me to understand we may be different from each other, but in many ways we are very much alike."

Kat then sat down and began to read from the book. While Kat was reading, Jorja looked around the room at the second grade class as they sipped their cocoa and nibbled on their cookies. Each child had their eyes on Kat, entranced with the story of the little bat that fell from the safety of her mother's embrace into a bird's nest. The children giggled as Kat read about how Stellaluna tried to behave like a bird, ate bugs and learned to hang by her little bat thumbs rather than her feet. As Kat finished reading the story, most of the children had finished their drinks and their cookies.

Kat closed the book and asked the children, "So, how did you all like the book? Do you understand what the story is about?"

A little boy with very dark curls raised his hand. Kat turned to him and asked, "Yes? Do you know what the story is trying to say?"

The boy quickly looked around at his classmates. Jorja knew children had active imaginations so she wondered what he was going to say. Finally, he looked at Kat. "Um, that it's okay to be yourself?"

Kat smiled brightly. "That's right! Good job. Yes, it's okay to be yourself. We're all different in the way we look, the way we act and how our home life is, but we're also very much the same too with many of the same feelings, thoughts and fears. We just have to appreciate others for who they are and not try to change them just because we want them to be more like us. Does that make sense?"

Some of the children bobbed their heads in agreement while others appeared too shy to involve themselves. Jorja smiled at the group as she stood up. "Thanks so much for letting Kat read to you today. If you'd like, you can take a look around the store or just sit here and play the games we have on the tables for you. Don't forget to get a bookmark before you go back to school. It's our special treat to say thank you for coming today."

Jorja then walked to Kat and sat in a nearby chair as the children took their time deciding what they wanted to do. "Great job, Kat. The kids love you and you did a terrific job reading. I'm going to talk to Mrs. Gibson about asking the other teachers to involve their classes in book readings as well. Did you enjoy yourself?"

Kat grinned. "It was fun. I just love little kids. Aren't they all cute? If any of the other teachers want to come for a book reading, I'll read for them. Just let me know when so I can get permission to leave school again."

Jorja nodded. This was good for Kat, she thought. The past few years had been difficult for Kat after losing her father to a heart attack, having to move in with her aunt who she didn't have the best relationship with and then discovering her mother had been murdered when she'd always been told her mother had run away. Jorja knew these types of distractions were good for Kat and she believed it helped with Kat's healing process to help others.

While Jorja and Kat sat chatting, Jorja noticed that the boy with the dark curls had remained where he had been sitting and he wasn't interacting with the other children. She decided to see if she could get him more involved. Leaning over, she said, "Hello. What's your name?"

The little boy turned to look at her with dark brown eyes. "My name is Justin."

"Don't you want to look at books or play any of the games with your friends?" Jorja asked.

Justin shook his head. "No, that's okay."

She thought she would try to get more from him. "Do you like your teacher, Mrs. Gibson? She was nice to bring you here, wasn't she?"

Justin nodded. "Yes, I like her. I like books too. But my mom said not to touch the books because we can't buy them."

Jorja frowned. "Well, you don't have to buy any books and you don't have to worry about touching them." She pointed at a nearby bookshelf. "See that bookshelf over there? Those books are just for kids to look at. You don't have to buy them, you can read them all you want and you can read them again anytime you come back to visit. Okay?"

Justin's eyes widened. "It's okay if I read them and I don't have to buy them?"

"Yes. Those books aren't for sale. They're just for kids like you who want to look at them while visiting the store. Here, give me your cup and I'll throw it away for you. You can go look at the books before Mrs. Gibson says it's time to leave."

"Okay." Justin stood up from the pillow he had been sitting cross-legged on, handed her his cup and headed to the bookshelf.

Placing her chin on her hand, Kat said, "Aren't they cute? I can't wait to have kids."

Jorja's head snapped as she quickly looked at Kat. "You mean in the distant future, right?"

Kat grinned at the obvious concern. "Yes, Jorja. I'm talking after high school, after college and after I meet the love of my life. Don't worry. I'm not in a hurry to have a family. I just can't wait until I get to be a mom."

"Well, don't make it too soon. That's all I'm saying. You have plenty of time for that later on." Jorja knew she sounded like she was mothering Kat, but she couldn't help it. She was about to apologize for being bossy when Mrs. Gibson sat down beside them.

"You had a nice little chat with Justin, I see. Did he open up to you at all?"

Jorja glanced at Justin, who was sitting alone while he read a picture book.

"Well, he was happy when I told him he could look at books because his mom apparently told him not to since he couldn't buy any. If I hadn't, he was probably just going to sit on his pillow until you told him it was time to leave."

Mrs. Gibson shook her head. "That poor kid. He's been attending school here for only a few weeks and he just doesn't seem to fit in with the other kids yet. I think, even at his young age, that he and his mother have moved around quite a bit." Mrs. Gibson looked at Kat. "I believe, Kat, that what you shared with your story was true fate because he has a mother but no father. Even in this day and age, having only one parent makes a child feel differently from others who have normal two-parent households. I believe he relates to the little bat in your story because he feels like a bat living among a bunch of birds himself."

Kat's compassion immediately kicked in. "Oh, that poor guy. What happened to his dad?"

Mrs. Gibson shook her head. "I'm not sure. When I met with the mother, she only told me that Justin had no father. She really didn't appear to want to elaborate."

"He and his mother live here in town?" Jorja asked, now curious about Justin and what brought him and his mother to the area.

"Well, not right in town, I don't believe. I think they have a place between here and Tumwater. She decided to enroll him in Tenino rather than the bigger school in Tumwater because she said she wanted him to be in a smaller school. She was just hired as a checker at the grocery store here in town so it seems to work out for her because she's working while Justin is in school."

"What's the mom's name?" Kat asked as she turned to look at Jorja. "Maybe you should invite her to attend the next book club meeting. You know, so she can make friends."

"Sure, we could always add new blood to the group. Makes it more interesting. What's her name?"

"Bailey is her name." Mrs. Gibson replied. "Bailey Maxwell. She's very shy and hasn't involved herself much with school functions yet. I believe she moved here from another state so it would certainly be nice if you invited her to your book club meetings to help her come out of her shell and make new friends. It might help Justin too because he seems hesitant to make friends as well. It's almost like he unconsciously avoids making ties."

Bailey...Jorja thought for a moment and then it struck her that Ruth had brought a guest named Bailey to the last book club meeting. It appeared they already had a head start on getting the newcomer involved with the group. While she had been curious about Bailey the first night they met, she couldn't deny the fact that she was now even more curious to discover the truth behind Bailey and her story.

CHAPTER 9

Jorja felt buried in paperwork again. Her mother had spent a few hours the day before sorting through the accounting records to prepare the year-end documentation they would need to file taxes. Jorja spent some time going through what her mother had provided to get a sense of the numbers and how the store did financially, but her eyes were beginning to blur from stress.

With frustration, she quickly shuffled the paperwork into one messy pile and shoved it to the side of the desk. She just didn't want to be bothered with the numbers right now. She trusted her mother enough to know the documentation would be accurate so she decided she would spend time going over the paperwork when she had more patience for that type of work.

For now, she wanted to get back to her case involving Michael Stafford. She had contacted Cynthia Stafford's sister, Gail Pierce, who had agreed to meet over a cup of coffee and as she glanced at the time on her computer, she realized she had just under a half hour to prepare for the interview. Reaching down to the floor, Jorja grabbed her messenger bag and opened it to pull out her file on the Stafford case. She had been able to speak briefly with the attorney about how he was going to defend Michael and it had been agreed that the attorney would attempt to acquire any medical records that might give them some indication as to Cynthia's mental state before she died. Until then, Jorja would get what additional information she could to see if it led to anything useful.

Opening her notepad, she made a few notes on a blank piece of paper with information she wanted to get from Gail. She mentally prepared herself for the fact that she would have to be sensitive to Gail, who likely believed Michael killed her sister. She continued making notes as she scanned through some of the police reports and reviewed Gail's initial statement one more time. Before she knew it, Taylor buzzed her on the phone.

"Jorja, Mrs. Pierce is here to see you."

"Thanks Taylor. Do we have customers downstairs?"

"No, it's empty right now."

"Good. I'll just be a second." She placed the paperwork in her folder, grabbed her notebook and a pen and went downstairs. Standing near the coffee stand, wearing a green winter coat with a bright red scarf, Jorja spotted a woman who she would describe as beautiful yet haunting. She knew Gail was in her late forties, based on the police report, but she would never have guessed correctly if she'd only just met Gail. Gail had cream-colored skin, fine features, a confident bearing and thick, wavy chestnut hair down to her shoulder blades. It was Gail's eyes which Jorja felt were truly haunting. They were dark brown, almost black, and in contrast to the rest of Gail's demeanor, full of sadness. Jorja realized she could only imagine what the loss of a sister might do to someone if they were very close. She couldn't bear the thought of losing Taylor, who was the closest she'd ever had to a sister.

"Mrs. Pierce? I'm Jorja. I thought we could sit down here on the sofa where it's more comfortable. Do you mind?"

"No, I don't mind at all. Please, you can call me Gail. There's no reason to be so formal." Gail began to walk toward the couch as she removed her coat.

Jorja placed her file on the steamer trunk in front of the couch and asked, "Would you like something to drink? We have a few holiday blends that are very good. We have cinnamon spice, pumpkin spice or a gingerbread latte and we also have peppermint mochas. Any of them sound good to you?"

Gail tapped her manicured index finger on her chin as she decided. Finally, she said, "I think the gingerbread latte sounds good. Thank you."

Jorja turned to Taylor, who was already beginning to make the drink. "I got it Jorja. Do you want one?"

"Yes, please. Can you make me a pumpkin spice latte? Thanks."

Jorja then sat down on the couch and grabbed the file off the trunk. Gail also sat down after laying her coat over the back of the couch. Jorja fingered the post-it notes she had placed to mark specific documents until she found the one titled "Pierce Statement." She pulled the statement from the folder and held it up for Gail to see.

"I have your statement here, the one you originally provided to the police. Have you had a chance to review it before today?"

Gail nodded. "Yes, I looked at it a few days ago when I was told by the prosecutor that Michael's attorney had hired an investigator who might wish to speak to me. The prosecutor said I didn't have to speak to you without him present, but I don't see any need for that. My husband was an attorney before he passed away. I understand your role is just to follow up on the case by questioning the witnesses to see if you can find something the police missed or something that might actually dig Michael out of this hole he's dug himself in to. I'm not sure you'll find either in this case. Thanks." Gail finished as she reached up to take the drink Taylor brought over to her.

"Thanks." Jorja said as Taylor placed her drink on the trunk.

Jorja turned back to face Gail. "I appreciate the fact that you appear to understand my role. It's not to corner you or trick you into saying anything. I'm hired as an unbiased third party to look into the reports and to follow up with witnesses to verify the facts and to verify what the witnesses will say on the stand should the case go to trial. Is that what you understand my role to be?"

Gail finished taking a sip of her latte before answering. She nodded slightly. "Yes, I understand that to be your job. As long as you treat me with respect, it's what you'll get from me in return."

"That's fair enough and I completely appreciate that attitude. I would expect no less myself." Jorja set the statement to the side and pulled out her notes. She placed a notepad on her lap as she leaned back to get a bit more comfortable before she began to write.

"I've read your statement and I understand how terribly difficult this has been for you. I guess I'd like to start with how you feel about Michael Stafford. Do you think he's capable of what the police and the prosecutor are accusing him of doing?"

Gail also leaned back on the couch cushion. She held her cup in both hands as she stared out the store window at an elderly couple walking by. Without looking at Jorja she said, "There are a lot of things about Michael that I'm in the dark about. I had always thought my sister and I were close, but there were incidents between the two of them that she would keep completely silent about. Some days he would treat her like a queen; others, he would treat her like a slave. And she would let him. I never understood their relationship. I didn't see any obvious physical abuse between them. Maybe a small bruise here and there, but it was easily explained away by Cynthia because she was, admittedly, pretty clumsy. She was always walking into door frames, dressers and tables. Ever since we were kids. She's quite a bit younger than I am and when we were children, if Cynthia ever got mad at me she would lie to our parents and say that I hit her because she always seemed to have a bruise somewhere on her body she could point to and blame me for. She was the baby, they adored her and I learned quickly they never believed her to be a liar. Thankfully, she didn't get mad at me very often."

Gail looked down at her cup before taking another sip. She then glanced at Jorja's cup before meeting Jorja's gaze. "You should drink your latte. It's going to get cold."

Smiling, Jorja said, "It's a fault I have. I can't drink and talk or write at the same time. I always tend to have to heat up my coffee, which completely irritates Taylor." For good measure, Jorja reached over to pick up her cup and take a sip before setting the cup back down.

"So what did you think about Michael himself? Was he a good husband? A good father?"

"Like I said, their relationship was a bit odd to me. It wasn't something Cynthia ever told me and I truly believe she never told me because she was embarrassed. I feel terrible about this, but I believe she saw what I had, a wonderful, caring, loving husband, and she didn't want to admit she hadn't found the same in her husband. I may be wrong, but it's what I think. And my husband was the best, compared to anyone I've ever met, and he will always be the best even now that he's gone. He was able to give me everything I ever wanted, except for children."

Rather than offer pity upon condolences, Jorja decided to move away from that delicate subject. "And how was Michael as a father? Were you around him and the girls a lot?"

Gail looked toward the window again. "Well, that's more of a sticky subject. My sister made certain claims in court about Michael. Ugly accusations I hoped weren't true involving my niece, Liz. There were a few times I felt Cynthia wanted to tell me something about her relationship with Michael, but I would have *never* guessed it had anything to do with Michael molesting Liz. I'm heartbroken to think that Liz may have possibly been the victim of such an unspeakable crime before she died." Gail wiped away a tear as it escaped out of the corner of her eye.

Jorja continued to write as she asked, "So Liz never made any statements to you about her relationship with her dad?"

Gail shook her head. "No, I'm afraid I wasn't as close to Liz as I would have liked. It became very difficult when she turned thirteen and began hanging out with boys and girls who seemed to get her into trouble. Cynthia did speak to me about that. She was at her wits end trying to figure out how to keep Liz home, but Liz would just sneak out and get into more trouble. She was shoplifting, abusing alcohol, even getting into fights. Cynthia tried to cover up for Liz, but Michael would find out and that's where many of their arguments generated from. Eventually, Cynthia told me Michael was moving out and she didn't appear too upset about it, but then when Liz died months later, Michael held her responsible and filed the custody case against her for Tabitha. The few times I spoke to Michael, he's told me Cynthia made up the molestation allegations to try to win the custody case. I didn't want to testify, but the attorney served me a subpoena and I had to testify to the fact that Cynthia never told me about her claims that Michael had molested

Liz. It was awful. Just awful. You can imagine how I felt when Cynthia lost the case and was later found dead. I just didn't know what to think. Did she kill herself because she couldn't deal with losing Tabitha? Did he kill her like her note on the bathroom wall says and if so, why?"

Even though her hand was beginning to cramp, Jorja continued to write as she asked, "Do you think she was capable of suicide or that he was capable of murder?"

Jorja finished her last note and looked up when Gail still hadn't responded. Gail remained silent as emotions seemed to rage inside her. Her eyes glazed with tears which spilled over her lashes when she finally blinked. "Was my sister capable? I don't have children, but if I were to lose them the way my sister did within a short period of time, would I think about suicide myself? It seems conceivable, but I don't think I could follow through with it. Does one have to be very weak or very strong to follow through with something like that? I always thought my sister was strong, but this isn't how I'd like to remember that strength. And is Michael capable? I guess we all are, if we're pushed into a corner. My sister had pushed him into a corner by calling him a monster, but yet he won the custody case so why would he need to kill her? To get her out of the way? Why would he do that to Tabitha?" Gail pulled a tissue from her bag to lightly dab at her cheeks. "Whether she did it or he did it, none of it really makes any sense."

Jorja leaned over to place the notepad and pen on the steamer trunk before she replied. "I understand how difficult this is for you and how many questions you must have about what happened. For now, I think maybe I've asked you enough questions, but maybe we could talk more at a later time, if I have more questions for you as I continue to investigate. Would that be okay with you?"

Gail smiled. "Yes, that would be fine with me. Don't get me wrong. If Michael killed my sister, I will help the police any way I can. If he didn't, I hope you're able to help his attorney figure out why my sister did what she did. Either way, I'll talk to you if you need anything further from me."

Jorja thanked Gail and expressed her appreciation for Gail's willingness to meet with her. As Gail said goodbye and left the store, Jorja knew she would need to continue to dig deeper to find out the truth in this case, if the truth actually wished to be found.

CHAPTER 10

The end of January brought cold weather and chilly rain. It was not Jorja's favorite time of year in Western Washington. There were days she would try to run from her Jeep to a building in order to limit how long she was in the rain, but when the temperatures dipped even lower, she had to remember to watch her step to avoid slipping on frozen sidewalks and steps.

Today was a frozen rain kind of day. The temperatures had not warmed up enough and the rain from the night before was now a thin sheet of ice on the uncovered sidewalks. As Jorja used a shovel to spread salt on the sidewalk outside the bookstore, she made a mental note to research what it would cost to add a larger awning over the front door of the store.

"Good morning, gorgeous. Want me to finish that for you?" Jorja looked up to see Brad Dawson, her old high school sweetheart and the reason behind Lydia's jilted jealous attitude toward her.

Jorja was cold, but when Brad looked at her, she always felt just a little warmer. Today was no exception. While their high school romance was long over, she still couldn't deny a certain attraction toward him.

"Well, sure, if you have the time. What brings you here this morning?" She asked as she stepped under the small awning over the door and out of Brad's way.

"Oh, just thought I'd stop by to say hi and get a cup of coffee. What they serve at the school employee lounge isn't always up to snuff. You should serve coffee there. You'd make a killing from all the teachers needing a caffeine boost before they take on their first high school class for the day."

Jorja smiled, but didn't want to get into whether she should be serving coffee anyplace other than her bookstore. She was happy just the way it was.

"What kind of drink do you want? I'll go inside and ask Taylor to get it started for you."

Brad turned to grin at her, his blue eyes sparkling. "That would be great. I'll let you choose."

She grinned back before turning to head inside the store. She found Taylor opening a new box of books that had arrived the previous day.

"Hey Taylor, Brad is outside salting the rest of the walkway for me. Can you make him a coffee? He said to surprise him."

Taylor placed the handful of books she'd been holding on the counter before moving to the coffee stand. Her brown eyes sparkled with mischief as she gave Jorja a devilish grin. "You want me to surprise him? How about a cinnamon spice latte with your phone number and the words 'call me' at the bottom of the cup?"

Jorja stuck her tongue out at Taylor. "You do that and I'll find a way to get you back."

Taylor giggled. "Well he hasn't asked you out yet so maybe he just needs a little push. What do you think?"

Jorja frowned. "I don't need him to ask me out. We're good friends and I like our relationship just the way it is."

Taylor only responded with a grin and a wink as she began to make Brad's drink. She knew Jorja wasn't in the market for a serious relationship, but she still enjoyed teasing about it.

The doorbell chimed and Brad walked inside the store, rubbing his hands together to warm them up. "Okay, the sidewalk's all clear. You won't be having any customers slipping outside your windows now."

"Good. Thanks for finishing that for me. Taylor is about done making your drink."

As Brad moved toward the coffee stand to get his coffee, the door opened and both Officer Fritz and Reynolds walked in. Jorja hadn't seen either of them since her last altercation with Fritz a week ago about the Stafford case. She waited to see if this was a social visit or not.

Reynolds spoke first, "Hey Jorja, how are you this morning?"

"I'm fine, how are you?" She responded as she glanced from Reynolds to Fritz and back again.

Reynolds replied, "Doing well, very well. Just here to get a cup of coffee. Fritz? Want me to order for you?"

Fritz turned to Reynolds. "Sure, just an Americano with two shots. Thanks." He then turned back to Jorja and asked, "So you're having a good morning?"

"Uh, yeah, so far so good. How about you?" Jorja wasn't sure if Fritz really wanted to know how she was feeling or if he was leading into another conversation.

"It's okay. Just started our shifts, so you never know." Fritz leaned against the counter by the check register as he continued, "So have you thought anymore about what I said the other day?"

She tried to pretend she didn't know what he was talking about, but she wasn't the best sort of liar. Finally, her expression showed some of her irritation as she raised one brow and pursed her lips before answering. "You mean about how you don't think I should work on cases involving what you believe are already solved crimes?"

Fritz straightened at her tone. "I'm not saying they're guilty just because we arrested them, although that's usually the case, but you don't have any idea what sort of people you'll be dealing with. You could be putting yourself in danger again. Do you really think it's a good idea?"

Jorja crossed her arms as she stared at him. He couldn't mistake the fire in her green eyes as she replied, "No, Fritz, it may not be a good idea, but I could walk across the street and get hit by a bus. No one knows whether what they are doing is going to be their last task on Earth, but while I'm here, I'm going to do what I'm good at. Right now, I think this type of work is what I'm good at and there's no reason I should stop just because you believe I'm hanging out with riff raff."

Fritz shook his head in frustration. "I'm not trying to tell you what to do. I just wish you'd understand the reason I'm bringing this up with you. You were almost killed by someone you thought you could actually trust to do the right thing. Now you're dealing with individuals who are most likely capable and very likely guilty of the crimes they're accused of. I just want you to be careful, that's all."

"Here you go, Fritz. Taylor made it nice and hot." Reynolds said as he moved next to Fritz to hand him his coffee. Reynolds then saw the look on Fritz's face as well as Jorja's. "Uh, I'll be chatting with Taylor whenever you're ready to leave." He hurriedly left them to head back to the coffee stand.

Jorja sighed at Reynolds' quick exit when she realized they made him feel uncomfortable. She hadn't yet been able to figure out her relationship with Fritz and she guessed even Reynolds felt the same way as Fritz's best friend. Ever since the two of them helped save her life and put behind bars the person who almost killed her and

Ryan, she and Fritz had formed a type of friendship she wasn't able to label. Things were easier with Reynolds, who made no bones about how much he cared for Jorja, and for Taylor, as their friend and protector. Reynolds was also married, which made the lines much cleaner.

Not so much with Fritz.

She wasn't sure where the line was between them. Sometimes he felt like a friend, other times an older bossy brother and then there were those days when she saw a look in his eyes that made her wonder...she wondered whether there was more to his feelings than even he was willing to admit. But she pushed away any such thoughts. It was no different with Fritz than it was with Brad; she didn't want to get into a relationship. At least not right now.

Jorja finally said, "I'll be careful, Fritz, I promise. You don't have to worry about me anymore."

"Why would he have to worry about you?" Jorja turned to see Brad standing behind her, sipping from his cup as he eyed Fritz warily.

She tried to wave him off as she replied, "It's nothing, Brad. Just a professional disagreement."

Brad's gaze moved from Jorja to Fritz and back to Jorja again. His brow furrowed with concern and then his mouth tightened with determination. Using the opportunity to get on Jorja's good side, he turned to Fritz and said, "You don't have to worry about Jorja. She's tough and can take care of herself. She's smart enough to know how to stay out of trouble. Besides, if she ever needs a bodyguard while she's working, she can always use me." Before she could say a word, Brad moved forward to put his arm around her as he continued to stare at Fritz.

Fritz stared back. Jorja watched as he narrowed his eyes at Brad before turning his gaze to her. He then quickly nodded and gave her a half smile. "You're right.

She's tough and I'm sure she can take care of herself. But Jorja, if you need help and can't pull Brad here away from the football field, don't hesitate to call me. You have my number."

Fritz turned to leave the store as he yelled out, "Reynolds! Let's get going."

Reynolds quickly said goodbye to Taylor and hurried after Fritz who was already heading out the door.

Once they were gone, Jorja grabbed Brad's hand and pushed his arm from her shoulders. "Brad, you didn't have to add to that conversation, especially since it was a private one."

Brad gave her a feigned hurtful look. "Aw, come on, Jorja. I didn't do anything worse than what he did. He was trying to make it look like you don't know what you're doing. I had to stick up for you, that's all."

She shook her head as she smiled. "Yeah, thanks for that, I guess."

"Good, I'm glad you're not mad at me. Well, I have to get going. Class starts in ten minutes. See you later." Brad then left the store and she turned her attention to the books Taylor had been going through earlier. She soon felt Taylor move next to her, waiting for her to say something. Jorja attempted to ignore her, but Taylor wasn't one to be ignored.

"So what happened between you and Fritz? Was that a heated conversation you were having? What did he do? Ask you out and you said no?"

She turned to look at Taylor, who gave her a wink with her grin.

Jorja looked away and back down at the books she decided to use as a distraction. "No, Taylor, that's not it. It's the same conversation as before. He's upset I'm working for who he believes are bad people. He's afraid I might get hurt again."

"You know why, don't you? Because he actually cares about you. He just hasn't been able to figure out how to tell you." Taylor said as she leaned over to force eye contact with Jorja.

Jorja suddenly turned to Taylor and blurted out, "You're sure having a lot of fun with this. What do you want? Do you want Brad to ask me out or Fritz? I'm not going to date both, you know."

Taylor grinned. "Well, whichever one asks you first, I guess. By then, if you feel any disappointment about the second one once the first one asks you, you'll finally know which one you actually wanted to ask you out first."

Jorja shook her head in frustration. "You're not making any sense."

"Oh yes I am. If you can't choose between one or the other, you just have to finally make a choice and you'll immediately feel disappointment if you choose the wrong one. But since you won't ask either one of them out, I guess you'll have to wait until they ask you out."

Again Jorja shook her head. "Nope. I'm not going to ask them out. Really, I told you already. I have no room for romance right now. I have enough to do working on your wedding preparations on top of everything else."

Taylor pouted. "So now you're trying to make me feel guilty for why you don't have a love life? Because you're too busy working on my wedding?" Taylor suddenly smiled again. "Well, that's not going to work. Eventually, one of those two, if not both, will get tired of waiting and they will finally ask you out. You just better be ready because I'm not going to let you say no."

Jorja decided she didn't have the energy to argue the subject any longer. If she did, she would have to admit to Taylor her real fear behind getting into a relationship and it wasn't something she was willing to admit to or discuss right now, even with her best friend.

CHAPTER 11

"Kat, can you and Bruce bring a few more chairs from the back room?" Jorja asked as she tried to finish getting the store ready for a PTA meeting scheduled that evening.

"Sure. Come on, Bruce, I'll show you where they are and you can carry them." Kat said as she smiled at Bruce.

Jorja watched the two as they walked toward the back of the store. She had noticed lately that Kat and Bruce had been hanging out together more often. Bruce, also a senior and a football player, was a good kid, from what Jorja knew of him. She hadn't been able to figure out whether he and Kat were just good friends or if it had turned into something more serious.

"They're cute, aren't they?" Taylor asked as she sidled up next to Jorja. "Before you know it, Kat might be making her own wedding plans."

She turned to give Taylor a quick glare as she shook her head. "Oh, no you don't. We're not going to be marrying Kat off anytime soon. She's got to finish school, hopefully go to college and then work on her career. There's time for marriage and babies later."

Taylor laughed. "Jeez, you sound like her mother, or at least an older sister." Holding her hands up to ward off another verbal attack, she continued, "I know, I know. She's young. I'm only kidding. But you have to admit, they are cute together." Taylor winked as she moved away to say hello to a newcomer who had just entered the store.

"Hello, I'm Taylor. Are you a parent or a teacher?" Jorja turned to see Taylor shaking hands with a middle-aged man wearing a black Columbia jacket, hiking boots and a stocking cap. Once he finally removed the stocking cap, Jorja saw salt and pepper hair cut military short.

"I'm Gabe Carter, a teacher at the high school." He replied to Taylor's question as he removed his jacket.

"Mr. Carter! I'm glad you made it." Kat exclaimed as she and Bruce returned to the lobby with a few more folding chairs for seating.

Kat turned to Jorja. "This is the new teacher I was telling you about." Kat turned back to Gabe. "Mr. Carter, this is Jorja, the one I was telling you about."

Gabe turned his gaze to Jorja and smiled. She immediately responded to his smile with one in return. "Hello. It's nice to meet you. Kat has had nothing but good to say about you."

Jorja laughed as she replied, "I sure hope she hasn't talked your ear off. So how do you like teaching here? You're pretty new to the area, aren't you?"

Gabe folded his arms in front of him as he hugged his jacket to his chest. "I like it. It's a great school and all of the students are great. It's been only a few weeks, but I already feel pretty settled in."

Jorja nodded in understanding. There were two things a small town could do to you if you let it. The town would either feel suffocating and limited or it would gather you in with warmth and familiarity to make you want to stay forever.

"I'm glad you like it here. I think Kat would be very disappointed if you were to leave."

The doorbell chimed as others entered the store. Jorja turned to see some people she recognized and others she did not. She waited as they all entered the store and began to get settled after grabbing a cup of coffee and choosing a snack to eat. Jorja located the head parent for the PTA club to make sure she had the meeting under control.

"Trina? Do you need anything else from us? If not, Taylor and I plan to sit in the back and just listen in, if that's okay. We don't really need to be involved." Jorja said as she took one more glance around the room to see that everyone was beginning to take their seats.

Trina breathed heavily as she gathered a portfolio and some pamphlets, but whether it was due to nervousness or the extra pounds she carried, Jorja wasn't sure.

"That's perfectly fine with me. I've got it from here." Trina held the bulk of what she needed in her arms as she moved away from Jorja toward the guests sitting closest to her. Jorja moved away to sit beside Taylor in an overstuffed chair at the back of the room where they could whisper to each other during the meeting.

"Hello everybody. My name is Trina Russell and I'm the President of the PTA. We have some parents here and we have some teachers here." She glanced at Kat and Bruce who were chatting with each other near the coffee stand. "And we even have a few students. I'm glad you all made it and I hope that we can put our heads together to come up with a great fundraising idea to raise money for the PTA this year. I'm going to pass around some pamphlets with past ideas and note paper so you can each jot down any ideas you come up with."

Taylor leaned over to whisper in Jorja's ear as Trina finished talking. "Do you think we should give them any ideas that can help us get some business here at the bookstore?"

Jorja pulled back to look at Taylor, who only grinned at her. Jorja smiled. She knew Taylor's head was always full of ideas to help the store make money. "Let's just wait and see what they come up with first."

Trina stood in front of the group again and asked everyone to introduce themselves. Jorja and Taylor listened in as the introductions went around the room. Jorja realized she hadn't met many in the group and she wondered why they hadn't yet visited the store. She had met Bailey, the young mother new to town who attended the last book club meeting with Ruth, but beyond that, she could only spot two more out of the fifteen who she had ever seen before.

Jorja decided she and Taylor did need to come up with some new ideas on how to get more parents, teachers and other residents into the store. She leaned over to say as such to Taylor when the door opened and Chief Douglas entered the store.

Jorja's spine straightened and her brow furrowed as she wondered what he wanted. She gave Taylor a quick nervous glance before she stood to approach the chief, who had quickly marched past the PTA group without much of a glance on his way toward her.

"Chief? What can I do for you?" Jorja asked.

Chief Douglas glanced at Taylor, who stood close behind Jorja. "Is there someplace we can speak in private?"

Jorja frowned in concern. She didn't know the Chief well enough to figure out if she was in trouble or if he had news to share with her.

"Sure, we can go back to the break room, if that's okay." Jorja pointed down the hall toward the back of the store.

The Chief glanced down the hall, looked quickly at the PTA group again and then nodded as he motioned for Jorja to lead the way.

Jorja glanced at Taylor and gave her a look not to follow, rather than risk embarrassment if the Chief told her to stay put. As Taylor watched them walk down the hall to the break room, more than a handful of eyes from the PTA group were watching them as well.

~ ~ ~

"Okay, Chief Douglas, what's up? Has something happened?" Jorja asked. She then felt a bullet of fear strike her. "Is it Ryan? Or Nicholas? Are they okay?"

He held up his hand to stop her from speaking. "No, it's not that. My visit here is about something else entirely."

She stood against the counter with her arms folded across her chest. "What about?"

He pulled a chair away from the table and sat down before crossing one boot-covered foot over his knee. "About you, actually. The boys happened to mention something to me and I thought I would see if what they said was true."

"The boys?" She arched an eyebrow. "You mean Fritz and Reynolds?"

He nodded. "Yep, they told me you're moving into dangerous territory. Are you actually working for a suspected killer?"

She felt her chest tighten and she let out a heavy sigh. She could not for the life of her figure this man out. He was a grumpy old bear half the time; more than half the time. She couldn't guess why he would care about what type of case she worked.

"I'm not working for a *killer*," she said, uncrossing her arms. "I've been hired by the defense attorney to look into a case where his client is *alleged* to have committed a crime. That's all. Why do you want to know?"

He stared at her with steely gray eyes. He didn't speak while she refused to continue until he answered her question. Finally, he said, "When one of my officers has concerns about one of our citizens, I take it very seriously. There's concern you may be getting yourself in deep and you might be putting yourself at risk. You've thought of that possibility, I assume. You certainly don't want to risk getting hurt again, do you?"

Jorja frowned. She knew this was all coming from Fritz. Why he'd have the nerve to speak to the Chief about it, she couldn't imagine, but if he thought she'd quit her investigation just because the two of them ganged up on her, he had another thing coming.

"Look, I don't mean to be rude or disrespectful, but this is what I'm doing to make a living in addition to the book store. I'll be careful. There's no reason for you to worry and there's no reason for Fritz to worry. What happened with Cooper was a fluke and there's no reason to think I'm putting myself in any danger."

He hefted his boot off his knee to let it land squarely on the floor. He then stood, looked down at her and said, "You just be careful, Jorja. You know from first-hand experience that there's evil in even those who you thought were good."

She held her chin up as she met his gaze. "I'll be careful, I promise."

She was finally able to lower her chin when he swung away from her to leave the room. As he walked out to the hall, she moved to follow him, but suddenly slammed into his back instead.

"Oh! I'm sorry." Jorja apologized while trying to figure out why he had suddenly stopped. She peeked around him and saw Bailey, who had apparently been heading to the restroom when he stopped to let her pass.

"Bailey, have you met Chief Douglas yet?" Jorja asked. "Chief, this is Bailey…uh, I'm sorry Bailey. I forgot your last name."

Bailey glanced quickly down the hall toward the bathroom and back at Jorja. "No, I haven't met the Chief yet, but it's nice to meet you. Could you excuse me? It's just that the coffee went right through me."

"Sure, Bailey, I'm sorry." Jorja barely finished the last part of her sentence before Bailey was on the move again. Chief Douglas watched Bailey as she opened the bathroom door and disappeared inside, but not before she gave him one more glance. Jorja thought the whole scene was a bit curious.

"Chief, I'm sorry, but I need to get back to our guests to make sure they don't need anything." She wanted to tell him he could show himself out, but she decided it would be best to hold her tongue.

"Go on. I'm fine," he said as he shooed her away.

She felt like she could breathe again once she found Taylor. She stood next to Taylor, who eyed her curiously, waiting for an explanation. As Trina wrapped up the meeting and made plans for another the following week, Jorja whispered to Taylor to fill her in on the chief's visit.

Taylor's eyes widened. "I can't believe he has the nerve to tell you what to do. What gives him the right?" Her eyes sparkled as she had a thought. "Maybe he's trying to play cupid in his own gruff way and he doesn't want to see you get hurt if Fritz has made his claim on you."

Jorja tore her gaze from the guests who were mingling now that the meeting was over. "Oh stop! Fritz has *not* made his claim on me. And the Chief is not playing cupid!" Jorja shook her head in exasperation. "You're too much, Taylor."

Taylor grinned. "Yup, that I am."

"What the hell do you think you're doing here?"

They both heard the chief's stern voice at the same time and turned to see what brought it on. Jorja was surprised to see him speaking to Gabe Carter. She glanced at Taylor and they both moved closer to the men to hear what was being said.

"Who the hell do you think you are coming back here? I told you I never wanted to see your face in this town again." The chief's cheeks became red and his eyes narrowed as he glared at Gabe.

Gabe returned the chief's glare with a glare of his own. He then glanced around at the crowd of teachers and parents to see who might be watching or within earshot and jerked his head at the Chief in an effort to make him move further away from the group.

Jorja watched as Gabe headed to the children's section while the Chief silently followed. When Jorja turned to look at Taylor, no words had to be spoken between them as they both nodded at each other before they silently followed the two men in order to be within ear shot.

"You can't tell me where I can live any longer. I've chosen to come back here to live and to teach. I meant to tell you, but since I began working a few weeks ago, I've just been very busy." Jorja heard Gabe say as he stood facing the chief. She watched him slide his hands in his jeans pockets in what she believed was an attempt to appear less on edge. The appearance didn't last long when the Chief took a step toward him, causing Gabe to pull his hands out of his pockets as he took an involuntary step backwards.

Jorja couldn't see the chief's mouth, but she could tell by the sound of his voice that he was speaking through clenched teeth when he said, "You have 49 other states you can live in, Gabriel. Why the hell are you defying my wishes by coming back here? What do you have to gain?"

Jorja watched as Gabe sadly shook his head. "I'm not looking to gain anything, uncle. I finally decided I needed to move back home. Can't you just let me live my life without interfering? I'll leave you alone if you leave me alone. Isn't that fair?"

Jorja and Taylor glanced at each other in surprise after hearing Gabe refer to the Chief as uncle. They both then quickly tried to get out of the way when the Chief suddenly came toward them as he roared back at Gabe, "Don't you *dare* talk to me about fair, boy. I can't make you leave, but you better do as you promised and stay out of my way."

Jorja felt the wind from Chief Douglas as he flew past her and Taylor. He rushed past the few remaining guests and quickly left the store.

When she turned her gaze from the door to Taylor, she knew Taylor mirrored her own shock and surprise. They both turned to look at Gabe who had remained where he was. She approached him with Taylor right behind her.

"Uh, Gabe? Are you okay?" Jorja asked.

Gabe ran his hand around the back of his neck. "Yeah, I'm okay. Sorry if we caused a scene."

Jorja's curiosity was piqued. There was no way she could put off asking the question. "Did I hear you right? Did you call him uncle?"

Gabe nodded and gave her a sheepish grin. "You heard me right."

Jorja had a sudden thought as she remembered the conversation with Betsy about the chief's nephew. Was this the nephew who ran away after the chief's wife died? Why would he be so upset with his nephew for returning home if he had been upset about the fact that he had run away?

Her curiosity was now in overdrive. She glanced quickly at Taylor, who gave her a slight nod urging her to go on. Jorja decided she may as well find out what she could while she had the opportunity. "I hadn't known the Chief had any family. Do you mind me asking why he doesn't want you here? That seems like an unfair request."

Gabe looked away toward a bookshelf as if something more interesting caught his eye. He continued to stare at the shelf for a few moments before turning his gaze back to Jorja and then to Taylor, but he remained silent.

Jorja and Taylor waited.

Finally, Gabe sighed heavily. "It's really a long story and not one I can share at this point. Let's just say my uncle and I have a difficult past and it's apparent he hasn't yet forgiven or forgotten."

Jorja shrugged. "Sure, you don't owe us an explanation or anything. We were just curious and the whole idea of the Chief having any family is just such a surprise. I hope the two of you are able to bury the hatchet, or at least I hope he's able to anyway. Forgive us for prying. It's just what we do." She smiled to try to lighten the mood.

Taylor followed suit with a grin. "Don't worry about us, Gabe. You're not hurting our feelings, but you can be sure you'll have a friend in us if you need one."

Kat and Bruce suddenly came around the corner giggling over a joke between the two of them. "Oh, Jorja, I just wanted to tell you we put the chairs away and we're going to go if that's okay. The varsity basketball team is playing a game tonight and we'd like to go watch what's left of the game."

Jorja waved a hand at Kat. "You two go ahead. Thanks for helping and have fun tonight."

After Kat and Bruce left the store, Jorja turned to Taylor. "Let's get this place closed up and go home. Gabe? Would you like something else to drink before you leave?"

Gabe shook his head. "No. Thanks though. Again, I'm sorry if my uncle and I caused a scene. If you don't mind, it might be best not to broadcast the fact that he and I are related. I need to mend fences with him, but if he discovers everyone around town is talking about him and I, it might just delay the process."

Taylor spoke first. "You don't have to worry about us. Just be sure none of the ladies at the hair salon find out because once they know, *everyone* will know."

Gabe gave Taylor a blank stare and she grinned at him in return.

Jorja laughed. "It's okay, Gabe. We'll keep quiet about it, but Taylor's right. The ladies at the hair salon do tend to talk a lot so just be careful who might find out before you want them to. Until then, good luck with the chief. He's one tough nut to break."

Gabe pulled his stocking hat over his head and put on his jacket. Before leaving, he said, "Thanks. Hopefully you two won't have to keep the secret to yourselves very long because I do intend on having it out with my uncle sooner rather than later. You two have a nice evening."

After Gabe left the store, Jorja had mixed feelings about the whole situation. She wanted to keep her promise to keep quiet about what she knew, but more than anything, she wanted to discover the real reason behind why the Chief was so upset about Gabe moving back to town.

CHAPTER 12

"Aunt Jorja, are you excited about the play?" Nicholas asked as he skipped ahead of Jorja and Ryan on their way to the school gymnasium.

"Yes, Nicholas, I'm very excited about the play. I know you're going to do a great job and you will entertain every one of us." She had only known her nephew a few months, but every day she discovered some new reason to love him even more than the day before. She hadn't realized how much a child could affect her.

"Nicholas, be careful. You don't want to slip and fall. Who would play the bear if you hurt yourself?" Ryan asked. He didn't expect a response from Nicholas, but was content when his son slowed down to a normal walk. Ryan turned to Jorja. "How has everything been going? I feel like we haven't seen much of each other lately."

Shrugging in response first, she then realized the only light was from a dimly lit street lamp. "Everything's going okay. The bookstore isn't as busy as it could be, but I'm also working on that homicide case so there's always something to do. I would still like you to become a part of the team at the bookstore when you're ready. You're my brother and I'd like you to be a part of the business."

She suddenly felt a chill and thought she sensed the presence of someone nearby. She glanced nervously to the side and then tried to look further behind her, but she saw nothing.

"What? What's the matter?" Ryan asked, also looking behind them in an attempt to see what spooked Jorja.

"Nothing. I just had this feeling someone was watching us. I'm just tired, I guess."

The two walked in silence until Ryan finally spoke up. "I appreciate your offer to partner with you, Jorja. I still need to finish tying up loose ends with my dad's property in Wyoming. Then I need to figure out what I want to do about work. I love editing books and it's something I can easily do either at the house or at the bookstore. I need to earn my own money because there's no way you're going to pay me to work for you."

She sighed in frustration. "I don't want to hire you as an employee. I'd like to bring you in as a partner. Between you and me and what Taylor and mom are doing for the store, we could all be a great team. Will you think about it?"

As they reached the gym and Ryan grabbed the handle to open the door, he turned to her and grinned. "Jorja, you and your family are all I have besides Nicholas and I would truly enjoy being a part of the business. Once I get things squared away with my dad's estate and establish that I'm moving my business here, we can talk more about what I can do to help you with the bookstore, okay?"

She nodded and smiled back. "Okay. We'll talk business again later."

"Dad, we have to go *this* way so I can get changed for the play!" Nicholas exclaimed as Ryan and Jorja began to walk down the hall to the gym. Nicholas stopped them and pointed to a door in the opposite direction. They turned to follow him and were soon surrounded by a dozen screaming kindergarten children. Jorja scanned the room and was finally able to spot Nicholas' teacher, Mrs.

Beatrice Plum. Jorja thought the spunky elderly teacher was as cute as her name.

Mrs. Plum clapped her hands as she tried to speak over the excited voices, "Children, children! Try to calm down. Now, line up here so I can see how you all look. Sally, fix your ear, it's lopsided. Good. Nicholas, you aren't even in your costume yet. Here, put this on."

Jorja and Ryan moved to helped Nicholas climb into his costume. Mrs. Plum handed him a pillow to plump up his stomach so he looked like a bear that ate well before hibernation rather than one on the verge of starvation.

"How do I look, Dad?" Nicholas asked through the mask. His bright little eyes could barely be seen through the eye holes.

"You look like a very sleepy bear about to hibernate. Aunt Jorja and I are going to get our seats. We'll be clapping the loudest when we cheer for you at the end. See you after the show."

Nicholas waved a furry paw at them as they left the room. "Bye Dad. Bye Aunt Jorja."

They hurried from the room to get a seat in the gym and were lucky to find two seats only three rows back from the stage. Before the show began, Jorja peeked around at the audience to see if she recognized anyone. She finally spotted Ruth's friend, Bailey and her son, as well as Kat and Bruce, who had promised Nicholas they would attend his play.

When the play began, Jorja was captivated by the energy and enthusiasm of each child and she was very proud of Nicholas, who played a very convincing bear. She had never attended a school function like this before and she knew with Nicholas now in her life, it would certainly not be the last.

Once the play ended, the whole gym stood and clapped, which warranted bows from all the children in the play who understood a bow was appropriate. Jorja laughed when Nicholas bent over too far, only to lose the bear mask off his head. He quickly grabbed the mask and placed it back over his head, but not before she saw he was grinning at the slip up.

Mrs. Plum thanked everyone for attending and asked the parents to wait for the children to remove their costumes and join their parents in the gym. While Jorja and Ryan waited for Nicholas, she made eye contact with Bailey. She was surprised when Bailey pretended not to see her and looked away. Curious, Jorja made her way toward Bailey. When she was close enough, she finally spoke, "Hi Bailey, how are you? Did you and your son enjoy the play?"

Bailey shyly smiled before she looked down at her son who had curled up on the chair and fallen asleep. "He did enjoy it, but it's past his bed time. He's usually in bed by seven o'clock and he just couldn't stay up any longer."

Jorja smiled. "I guess it's a good thing he doesn't have a problem sleeping where ever he is. Imagine if we could do that as adults? But then it probably wouldn't go over too well with others."

Bailey laughed, but just as quickly lost her smile. Jorja wondered about Bailey and what caused her to be so cautious around others. She decided to see what she could find out.

"So how do you like our little town? Are you and your son settling in? It must be difficult when you're moving from another state. Was it Montana? Nevada?"

Bailey shook her head. "No, Colorado. Just a small town, really. Not much different than here."

"Oh. Are you married? I'm sorry, I don't mean to pry. I just wondered if you moved here by yourself. That's quite a move as a single parent."

Bailey hesitated. "Uh, well, I was married." She glanced down at her son. "But his father is no longer in the picture."

Jorja waited, but that was all Bailey was willing to offer. Finally, Jorja relented. "Well, I'm sure it's his loss and our gain. You've made a good friend in Ruth and I can vouch for that. If you ever need anything or help in any way, you should make sure to let her know because if she can't help you, she'll steer you toward someone who can."

Bailey suddenly turned away, but not before Jorja saw the worried look that crossed her face. Bailey then looked at Jorja and smiled. "Thanks. I'll keep that in mind. Well, I need to get Justin home and to bed. I'll see you around."

Jorja watched as Bailey bent over to wake up her son before helping him sit up and then stand before they walked out of the gym. She wondered exactly what had happened with Bailey's husband. If she had to guess, the guy was a loser who ran out on them and forced Bailey to find a new way of life. If that was the case, Jorja was certain Bailey and her son could probably do better.

CHAPTER 13

"Come on, Piper, let's go for a nice Saturday afternoon walk." Piper, who had been gnawing on a toy in the kitchen, suddenly jumped up as quickly as was possible for a semi-overweight dog before running to the front door. Jorja peeked around the corner into the living room to find Nicholas on the floor playing with Lego's. "Nicholas, do you want to come with me and Piper?"

Nicholas dropped what he had in his hands and stood up. "Sure! Can I hold Piper's leash?"

Jorja smiled. "Yes, you may hold Piper's leash, but how about we hold it together? Remember, she can pull you to the ground if she sees a squirrel or anything she might like to chase."

Nicholas' shoulders hunched just a fraction. "Okay." Just as suddenly he straightened up when a new thought occurred to him. "But can I pick out her treat when we get back? And give it to her?"

"Yes, Nicholas, you can do that all by yourself."

"Good! Come on, Piper, let's go!" Nicholas exclaimed as he grabbed his jacket and mittens for the walk.

"Don't forget your hat." Jorja said as she put on her jacket and hat.

Piper had remained patient long enough while she watched the two of them get ready. She finally grabbed her leash, which had been hanging off the side of the hall bench, and brought it to Jorja.

Jorja laughed. "Okay, okay. I know you want to go." She latched the leash onto Piper's collar and opened the door. It was all she could do to hold Piper back when she attempted to sprint out onto the front porch. She held the leash tight to keep Piper at bay. "Hold on, girl. Let's go, Nicholas, she doesn't want to wait for us."

Jorja yelled back toward the formal dining room where Ryan had been working on his laptop. "Ryan, we'll be back in awhile."

"Okay!" Ryan yelled back.

After Jorja and Nicholas left the house with Piper, she placed the leash in Nicholas' hand while keeping a section of the leash in her own. She didn't want to risk him taking a face plant on the sidewalk should Piper see anything that might cause her to run.

"Let's go this way." She pointed to the left of the house and they walked down the sidewalk free from all the leaves that had fallen so freely the past few months. The trees were now bare of leaves and the sidewalks were clean and bare, as well. She appreciated the fact that the city took care to keep the sidewalks and drains clear, especially when the rain could be heavy this time of year if snow wasn't in the cards.

It was cold and Nicholas' nose looked to be as red as hers felt, but it felt even better to get a walk in. She needed it, as did Piper, and she welcomed any extra time she got to spend with Nicholas.

"Aunt Jorja, is Dylan going to move in with us after him and Taylor get married?"

Jorja peeked down at Nicholas, who was now holding onto Piper's leash with both hands while he attempted to keep up with Piper's excited gait.

"Why do you ask? Would you like him to?"

"Not really," he said with a shake of his head. "But if he doesn't live with us, does that mean Taylor has to move out?"

She thought she understood where Nicholas was coming from. "You don't want Taylor to move out, do you?"

He frowned. "No. What if she moves out and we don't see her...ever?"

"Oh, Nicholas, that won't happen. She works at the bookstore with me, remember? And she'll visit us. We'll also visit her in her new home. Don't worry. We will see her probably about as much as we do now."

"I guess. Hey, look! A quarter! Can I keep it?" He let go of Piper's leash to bend down to pick up the quarter. Another reason Jorja made the rule to hold the leash together. She knew his attention could also be diverted at any minute.

"Sure you can keep it. Finders keepers, right?"

He shoved the quarter into his pocket and she laughed at his delighted grin. She wished she could feel as happy with only just a quarter.

When she turned her attention to watch where they were going, Jorja caught sight of Bailey and her son walking toward the playground at the park. Nicholas also spotted the playground and asked, "Can I play on the toys? Please?"

Once she told him he could play on the toys, he quickly skipped away to the slide while Jorja followed at a slow gait and attempted to make eye contact with Bailey. Bailey stood near a picnic table while she watched her son on a swing and Jorja soon realized Bailey was trying to avoid eye contact.

Curious, she walked toward Bailey anyway. "Hey Bailey. How are you?"

Bailey turned to look at her with a feigned look of surprise. "Oh, hello Jorja. I'm fine. How are you?"

"Good. Just taking Piper here for a walk. That little guy over there is my nephew. You might not recognize him without the bear costume."

Bailey smiled and nodded, but said nothing in return.

Jorja continued, "Is your son adjusting well to his new school? Are you settled in your house okay? It must be difficult moving to a new state and an area you're unfamiliar with."

Bailey smiled and nodded again as she finally said, "Yes, we are both adjusting well and settled in."

Feels like I'm trying to pull teeth. Jorja thought to herself.

"How about the job? Do you like working at the grocery store?" She knew Nicholas would be trotting over to her soon to continue with the walk so she wanted to see how much she could get from Bailey before he became bored with the playground.

Bailey was about to answer when something over Jorja's shoulder caught her attention. Bailey stared long enough to make Jorja turn around. Seeing nothing in particular other than an elderly man and woman walking together and a car pass by, Jorja turned back to look at Bailey. She was shocked to see that Bailey's face had lost all color.

Concerned now, she asked, "Bailey? Are you okay?"

Bailey didn't answer. Her eyes were glued to the same spot so Jorja turned around in an attempt to catch sight of what had caught Bailey's attention.

Again, she saw nothing. But she couldn't deny a chill she felt as it ran up her spine. She suddenly felt as if she were being watched. She narrowed her eyes and tried her best to see who or what might be across the street, but still could see nothing.

Jorja turned back to Bailey and moved enough to get right in her line of sight. "Bailey, is everything all right? You look like you're going to faint."

Bailey's eyes finally focused on her. Jorja could hear her breathing heavily when she finally attempted to answer the question. "I-I'm fine. I j-just saw a really big dog. I was bitten by a large dog awhile back and I'm still very skittish around them, that's all." Bailey turned from Jorja's scrutiny toward her son. "Justin! Come on, we need to get home."

Justin heard the tone in his mother's voice and didn't argue. He waved goodbye to Nicholas and quickly ran to his mother's side.

"It was nice seeing you, Jorja, but we need to go." Bailey grabbed Justin's hand and they began to quickly walk to their car.

Jorja was hesitant to let Bailey go. She didn't believe Bailey's story about the dog, but realized there was really nothing she could do about it. "Okay, Bailey. I hope we see you at the next book club meeting. Bye Justin."

Justin peeked around his mother to catch a glimpse of Jorja as he waved. "Bye," he said.

Jorja watched as the two of them climbed into a mid-sized car parked in the nearby parking lot. As she struggled to resist the urge to yell at Bailey to stay and talk, she could only watch when the car pulled out of the lot and onto the street. When the car finally disappeared out of sight, Jorja tried her hardest to shake off the disquiet she could no longer ignore.

CHAPTER 14

"Hello? Is this Mr. Carlton Ayers?" Jorja asked over the telephone.

"Yes. Who am I speaking to?"

"This is Jorja Matthews. I'm a private investigator and I've been hired by the attorney who represents Michael Stafford. We're investigating the allegations that have been made against him with regard to the death of his wife, Cynthia."

"Oh, yes. I was informed by the deputy prosecutor you might be calling. What can I do for you?"

Jorja moved her notepad to easily write as she asked her questions. "Well, you were the Guardian ad Litem appointed by the Court, correct? I was wondering what you could tell me about your findings with regard to the custody case. It's my understanding you recommended that Tabitha be placed with her father. Was there something about the mother's care of her daughter that concerned you?"

She heard him clear his throat over the phone. "Well, I'll tell you what I told the police. I believed Cynthia was manipulating the court in an attempt to gain full custody of Tabitha by making false allegations against her husband. After the death of her eldest daughter, it's my opinion that Cynthia felt some guilt about her daughter's death because she didn't limit who Liz spent time with and she didn't work with Michael to look into the possibility that Liz might be abusing alcohol. Cynthia blamed Michael for pushing Liz away, but I wasn't able to find any proof to Cynthia's claims other than that Liz was a troubled teen who lost control after her parents' separation. After Liz's death, Michael filed the custody case because he worried about Cynthia's influence over Tabitha. I had to agree with him. I believed Tabitha would fare much better with her father, who has shown his stability, rather than with her mother, who I already had some concern with regarding her mental state."

Jorja scribbled down the information as he spoke, but she was surprised by the last statement. "Her mental state? What about it? Did you have concerns she might actually try to harm herself or others?"

"I wouldn't go that far, but Cynthia needed help. She was already trying to deal with the end of her marriage when she lost her daughter in the car accident. She felt some guilt when it came to both matters. That guilt and the grief she was feeling were enormous. She wasn't able to fully be there for Tabitha and would never be there for Tabitha until she got help for what she had already gone through. She denied needing help and wouldn't let me refer her to a counselor for treatment. Her denial that her mental state might be fragile was one thing, but the fact that she wouldn't even consider looking into the possibility in order to make herself whole again for her youngest daughter left me no choice."

Jorja put a check mark next to the questions the Guardian ad Litem had answered and she moved to the next question on her list.

"Do you believe Michael is capable of doing what the police say he did? Or do you believe it more likely that he's telling the truth and Cynthia killed herself?"

"Well...I will say I don't see Michael as having the behavior of a killer. He really didn't have a motive, did he? He had already been awarded custody of Tabitha. I don't see what killing his wife would have given him unless he was a true sadist. I would say I did question Cynthia's well-being to the point that I was concerned how she would react when custody was granted to Michael, but yet I heard she wrote an accusation in blood that Michael killed her. A victim's last words, you might say. So do I think he was capable? It's possible. Anyone is capable of murder if they are pushed to their limit. Do I think Michael killed his wife? I don't know. I'll have to leave that question up to the jury."

Jorja looked over her notes before she said, "So if I understand you correctly Mr. Ayers, you don't see Michael as someone with a motive to kill, but he, like anyone, could certainly be capable and while you did have concern about Cynthia's well-being or her mental state, you won't go so far as to say you believe she was a danger to herself or anyone else?"

"I guess that's about right. I really can't say one way or another what happened that night. Only those who were present know the truth, but one is dead while the other may or may not be telling the truth. Again, it will be up to a jury to figure that out, if in fact they are able to pull that off. Time will tell, but one thing I will say, the true victim here is Tabitha. She's already lost her sister and her mother. If she loses her father as well, should he be found guilty, that girl will need a good amount of therapy to get through the next few years."

She had to agree to the truth in that statement. It was Tabitha who would be greatly affected by how this matter was finally resolved. While it was true children were more resilient than some gave them credit for, Jorja wondered how anyone, young or old, could manage a normal life after the loss of so many family members in such a short amount of time. It was, she knew, a question only time could answer.

CHAPTER 15

Jorja was eating a snack in the break room when Kat poked her head around the corner. "Betsy's here to see you."

Jorja finished swallowing the granola bar she had been chewing and followed it with a large drink of water. "Okay, be right out."

Kat disappeared back down the hall and Jorja slowly stood to follow. She had been feeling sluggish all day after getting a poor night's sleep from bad dreams. She knew she'd be paying for it if she didn't start sleeping better soon.

Once she made her way out of the break room and into the main lobby, Jorja found Betsy sitting at a table near the coffee stand chatting with Taylor.

"Hi Betsy, what are you up to today?" She asked as she sat down at the table.

Betsy raised her coffee cup. "I just thought I'd stop in for a mocha and one of Dylan's cookies. This is a nice afternoon snack, I have to say. It gets lonely over there at the police station sometimes. When the Chief and the boys are all gone, there's just not a lot to keep me busy if the phone isn't ringing much." Betsy winked at Jorja. "I thought I deserved a little break and if anyone does call the station, they can leave a message and wait till I get back."

Jorja smiled at Betsy and her tenacity. She thought if it were anyone else, the Chief would have a fit if they left the office empty to take a break, but when it came to Betsy, she could do no wrong. Not for the first time, Jorja wondered if there were any makings of a relationship between the two of them. The Chief was at retirement age, but refused to quit. Betsy wasn't too far behind him, but for whatever reason remained at what she described as a boring job. Jorja would bet there was more to it than that.

"So nothing much is happening at the office lately? I guess that's a good thing. It's one of the reasons I enjoy living here. Not really much crime to speak of, with a few exceptions, of course." Jorja said as Taylor nodded in agreement.

Betsy took a sip and set her cup down. "No, not a lot going on. Less crime means fewer reports to type and less filing. But you're right, it's a good thing. It's why I love this little town of Tenino myself."

Taylor leaned forward. "So how are Fritz and Reynolds doing? We don't see them often enough, do we Jorja?" Taylor smiled at Jorja before looking back at Betsy.

Betsy smiled. "Why, they're two of the best officers we've ever had. They're good boys, both of them. I'll have to tell them to stop in more often to check up on you girls, especially when you're open in the evenings. You can never be too safe, even in a small town."

Jorja flushed and kicked Taylor under the table. Taylor jumped in surprise, but grinned wickedly at Jorja as she said to Betsy, "That would be great. You tell them they should stop by here as often as they like. We don't mind the extra company, do we, Jorja?"

"Uh, no, I guess not." Deciding to change the subject, Jorja said, "You should stop by here yourself, Betsy. You know we'd appreciate a visit anytime you can stop by."

"Oh, you're sweet. You know that's something an old lady loves to hear. Well, I'll try to visit more often. How about that?"

"If you like to read, you could come to one of our book club meetings. We hold them twice a month and we have one coming up next week." Taylor added.

Betsy smiled at the offer. "That's a wonderful idea. I would love to." Her smile slipped a fraction as she had a thought. "By the way, do you know a woman by the name of Bailey? She stopped by the other day, but she forgot to give me a way to reach her."

Jorja nodded as she asked, "Bailey Maxwell? We met her when she attended the last book club meeting with Ruth. You need to contact her? "

Nodding, Betsy said, "Reach her or get a message to her. She came by hoping to speak to the chief, but he was out. I happened to mention to him that she wished to speak to him and he told me she could either come back by the station when she has the time or she could stop by his house. I've always tried to tell him he shouldn't conduct business at his home, but he refuses to listen to me." Betsy let out a breath in exasperation. "That man is *always* working."

"Well, we might not see her until the book club meeting, but if she happens to stop in for a coffee, we'll be sure to tell her. She works at the grocery store so you could also leave a message for her there."

"That might work. I'll do that, but if you see her, make sure you pass on my message, okay? Well, I should get back to the station. You girls take care and I'll see you again soon."

Betsy left the book store, leaving Jorja the privacy she needed to chide Taylor. "Would you stop trying to play cupid? We don't need Fritz here more often. All he'll do is get after me about taking on criminal defense cases."

Taylor tilted her head as she pondered Jorja's response. She then pointed at Jorja. "You're not going to admit it, are you? You don't want to hear what Fritz has to say because you actually care what he thinks about you."

Jorja frowned. "I do not. I can do whatever I want and I don't need him telling me what to do. I'm not a child he can order around." She sat back in her chair as she crossed her arms.

Taylor grinned. "No, you're not a child, but sometimes you act like one when he's around. He's been a good friend to us since that day with Cooper. Don't you think he cares and is worried about you?"

"Sure, I know he cares. But it's not his responsibility to tell me what I should or shouldn't be doing."

Taylor nodded. "You're right, it's not his job. But it sure is fun to watch him try to make his point with you. For some reason he seems to think you should listen to him. Don't you wonder what that reason is?"

Jorja remained silent as she uncrossed her arms, placed them on the table and turned to stare out the window.

Taylor lost her grin as she saw the look on Jorja's face. "Hey, what's up with you? Do you really not like the guy? I'm sorry, I don't mean to tease you, but I seriously thought you had at least an attraction toward him. Don't you?"

Jorja turned to look at Taylor. "I'm not saying it isn't true. It's just that..." She felt her heart flutter at the thought of voicing a fear she wasn't yet ready to share. She closed her eyes and shook her head quickly back and forth. When she looked at Taylor again she couldn't come up with the right words.

Taylor reached over to touch Jorja's hand. "What's wrong? You know you can tell me anything."

Jorja knew Taylor would be a good listener, but decided instead to avoid where the conversation was going. "It's nothing. What I'll tell you is that Fritz is a friend and he just needs to stay in his place. That's it, nothing more." Jorja hoped she sounded convincing. She couldn't admit to Taylor she knew Fritz's attention toward her had turned into something more and that it absolutely terrified her.

CHAPTER 16

Sirens could be heard in the distance as Jorja and Taylor were restocking bookshelves in the children's section. It wasn't often sirens were heard and more often than not, it would be a fire truck or ambulance rather than a police vehicle. When the sirens appeared to be getting closer, they both stood up to move to the window looking out onto the main street. It was only moments later when they were both surprised to see a patrol vehicle whiz by at a high rate of speed.

"Wonder what happened? An accident?" Taylor asked.

"Maybe," Jorja replied. "But if that's the case, we should see an ambulance go by soon too."

They heard another siren as an ambulance also passed the bookstore.

"Why don't you call Betsy and see if she'll tell you what's going on?" Taylor asked, already picking up the phone to hand it to Jorja.

Jorja eyed the phone only briefly before agreeing to call. Betsy didn't have to tell her, but it didn't hurt to ask.

Jorja waited after dialing the number and was disappointed when she was instructed to leave a message. She hung up the phone without leaving one, not knowing what kind of message would even be appropriate for someone just being nosy.

"No answer?" Taylor asked.

"No. Maybe Betsy is on one of her breaks. We can try again in a little bit. Let's finish with the books so I can get to work on some other paperwork I'd like to get done today."

A half hour later when they were finished restocking the shelves and tidying up the children's section, Jorja grabbed a bottle of water from the fridge in the break room before heading upstairs to the office. She was half way up the staircase when the front door burst open and Kat ran inside, breathless from running to the store, her long blond hair wild from the run. Jorja wasn't surprised. Kat was often running from one place to another, never running out of energy. It was the look on Kat's face that made Jorja turn to head back downstairs before asking, "Kat, is everything okay?"

Kat excitedly began to speak between breaths. "Have you…heard? Oh my God…did you hear…what happened?"

Jorja reached the bottom of the staircase as Taylor moved toward Kat and asked her to sit on the sofa. "Here give me your jacket. Take a few deep breaths. Now, tell us what happened."

Jorja sat down in the chair next to the sofa while Taylor sat by Kat. They both waited for Kat to catch her breath. She finally took one deep breath and let it out with, "Chief Douglas was attacked!"

"What? Who told you that? What happened?" Jorja and Taylor both spoke up at once.

Kat took another deep breath. "I don't know. I heard it at school just before I left my last class. They said someone attacked the Chief at his house."

Jorja's brows furrowed in concern. *Who would hurt the chief? And why?* She asked Kat, "Are you sure? Who did you actually hear this from? It could all be a sick joke."

Jorja parked her Jeep far enough from Chief Douglas' home in order to avoid any sort of reprimand from the police investigating what was likely a crime scene. She quickly spotted Reynolds standing outside on the lawn speaking to a medic. Jorja exited her Jeep and cautiously moved toward the home, knowing full well if the wrong person spotted her she would be quickly shooed away.

When she was about ten feet from Reynolds and the medic, she paused and waited. Moments later they finished their conversation and the medic left Reynolds to enter the house. As Reynolds scanned the perimeter of the yard, his eyes widened when he caught sight of her.

He approached her, sporting a stern expression. "Jorja, what the hell are you doing here?"

She tried to hide the guilt she was feeling. She was here for a good reason, she told herself. She wasn't just being nosy.

She eyed Reynolds steadily. "I heard something might have happened to the Chief and I was concerned when I couldn't reach Betsy. Kat came to the store in a panic telling us she thought someone tried to kill the chief. I just want to know what's going on."

Reynolds quickly looked behind him before he answered her. "Something did happen, Jorja. But it hasn't been officially announced yet."

She frowned and became uneasy. "What do you mean? D-did something happen to the chief?" She looked around the yard and caught sight of the police vehicle. She realized someone was sitting in the back of the vehicle and she moved to get a better look. When she caught sight of the profile her eyes widened in surprise at the sight. She was shocked to see the vehicle's occupant was Kat's history teacher, Mr. Carter.

Jorja began to worry as she recalled the sirens they hea
earlier.

Kat shook her head. "No. Betsy is friends with on
the teachers and that teacher had to leave because B
needed her. I guess she's really shook up. Once the teac
left school the news spread like wildfire. I was in
history class and we had a substitute because Mr. C
wasn't there so I snuck out of class after telling the s
had to use the restroom. I wanted to get here to see if
had heard or not."

Kat quickly stood as she exclaimed, "I just
believe it. Someone tried to *kill* our police chief!"

Jorja also stood. "Kat, we need to find out the
before you get too panicked, okay? You know how 1
spread. Let's wait to see what really happened and
chief's okay or not. We don't want to assume anythir

Kat sat back down on the sofa. "Okay. I'm
You're right. But how will we know the truth? Ca
call someone?"

Jorja grabbed her jacket hanging on the nearl
rack. "I'll do something even better. I'm going to c
the chief's house and see if I can speak to either
Reynolds. Taylor, can you stay here with Kat?"

Jorja knew Taylor would like to be in on the
but the store and Kat were also a concern. Taylor
nodded. "Yes, you go and we'll wait for you to co
with news."

Jorja put on her jacket and grabbed her bag. "
here with Taylor until I get back. I'll find out w
and be back as soon as I can."

She then left the store, realizing at once
foreboding feeling she felt before was now in full

~ ~ ~

Turning back to Reynolds she said, "What happened? Is the Chief okay? And why is Gabe Carter in the back of your patrol car? Is he under arrest?"

Reynolds shook his head. "The Chief is hurt and the EMT just confirmed he's critical, but stable. And as far as Mr. Carter and what actually happened here, that's still under investigation."

"Jorja? What are you doing here?"

Jorja and Reynolds turned to face Fritz, who was eyeing them suspiciously. Fritz asked his partner, "Reynolds...what did you tell her?"

Reynolds stood back from her as he answered Fritz. "She heard something happened to the chief. I was just telling her he was critical but alive."

Fritz turned to Jorja. "You shouldn't be here. We need to investigate and you being here isn't appropriate, especially if you think it might lead to another job defending some crackpot."

Jorja sucked in her breath in surprise.

Then she became angry.

"What right do you have to say that to me? I'm here because I was concerned, that's all. Kat heard the Chief had been attacked and I wanted to ease her fears if I could. The fact that someone may or may not need to be defended is a completely separate matter!" Jorja huffed as she glared at him before she turned and stormed off.

She willed herself to keep her anger in check as she climbed back into her Jeep and sped away. With or without Fritz's approval, she was already determined to look into why the Chief had been attacked and why Gabe Carter was in the backseat of a patrol car.

CHAPTER 17

"So? What happened?" Taylor asked with Kat standing right beside her, both waiting for Jorja's answer.

She shook off her jacket and threw it on the sofa. "I can't believe the nerve of that man. He actually thought I was there looking for *work!* Can you believe that?"

Taylor raised one eyebrow and turned to glance at Kat. Kat shrugged and Taylor turned back to Jorja. "What man? What are you talking about? Is the Chief okay or not?"

"Yes, he's okay. Or at least, he's critical but alive. Something happened, but I wasn't told exactly what. What's even more surprising is the fact that Gabe Carter was sitting in the back of the patrol car. I think he's actually been arrested."

"What! Mr. Carter? Why would he be arrested? He didn't hurt the chief, did he?" Kat exclaimed.

Taylor eyed Kat with concern before moving closer to Jorja. "Did they arrest him? Did they say if they actually thought he attacked the chief?"

Jorja shook her head. "No, I didn't get that far because Fritz had the nerve to say he thought I was there looking for work as a private investigator. I could have slapped him if I wasn't worried about being arrested for assault."

Taylor placed her hand on Jorja's arm and lightly pushed her to sit down on the sofa. Taylor then sat down beside her as Kat began to pace the floor. "Kat, sit down, please. You're just making us more nervous."

Kat stopped pacing and plopped herself on the couch. Taylor turned to Jorja and asked, "So you really don't know anything other than that something happened to the Chief and Gabe may have been arrested?"

Jorja sighed. "Yeah, that's all I know. I need to touch base with Betsy and see how she's doing. Maybe I can confirm the Chief is going to be okay because she'll be one of the first to know."

Taylor nodded. "Okay, sure. You want to do that now?"

Jorja stood up. "Yes, I'd like to at least check on her. She cares for the chief, even if she doesn't admit it to him."

She picked up her jacket and was about to put it back on when the door suddenly swung open. Bailey quickly came inside, shut the door and discovered three pairs of eyes staring at her in surprise.

Jorja was first to speak. "Hello Bailey. What can we do for you?"

Bailey wrapped her arms over her chest as she shivered. "I, uh, was wondering if I could...well, do you have a minute, Jorja? I'd like to speak with you."

Frowning slightly when she thought about delaying her trip to see Betsy, she knew she wouldn't feel right turning Bailey away. "Sure, why don't you come up to my office? Would you like some coffee first? You look cold."

Bailey shook her head. "No, I'm okay."

"Okay, let's go upstairs then." Jorja gave Taylor a quick glance. "Do you think you could try calling Betsy? Maybe she'd be willing to speak to you over the phone."

Taylor nodded. "Sure, I'll see if I can reach her."

Jorja climbed the stairs with Bailey right behind her. With each step she became more curious about this surprise visit. Once they topped the stairs, Jorja hung her jacket on the coat rack and sat down at her desk, waving at a chair for Bailey to take a seat.

Bailey tentatively sat down as she glanced nervously around the room. She folded her hands in her lap and remained quiet as she appeared to contemplate what she wished to say. Jorja waited, knowing the wrong statement on her part might make Bailey change her mind about speaking to her.

Finally, Bailey spoke. "Ruth told me you're an investigator. Is that true?"

Jorja nodded. "Yes, that's true."

"I, uh, I may need some help. But I don't know how much I can tell you." Jorja was surprised when Bailey suddenly began to cry. She quickly reached over to grab a tissue box and held the box across the desk toward Bailey.

"Thank you," Bailey said as she pulled two tissues from the box. "I'm so sorry. I don't mean to cry, but this is all very difficult for me."

"Take your time, Bailey." Jorja sat back in her chair as she waited for Bailey to compose herself. She wondered whether she should take any notes, but decided she would just let Bailey speak her mind.

Bailey blew her nose and threw the tissue into a nearby basket. She sighed heavily and then began, "I'm scared. Something happened where I used to live and I had to leave. That's why I moved here. I'm afraid of someone. Someone that could harm me or my son and I think he might have followed me here. I just don't know what to do."

"Did you go to the police?"

Bailey nodded. "I tried before I left home. But he never did anything the police could actually find proof of. He was abusive, both mentally and physically, but he was also very smart. I began to sound like a crazy person when nothing I alleged could ever be proven. And there's nothing the police can do here. I don't know if he's here. I just *feel* that he's here. I'm scared and I don't know if I should move again or not because I thought he wouldn't find me here in the first place."

Jorja decided she did want to take notes. She grabbed a notepad and a pen. "Why wouldn't he be able to find you? Have you changed your name?"

"Yes, I'm using a different name."

Jorja's brow furrowed. "How did you get a job using someone else's name?"

Bailey fidgeted as she straightened in her chair. "My cousin and I are similar in looks so she agreed to let me use her identification while she's living out of the country. She was able to get a second copy of her driver's license when she said it had been stolen." Bailey hung her head as she continued, "I told her I would never need to pretend to be someone else, but she knew before I did that I'd have to someday get away."

"So you're using her name and social security number? For your job?"

Bailey looked up and her eyes narrowed at the question. "Yes. Why?"

"Because if the man you're talking about has any ability at all, he could try to find you by trying to locate your family members, on the assumption you might go to them for help. Can you tell me who this person is to you? Did you marry him? Is he Justin's father?"

Bailey shut her eyes. Quietly she said, "Yes, I married him and yes he's Justin's father. He's also a monster and I had to get away from him."

Jorja scribbled a few notes as she asked, "Have you tried to speak to the police here? If you think he's here and you're afraid for your safety, you should speak to them or go to court and get a restraining order."

Fresh tears formed in Bailey's eyes. "I can't go to the police. If I go to the police or to the courts, they'll just take Justin from me. I can't take that risk and I'd do anything to stop Justin from going back to his father."

Jorja set her pen down and leaned forward, folding her hands under her chin. She held Bailey's eye contact as she asked, "Bailey, what is it you want from me? What do you think I can do for you that the police can't do?"

Bailey broke eye contact with Jorja as she looked around the office. Jorja waited for Bailey to answer her. Bailey briefly made eye contact again before looking down at her hands in her lap. "I don't know. I thought maybe you could do some research to dig up some information that I could use against my husband if he's here to take Justin from me. I don't know how else to fight him, but I will *not* go back to live with him. If he tries to make me, I'll just take Justin and run away again!" Bailey eyes widened and she slapped a hand over her mouth.

Jorja inwardly questioned the outburst, but decided against asking Bailey to elaborate. Instead, she pretended not to notice and waited for Bailey to continue.

Bailey lowered her hand and with a shaky voice asked, "Can you help me? I don't have a lot of money, but if you could research my husband and see if there's anything in his past that might give what I'm saying some weight, that's all I'm asking. He's dangerous, but I don't know how to go about proving it. Maybe you can help me find something I can use."

Jorja nodded and picked up her pen again. "Okay, Bailey. I'll see what I can do. Give me the information you have and we'll go from there." As she wrote down the information Bailey provided, Jorja had a nagging feeling that there was more to this story than met the eye.

CHAPTER 18

Jorja wasn't able to find a lot of time to look into the matter of Bailey's husband right away. She and Taylor had anxiously waited for news about the attack involving the chief, but Betsy was only able to give them bits and pieces of information as she knew it. According to Betsy, the Chief had gone home to have lunch and when he had not returned to the station after a few hours, Betsy called him to see what was holding him up. After getting no response, she asked Fritz and Reynolds to check on the chief. She was later informed that when they arrived at the home, they caught Gabe Carter running from the house and found the Chief unconscious on the kitchen floor.

Jorja shook her head as she thought about what Betsy had described. She hadn't been able to speak to either Fritz or Reynolds to verify the information Betsy had provided. She didn't particularly wish to ask Fritz any questions at this point and had secretly hoped to run into Reynolds, but the two were inseparable and Jorja knew getting Reynolds alone was unlikely.

Squinting at the bright lights of the vehicle heading toward her, Jorja was brought out of her thoughts and she paid close attention to the road while passing by the oncoming car. She had just met with the attorney who hired her to work on Michael Stafford's case, just to update him on the witnesses she had already interviewed so he could decide what else he wanted her to do. During the meeting, the attorney disclosed to her that he thought Michael might be successful if the case were to go to trial. The facts surrounding the case did not bode well for the State's case against Michael, even if he had the means and was lacking an alibi. A preliminary inspection of the medical records the attorney was able to obtain with regard to Cynthia Stafford's mental health was, in the attorney's words, 'revealing.' When they discussed additional witnesses they might interview, Jorja agreed with the attorney that for the time being they would wait on conducting an interview with Tabitha since it was unlikely she would have any useful information.

She felt tired and would have preferred to go home and just enjoy the evening with Ryan and Nicholas, but that was not to be. She had received a phone call from Gabe Carter just before she left the bookstore to meet with the attorney. He asked her if she would be willing to meet with him. She was curious and to satisfy that curiosity, she agreed to meet with him at her house after her meeting with the attorney.

Jorja turned on her wipers when it started to sprinkle and she was glad to be close to home. She hated driving in the rain. Only a few minutes later she pulled into the driveway, grabbed her bag and jumped out of the Jeep to run up to the house. She heard Piper barking from inside the house and smiled. The barks were not meant to scare anyone away, since Piper knew exactly what her Jeep sounded like. She opened the front door only to have Piper's nose immediately attached to her boots and jeans.

"Hi girl. How was your day?" Jorja said as she scratched the top of Piper's head. Piper's nose shot upward to smell Jorja's hand before lowering her head again for another scratch on the head.

"I know, you miss me. I miss you too, you big baby." She used both hands to give Piper a couple of good pats on the back, which only made Piper drop to the floor and onto her back, with the expectation that her belly might get a couple of good pats as well.

Jorja laughed and she bent down to rub Piper's belly. "Okay, there. That's enough for now. There are others in this house who want my attention too, you know." She stood up to remove her jacket. "At least I think there are. Ryan? Nicholas? Where are you two?"

She listened and heard only silence, which was rare when Nicholas was around. "Okay, Piper, show me where they are."

Piper quickly stood up, but only to plant her rear beside Jorja's feet. "Well, that's not getting us anywhere, you goof. Where are they?"

In response, Piper only panted with her tongue hanging out the side of her mouth as she gazed adoringly up at Jorja.

Jorja chuckled. "Okay, come on." She moved to the kitchen with Piper obediently behind her. She smelled the roast simmering in the crock pot and immediately her belly grumbled. "Ryan?"

Seeing no one in the kitchen, she was about to turn around to head upstairs when she heard a child's squeal. Her heart raced in panic at the first sound until she heard laughter follow the squeal. She then realized the sounds had come from the garage.

She moved through the kitchen and informal dining area to the laundry room where she opened the door to the garage. There she spotted Ryan and Nicholas, laughing together as they worked on a project on the work bench. Jorja's heart swelled at the sight.

"Hi you two. What are you up to?" She asked as she tried to get a look at their project.

Nicholas quickly jumped off his stool and ran to her. "Hi Aunt Jorja! Dad's helping me make a car for Cub

Scouts. You want to see?" Nicholas grabbed her hand and pulled in an effort to make her walk with him. She moved forward to get a look at the wooden car they had been working on.

"Pretty neat, huh?" Nicholas said with a grin. Curious about this new bit of information, Jorja glanced at Ryan who explained, "He heard some other boys talking about the Cub Scouts and he really wants to join, but he's not old enough. When I found out Pastor Pete was the pack leader of one of the local dens, I asked him about it and he said Nicholas could join when he's six or in the first grade next year. In the meantime, he said we could hang out with him during some of the upcoming activities. The first one is a pinewood derby and it sounded like fun, although Nicholas can't technically race, but Pastor Pete said he can compete with the other kids once the actual races are over."

Jorja smiled before she looked at Nicholas again. "I think it looks perfect. You're doing a great job."

Nicholas grinned and turned back to his work on the car. He picked up a paintbrush and began adding more blue to the side.

Jorja glanced at Ryan again. "The roast smells amazing. Are you ready to eat? I have someone stopping by soon and I don't want to be in the middle of dinner when they arrive."

"Sure, I'm hungry. This wood building is hard work." Ryan ruffled Nicholas' hair. "Come on, squirt, let's go inside and eat."

While they ate their meal, Jorja informed Ryan that Gabe would be stopping by for a visit.

"Wait...what? Why would you have him come here? Isn't he being accused of...you know, *attacking* the chief?" Ryan glanced at Nicholas, who was too busy flattening his peas on his plate to pay attention to their conversation.

"He's a person of interest at this point, Ryan. They haven't arrested him yet. Remember me telling you the Chief is Gabe's uncle? I have a hard time believing Gabe moved back here from where ever he was living just to attack what is likely the only family he has left. From what I understand, the Chief didn't see who attacked him so no one really knows what happened, other than the person who is responsible, of course."

"Well do you think it's safe having him here in case there's a reason he *is* a person of interest? Why bring him here?"

Jorja found it difficult to explain her reasoning. "I just don't feel the need to worry about him or be afraid of him. I just want to hear what he has to say or what he wants to speak to me about. You can sit in on the conversation if you're concerned about me."

Ryan nodded quickly. "Your damn right I will. I'm not leaving you alone with a virtual stranger in our house. Nicholas, finish up and once you're done, you can go upstairs with Piper and play, okay?"

"Okay, Daddy." Nicholas hurriedly finished the last few bites of his meal before hopping off the chair. "Come on Piper, let's go play!" Piper needed no further request as she followed his running feet up the stairs.

Ryan stood up from the table to place his dishes in the sink. "Okay, Jorja. I don't know what you're getting yourself into, but I want to be involved. There's no reason you have to do this by yourself."

Jorja nodded, smiling. Ryan was too protective, but she knew he had good reason after the two of them almost lost each other at the hands of someone she thought she could trust. She knew he would do anything to make sure there was no repeat performance.

CHAPTER 19

Jorja was placing her dishes in the dishwasher when the doorbell rang. Ryan was quick to move down the hall. "I'll get it," he said.

Smiling at his overprotective attitude, she finished putting the dishes away before moving down the hallway where Ryan was introducing himself to Gabe.

"Hi, Gabe. Would you like to come into the living room?" Jorja said. "If you'd like to take off your jacket you can just leave it here on the hall bench."

"Okay, sure." Gabe removed his jacket and placed it on the bench before moving into the living room to sit on the couch. Ryan sat in the recliner and Jorja chose the overstuffed chair.

Gabe sat back on the couch and crossed his foot over his knee, but as he caught both Ryan's and Jorja's stare, he uncrossed his leg and sat straight up. Placing both hands on his knees he looked at Jorja for a moment before turning to Ryan. Ryan continued to stare at Gabe impassively, saying nothing, as Jorja watched the silent exchange between the two of them. She knew Ryan didn't wish to appear friendly until he knew exactly what it was Gabe wanted.

Jorja cleared her throat, causing Gabe to return his hazel eyes to her. "So...Gabe. What can I do for you?"

"Well, I would like your help, actually. I understand you're an investigator and as you know, I'm a suspect in the attack involving the chief. I hope it doesn't happen, but they may file charges against me and if they do, I'm going to have to be ready to defend myself. I've already spoken with an attorney and I told him I was going to meet with you to discuss possibly working for us. If you'll agree, we'd like to hire you now to begin investigating this matter so that maybe we can avoid charges being filed in the first place."

Jorja saw Ryan's head turn toward her and she could feel his penetrating stare, but she refused to look at him. She could already tell he thought Gabe's proposal was a bad idea.

"Are you saying you didn't attack the chief?" Jorja asked, not expecting him to be truthful if in fact he was the one responsible.

"Hell no, I didn't attack him." Gabe quickly glanced at Ryan before turning back to Jorja. "Look, I'd really like to speak with you about this in private. What I have to say is something I'd like to be kept confidential in case I'm arrested. No offense, Ryan, but I don't want to make you a witness to any conversations between Jorja and myself."

Ryan raised an eyebrow in question at Gabe before he narrowed his eyes and frowned. When he glanced at Jorja, she shrugged and offered, "Gabe and I can talk in the formal dining room. It really is best that you not be a witness to our conversation just in case they file charges and actually take it to trial."

Ryan was unable to hide his frustration as he threw his hands up and sighed heavily. "Okay, but I'll be right out here if you need me." He turned to glare at Gabe. "I don't know if you're guilty or not, but I will tell you that you better not be bringing my sister into a situation that will cause her any harm...from you or anyone else."

Gabe blinked quickly in surprise, but just as quickly nodded and gave Ryan a brief smile. "You know, if I had a sister I would probably act the same way. I completely understand and don't worry, I'm not a monster and I'm only asking Jorja to help me prove my innocence before the case goes any further."

Ryan only nodded in response and he eyed both of them warily as Jorja asked Gabe to follow her to the formal dining room. Once in the dining room, she pulled out a chair for Gabe and then chose another one for herself on the opposite side of the table.

Leaning back in her chair, Jorja laced her fingers together and placed her hands on the table. "Okay, Gabe. What do you want to talk to me about with regard to the case? How can I help you prove your innocence?"

Gabe leaned forward and asked, "Does this mean you'll help me? Will you take the case?"

Jorja nodded. She didn't know if Gabe was innocent or not, but she already felt in her heart that he was no cold-blooded killer. "Yes, I'll help you."

Breathing out a sigh of relief, Gabe leaned back in his chair. "Oh, thank God. I didn't know what I was going to do if you said no. I really need someone on my side to help me." Jorja was surprised when he choked back a sob. "You have no idea how much this means to me."

She gave a hesitant smile as she replied, "I'll help out as much as I can. Why don't you tell me what happened. From what I understand, the police caught you running from the scene. Why were you running?"

Gabe's shoulders visibly sagged as he thought back to that day. "Yes, I was running from the house when the police arrived. I was just so scared and I didn't know what to do. I tried to call 911 from the house phone, but it had been pulled from the wall and I had left my cell phone in my truck. When I ran to the truck, the police intercepted me and, of course, thought I was running from the scene after committing a crime."

"But why were you there? You're saying you found the Chief that way?"

Gabe held Jorja's gaze for a moment. He opened his mouth to speak, but just as quickly closed it and remained silent. Curious, she waited while he wrestled with his inner emotions.

Finally, he began to speak. "I did find him that way. He wasn't expecting me, but I had heard that he often went home for lunch so I took a chance and stopped by. I knocked and when he didn't answer, I tried the door and found it to be unlocked. When he didn't respond after I called out his name, I decided to go inside because his patrol car was at the house so I knew he must be there."

Gabe's voice cracked as he continued, "I found him in the kitchen, lying on the floor with blood around his head. The phone was sitting on the counter in the kitchen, but I could see that the wire had been ripped from the wall and because my cell phone was in my truck I had no way to immediately call for help. I checked to see if he had a pulse and I found one, but it was very light. I knew I had to get the hell out of there to get him some help so I ran outside to my truck. That's when the police found me."

"Do the police have any reason to believe you might have a motive for attacking the chief?"

He quickly looked away before turning his attention down to his hands. Jorja's brow furrowed when she saw the obvious display of a guilty reaction. When he didn't answer she asked, "Gabe? Is there a reason you'd have a motive to hurt the chief?"

Looking up, he finally made eye contact with her, but only for a second before he quickly looked away toward the dining room window. He kept his gaze on the window when he finally answered her question. "Your Chief and I have a…past, if you will. He wasn't happy with me for moving here."

She nodded. "Yes, I remember the conversation you and the Chief had at my store. You called him your uncle and he seemed very upset with you for having moved back here. Why is that?"

Gabe finally looked at her. "I had forgotten you heard that. Yes, he's my uncle. Even though we're family, I haven't seen him in about thirty years and he's very upset with me because he forbade me from ever coming back here. But after more than thirty years, I thought he could set aside his anger with me. I guess I was wrong."

"What could you have possibly done thirty years ago that he'd be so unwilling to forgive you for? It couldn't be anything so horrible, could it?" Jorja asked.

When he broke eye contact again to look down at the table, Jorja quickly noticed the color in his cheeks and how his hand shook when he scratched an itch on the side of his face. She was surprised when he suddenly pushed back his chair to stand and as he paced he said, "It *was* horrible, Jorja. I was responsible for killing the love of his life...his wife."

CHAPTER 20

Jorja was speechless. She hadn't expected this admission or anything like it. Gabe continued to pace as he let out a few deep breaths and when he finally stopped to look at her, she could only stare at him in return.

He took another deep breath, rubbed the back of his neck with his palm, and sat back down.

"Don't you want to know how?"

She found it difficult to nod her head. She had thought he was incapable of a cold-blooded attack on the chief, but was he about to tell her he had already killed before?

"You—you're saying you killed your aunt? H–how?"

He nodded, shame clouding his face. "Yes. I'm responsible for my aunt's death. But it was an accident. My aunt and uncle bought me a new car as a graduation and birthday gift after I turned 18 years old. I wanted to go for a drive and I insisted my aunt come with me. It was a beautiful day and I didn't realize it then, but I was going too fast. There were too many curves and I didn't plan for how I would react when a doe and her two fawns were standing right in the middle of the road as I rounded a sharp corner. I hit the brakes, but instinctively I also tried to avoid hitting all three deer." Gabe paused to take a deep breath before going on. "The car skidded, I lost control and the car rolled. I don't know how many times, but it seemed to last forever. It also felt like we were moving in slow motion. And then suddenly, it was over."

Gabe took a deep anxious breath before continuing. "We stopped rolling because we hit a tree. The force hit my aunt's side of the car and she was killed. Instantly killed, is what I was later told. I can't tell you how awful it was to wake up after being knocked out cold, only to discover her lifeless body beside me. I was climbing out of the car when I heard a vehicle approach and you can't imagine the horror and absolute guilt I felt when I saw it was my uncle, who had been patrolling the area. Once he discovered what happened, he was enraged. I honestly think he could have killed me. After my aunt was taken away and my uncle took me home, I knew something in him had changed. He finally told me he wanted me to leave and never come back. He said if I didn't leave, he would have me arrested for vehicular homicide. I didn't know what to do. I wanted to take responsibility for my aunt's death. I knew it was my fault. I wanted to be there for her funeral. But the thought of being arrested and going to prison scared the crap out of me. He told me I was an adult and I'd spend a lot more time in prison than if I had still been a juvenile and that if I didn't leave, he would ask that I receive the highest sentence possible. It was awful. I finally decided to do as my uncle said and I left. It was difficult because I felt like a fugitive. I worried I would be hunted down and arrested at any time. I stayed away because my uncle told me he never wished to see me again, but it has been very difficult not to make contact with him. I've needed for so long to make peace with him because he's all I have left. After my own parents were killed in a car accident when I was little, my aunt and uncle were like parents to me and losing both of them the way I did has been very difficult to live with all these years."

Jorja took in everything Gabe said with a heavy heart. She now understood why the Chief acted the way he did. Why he was so difficult and hard to get close to. He had lost his wife in a horrific accident and he would have lost his nephew to the criminal justice system as well. She wondered if the chief's decision was a way to save his nephew from a prison sentence as well as saving himself from the pain of having to look in the eyes of the one who killed his wife.

"I honestly can't imagine how you've lived with that all your life, especially since you were never forgiven by your uncle after it happened. Is that why you went to see him? Were you hoping to speak to him about all this?"

Nodding, Gabe replied, "Yes. I decided to move back here when I saw the school needed a substitute teacher. It had been long enough, I thought, and I hoped that my uncle could speak to me and possibly some day forgive me. He obviously hasn't forgiven me yet, if his attitude toward me at your bookstore was any indication. I stopped by his house that day because I wanted to get it all out in the open. I wanted to know what I needed to do to help him forgive me. I decided I couldn't go any longer without having contact with the only family I have left. Now, I might lose him without being able to mend the relationship between us. You have to help me Jorja. I need to prove I didn't hurt my uncle."

"Okay. I'll help you. I'm not sure how yet, but I'll do what I can. We can talk more about this later, but we need to set up a time to meet with your attorney so we're all on the same page. Do you want to contact him tomorrow and see what date and time might work for him?"

"Yes. I'll do that." He pushed his chair back as he stood. "Thank you so much. You have no idea how lonely it is to be a person of interest in a crime involving the chief of police in a town where no one really knows me.

Jorja also stood. "I can only imagine. I hope the Chief might be able to give you the benefit of the doubt and not assume you're responsible for the attack, even if law enforcement believes you are. Let me know when you're able to speak to your attorney about a meeting and then I'll schedule a time to meet with the Chief once he's feeling up to it. Maybe he'll help us if he can admit he doesn't believe you were involved."

Gabe's look betrayed his doubt, but he nodded anyway. "Perhaps. We'll have to wait and see what he says."

He pushed his chair back in place under the table and as he turned to leave the room, a shadow box on the wall caught his attention. His attention remained focused on the small cabinet as he moved closer to it. Jorja glanced at the shadow box, where she had placed Gloria's glass hummingbird collection, and then looked back at Gabe. She watched as he quickly glanced from one figurine to the next with an odd expression on his face. Finally, he turned to her and asked, "Where did you get these?"

"That collection belonged to my aunt. I received them after she passed away."

Gabe's stare was intense as he asked, "And your aunt's name was...?"

Jorja took a step back from the intensity of his stare. "Her name was Gloria. Why?"

"Your aunt was Gloria? She passed away? When? How?"

She frowned at the number of questions he asked her. "She died last year. In a car accident. Why? Did you know her?" She wasn't sure she wanted to share information with him, but she couldn't ignore the stricken expression on his face.

"You could say that." He reached for a dining chair and pulled it out in order to sit down again. "She was someone who was very close to me, but who I lost contact with when I left town. I'm sorry, I don't mean to be rude. I just haven't had a chance to speak to my uncle about anything and this is the first I've heard about Gloria's death. I heard rumors about what happened to her after I left, but I never knew if they were true. I thought her sister might still be living in the area so that I could ask where Gloria might be living. I didn't realize you were family. Is Helen your mother?"

Jorja nodded, not feeling the need to fill him in on the real truth. "How did you know my aunt?"

"We knew each other from school and, to be quite honest, we became an item when we were both probably too young. I swore her to secrecy because she was only fifteen at the time and I was seventeen. My uncle had already made it clear he didn't want me to form any relationships because it had been his plan to have me apply for the academy after graduation and eventually become a cop like him. I couldn't let him know Gloria and I were in a relationship because more than once he threatened to send me to military school if he thought I was going to interfere with his plans for my future. I was fine with becoming a cop. Heck, I wanted to go further and become an agent with the CIA or the FBI. But I was young and a romantic and your aunt and I fell in love. I will always regret that I left town without being able to tell her where I was going and why I was leaving. I feel worse now that I see she kept the hummingbird collection I gave her which would only remind her that I left her behind. I hope she was able to find someone else and lead a happy life after I left town." Gabe's look was questioning as he waited for her response.

Jorja was beyond speechless and had no idea how to respond to what he had just told her. She certainly didn't want to start with the fact that Gloria had been pregnant and later admitted to a mental institution for over twenty years. Her heart began to race at the realization of just who Gabe Carter really was and she knew she had to get him out of the house in order to find time to figure things out.

She finally responded by saying, "I wasn't really close to my aunt, but the years leading up to her death I would say she was pretty happy."

"I'm glad to hear that, at least." Gabe slowly stood again and he held his hand out to Jorja. "Thank you for telling me about Gloria and thanks again for helping me. I should probably let you get back to your evening, but I look forward to meeting with you again soon."

She hesitated only slightly, but she saw his quizzical look before she finally reached out to shake his hand. She made her best attempt to stop her hand from shaking, but thought he might likely hear her rapid heart rate anyway.

"You're welcome. We will definitely talk again soon."

Jorja let her hand drop to her side. She felt her body grow tense as she followed Gabe out of the dining room, down the hall and to the front door. She did her best to make small talk with him as he put his jacket on and waved goodbye to Ryan who was still sitting in the living room.

When Gabe walked out of the front door and down the porch steps to his truck, Ryan finally moved toward Jorja where she stood by the door watching Gabe. Ryan waited and watched along with her as Gabe got into his pickup and drove away. He waited while she continued to watch the pickup as it traveled down the street and he waited as she watched the pickup turn a corner and disappear from sight. When she made no attempt to close the door or even move, Ryan finally turned to look at her. He was struck by the fact that she had tears in her eyes.

"Jorja? What's wrong? Did he say something to upset you?" He hit his fist into the palm of his other hand. "Damn it! I told you this wasn't a good idea."

She turned to stare at him, but when she still didn't say anything, his anger turned to concern again. "What the hell is wrong? Would you *please* say something?"

Taking a deep breath she finally said, "Ryan, you won't believe this, but I think Gabe Carter is our father."

Ryan gave Jorja a blank stare which soon turned to disbelief. "What are you talking about?"

She moved away from the door frame to shut the front door before moving to the living room to sit down. She felt her heart rate pounding and she tried to take long deep breaths. Ryan slowly sat down on the couch next to her as he watched her carefully. She shut her eyes and leaned back on the couch cushion. "Just give me a minute. I feel like I could pass out."

Keeping her eyes closed, Jorja felt Ryan get off the couch and she heard him walk to the kitchen. She then heard the tap water running and the cupboard open and shut. Moments later she heard him say, "Here, drink this."

When Jorja opened her eyes she saw Ryan holding a glass of water. She suddenly realized her throat was dry when she tried to say she didn't need water so she sat up and grabbed the glass. Ryan sat down next to her again and watched her drink from the glass. After a few gulps, she set the glass down and turned to look at him.

Finally, she said, "I know this is coming out of nowhere, but I really do believe Gabe is the one who got Aunt Gloria pregnant. He told me he gave her that hummingbird collection I got from her. He told me he had a relationship with her that he had to keep secret because his uncle, Chief Douglas, thought any sort of relationship would interfere with his potential career. He also told me he left town quietly and quickly after he accidentally took the life of the Chief's wife. The Chief threatened to have him arrested if he stayed in town and also told Gabe never to come back. Until now, he never did."

Ryan's brow creased as he took in all the information. He then rubbed his temples with his fingers. "He killed his aunt? What are you saying? That he ran from the law to avoid being arrested? Why wouldn't he tell Gloria?"

"He ran because he was young and he had recently turned eighteen. The Chief told him he would go to prison and Gabe believed him. I think the Chief did that as a way to protect Gabe, but also because he couldn't live with the person responsible for his wife's death. It's sad if you think about. I don't know why Gabe didn't tell Gloria other than I would guess he couldn't tell her. I don't think he knew she was pregnant and maybe at the time he left, neither did she."

Ryan frowned at her as shook his head. "You sure are giving him the benefit of the doubt. He killed someone, didn't take responsibility for it and ran from the law. You don't think he knew Gloria was pregnant, but maybe he did and he left because he didn't want to take responsibility of us either. As far as I'm concerned, his past actions leave a lot to be desired."

"Yeah, I know. I understand what you're saying. But until he gives me a reason to think otherwise, I want to give him the benefit of the doubt. I need to speak to the Chief . I believe Gabe when he says he had nothing to do with the attack on the Chief . I need to see what the Chief believes."

"So you are going to help him. Will you please be careful and not do anything rash? You really don't know this guy from Adam. He could be a dangerous person and you can't help people like that. I don't care if you think he's our father or not." Ryan's frown deepened as he asked, "You don't plan to tell him, do you?"

Jorja gave him a half smile. "Tell him what? That I believe him because I think he's my biological father and I don't want to believe he's capable of trying to kill someone? No. I'll wait, but eventually we'll need to tell him. He needs to know."

Ryan stood up. Staring down at her he replied, "I know you'll do whatever it takes to help him, but I'm telling you right now, you better keep me and Taylor in the loop on what you're doing and where you're going. Let one of us tag along with you if you can. You tend to play with fire and eventually you'll get burned. You should know that already."

She also stood as she placed her hands on his shoulders. "I know you care. I promise I'll be careful and I'll keep you and Taylor in the loop. Don't worry so much."

Ryan rolled his eyes. "You know for a fact that's much easier said than done."

CHAPTER 21

The rain was becoming a part of everyday life and Jorja began to dream of vacationing in a warmer climate. It wasn't just the rain; it was also the gloomy, gray, cloudy days to go along with it. The long stretch between the holidays and the changes she looked forward to in the spring seemed to take much too long. As Jorja sat in her Jeep soaking up the warmth inside the vehicle, she prepared herself for the time it would take to run from her Jeep to the back of the store. She often forgot to bring an umbrella, but there were days like today when she wished she had remembered. The rain drops were as big as cherries, or they seemed to feel that way when they hit her head.

She turned to the passenger seat. "Okay, Piper, are you ready to run for it?"

She quickly thought it may have been a bad idea to bring Piper today because she'd risk making the store smell like wet dog. When Piper gave her a loving look, Jorja immediately took back the thought. Realizing she could never regret bringing along such a great companion, she attached the leash to Piper's collar and pulled her purse straps over her shoulder.

Bracing herself, Jorja opened the door to the Jeep, jumped out with Piper right behind her and quickly ran to the back of the book store where she hurriedly unlocked the back door. As she turned the key and opened the door, she felt a chill go up her spine. She quickly turned to look behind her, but saw no one as she glanced up and down the alley on both sides of the building. Holding her breath, she tried to tell herself she was being silly, but she couldn't shake the feeling she was being watched. Piper's stance changed as her ears dropped back and the fur on the nape of her neck rose. Jorja then heard Piper sniff the air while she let out a few growls in between sniffs. It was enough to make Jorja finally move.

She turned the key so that she could remove it from the lock and just as she moved into the doorway she saw movement out of the corner of her eye. A man, wearing a long coat, was walking away from the building and was already on the other side of the street. She could see the back of his head, but only what appeared to be short black hair visible below the rim of a hat. She tried to tell herself it was just a pedestrian crossing the street, but she couldn't shake the heightened sense of panic. Piper also saw the retreating man and quickly let out a bark. When he didn't turn toward the unexpected noise, Jorja's suspicion in him rose to a higher level.

She pulled on Piper's leash to get her into the store and then quickly shut the door, locking it from the inside. Jorja knew Taylor would be arriving soon to help open the store, but she would keep the doors locked until then. She shook her head in exasperation. She *had* to get a grip. No one was watching her and she was just being paranoid and there was no reason for it.

Shaking off her jacket, she hung it on the coat rack near the back door. She bent down to unhook Piper's leash and grabbed a towel lying near the back door to quickly rub down Piper's fur. Once Piper was as clean as possible, Jorja entered the break room to make a pot of coffee and once that was done she moved to the front of the store to prepare for another day. When she was only a few steps from the cash register, she nearly jumped out of her skin when she heard a knock at the front door and Piper let out a quick bark.

"Jorja? You in there?" She heard someone yell. "Open up. It's Fritz."

Holding her hand to her chest in an attempt to quiet her rapidly beating heart, Jorja walked to the door to unlock it. She opened the door a few inches and peeked through the crack to see Fritz and Reynolds standing under the small awning together in their attempt to stay out of the rain.

She opened the door the rest of the way to let them in as she admitted, "You scared the life out of me."

Fritz looked at Jorja and was about to tease her when he realized her face had no color. "What's wrong?"

She only shook her head. "Nothing's wrong. You just scared me, that's all."

Fritz leaned toward her, eyeing her with suspicion and she knew he didn't believe her. She knew he could also tell by the look on her face that she wouldn't offer any additional explanation. He finally leaned back as he thoroughly scanned the store. "Everything's okay here? Is it just you this morning?"

"Yes, just me and Piper. Taylor will be in soon." Jorja moved back to the register where she checked to make sure there was enough paper before she opened the register to check the amount of money left in the drawer.

Reynolds had been distracted by Piper who immediately demanded some affection, but he finally spoke up. "Do you think we could get a cup of coffee? Or is it too soon?"

"I have some perking in the back room if you'd like just a regular cup of coffee. If you want something from the stand, you'll just have to give me a few minutes to finish what I'm doing here."

Reynolds shook his head. "No, regular coffee is perfect. Do you mind?"

Jorja looked up to see Reynolds' questioning look as he pointed at the back of the store. "No, go ahead. It should be about ready. There are some paper coffee cups in the cabinet next to the fridge."

Fritz continued to scan the rest of the store as Reynolds made his way to the back with Piper right on his heels. Jorja could tell Fritz was tense and ready for anything. She decided she should let him off the hook.

"You don't have to worry. It's just me and Piper and everything is fine. You can check the whole store, but there's nothing to find."

Fritz glanced at her, saw the color was back in her cheeks and his posture finally relaxed. "Okay, I won't worry. But I know something was bothering you. You should trust me, Jorja. I'm only here to protect you."

She was beginning to believe he felt it was his duty ever since he and Reynolds found her after she had been attacked by Cooper. She didn't want him to continue to feel the need to protect her and, if she really had to admit it, she didn't want to continue to feel she owed him anything.

"I know. I appreciate that."

Fritz suddenly smiled. "I'm glad you appreciate it. I hope you remember I'm just a friend looking out for your best interests."

Jorja braced herself. She waited for another lecture about his concern when it came to her working for Michael Stafford.

"In fact, I've been meaning to speak to you about something. I just wasn't sure how to approach you about it."

With a raised eyebrow she asked, "Oh? What about?"

"Well, even if we do have a difference of opinion when it comes to your new job, I hope you know anything I say to you is only out of concern as a friend. I just don't want you putting yourself in harm's way or working with people who you might mistakenly give too much benefit of the doubt."

She took a step back in surprise. *Had Ryan told him about Gabe? Why?*

"What are you talking about? You know I take my job seriously and I'll do my best to keep safe. I wish you'd let go of the fact that I was attacked. I'm not going to give up jobs just because of one incident. It's not a way to live and it's also not a way to work. You do it every day."

Fritz crossed his arms. "My job is much different than your job and you know it. It comes with the possibility and expectation of danger. Your job shouldn't. Besides, that's not what I wanted to talk to you about—"

"What I do for a living is not something you have a say over. And stop treating me like I'm a child. I can work for anyone I chose, even Gabe Carter."

The words slipped out before she could stop them. She hadn't planned to bring up Gabe's name, but she was beginning to assume he knew. She quickly realized by his puzzled expression that he did not.

His arms dropped to his sides as he scowled at her. "What do you mean, Gabe Carter? You're not helping him, are you? You can't help him. He attacked the Chief!"

Jorja placed her hands on her hips. "You assume he did, but you have to prove it. There are two sides to every story. If you don't believe that, then you can't be a very good cop."

Fritz didn't respond except to glare at her. She stood her ground with her hands on her hips as she glared back. She refused to break the stare even when she heard Piper run down the hall ahead of Reynolds and then felt Piper sit on her foot and lean against her leg. Reynolds soon followed, holding two cups of coffee as he approached them.

Reynolds stopped next to Fritz and held out one cup. "Here you go, Fritz, It's nice and hot."

When Fritz didn't respond or take the cup in his own hand, Reynolds looked at Fritz more closely before he turned back to glance at Jorja. In an effort to lighten the mood he said, "Boy, it's a good thing I stopped short or the daggers between the two of you would spear me."

Getting no response from either he finally moved in front of Fritz. "Hey, buddy, do you want your coffee or not?"

Fritz finally focused on Reynolds. He looked down at the cup in Reynolds' hand and reached out to take it. Reynolds then leaned over to whisper, "I take it you weren't able to bring up dinner?"

Jorja heard enough of what Reynolds said and couldn't contain her surprise before she caught Fritz's gaze again. She saw not only anger, but a wounded look and she wanted to apologize although stubbornly, she thought he should apologize first.

"Uh, well, we should get going. Thanks for the coffee, Jorja. Fritz? You ready to go?"

Fritz glanced at Reynolds. "Yeah, I'm ready. We've got work to do." Fritz did not say goodbye and only glanced briefly at Jorja one last time before leaving the store. She could only shake her head and sigh as she wondered how she should deal with this odd relationship forming between her and Fritz.

CHAPTER 22

"Good morning. How's it going so far?" Taylor said as she breezed into the store. She shook off her jacket, tore the hat off her head and tossed the items on a chair behind the coffee stand. She quickly ran her fingers through her long brunette hair to smooth it out and then placed her bag on a shelf below the stand before peering back over the counter at Jorja, who sat quietly at a nearby table holding a coffee cup between both hands.

"Hey, is everything okay?"

Jorja looked up from the cold coffee she'd been staring at, but stared out the store window rather than at Taylor.

"Sure. Everything is a-okay."

Taylor moved around the stand to sit in a chair at the table. When Jorja continued to stare out the window, Taylor used her hand to force Jorja to turn her head and look at her.

"Jorja, come on. What's wrong? Is it what happened last night with Gabe? I know you must still be in shock over it, but you look absolutely glum. Why?"

Jorja shook her head and felt embarrassed when her eyes began to tear. "It's not Gabe. It's, um…something that happened with Fritz this morning."

Taylor leaned back in her chair and stared at Jorja. She blew out a breath in surprise. "Oh. And when did you see Fritz? Did he stop by?"

"Yes, he and Reynolds stopped by early. We had words."

Taylor chuckled. "What did you have words about now? Why is it the two of you can't seem to get along?"

Jorja quickly stood up. "Oh Taylor, how can I get along with a man who continuously tries to tell me what to do? He was upset when he found out about Michael Stafford and he was extremely upset when he found out about Gabe."

Taylor gave her a quizzical look. "How did he find out about Gabe?"

"I told him, but it was an accident. By the way he was talking I thought he already knew and that Ryan must have told him."

"So you had words. So what? He's been a good friend to us, Jorja. I'm sure the two of you can work it out."

Jorja paced back and forth. "I don't know, Taylor. He keeps pushing me to do what he thinks will keep me safe and he doesn't understand why I don't want to listen to his advice. I just wish he'd leave me alone about it and stop interfering so much."

Taylor smiled knowingly. "Jorja, that's what friends do if they care about you. They interfere if they think you're putting yourself at risk. And if he cares for you like I think he does, that gives him even more reason to show you he wants you to stay safe."

Jorja stopped pacing and glared at Taylor. "If he has feelings for me, he has a funny way of showing it. Always telling me what to do, but not actually saying he cares about me." She shook her head. "No. He just feels obligated to look out for me ever since that day with Cooper. I'm sure he feels some sort of misplaced guilt over the fact that I was attacked and almost killed by one of his own. Those are his feelings for me. Nothing more."

Taylor frowned as she moved to Jorja to grab her shoulders. "I'm sorry you think that way, but I don't agree with you. I think he really does care and maybe if you gave him a chance you'd see it too."

Jorja didn't immediately respond. She only stared at Taylor for a few moments before breaking eye contact and pulling away from her grip. "I don't need to see anything. I'm not going to give him a reason to think we could be anything more than friends, but even as a friend, he needs to stop crossing the line. Nothing gives him the right to tell me what to do."

Taylor watched Jorja as she attempted to straighten a row of books before finally throwing her hands down in frustration. "Look at me! I can't even work right now...he's got me so upset."

"Why are you so upset? What's going on that you aren't telling me?" Taylor tried to catch Jorja's eye, who only turned to look at another book display.

"Come on, give it up. What's got you so upset?" Taylor moved so that she stood right in front of Jorja, forcing her to look her in the eye.

Jorja finally turned to look at Taylor. She began to speak, but then hesitated, blew out a breath and closed her eyes. She took a deep breath, opened her eyes and stared directly at Taylor. "I'm not upset. I'm just being realistic, that's all."

Taylor's brow arched as she asked, "Realistic about what?"

Jorja broke eye contact and moved back to the table where she began to straighten the chairs around the table. "I'm just being realistic about my future. I don't think I'll ever get married and have children so I'd rather focus on the businesses and the house."

"*What* are you talking about? Of course you'll get married and have children. Why wouldn't you?"

Jorja shook her head. "No, I don't think that'll be in the cards for me." She suddenly felt tired and pulled out a chair to sit down. She looked up at Taylor. "Not everyone has to get married, you know."

Taylor's puzzlement at her friend's attitude was evident in her furrowed brow and intense frown. She moved to sit in a chair next to Jorja. "I don't know what's come over you, but you're not making any sense. You actually have two men who might be interested enough in you to put forth the effort to establish a very serious relationship, but for some reason you're going to turn into the spinster cat lady?" Taylor quickly glanced over at Piper who was napping on her dog pillow nearby. "Or, a spinster dog lady, anyway. What's wrong with you? Why would you even think you'll grow old by yourself and not with the love of your life?"

Jorja's heart was racing as she prepared to finally confide her fears to Taylor. This wasn't how she thought it would be when she finally expressed them. She'd rather be at home, safe from intruders and where she could later hide in her bedroom to mull over the conversation. Instead, she was going to tell Taylor at work, right before customers were due to arrive and right before she'd have to focus on work.

"Jorja, please tell me what's wrong. I'm your best friend. You know you can tell me anything."

Jorja knew she had to reveal her fear to Taylor. She knew it would be good to talk about it and she doubted any time would feel like a good time.

She leaned back as she blew out another breath. "Okay, I'll tell you, but you can't tell me I'm being irrational."

When Jorja didn't continue, Taylor nodded. "Fine, I won't say you're being irrational."

Jorja waited a heartbeat before she spoke.

"I have a fear. It may not be something that'll ever happen, but I think it's a fear I can't deny when it can put someone else at risk."

Taylor's look was questioning, but she remained silent as she waited for Jorja to continue. She nodded to encourage Jorja to move on.

Jorja finally blurted out her fear. "I'm afraid because of what happened with Gloria. I'm afraid to get married because I'm even more afraid about the thought of having a baby. I can't take the risk that I might...well, you know. That I could turn out like Gloria."

Taylor leaned back in shock as she stared at Jorja. She suddenly wanted to cry over her friend's distress. "Why would you think that? You're going to make a great mother some day. Just look at what a wonderful aunt you are to Nicholas. There's no reason for you to believe you'd ever turn out like Gloria."

"Why not? We don't know why she did what she did. We don't know what triggered it or if she had some chemical imbalance after she got pregnant or after she gave birth or if she was already disturbed and our birth just pushed her over the edge. It doesn't matter. I'm her daughter and I have her blood and I might very likely have the same sort of tendencies she had. I've tried to find something I can understand in her journal entries, but none of them have provided me any real answers. Without knowing what caused her to do what she did, I'm petrified of having a baby and possibly doing something so terrible myself." Jorja violently shook her head. "I just don't want to risk it so it'll be easier not to get into any type of relationship with anyone."

Jorja looked down at her hands as she wiped her palms on her jeans. She was suddenly very nervous about how Taylor would respond to her confession. She waited as she stared at her hands and when Taylor didn't say anything, she finally looked up. She was struck by the fact that Taylor's eyes were glistening. Jorja took a deep breath and looked out the window. Nothing could make her cry more quickly than someone else showing her compassion.

"Don't do that, Taylor. If you cry, I'll cry." Jorja quickly stood up and pushed the chair back under the table.

Taylor also stood and just as quickly she leaned over to give Jorja a hug. Jorja did her best to ignore the overwhelming feelings that would make her cry. She hugged Taylor back before they pulled back to look at each other.

Taylor finally said, "Jorja, I love you like a sister and I'm upset you've been holding this in for the past few months without telling me. I'm sorry you feel like you do. I don't believe you will ever turn out like Gloria, but I understand your fears. I'll do my best to back off from the jabs about getting a date with Fritz or Brad, okay?"

"You know I won't hold your teasing ways against you," Jorja said. "I guess I just wanted you to know how I was feeling because I really don't want to jump into anything serious with either of them."

"Okay, I understand. But please believe what I believe. You won't turn out like Gloria. I wish you'd believe that because I'd hate to see you give up a happy and fulfilling life with someone who might be your soul mate."

"Whether I'm like her or not, I'd just rather not take the risk. Don't worry, I'll still live a happy life."

Taylor hesitated to agree, but finally nodded. "Yes, I'm sure you'll have a happy life. I just hope you'll finally decide to take the risk necessary to have an even more fulfilling life, that's all."

The shrill of the phone made both of them jump.

Jorja glanced at the clock on the wall as she moved to the telephone. "Good morning, Books 'N Brew, how can I help you? Oh...hello, Lydia. What can I do for you? Kat? Yes, she's working until six o'clock, I think. Why? Well, if she has something else she needs to do, I'm sure we can let her leave early." Jorja eyed Taylor who nodded in agreement. "Uh, sure, I can let her know when she gets here."

After Lydia hung up, Jorja pulled the receiver away from her ear to look at it. "You're welcome."

"What's up with Kat?" Taylor asked.

Jorja hung up the receiver. "I guess they're having some sort of fundraiser at the salon to raise money for Wolf Haven and Lydia wants Kat there to help out. Maybe she thought Kat was going to use work as an excuse not to help so she made the call to make sure I'd let her go. Who knows. Anyway, I think it's great they're raising funds for Wolf Haven. I hadn't thought about it, but it would be a great place to take Nicholas so he can see all the wolves. I wonder if they still have the Howl-ins during the summer. That would be fun for Ryan to take him to."

As Jorja moved toward the computer, Taylor asked, "Howl-ins? What are those?"

Jorja punched in a few keys after she brought up the website for a search engine. "I haven't actually been to one, but you visit the wolf sanctuary for a tour, sit around a camp fire, listen to stories and eventually the group of visitors howl and hope that the wolves will answer with their own howling."

Taylor's eyes widened. "If the wolves howl back, I bet it sounds kind of creepy, especially if it's at night."

Jorja nodded. "Yeah, it probably does. I remember hearing the coyotes here when I was a kid whenever they were back behind Scatter Creek and the howls and yips they make when they're in a pack can sometimes raise the hair on your neck. They always sounded like they were up to no good. I'm betting the wolves sound more beautiful and soulful, but could probably also raise the hair on your neck."

Taylor moved next to Jorja to see what she was looking at on the computer.

"Oh, it looks like the Howl-ins aren't an event any longer." Jorja said as she pointed to the screen. "They have something new, but it sounds even better, if Ryan and Nicholas want to actually camp at the sanctuary. Look at this...they get dinner, a tour, sitting by the campfire, breakfast in the morning, and another tour in the morning. I'll have to let Ryan know because it's something he and Nicholas can do this summer."

"I bet Nicholas would love it. He'd probably want to take a wolf home."

Jorja's head snapped up. "That's a great idea."

Frowning, Taylor asked, "What's a great idea?"

"I can adopt a wolf and use it as a write-off for the business. We can let Nicholas pick out which wolf he wants us to sponsor. We'll get a photo and information about the wolf and a subscription to a wolf magazine. Nicholas would love it. Check this out...here's their gallery of wolves to choose from. He'll have a hard time choosing, but he can pick his favorite and if the wolf is at the sanctuary when he and Ryan go visit later this year, that'll be even more of a treat for him."

Taylor leaned over to get a look at the gallery of photos. "They're all beautiful. I think it's a great idea to adopt a wolf and you're right, Nicholas will love the idea."

Jorja stepped back from the computer. "Well, I'll look at it more later after I talk to Ryan about letting Nicholas choose a wolf. I must admit, that was a good distraction after our little chat. Now I need to get back to work. I think I'll go upstairs to do some research. Do you mind?"

Taylor shook her head. "No, I don't mind. Let me make you a fresh latte to take with you, okay? If you need any help with the research, let me know and I'll work on the computer down here."

"Thanks. Actually, when you do have some free time, do you want to see if you can find any information on the Internet about what happened with the Chief's wife? It was so long ago you might not find much so we might have to go to the library, but if you do find anything, print it out for me, okay?"

Taylor was already preparing a latte for Jorja as she replied, "Sure, I can do that. Here's a nice hot cinnamon spice latte to help lighten your mood. Go work for awhile and we'll talk more later."

Jorja frowned at the idea of more talk, but she gladly took the latte and headed up to her office. After she sat down at her desk, she booted up the computer, found a notepad and began researching what Bailey told her.

Or what Bailey wanted to tell her.

Jorja didn't think Bailey was telling the whole truth and she was determined to find out why. She looked over her notes. Bailey told her the city and state she had moved from and what her husband's name was. Jorja ran a few news searches to see what she could come up with. She found a few articles about Bailey's husband, Scott Wheeler, and awards he had received as a volunteer and financially generous member of the community. Her interest grew when she saw more articles about donations he made to a local children's daycare and to the community center and also to the local senior center. He was on the city council as well as a member of a number of business organizations. Overall he seemed to be a pillar of the community. However, Jorja knew it was possible for a man to be a monster at home while the rest of the community believed just the opposite.

She finally found articles relating to Scott and Bailey, or Bethany as she was really known. Jorja found a few photos where the two were seen at local events and ribbon cuttings. There were a few more articles about how beneficial Scott's large construction business was to the community as a whole. He appeared to donate quite a bit of time and material to those who needed it the most. Jorja was beginning to wonder if this guy really was too good to be true.

Another article threw those thoughts to the side and she was deflated as she read an article dated two months prior:

The community as a whole is shocked at the allegations which have been made against the wife of one of our prominent community members, Scott Wheeler. Most will agree they had no idea she was capable of thinking about such acts, let alone committing them. Bethany Wheeler, wife and mother, PTA member, school fundraising coordinator and volunteer librarian, is now on the run from the law. According to police sources, it is alleged Mrs. Wheeler assaulted her husband, left him for dead and kidnapped their only son to whereabouts unknown. The horrific crime of assault and attempted murder is only shadowed by the thought of whether Mr. Wheeler will ever see his son again. The police are investigating this matter thoroughly, but if you or someone you know has any information with regard to these crimes or the location of Bethany Wheeler, please contact the local sheriff's office immediately.

Jorja leaned forward to place her head on her arms as she took in what she had just read. She couldn't believe it. Bailey had kidnapped her son after attacking her husband? Was it true? How could it not be true? Something had happened to the husband and if it wasn't Bailey, who was responsible?

Moaning in frustration at the thought of having to either confront Bailey with what she knew or involving the police, Jorja felt the stirrings of a headache. She also felt the stirrings of unease as she wondered how she would confront Bailey…a suspect in an assault, kidnapping and apparently even attempted murder. This was exactly what Fritz was talking about when decisions she made could put her at risk. Should she confront Bailey? Was she at risk? Jorja closed her eyes in disbelief. She just couldn't see Bailey as the type to attack someone unless it was in self-defense. Maybe her husband attacked her and she fought back. But taking her son and being charged with kidnapping were also serious, even if it was initially in self-defense.

"Oh brother. Now what the heck do I do?" She muttered to herself.

"About what?"

Jorja opened her eyes and raised her head in surprise to see Taylor standing in front of the desk. Leaning back in her chair she said, "Oh, something I discovered about Bailey. It's not good. Not one bit. How about you? Did you get a chance to research the accident involving the Chief's wife?"

Taylor nodded. "Yeah, but there wasn't much about it online. I think it's too old of a case to be on the Internet. What did you find out about Bailey?"

Jorja asked Taylor to sit down while she filled her in. Once she let Taylor read the news article she found,

Taylor handed the printout back to Jorja in stunned silence.

"I know, right? Hard to imagine Bailey is capable of all that. Now I don't know if I should speak to her directly about it or just turn her in to the police. What do you think?"

Taylor stood to pace in front of Jorja's desk. "If she's capable of doing something like that you have to be careful. Why did she ask you to look into this? Didn't she know you'd trace her back to this crime? What did she expect you to do? I think you should just tell Fritz or Reynolds. Let them take care of it. You can't confront someone who has already shown they are capable of violence."

Jorja looked down at the news article. "I know what you're saying is right, but I just think there's more to the story. I'd like to hear it directly from Bailey. We could talk to her together, here, and I could ask Ryan to be here as well, just to be safe. She can either explain herself or we'll call the police to pick her up as soon as she leaves the store. Are you willing?"

Taylor stopped pacing. "Only if we stick to a plan. I don't want any of us in danger."

Jorja nodded. "Okay. It's a deal. We'll talk to Ryan and make sure we have a plan. I'll call Bailey to set up a time to talk sometime on Monday."

CHAPTER 23

"You want to do what?" Flustered, Ryan waved his hands wildly as he paced in front of Jorja's desk. "How can you and Taylor agree it's a good idea to have a discussion with someone to ask them if they committed serious crimes? That's crazy. They'll either run or they might try to hurt you to keep you quiet."

Jorja wasn't able to get a word in when Ryan only shook his head in frustration and continued, "I can't believe it. I come in here to help you run a bookstore, but instead you've got me meeting up with known criminals. I don't like the idea. It's just not safe."

She stood up and walked around the desk. "You don't have to worry. I'll speak to her and if I think we should call the police, we'll do that. If it will make you feel better, we'll invite Fritz and Reynolds here for coffee at a certain time just in case. She'll either be gone already or they'll be here in case they're needed."

Ryan crossed his arms. "Yeah, that makes me feel much better. We shouldn't even be making precautions like this. We should just let the police handle it."

"But I need to let her explain it to me. She came to me. I don't know why, but she was asking for my help so I need to be up front with her and let her know what I know. I called her and she'll be here on Monday at one o'clock. You can call Fritz or Reynolds and make up some excuse about how you want to meet them here at two o'clock to discuss doing a ride-along with them for a book you're writing."

"A lot can happen in an hour. She should be able to explain herself in less time than that and she can do a lot of harm with the amount of time she has left."

Jorja blew out a breath, exasperated. "Okay, fine. Tell them to be here at one-thirty. Will that work?"

Ryan hesitated before finally nodding his consent. "Fine. I'll touch base with Reynolds today. Based on what Taylor told me when I got here, Fritz might not want to come to your rescue anytime soon."

Jorja couldn't hide her surprise. "I doubt what happened between me and Fritz will stop him from coming here to meet with you. Okay, drop it," she said when she realized he wanted to discuss the issue further. She placed a few items she'd need for later in her purse before she grabbed her jacket. "Let's just move on. I need to head to the library so you can stay here and work if you want. Where's Nicholas?"

"I dropped him off at one of his friend's to play. I need to pick him up around two-thirty so I'll work from here until then." Ryan grabbed his briefcase from the chair nearby and moved to sit at Jorja's desk. "Do you mind if I use your computer? I left my laptop at home."

"Knock yourself out. I'll see you when I get back."

Jorja grabbed her purse and headed down the stairs where she found Taylor helping a customer in the mystery section.

"You know we have book club meetings here two times a month don't you? You don't? Well, you should sign up. We have a sheet near the cash register for anyone who may be interested. Just leave me your e-mail address and I'll add you to the list so you'll receive notice of our next meeting and the book list."

Taylor turned from the customer to find Jorja watching her. She quickly moved away from the customer to stand in front of Jorja before asking, "What? Did you talk to Ryan?"

Jorja caught the guilty look cross Taylor's face.

"Why did you tell Ryan about Fritz?"

Taylor suddenly busied herself with a few books sitting out of place on a shelf. She tried to find their home while avoiding eye contact with Jorja. "Well, it just happened to come up. Does it matter? I thought you told him everything."

"I might tell Ryan a lot, but I certainly don't tell him everything."

"Okay. I'm sorry. I didn't mean to stick my nose where it doesn't belong."

Jorja sighed. She knew Taylor would stick her nose wherever she chose whether Jorja liked it or not.

"That's okay, I'm sure you meant well."

Taylor finally looked at her and grinned. "Thanks."

"So, I was thinking of going to the library to see if I can find anything about the Chief's wife. I'm not sure it will shed any light on what Gabe has already told me, but I'd like to research it anyway. I'll probably be gone about an hour."

Jorja walked to the back of the store and she heard the front doorbell chime, but ignored it as she moved into the break room to grab a water bottle.

"No, girl. You stay here until I get back," she said to Piper, who had been right on her heels the whole time. She moved around the door frame of the break room to open the back door just as Taylor yelled from the other end of the hall.

"Jorja! Don't leave yet."

Turning to face Taylor she asked, "Why? What's wrong?"

"Nothing. It's just that Betsy's here and she really wants to speak to you."

Jorja was surprised and immediately wondered if Fritz had blabbed to Betsy that she was helping Gabe Carter in his defense.

"Uh, okay. How about if I talk to her back here in the break room?" Jorja removed her jacket and again hung it on the coat rack.

Taylor turned to move back down the hall. "I'm making her a mocha so I'll tell her to come back here and I'll bring her the mocha once it's done."

Jorja waited only a few minutes before Betsy hesitantly looked around the doorway into the break room.

"Hi, Jorja. How are you?"

"I'm fine. How are you? Here, go ahead and have a seat."

Betsy took the seat Jorja offered.

"Do you want to take off your coat?"

Betsy shook her head. "No. I'm chilled and can't seem to get warm. I'm hoping a mocha will do the trick. Ah, thanks Taylor." Betsy reached up to carefully take the hot drink from Taylor's hand as she entered the room.

"You're welcome." Taylor said before she left the two to their privacy.

Jorja waited for Betsy to take a sip of her drink before asking, "So how have you been doing? How about the Chief? Has he made progress in his recovery?"

Betsy nodded. "Stan is doing wonderful. Those first few days in the ICU were terrible, at least they were for me. Now that he's past the critical stage and into the recovery phase, I'm much more optimistic that he'll get back to one hundred percent. You can't imagine the pain he's been in from that head injury."

Jorja unconsciously raised her own hand to rub the area on her head where she had been struck with a gun by Cooper. She knew exactly what it took to recover from that type of injury.

Betsy's eyes widened. "Oh, dear, I'm so sorry! I forgot you also had your own run-in with a head injury. Well, I guess you know more than most how the recovery process works."

"That's okay, Betsy. There are days I forget myself." She hated to lie, but she didn't wish to make Betsy feel bad.

Jorja continued, "So what do we owe the pleasure of this visit? Did you want to speak to me about something specific?"

Betsy nodded. "Yes, actually. I wanted to ask your advice about something. I've taken quite a bit of time off lately, you know, to be with Stan. When he finally goes home I expect I'll be going back and forth from my house to his and from the station to his because I'll be checking up on him constantly. I really can't work the hours at the station like I should and I'd like to hire some extra help. We have some funds in the budget for it, but from what I understand, the students have community service hours they need in order to graduate so I thought maybe I could make use of one of the students. My friend, who is a teacher at the high school, recommended Bruce Olsen. I think Kat is a friend of his so I thought maybe you also knew him. Would you recommend him? Is he a good kid? I just don't have the time to babysit and I'd like to make sure I have someone who is capable and who I can count on."

Jorja smiled. "Sure I know Bruce. He's a great kid. He's a football player, keeps his grades up as far as I know and he's always been really responsible when he's helped out around here and also in the way he's treated Kat. I don't think you'd go wrong hiring him. I know football practice and the game schedule kept him too busy to earn community services hours so if he hasn't found something already, I bet he'd jump at the chance if you gave it to him."

Betsy took another sip from her cup. "That's good. I just wanted to hear it from you because my friend knows how he acts at school. I needed to hear from someone who's seen how he acts when he's not around teachers."

Jorja laughed. "Don't worry. He's a good kid no matter who he's around."

They sat in silence for a moment as Betsy took another sip. Jorja wondered if Betsy had anything else she wanted to talk about and she worried the news about her helping Gabe had spread. She was relieved and a little confused when Betsy asked, "Have you seen Bailey lately?"

"Well, I did the other day, why?"

"Hmm. Did she happen to tell you what she met Stan about?"

Jorja's brows furrowed. "What do you mean? When did she meet with the Chief ?"

"Remember when I told you to tell Bailey she could stop by to see Stan when he was at home for lunch? Turns out the day Stan was attacked, she stopped by there to see him. Problem is he won't tell me or the police what she spoke to him about. Don't you think that's odd?"

Jorja hesitated with an answer, knowing she had to be careful what she shared with Betsy since Bailey was technically a client.

"I agree it does sound odd. Maybe it was a personal matter and he doesn't wish to betray her confidence. Did he say he thought she had anything to do with his attack?"

Betsy sucked in her breath at the thought. "Oh goodness, no. Nothing like that. He just talked about what he had done that day up until he was attacked and her name came up as someone who had stopped by. He said she was there for no more than fifteen minutes before she left. It just bothers me that he won't even hint at what she discussed with him. I guess you're probably right. It's something personal she didn't want him sharing with others and that's why he's been such a good chief of police all these years. People trust him and he wouldn't do anything to betray that trust."

Jorja nodded, but her mind was reeling at the thought that Bailey had visited the Chief and hadn't bothered to mention it.

"Has the Chief been able to remember anything else to help with the investigation? Do you think he might be up to a visitor so that I can ask him a few questions?"

"He doesn't remember much else. He might like a visit from you, but why would you be asking him questions about the attack?" Betsy's look was inquisitive as she waited for Jorja to reply.

Jorja delayed her response by taking a drink of water before she finally said, "I'm going to do a little side work and investigate the attack on the Chief myself. I was hoping he'd be willing to meet with me about it."

Betsy's look of curiosity turned to distress. "What are you getting yourself involved with now? Is it for Gabe Carter? Did he ask you to help him?"

Jorja leaned forward. "Betsy, I'm only looking into it and I'm not getting myself *involved* with anything. Besides, Gabe has every right to a defense if the State presses charges against him."

Betsy rubbed her hands together in a nervous gesture. "Oh dear. Stan may not be pleased, but I'm glad if Gabe came to you."

Jorja leaned back in surprise at Betsy's statement. "You are? Why would you be happy I'm helping the person who the police think attacked the Chief ?"

Betsy began to speak, but quickly held her hand over her mouth as she turned to glance down the hall. Seeing no one, she looked at Jorja and whispered, "Because I know who Gabe Carter is. He's Stan's nephew."

Jorja let out a breath. "Oh, so you know. Did Stan tell you?"

Betsy shook her head. "He didn't have to. I've been at Stan's enough times and when he was laid up a few years back with a broken leg, I helped keep his house clean. I came across old photos of his sister and her husband, along with photos of Gabe growing up during the time he lived with Stan and his wife after the parents were killed. Gabe looks older, but he hasn't changed much and he has a lot of Stan in him. If Stan wasn't such a crotchety old bear to everyone, they might actually see how much Gabe looks like him."

"Have you told Stan you know?"

"No, I'll wait until he's ready to tell me. I know that man resents his nephew for the accident, but it was just that. An accident. I don't see why Stan would ever believe his nephew would try to attack him. Since he won't be straight with me and he won't let go of old hurts, I think it's just as well that you're in Gabe's corner to help prove he wasn't responsible."

"I'm so glad you feel that way. Do you think you could help me schedule a time to meet with the Chief ? Sometime in the next few days?"

Betsy took another sip from her cup before standing up. "You bet. He'll be going home in the next day or two. I'll let you know once I figure out how I'll set it up. Just wait to hear from me, okay? I better get back to the hospital now. He's been getting awfully used to having me around so he'll be wondering what's holding me up. I'll be in touch."

"Thank you so much, Betsy."

Jorja watched as Betsy left the break room to walk toward the front of the store. She could hear Taylor mumble a goodbye to Betsy before the doorbell chimed as Betsy left the store. Jorja sat at the table for a moment, thinking about what she and Betsy discussed. She was surprised by Betsy's admission at knowing Gabe was the Chief's nephew, but what struck her the most and what she now wanted to verify was the statement that Bailey had actually visited the Chief shortly before he was attacked.

Either Bailey was the last person to see the Chief before the attack or Bailey might possibly be the number one suspect. But why would Bailey want to attack the Chief ? Did he find out she was accused of kidnapping and assault? Was he threatening to turn her in so that she would lose her son? Jorja knew it was possible for a mother to do anything to prevent her child from being taken away. She just hoped in this case it wasn't true.

CHAPTER 24

Jorja and Taylor quickly crossed the road as they moved their way closer to the library. The rain had let up and the sun was trying to peak out, which made for a nice last-minute walk.

"I'm glad you asked me to come with you, Jorja. We haven't done much together as far as investigating goes. This makes me feel like we're actually a team." Taylor smiled as they entered the library.

Jorja moved through the doorway. "I know. It's difficult when we have the store to run and one of us always needs to be there. But I think Kat can manage without us for an hour or so, don't you?"

"Of course she can. That kid can do anything and she's become a real whiz on the espresso machine. I might actually be able to go on my honeymoon without worrying too much if she's still working for us."

Jorja shook her head. "Don't get your hopes up. If you're going to be married in the fall, she'll be attending college. We don't know yet if she's staying local or moving away to a university, but maybe you should pin down a date for the wedding so she'll be able to work around it with her school schedule. You want her to be in your wedding, right?"

Taylor laughed. "Don't worry. I already thought about that. I know how important it will be for Kat and I also want to make sure she'll be here to be a part of the wedding. I wouldn't have it any other way."

"Good. Now, let's see what we can find out about Gabe's past. Can you find the reels we need and I'll get the machine ready? Let's start with the month Gabe would have graduated the year before Ryan and I were born. If he didn't know Aunt Gloria was pregnant, she must have been in her first trimester or she probably would have told him already."

Taylor found the reel they needed and Jorja worked the machine to move it through the microfilm machine. Once the film caught, Jorja turned the knob to quickly turn the film to the first local news section of the paper. Seeing nothing relating to an accident, she turned the knob slowly as she and Taylor quickly scanned the articles as they flicked across the screen.

"There!" Taylor exclaimed. "What about that one?"

Jorja stopped the film to reveal an article with a photograph of an overturned vehicle. She nodded as she read the beginning of the article. "I think you're right. This appears to be the one."

Jorja and Taylor each read the article silently to themselves.

GREAT LOSS TO THE COMMUNITY FELT BY ALL

A one-vehicle accident Thursday afternoon on Tilley Road resulted in the death of Norma Douglas, the beloved wife of local police officer, Stan Douglas. According to Mack Wilson with the Tenino Police Department, Mrs. Douglas was a passenger in the vehicle and died from blunt force trauma after the vehicle driven by Douglas' nephew rolled and struck a tree. Douglas' nephew had minor injuries that were not life-threatening. Based on information provided so far, drugs or alcohol do not appear to be a factor. The case remains under investigation by the County Sheriff's Office as police determine whether charges should be referred against the young driver.

Once they both finished reading, Jorja scrolled through in an attempt to find additional articles. She found none about the accident, but she did come across the obituary for the Chief's wife.

NORMA R. DOUGLAS of Tenino passed away suddenly on July 17th; surviving are her husband, Stan Douglas, and her nephew, Gabriel Carter, both of Tenino. A memorial service will be held on July 29th at 3:00 p.m. In lieu of flowers or donations, it's requested that donations be made directly to the Family Gospel Church.

Taylor leaned closer to Jorja to get a better look as they both read the obituary. Jorja shook her head and Taylor leaned back as she said, "Wow, that's sad. I feel sorry for the Chief . I wonder what everyone was saying about the accident or why Gabe wasn't at the funeral."

Jorja tried to swallow the lump in her throat. She couldn't imagine what the Chief was feeling at that time or how awful it also must have been for Gabe, especially since he was never able to pay his last respects to his aunt.

"Guess there wasn't much they could say. It sure doesn't give us much more than we already know. I wonder if the reporter or the officers who were at the scene are still in the area. It's been over thirty years so it may be a long shot. Let's make a copy of what we've found and we'll do more research at the store."

Jorja set up the machine to print the pages she wanted as Taylor stood up to stretch her back. "So now we see if we can track down the officers or the reporter to see if they know anything more than that article gives us? What is it you're hoping to find?"

Jorja folded the printed article and placed it in her notepad. She shook her head. "I don't know. Even though I trust Gabe and what he's telling me, I just feel that there's more to the story than he's letting on. If I can have all the answers before I meet with the Chief , it might make that interview go much smoother because I won't feel so much in the dark."

Taylor snorted before she could stop herself. She covered her nose and mouth as she giggled. "Sorry. It's just that I can't imagine an interview with the Chief going smooth at all, regardless of how well-armed you are with information."

Jorja smiled. "Yeah, you're probably right about that. Come on. Let's get back to the store."

They left the library and walked back to the book store as they enjoyed the continued break from the rain. After a block Taylor broke the silence by asking, "Do you want to talk about Fritz?"

Jorja gave Taylor a pained looked. "There's nothing to talk about. We just have a difference of opinion, that's all. He thinks he can tell me what to do and I disagree."

Taylor laughed. "I get that, but I hope you two can mend fences rather than continue to argue. Don't get upset with me. I just want what's best for you, that's all."

"I'm not upset with you. I'd just rather move onto another subject. This one is too distracting."

"You think everything else you're dealing with now isn't too distracting? That's funny." Taylor said as they crossed the street and walked up to the door at the book store where she opened the door and walked in with Jorja behind her.

"It's about time you got back." Taylor heard the voice and turned to see Dylan. Her smile became radiant.

"Hi, babe, how long have you been here?" She quickly reached over to grab Dylan's hand.

"About twenty minutes. Kat made me a coffee and Ryan has been keeping me entertained with some stories about Nicholas. Jorja, you might want to invest in a television for the store. You could get more guys to hang out here if they know they can watch a game on ESPN."

Jorja quickly shook her head. "No way. That's *all* they'd be here for and certainly not to buy books."

Dylan shrugged. "Just a suggestion." He turned to Taylor. "I was putting together some ideas for Valentine's Day cookies and I thought maybe you could stop by later to give me your opinion. Then maybe I could take you out to dinner."

Taylor smiled. "You bet. I'll sample your treats any chance I get." She gave Jorja a devilish grin as she winked. "And dinner sounds great too."

"Walk me out?" Dylan asked as he pulled on Taylor's hand. "Bye Jorja...Kat. Bye Ryan. See you later."

Taylor followed Dylan outside where the two said goodbye before she came back inside the store with two women right behind her. Taylor moved to the espresso stand when she heard them talk about ordering coffee as Jorja walked toward Ryan who was sitting on the couch.

"Were you able to get any work done?"

Ryan nodded. "A little bit. But it was nice to sit and talk with Dylan for awhile. Before he got here I was able to call Reynolds and ask him about stopping by on Monday. I don't think he believed me when I told him why I wanted him to come by, but he said he'd be here."

"And Fritz? Will he be here too?"

"I'm not sure, but you know how they are. Where one is the other is never far behind. Those two are closer than brothers. Don't worry. I'm sure he'll be here."

Jorja snapped her chin up at the comment. "I'm not worried. I just thought it might be better if both of them were here. Like you said, we don't really know what to expect with Bailey. I'm going to go upstairs to get some work done. I'll see you at home tonight."

Jorja walked away, but with each step closer to her office, she felt guilty about how she snapped at Ryan. She had to get a grip. She knew that lashing out at those closest to her wasn't an effective way of dealing with things.

CHAPTER 25

Jorja used Sunday afternoon to conduct more research and it didn't take long for her to locate one of the officers who had been at the scene of the car accident involving Gabe and his aunt. Officer Mack Wilson, now retired, was currently living in Bend, Oregon. Jorja leaned back in her chair as she listened to the phone ring. After the third ring someone finally answered, "Hello?"

"Hello, is this Mack Wilson?"

"Yes? Can I help you?"

"My name is Jorja Matthews and I found your name in a news article relating to an accident that happened thirty years ago. You were working for the Tenino Police Department and you gave a brief statement to a reporter about the accident. I was wondering if I could ask you a few questions." Jorja leaned forward and held a pen over her notepad.

"What's this about? What do you want to know?" Mack's burly voice made him sound like she'd woke him from a nap.

"It was an accident involving a young man named Gabe Carter and his aunt. She was married to Stan Douglas, an officer at the time. The article implicates Gabe as having caused the accident, but it's not clear if he was ever held responsible for the accident or found to have committed any sort of negligence."

Jorja heard Mack clear his throat. "Well, that was a long time ago. I don't recall there being anything about the nephew being negligent. It was just an accident as far as I can recall. Why do you ask?"

She scribbled a few notes before answering. "I'm just looking into a few things and the accident happened to come up. Many times when someone dies in a car accident the driver is held at fault in some way. That doesn't appear to be the case here."

"That's because there was no reason to hold him at fault. It was just an accident."

"I see. Well, unless you have anything else to add, I guess I don't have any other questions for you. I do appreciate the fact that you were willing to speak with me."

"Not a problem, miss. Not a problem. I do have a question for you, though. Is Stan still living in the area? I haven't been back for quite some time. Got no family there. Is he still the chief of police or has the old dog finally retired?"

Jorja frowned. She hadn't thought about the fact that Mack might ask about the chief. "He's still chief and no he hasn't retired. But he's temporarily on leave due to a recent incident."

"Oh?"

"Uh, yes. He was recently attacked by someone."

"What? Is he okay?" Mack's burly voice suddenly raised a few octaves.

"He's doing okay. He's recovering quite nicely from what I hear. He probably has a nasty lump on his head, but he's doing well."

"That old goat better think about retiring now. He's too old to be taking on punks that'll shoot you soon as look at you."

Jorja was beginning to think Mack might be one of the few friends the Chief might actually have. That gave her a thought.

"You know...if it's been awhile since you've been up this way, maybe you could plan a trip to the area soon. Come by and visit with the Chief. It appears you too have some catching up to do and I'm sure he would appreciate the visit."

There was silence on the other end.

"Mr. Wilson? Are you there?"

"Yes, I'm here. I'm thinking."

"Oh. Well, it was just a thought. I'm sure he'd like to see you, but if you can't travel up here I understand."

"It's not that. I'll think about it. But don't say anything to him in case I'm not able to come up."

Jorja shook her head before she remembered he couldn't see her. "I won't. Thanks again. It was nice speaking to you over the phone and I hope maybe I'll be meeting you soon in person."

"Maybe. You have a nice afternoon. Good bye."

Mack hung up and Jorja did the same. She leaned back again as she thought about Mack. She truly hoped he would come up for a visit with the Chief when the only company he had at this point appeared to be Betsy. Jorja suddenly sat up straight, her eyes wide as a thought struck her. She quickly jumped up and ran to the railing. She spotted Taylor at the register and let out a quick whistle once she realized she wouldn't be able to voice a legible word. Taylor looked up in surprise to see Jorja waving her hands feverishly at her to come up the stairs. Jorja then backed away from the railing to sit in a chair at the front of her desk as she waited for Taylor. When Taylor finally reached the top of the stairs, Jorja jumped up from the chair.

"What's wrong?" Taylor's brows furrowed in concern.

"I just realized something. I can't believe I'm just realizing this!"

"What? What are you realizing?"

"If Gabe is mine and Ryan's father, do you know what that means? It means Stan Douglas is our great uncle!"

Taylor stepped back with her brows now raised in question as well as surprise. "You're telling me you're just now figuring this out? Jorja, come on, you can't just now be realizing this." She laughed when she saw the look on Jorja's face made it clear she was serious.

Taylor shook her head. "You're funny. You're so observant in some ways and then there's this one vital, very important, completely relevant fact where your bloodline is concerned and you completely miss it. I just assumed you weren't talking about it yet until you knew exactly what the deal was with Gabe."

Jorja sat down again. "I really hadn't given it a second thought. I wasn't thinking about who might be related to Gabe. I haven't been able to take in that he's probably my biological father yet, much less that I might have more family. Wow. I wonder if Ryan thought about it and just didn't mention it to me."

"Well, what's the big deal? So the Chief is your great uncle. There's nothing wrong with that, is there?"

Jorja grimaced as she shook her head. "No, Taylor. There's nothing wrong with it except that I was able to brush off the Chief's gruffness before. Now that I know we're likely related, I won't know how to act when I'm around him."

Taylor patted Jorja on the shoulder. "You'll treat him no differently than you did before and he'll probably treat you no differently because he's an old man set in his ways."

"But I'm going to interview him about the assault. I'm going to try to prove my biological father didn't try to kill an uncle I didn't know I had. To top it off, neither of them really knows what it is I'm trying to do." Jorja let out a huff of air as she shook her head. "Boy, I guess Betsy was right when she asked me what it was I getting myself into now."

~ ~ ~

Jorja couldn't let go of the new knowledge that Stan Douglas, the chief of police, the gruff and sometimes irritable old man who had a real hard edge, was probably her blood relation. She knew she would need to speak to Gabe about what she suspected, but for now, she decided to focus on the case.

In order to distract her attention from her thoughts, she grabbed the copy of the news article from the corner of her desk to read the name of the reporter at the top of the page.

"Robin Williams. Hmm, now that's funny." She mumbled to herself as she did a quick search to see whether she could locate where the reporter currently lived. Once she discovered the name was fairly common, for men and women, she quickly realized she needed to narrow down her search if she was going to catch a break.

The only real option, she finally decided, was to call the local paper to see if the owner would be able to fill in the blanks.

Jorja picked up the phone and dialed the number for the local paper. Just after the first ring she wondered if they'd be open since it was Sunday...but on the second ring she got her answer.

"Timely Independent, can I help you?"

"Hi, is the owner available?" Jorja asked.

"You've got him. What can I do for you?"

"Well, I was wondering if you could help me. I'm trying to locate a reporter who was staffed by your paper thirty years ago."

Jorja heard the owner chuckle over the phone. "Thirty years ago? That's a long time to remember an employee and that was when my dad owned the paper, not me. Who is it?"

"The name is Robin Williams. Would you have any idea if you could find out whether he took another job or moved from the area and where?"

"Well...I don't know. I guess I could ask my dad, if his memory goes back that far anymore. I can't really guarantee it and I'm not sure we still have any records that far back. Why don't you give me your number and I'll get back to you."

Jorja gave him her number before she hung up the phone. She was beginning to wonder if the efforts she was making were worth it, but she decided she wanted to know if there was more to the story about what caused Gabe to leave the area and not return for over thirty years.

CHAPTER 26

"Are you really sure this is a good idea?" Ryan asked Jorja as he sat on the couch in the bookstore.

Jorja rolled her eyes. "Of course I'm not sure if it's a good idea. It's just the only idea I believe will work. I have to talk to her."

Taylor sat down beside Ryan and patted his knee. "Don't worry, Ryan. The boys will be by in plenty of time if Bailey turns out to be some psycho."

"They'll be here, but we'll be fine because she's not a psycho." Jorja argued.

Shrugging, Taylor leaned her long frame back on the cushion. "Let's hope so. I'd hate to see what would happen to her kid if she was arrested and put in prison."

Ryan nodded his head in agreement. He then looked at his watch. "She should be here any time. Where are you going to sit with her?"

"I'm going to take her back to the break room. You stay out here and watch for Fritz and Reynolds."

The door suddenly opened, making all three of them jump. Bailey slowly entered the store as she made eye contact with Jorja and smiled. She quickly glanced at Taylor and Ryan and her smile faltered before she looked at Jorja again.

"Hi, Jorja. I hope I'm on time. I had to walk over from work because my car battery died."

"Oh no, you're fine. Too bad about your battery though. Maybe after we're done my brother can drive you back and jump start your car." Jorja was glad Bailey missed the quick glare she received from Ryan.

Bailey shyly glanced at Ryan. "Thanks. That would be great."

Ryan quickly plastered a smile on his face. "No problem."

Jorja motioned toward the back hallway. "We'll just go back to the break room and talk, if that's okay." She began walking and Bailey followed.

In the break room Jorja pulled a chair out for Bailey and then she moved to the opposite side and sat down.

Bailey sat in the chair and placed her purse in her lap with both hands lying on top of it. She then looked at Jorja and asked, "So were you able to find out anything about my husband?"

Jorja shook her head. "Not really. I found information, but it wasn't what I expected."

"Oh? What was it?" Bailey's look expressed only curiosity and Jorja wondered why there was no expression of guilt.

"Well, I'll get into that in a minute. First, I wanted to ask you something."

Bailey hesitated, but then nodded her head. "Okay, go ahead."

"Remember when you told me you tried to speak to the police about your husband? And how they couldn't do anything?" Bailey nodded so Jorja continued, "But you made it sound like you didn't speak to the police here. Is that true?"

Jorja noticed Bailey tense slightly. Frowning, Bailey replied, "Yes, that's what I said."

"But is it true? You've had no conversation with the police since you've been here?"

Bailey suddenly shivered and wrapped her arms around herself. "Oh, you must think I'm awful. I'm so sorry. How did you know?"

Jorja raised an eyebrow. "How did I know what?"

"Well...that I, uh, you know. That I went and saw the Chief ."

Jorja leaned back. She was relieved Bailey admitted to it, but was now more confused about why she lied about it in the first place.

"I know because the Chief told Betsy and Betsy told me. If you were there, you could either be the last person to see the Chief before he was attacked or you might become a person of interest in the attack."

Bailey raised a hand to her mouth as she explained, "But they really can't think I was responsible, can they?"

"Why didn't you say you'd been to the Chief's that day?"

Bailey pursed her lips as she placed her hand back on her purse. She closed her eyes briefly as she sighed. When she opened her eyes to look at Jorja again she said, "I was afraid. I'd been there to see the Chief , I told him my situation and he said he couldn't help me. After I left and went to work, I heard the news about his attack and I was scared about being the center of an investigation if I were to admit I'd been there."

"But why, Bailey? Why were you scared? Why would the truth about why you met with the Chief get you in trouble?"

Suddenly, Bailey placed her hands over her face and began to sob. Jorja quickly stood to grab a tissue box off the counter to place it in front of Bailey. She anxiously waited for Bailey to stop crying and after a few minutes Bailey finally pulled her hands from her face to grab a tissue and blow her nose. Jorja quickly glanced at the clock and was concerned to see fifteen minutes had already passed.

She decided to press the issue. "Bailey, please be straight with me. Why were you afraid to say you'd been to the Chief's house? You didn't do anything, did you?"

"No! I did *not* do anything to the Chief . He was fine when I left. Said he was going to finish his lunch and get back to work. I swear, Jorja. I didn't do anything to that man."

"So why keep your visit a secret?"

Bailey hung her head. "It was hard enough going to him and admitting all the terrible things my husband did to me to cause me to run away. I felt it was the only way I could get him to help me. He said it wasn't in his jurisdiction and that I'd have to go back home to get the police there to do something. I was worried that if the police knew I'd been to the Chief's they would question me and possibly make contact with someone from home to verify my story. I didn't want that to happen because my husband is friends with many local police officers at home. Someone would tell him where I was. That's why I kept quiet about being at the Chief's." Bailey raised her head to look at Jorja. "I really didn't think it would matter that much. Please believe me."

Jorja wasn't sure if she should believe Bailey's story, but she nodded anyway. "Okay, but there's something else I'd like you to be straight with me about. The information I tracked down about your husband was an eye-opener, but it had more to do with what you did rather than what he did."

"What do you mean? What did I do?"

Jorja tilted her head as she looked at Bailey and wondered how one was to nicely accuse someone of a crime. "Bailey, the reports I read say that you not only kidnapped your son, but that you assaulted your husband with a weapon in order to do so."

"What!?" Bailey suddenly stood up, her purse falling to the floor. "What are you talking about?"

"The reports say you attacked your husband and kidnapped your son. I don't know what more I can tell you. Is that what happened? Are you telling me you didn't do these things?"

Taylor ran around the corner from the hall and stopped short of running into Bailey. "Is everything okay?"

Ryan was soon behind Taylor asking, "Everything all right?"

"Yes, everything's okay. Just give us a few more minutes, okay?"

Jorja watched as both Taylor and Ryan reluctantly backed away in order to go back to the main lobby of the store.

Jorja then looked at Bailey. "Bailey, sit down and tell me what happened. Did you do what the news reports say?"

Bailey shook her head, tears streaming down her face. "No. I never assaulted my husband. He'd been abusing me for many years and I was afraid of him. So afraid I never wanted to find out what he would do if I ever fought him back. But I knew the only way I could get to him was through our son. I blackmailed him, Jorja. I planted a video camera in our room and the last time he laid a hand on me, I was ready. I was able to record him doing to me what he's done for eight years. The abuse was horrible, but the indignity of how he treated me was more than my soul could finally take. I was so scared, but I finally showed him the video. I thought he might actually try to take it from me by force so I showed him when we were at a public park. I just let him view the video screen as I held it for him. I told him if he didn't let me leave with Justin that I would turn the video over to the prosecuting attorney, the sheriff and I would also make a copy for safekeeping. I knew it would hurt him and his business to be labeled as violent and abusive."

Bailey shivered involuntarily as she continued, "He didn't say anything to me, but his glare was enough to make me pee my pants. He told me I could leave, but only if I gave him the recording. I didn't argue. I gave it to him, grabbed Justin by the hand and left. I had already packed the car so I left at that moment and drove all night. I've been so scared he might come looking for me so that's why I went to the Chief . I wanted to know what I could do to protect myself."

Jorja was stunned. She could only imagine what Bailey had gone through. "If what you're telling me is true, after you left he somehow set up a scene to make it look like you assaulted him and kidnapped your son. It's a serious crime, Bailey, and you're officially a wanted person back home."

Bailey moaned. "I can't believe this. He's still abusing me even when we're hundreds of miles apart. What can I do?"

"Did you keep a copy of the recording? It would be the only thing that might back what you're trying to say."

Bailey hesitated before answering, "I do have a copy of the recording. I guess I should probably get it now, shouldn't I?"

Jorja nodded. "Yeah, it would be a good idea. If you had nothing to do with the Chief's attack, that's good, but if the police question you, they'll eventually discover you're wanted in Colorado."

Taylor suddenly poked her head around the corner. "Jorja, Fritz and Reynolds are here."

Jorja waved a hand at Taylor in dismissal. "They can go with Ryan. We don't need them."

Taylor stepped into the room, frowning. "They aren't going to leave. They said they want to see Bailey."

Bailey looked up at Taylor. "Who wants to see me?"

Taylor glanced at Jorja and so did Bailey.

"Jorja? Who's here to see me?"

"It's, uh, well…the police." Jorja stood up, suddenly nervous for Bailey.

Bailey also stood. She whispered fiercely at Jorja. "Why would the police be here to see me?"

"I don't know. They were here to see Ryan. I don't know why they'd be asking for you."

"Did you ask them to come here?" Bailey hissed.

Jorja tried to avoid looking guilty. "Well, we did ask them here, but like I said, they're here to meet with Ryan. Let's just see what they want. Maybe it's to talk about why you were at the Chief's that day."

Bailey tensed as she gripped her purse tightly. "Even if that's the reason they're here, do I have to discuss my relationship with my husband?"

"Maybe just tell them you were trying to get some advice about a situation, one that you really don't wish to discuss without an attorney." Jorja said.

Bailey's look was doubtful. "Okay," before she turned to leave the room with Taylor in front and Jorja behind her. They had only moved halfway down the hallway when Fritz and Reynolds met them.

Fritz spoke first. "Are you Bailey Maxwell?"

Bailey replied in a hesitant voice, "Yes."

Fritz moved closer. "Also known as Bethany Wheeler?"

Bailey's eyes grew large, her face paled and she quickly looked back at Jorja. Jorja tried to catch Fritz's eye, but he would not return her gaze. Bailey's shoulders sagged as she turned back to face Fritz. "Yes, I'm Bethany Wheeler."

Fritz moved closer to Bailey. "We need you to come to the station with us to answer a few questions. We have the car out front and we'll drive you there." Fritz gently held Bailey by her elbow to escort her through the store.

Jorja caught up to Reynolds who was following Fritz. "Reynolds, what's going on? Why are you taking her to the station?"

Reynolds glanced at her and then looked at Fritz. He stopped to lean closer as he whispered, "We got a tip Bailey would be here and that she's wanted for an assault and kidnapping in another state. We have to take her in. If she kidnapped her son, she took him across state lines and the feds will get involved. Either way, she'll be going back to face charges of kidnapping and assault."

"A tip from whom? Who told you she was here?"

"I don't know," Reynolds said. "It was anonymous. But once we checked her out we found out the tipster's information was correct. I've got to go. Tell Ryan I'll talk to him about the ride-along later."

As Fritz and Bailey reached the door, Bailey turned to look at Jorja. There were tears in her eyes when she said, "Jorja, please call Ruth and ask her to pick up Justin at school. Ask her to keep Justin with her until we figure this all out. *Please*, call her right away."

"Okay, Bailey, I will."

Jorja stood in shock as she watched Fritz and Reynolds leave the store with Bailey. She didn't know how Bailey could get out of this mess, but she was determined to help if there was a way.

CHAPTER 27

Jorja gave a couple of good raps against the Chief's front door and waited only a few moments before Betsy opened the door. "Hello, Jorja. Come on in."

Betsy moved back so that Jorja could enter the house. "He's lying on the couch in the family room. Right through that doorway there." Betsy pointed and allowed Jorja to move through the doorway ahead of her.

Jorja was shocked at the Chief's appearance when she saw him. He was lying on the couch with a blanket over his legs. His face looked pale and while he did have a few pounds to spare, he appeared much thinner and gaunt.

She sat down on a chair across from the couch. "Hello," she said. "How are you feeling?"

"I'm doing about as well as anyone my age might be after such an experience." Chief Douglas moved slightly as he attempted to sit up. Betsy quickly walked around the couch so that she could place a pillow behind his back.

"There, is that okay Stan?" Betsy asked. Jorja watched as Betsy placed a hand on the Chief's shoulder, waiting for him to respond.

"It's good, Betsy. Thank you."

Betsy nodded, patted the Chief's shoulder affectionately and then turned to Jorja. "He still tires easily so I'll give you about ten minutes before I come back to check on him."

Jorja nodded in acceptance, knowing she really had no choice.

"Thank you." Jorja watched Betsy leave the room before she turned back to the Chief . "Since it appears my time will be very limited, I'll get right to the point. Is that okay?"

Chief Douglas nodded, but said nothing.

"Okay. I'm sure you've already answered this question countless times, but do you have any idea who may have assaulted you? Did you see anyone, hear anything, or see anything that may give you some idea?"

He shook his head. "No, I was completely unaware of the fact that anyone was even behind me when I was struck. I can't even say if it was a man or a woman, but I'm sure the investigation will help prove either scenario based on how and where I was struck compared to the size and height of the person who hit me. I heard they may have a person of interest in custody, but if they're talking about that little gal, Bailey, I will say I highly doubt she had the strength to do the job. She's pretty short too. She'd probably have to stand up on a chair to give me a good whack on the head and believe me, it was a pretty good whack on the head." He raised his hand to gingerly touch the area on his head where he was struck.

"But Bailey was here, right? You told the police she'd come by to see you?"

He shrugged. "I didn't at first. She was here for a personal matter and as far as I knew, she had left the house. I didn't feel the need to bring her into this. Of course, now I'm hearing she might be wanted for kidnapping and assault in another state so the guys here think she's highly capable of assaulting me."

Jorja leaned forward as she asked, "But do you think she's highly capable?"

Again, he shook his head. "No, I don't. When I met with Bailey she was scared, nervous and I would venture to say, afraid of her own shadow. I don't see her as the type to commit any type of crime. I've told Reynolds and Fritz as much, but you know we can't do anything when the federal government gets involved and she's been accused of some serious crimes. We really don't know what may or may not have happened in Colorado. I just know I don't believe she's responsible for what happened to me."

Jorja leaned back in her chair. "Do you believe what she told you about her husband? What he did to her?"

He suddenly jumped and he closed his eyes as he placed a hand over them.

"Chief? Are you okay?" She again leaned forward, this time in concern.

She waited, but he didn't immediately reply. Finally, he pulled his hand away from his eyes and opened them to look at her. "I just get these bad pains every now and then. They rip through my head like a lightning bolt and I feel like I might pass out. The doc says it will take some time, maybe another week or so and I'll be able to get back to work."

Jorja unconsciously raised an eyebrow at the thought. "You plan to go back to work? Couldn't you just retire?"

He gave her a cold stare as he replied, "And do what? Sit here and watch the news all day? I'll always be out there doing my job to keep this community safe as long as I'm able. I'll retire when I'm dead and not a day sooner."

She didn't doubt his words. Quickly glancing at her cell phone to check the time, she realized Betsy would be coming back any minute so she moved onto the next question. "What about Gabe? Do you think he had anything to do with your attack?"

She noticed a slight hunch in his shoulders as he heard the question. He frowned deeply. "I don't know what that boy is capable of. I haven't seen him in thirty years and it may not be a coincidence that I was attacked not too long after he moved back here."

"Do you really believe that? Do you really think he's capable of harming you like this?" She watched as he made an attempt to answer. He continued to hold his frown, but she didn't miss the confusion and doubt on his face.

Before he could answer, Betsy entered the room. "So how are we doing? Stan? Do you need a break?"

Jorja hoped the Chief would answer her question about Gabe first, but instead he said, "Yes, Betsy. I could use some rest now."

Betsy moved to the couch where she carefully removed the pillow from behind the Chief's back so he could lay down. When he closed his eyes, Jorja stood but remained standing where she was, hoping she could delay her exit to give the Chief time to answer her question. When he ignored her, she decided to take a chance and push him just a bit further.

"Chief? Can you answer my last question?"

She looked down at him from where she was standing as he opened his eyes to return her gaze. He stared at her, but didn't say anything. She began to fear he might actually refuse to answer. Finally, he sighed heavily. "No, Jorja. I don't believe Gabe is capable, but that's based on a young man I knew a long time ago. I don't know what type of man he's grown into and I will not venture to say whether his mind or his motives are as innocent as they may have been when he was a teenager. Now, leave me be. I need to rest."

At that request, Betsy hurriedly motioned at Jorja to leave the room. Jorja complied, but as she was about to open the front door to leave, she turned to Betsy. "Did you hear that? He won't say Gabe isn't responsible. He's leaving room for doubt so that Gabe might actually be arrested. He could actually go to jail."

Betsy grabbed Jorja's hands as she replied, "You know how stubborn the Chief is and his reaction is due to old hurts and tragedies. You just do what you can for Gabe. If the answer is out there, I know you'll find it. And if there's anything I can do to help, you just let me know."

Jorja smiled. "Thanks. I'll do my best and I'll be in touch."

As she said goodbye and left the house, Jorja knew she had to dig deep. Not only was she going to prove to the Chief his nephew wasn't capable of such an intentional crime, she was going to prove to herself she didn't have a second parent actually capable of causing harm to another.

CHAPTER 28

Jorja shivered as a chill came over her so she reached over to turn up the heater in her Jeep. With only a five mile drive from the bookstore to Michael Stafford's residence, her Jeep hadn't quite warmed up during the drive to meet with him to discuss the status of the case.

She wasn't sure what she thought about Michael and whether he was capable of killing his wife. There were circumstantial facts surrounding the case, but whether that would be enough for a jury to convict, she wasn't sure. It was always a tough decision when an accused made the choice to take a case to trial. Jorja wanted to get a better sense from Michael how he felt about taking the case to trial and whether he was going to force the issue about testifying. She knew his attorney had advised against it based on the circumstantial facts surrounding the case, but from what the attorney told her, Michael wanted to tell his side of things. She knew from cases that had gone to court while she worked at the law firm that this decision didn't always pan out. Some jurors wanted to hear from the defendant and when a defendant chose not to testify, they might easily believe it was because the defendant had something to hide. But it could also backfire for a defendant if they were to testify in such a way as to give the jury a reason to distrust or dislike them. Either way, it was a big risk and whether he planned to testify or not, Jorja wanted to know more about what Michael was thinking.

Rain clouds began to build as she neared the house numbers she knew were close to Michael's house number. She hoped the rain would hold off until she found the correct house. As she neared a dark brown rambler, she finally saw the house number she was looking for. Jorja pulled into the driveway beside a silver car and turned off the engine. As she grabbed her bag and opened the door, she looked curiously at the silver car, not recognizing it as the vehicle she had seen Michael driving before when he'd come by the bookstore. Walking by the car she looked inside and saw only a tidy interior with nothing but a few chains around the rearview mirror with flowers attached to give an indication the car might belong to a female.

As Jorja neared the garage, she was about to turn toward the front door when she heard voices coming from behind the house. Curious, she moved closer to the corner of the house and then along the side of the garage to the back yard fence. It was a tall fence, six feet and made of wood, so she couldn't see anyone.

She finally heard a male voice say, "You don't know what you're asking of me. How can you expect me to admit to something I didn't do? You can't ask this of me."

She instantly recognized the voice as Michael's.

She then heard a female voice. "You either admit to it or I'll prove you were capable of much worse. How do you think people will look at you if they know what you did? Would you rather be known as a killer or as a rapist?"

Jorja sucked in her breath. She now recognized the female voice as Gail's. What was she talking about? Jorja took another step toward the fence.

"You can't ask me to say I killed my wife. I didn't kill her! You're asking me to go to prison for something I didn't do."

"It's up to you. You can either say you killed my sister or you can let people know the real monster behind your mask. I mean it, Michael. I'll let everyone know what you're really capable of. I should do it anyway. It's despicable and you ruined a young girl's life."

Jorja held her breath as she continued to listen. She waited for Michael's response and barely heard him as he replied through what sounded like clinched teeth. "You can't prove it. You can't prove it so that a jury would convict me."

"Really? You think I care about that? If you go to prison, that's just a bonus. Even more so when I think about the stories I've heard about what other inmates do to perverts like you. But either way, I will ruin you. Not only will I hand the information over to the police, but everyone will eventually know what you did. With the journal and what little Tabitha can offer, I'm sure there's enough for the police to look into it."

"I don't believe you. You don't have Liz's journal."

"Oh? You don't think so? Remember the last visit I had here with Tabitha when you went to see your attorney? I decided to take a look around and you'll never guess what I found tucked between your mattresses. I should have taken it rather than make a copy. I may not have the original, but I do have a copy and I'll use it however I have to in order to make you pay for my sister's death."

Jorja heard only silence after that statement. She strained to listen in case one of them headed her way, but she heard nothing. She waited; her muscles tight and ready to move should one of them walk toward the gate. Finally, she heard Michael respond.

"Liz is dead, Gail. What do you expect the police to do?"

"They'll take Tabitha away from you and that's exactly what they need to do. You can't do to her what you did to Liz. I won't let it happen. I *can't* let it happen. You sicken me. If Cynthia actually killed herself, I understand why if she felt so helpless to stop you. In her mind, you taking responsibility for her death is the *only* way she could get you away from Tabitha. I plan to finish what she started, but I'm giving you a choice, which is more than what you gave my niece when you defiled her."

Jorja jumped back slightly when she heard the latch move on the gate. When the door began to open, she feared she would be caught as she attempted to quietly move backwards toward the front of the house. When the door stopped after opening just a few inches, she paused only long enough to hear Gail say, "I'll give you until the end of the week. And don't make any plans to ransack my house or threaten me. I have the evidence in a safe place and if anything were to happen to me, word will get out anyway. You can be sure of that."

Certain the conversation was just about over, Jorja backed away from the side of the house to the front of the garage. She quickly sprinted to her Jeep and opened the door to jump into the driver's seat. As she saw Gail walk around the corner of the house, she jumped out of the Jeep as if she had only just arrived.

"Hi, Gail. What a surprise to see you here." Jorja threw her purse over her shoulder as she shut the driver's side door.

"Hello, Jorja." Gail quickly glanced behind her as she walked toward Jorja. "I was just talking to Michael about a few things."

"Oh? I didn't think you'd be speaking to him at all."

Gail opened the door to her vehicle and tossed her bag on the passenger seat. She then looked at Jorja. "As much as I despise him for what he may have done to my sister, I still want to see my niece. I thought he'd agree to some sort of regular visitation schedule."

"And were you able to come to some sort of agreement?"

"I'm not sure yet. He'll let me know soon enough. Well, it was nice seeing you, but I need to get going."

"Uh, sure. Nice to see you too." Jorja backed away from the vehicle as Gail got inside and shut the door. She gave a little wave to Gail as she walked to the front door of the house. Completely distracted now, she rang the doorbell and waited for Michael to answer the door, but her mind was replaying the conversation she'd just heard between Michael and Gail. What was she supposed to do with this sort of information? From a legal standpoint, she knew she could likely do nothing; not if she didn't wish to be sued or lose her private investigator's license. With difficulty, she knew she'd have to wait to see whether Michael decided to meet or ignore Gail's demands.

~ ~ ~

Pretending not to have heard the exchange in the backyard was difficult for Jorja when Michael finally opened the door. She tried to act casual as she stepped inside the house to follow him to the dining room.

She took a seat at the dining room table while Michael stood at the window to look out at the back yard. When he remained silent, she finally began by saying, "I met with your attorney to go over my notes from the interviews so far and other than some additional interviews with some of the police officers, I believe we just need to obtain additional records that might be available with regard to Cynthia's medical or mental history. Is there anything else you think we should do? Any other witnesses we need to speak to?"

Jorja waited, but Michael only continued to stare out the window with his arms crossed over his chest as he leaned against the wall. She watched him for a moment and realized she was having difficulty with the fact that he might be innocent of murder, but guilty of an act that she personally believed was even worse.

"Michael?"

He finally turned to look at her. "What? Oh, sorry. Yes, I spoke to him the other day and he said there might be just a few more interviews he'll want you to conduct. He also said he thought there were more medical records he might be able to obtain to show how unstable Cynthia was right before she died."

Michael turned his attention back to the window. Jorja thought the word 'unstable' was a poor choice if the reasons behind Gail's accusations about him, and why Cynthia did what she did, were true.

She coughed lightly as she tried to figure out how to make the meeting more productive. Finally, she decided to ask, "What about Tabitha?"

Michael's head turned quickly toward her. "What about Tabitha?"

"Well, do you think she might have any useful information with regard to her mother? Would you like me to speak with her?" Jorja knew for a fact that the attorney wasn't going to use Tabitha in any way as a witness, but she was now curious what Michael's response would be to the idea.

Unfolding his arms, he leaned forward as he placed his hands on the back of a chair. Firmly, he stated, "There is absolutely nothing Tabitha can tell you that would help my case and I'm not going to even think about putting her in the position of having to testify. I can't let her grow up thinking I wanted to use her to say something bad about her mother to a judge, can I?"

Jorja wondered if he'd already forgotten that was exactly what he'd expected of Tabitha when he was in the middle of the custody case with Cynthia.

Nodding slightly, she replied, "No, you can't let her think that. Well, unless there's anyone else you think we should interview, I'll probably wrap up the last few interviews by next week. If your attorney wants anything else, he'll let me know and when you go to trial, I'll make myself available to testify if it becomes necessary."

She waited for his response, but he was again staring off in the distance, already checked out of the conversation. Jorja sighed. She pushed the chair back as she gathered the file she'd brought with her but hadn't had to open. "Does that sound good to you?"

He finally heard her gathering her things and he turned to make eye contact. She was alarmed by the intense look he gave her before he shook his head and smiled. "Yes, that's fine. Sorry, I just have some other things on my mind right now. I was in the middle of a project in the back yard and I should get my equipment back in the garage before it finally rains. Can you let yourself out?"

"Sure, no problem. Call me if you think of anything else, okay?" She grabbed her bag and held it in her arms with the file as she walked through the living room and toward the front door.

"I'll do that. See you later, Jorja." Michael then left her sight and she heard him open and close the sliding glass door as he went out into the back yard.

She had every intention of walking out the front door, but found herself hesitating when she passed the hall leading back toward what she assumed were the bedrooms. In a flash she wondered if she would also find a journal tucked between the mattresses in Michael's bedroom, but just as quickly, she knew she couldn't put herself in such a risky position. Against the forces of her curious nature, she quickly moved past the hall and out the front door before she could change her mind and actually do something so risky and stupid.

CHAPTER 29

"I need to speak to Bailey...or, I guess I'll have to call her Bethany now. Can I see her?" Jorja asked Betsy as she stood in front of the counter at the police station.

Betsy scanned the day's mail as she answered, "She still wants us to call her Bailey but I'll have to check with the Chief on that, Jorja. You know the feds have gotten involved. I'm not sure who's allowed to see her. Can I get back to you once I find out?"

Trying not to show her disappointment, Jorja nodded. "Sure. Can you let me know as soon as you find out? I really need to see Bailey as soon as possible."

The door slammed shut behind her just as she heard someone say, "Why's that?"

Jorja turned to face Fritz. Reynolds opened the door and stepped inside as well. He smiled when he saw her. "Hi, Jorja. How are you?"

"I'm fine. How are you?"

Reynolds continued to smile. "Very good, thanks. It's funny to see you. Fritz and I were just talking about you."

Jorja furrowed her brow in response just as Fritz quickly turned to Reynolds. She couldn't see Fritz's expression, but the look on Reynolds' face indicated to her that Fritz was telling him to shut up. Reynolds only grinned at Fritz before he turned to Jorja. "Just about how persistent you are. It's a good trait, believe me. At least I think it is, anyway."

She heard Betsy chuckle behind her. She wasn't sure what the joke was, but knew she was missing something. "Well, thanks, I guess."

Fritz strayed away from the small talk as he pointedly asked, "Why do you need to speak to Bailey?"

Jorja could only sigh before she replied, "I'm just following a lead, that's all."

Reynolds looked as if he might speak, but before he could say anything, Fritz continued, "What lead? What case are you working on now?"

Feeling her spine tighten at his tone, Jorja gave him an unwavering look. "That's not something I can discuss with you." Turning to Betsy, she said, "Will you call me when you find out if I can come back to see her?"

Betsy nodded. "Yes, I'll call you right away."

"Thanks. I'll talk to you soon." She had to walk around Fritz as she moved to the door to grab the door handle and she could feel the heat from his body as she passed by. She looked at Reynolds as she opened the door. "It was nice seeing you, Reynolds." She made brief eye contact with Fritz. "Goodbye, Fritz," she said before slipping through the door and outside the station. Jorja made every attempt to ignore the quickening pulse she could feel in her throat. Why did that man cause her to react at all? She was frustrated with his attitude toward her work, but she didn't want to admit why it bothered her so much.

Before the door shut completely, Jorja's cheeks burned as she heard Reynolds laugh and say, "Man, that girl really gets under your skin. When are you going to finally ask her out?"

She didn't hear Fritz's response. She wasn't sure she wanted to. She also wasn't sure what her answer would be if Fritz ever got up the nerve to ask her. Regardless of how she felt about getting into a relationship, how could she ever date anyone who questioned her about her job or her ethics?

~ ~ ~

"You can have fifteen minutes with her. That's it." Chief Douglas tried to look stern as he ushered her into a small room, but Jorja could tell he was easily tired after working only a few hours at the station.

"Thanks," she said. "I really appreciate this. You know you didn't have to meet me here if you're not supposed to be working yet. Reynolds or Fritz could have taken care of it." Jorja said as she sat down at the table.

He dismissed her statement quickly. "I'm well enough to put in a few hours a day. I'll just be outside at my desk and I'll let you know when your time is up." Chief Douglas then stepped out of the room and shut the door.

It was only a few moments later when another door opened and Reynolds entered with Bailey. Jorja frowned at the handcuffs she saw on Bailey's wrists, but she knew it was for safety reasons. She watched Bailey as she sat down and attempted to get comfortable on the chair with her cuffed hands on her lap.

"Thanks." Jorja said to Reynolds, who looked at her and smiled in response before shutting the door as he left the room.

When Bailey finally made eye contact with her, Jorja could see desperation and despair. She was suddenly struck with just how lonely Bailey must feel if she truly had no one to help her. Jorja leaned forward. "Bailey...do you want me to call you Bailey rather than Bethany?"

Bailey nodded. "Yes, please. Bethany is from my old life, one I don't care to remember. I plan to legally change my first name to Bailey if I'm able to get out of this mess I'm in."

Jorja nodded. "Okay, Bailey it is then. I want to help you. I believe what you told me is true and I want to help. Do you want that?"

Bailey's eyes began to tear up. "You believe me?"

Jorja nodded.

"Why? Why do you believe me?"

Jorja was struck by that question. Why did she believe Bailey? She knew people in bad circumstances often got into trouble by lying or might lie to get out of trouble. Was Bailey a liar? Jorja didn't think so.

"I believe you because I believe you did the only thing you could in order to get out of a bad situation. I want to help you because I don't want your son to have to go back to live with a man who might turn him into the monster he has become."

Bailey's head dropped as she placed her shackled hands over her face and sobbed. Jorja waited uncomfortably as Bailey cried. She was glad when Bailey finally stopped crying and used her shoulders in an attempt to wipe her cheeks and eyes.

"How do you want to help me?"

"Well, you said you had proof about how your husband abused you. I'd like to get that proof from you so we can show it to the police. Maybe if they see it, they won't believe the lies he's told about you. Have you been able to meet with an attorney yet? Do you plan to hire one? The attorney might be able to work something out for you."

Bailey shook her head. "I can't afford an attorney so I'll have no choice but to have one appointed to me when they take me back home. I don't trust any of them because my husband has a lot of influence."

"Well, let's see how much influence he has once they see how he's abused you. Can I get the tape from you? Do you want to tell me where it is?"

"I can't afford to pay you either. And I can't expect you to work for me for free. That's not fair to you."

Shaking her head, Jorja said, "I won't be working for free. You don't have to pay me but you can make it up to me later."

"How?"

"Well, I thought we might reach an agreement. I'll put whatever time is necessary into helping you and when it's all over, you can work for me to compensate me for my time. Once we're even, you can continue to work for me, if you'd like, at my bookstore. I need to hire more help and I'd like to offer you a job."

Bailey's eyes widened. "You want to...hire me? For a job?"

Jorja hadn't quite thought this through, but now that the words were out, she couldn't take them back. "Yes. A job. Is that something you'd be interested in?"

Jorja was afraid Bailey was going to sob again but Bailey surprised her with a huge grin and a bubbly laugh. "Are you kidding? I'd love to work for you at the bookstore. Oh, thank you. Really, I appreciate it." Bailey suddenly lost her smile. "Of course, that's if everything works out and I'm not in jail back home."

"Well, let's not think that way. Let's start with what can help you. Tell me where you've hidden the video tape so I can get it for you. I'll show it to Chief Douglas first and he can help me get it to the right people. Is that what you'd like to do?"

Bailey nodded. "Yes, I trust the Chief and I think he'll do what's right." She looked at Jorja shyly and seemed unwilling to say anything more.

"Bailey? Do you want to tell me where the tape is?"

She wondered at Bailey's resistance to continue but then Bailey finally said, "Yes, I'll tell you. It's just..."

"Just, what?"

Shaking her head, Bailey sighed. "Never mind. You'll have to go to my car. It's probably still parked where it was when the battery died. At the grocery store parking lot. I'm betting they won't let you take my keys from here so look for my spare key tucked in a small compartment near the driver's side back tire. In the trunk, look for a green duffel bag and inside that you'll find a smaller blue bag with daises on it. There's where I left the video tape. The tape is hidden inside a full box of tampons."

Jorja was amused with Bailey's hidden location. "Okay, I'll get it as soon as I can after I leave here. Do you want Ryan to jump start your car so we can move it someplace else?"

Bailey hesitated again before she replied, "Uh, sure. Would you mind just parking it at your house? Would that be a problem?"

"No, that's not a problem. We'll do that for you."

A knock on the door made Jorja jump slightly just as the Chief opened the door to peek inside. "Time's up."

Jorja stood. "Okay. Bailey, I'll see you again soon."

"Thank you. You don't know how much I appreciate this." The relief on her face confirmed for Jorja the decision to help Bailey.

Jorja turned to the Chief , who gave her a curious look. As she walked by him and out the door into the hall, he shut the door and followed her to the front lobby of the station.

"You're planning to see her again? I'm not sure that's going to happen, Jorja. The feds will be here soon to transport her back to the jurisdiction where the assault and kidnapping occurred."

"Well, if I can take care of what I need to do, I'm hoping to see her again before she's transported. I'll need to see you too, if that's okay."

Chief Douglas raised his brows in question but when she refused to elaborate he said, "Fine. Just let me know when and I'll set some time aside."

"Thanks." Jorja waved goodbye to Betsy before she left the station. She was already mentally preparing for how she would retrieve the video tape. She had to retrieve the tape to prove Bailey was telling the truth about the reasons behind her actions. She just didn't know yet how she would prove Bailey had no motive for assaulting Chief Douglas.

CHAPTER 30

"Hey, Ryan, do you have time to help me?" Jorja said after she entered the house to find Ryan sitting at the kitchen counter.

Ryan looked up from the newspaper he was reading. "Help you with what?"

"We still need to jump start Bailey's car and I told her we'd park it here for her."

Ryan frowned. "Keep it here for how long? What if they take her back to Colorado so they can charge her with kidnapping and assault? What will we do with her car then?"

"I don't know. We'll think of that when we need to. For now, we just need to move it for her so it doesn't get towed. I'd hate for her to have to spend money to get it out of some impound."

Ryan's frown remained as he folded the newspaper. "I don't understand why you're helping her. She may have assaulted the Chief and the police in another state say she already assaulted someone else. She might not be the innocent you think she is."

Jorja pulled a clean glass out of the cabinet and filled it with water from the fridge. She took a long drink before she finally looked at Ryan. "I understand your hesitation, but I believe what Bailey is telling me. I just want to try to help her prove her innocence. Okay?"

"Okay, but just be prepared. You have to realize she might be scamming you."

"Sure," she said. "That's always a possibility, but I still want to try to help her. Now let's go take care of the car."

Jorja and Ryan drove to the store parking lot in her Jeep where it didn't take long to locate Bailey's abandoned car. Jorja parked her Jeep in front of the car and popped the hood of the Jeep. She stared at the car for a moment before turning to look at Ryan who said, "Wow. What do you think of that?"

Jorja looked at Bailey's car again and a sudden sadness overtook her. She could tell from this vantage point that the car was heaped with items in the back seat. The front seat was full, but left some room for Bailey and Justin to fit. Jorja wondered how long the two had been living out of the car because from the way the car looked, there was no other reason for the appearance of the vehicle.

"Bailey told Ruth she was renting a house someplace between here and Tumwater."

Ryan shook his head. "Looks like she wasn't truthful about her situation. Poor kid. I can't believe she's letting him live in a car when you know damn well Ruth and Peter would have helped them find a place."

Jorja looked at Ryan again. "She might have been afraid or too proud to tell Ruth. I don't know. I guess it's a good thing Ruth has Justin. At least we know he's in a safe place. Well, let's get this over with. Can you grab the jumper cables in the back?" She asked as she opened her door to jump out.

As Ryan dug out the jumper cables, Jorja walked to the driver's side back tire and bent down to locate the hidden key. After feeling around, she finally struck an object which moved slightly when she hit it. She grabbed it more firmly and pulled the magnetic key holder from its place. Standing up from her crouched position, she opened the holder and flipped it over to let the key drop into her other hand.

Jorja used the key to open the driver's side door so that she could pop the hood with the hood release. As Ryan opened the hood the rest of the way and propped it up, she got out of the car and moved to the trunk. She used the key to open the trunk, finding yet another hoard of belongings. Jorja shook her head in sadness as she moved items around to find the green duffel bag.

"I have the cables attached and ready to go. What are you looking for?" Ryan asked.

"A bag. I need to find something that should help Bailey with her case." Jorja continued to move items until she spotted the green duffel bag. She pulled the bag out so that she could unzip it to look inside.

"What will help her with her case?"

Jorja found the blue bag with daises. She unzipped the bag and quickly found the box of tampons. She pulled the box out of the bag. "This will."

Ryan took a step back as he glanced warily at the box. "Tampons? Those are going to help her with her case?"

Jorja smiled and laughed lightly. "No, Ryan. It's what's inside that will help her."

Just as she was about to open the box to find the tape, she heard a vehicle approach and stop right behind her. She saw Ryan glance at the vehicle and when he nodded an acknowledgment, she turned to see who had arrived.

Her smile faded at the sight of a police car and she frowned when she saw Fritz and Reynolds exit the car. She tried to hide the guilt she felt as she dropped her hand holding the tampon box behind her back.

Fritz was the first one to speak. "What are you two doing here?"

"Hey, Fritz, good to see you. We're just jump starting Bailey's car for her because the battery died. We thought we'd park it at our house so the store wouldn't have to tow it." Ryan caught the look between Fritz and Reynolds, as did Jorja.

"What are you doing here, Fritz? Is there something you need from us?" Jorja asked.

Fritz shook his head. "No, we're here for the car. We have a warrant to search and seize anything we find that might be related to the Chief's case and the feds will be looking for anything that might be related to the case in Colorado."

Jorja tightened her hold on the box behind her back. She tried to take a step away from the trunk so that she could walk to the other side of the vehicle. Instead, she backed into Ryan who grunted as she accidentally elbowed him in the stomach.

Reynolds moved to the hood of Bailey's car. "It was nice of you two to offer to jump start the car, but we'll just have the tow truck take it to the impound lot for us." Reynolds then removed the jumper cables from the battery of both vehicles before walking back toward Jorja and Ryan. He held the jumper cables out and when Jorja didn't move to take them, Ryan reached out to grab them instead.

Fritz moved closer to Jorja as he glanced at the open duffle bag and asked, "Jorja? What do you have behind your back?"

She quickly glanced at Ryan who returned her gaze with mild concern. He nodded at her to answer Fritz, but she hesitated.

"Jorja? If you took something from this vehicle, you need to let me see it. You know you can be charged with tampering if you remove any evidence from this car, don't you?"

She stuck her chin out at Fritz as she answered, "You have a search warrant for what's in the car. You can search the car. You don't have any right to search me."

Fritz held out his hand. "Show me what's in your hand." Fritz's voice was firm and made it very clear he wasn't going to let her leave without seeing what she held.

She glanced at Reynolds who only returned her gaze with mild interest. She knew he wasn't going to go against what his partner was requesting. Reluctantly, she brought her hand from behind her back to show what she was holding.

If the situation hadn't been so serious she might have laughed at the looks on both Fritz's and Reynolds' faces. Reynolds raised his brows in question before attempting to hide a grin as Fritz's gaze shot from the box, to Jorja, to Reynolds and back to Jorja again.

"Uh...why are you taking tampons from Bailey's car?" Fritz asked as Reynolds looked away, still attempting to hide his grin.

Jorja wondered if she could get away with it as she replied, "Because she needs them?"

She could have kicked Ryan when she heard him chuckle beside her. She knew she should tell Fritz the truth, but she didn't want to take a chance that the only evidence Bailey had might disappear if it got into the wrong hands.

Fritz narrowed his eyes as he stared at her. He glanced at Ryan and when he quickly looked at Jorja again, she knew Ryan must have been unable to hide the guilt on his face. Fritz suddenly held out his hand. "Give it to me."

She took a deep breath and sighed as she reluctantly passed the box to Fritz. He grabbed the box and opened it, exposing that it was full of tampons. When Fritz glanced at Jorja she tried to hide the relief on her face, but she could tell he knew something was up. He then moved closer to the trunk as he held the box upside down so that the items fell into the duffle bag. She held her breath as an item wrapped in plastic also fell out. Fritz immediately pulled plastic gloves from his pocket, placed them on his hands and reached inside the bag to grab the item. Everyone watched as he pulled the plastic away to reveal a small cassette tape. Fritz looked at Reynolds, who had moved closer to get a peek, before he turned to Jorja and held her gaze. She held it for as long as she could before she finally broke eye contact to look anywhere but at his accusing eyes.

"Were you planning to tell us about this? What is it?"

She could only shrug. "It's just something Bailey asked me to get for her. It might help her with her case."

Fritz straightened as he pointed a finger at Jorja. "You were planning to take what might be a key piece of evidence from this vehicle without telling us. You're lucky I don't arrest you right now."

She knew she was in deep, but she couldn't stop herself. "So arrest me. I was only doing what Bailey asked me to do. How was I supposed to know you planned to seize her car?"

Fritz shook his head as he glanced at Reynolds. "I'm not going to arrest you. But I can't believe you tried to hide this from us. You two can leave now. We have work to do."

Jorja tried to ignore the fact that his disappointment in her bothered her. She also tried to ignore the immediate feelings of regret she had for trying to hide the cassette, but she decided she should try to make it right.

"Look, I'm sorry. I was just trying to help Bailey."

Fritz didn't look at her and Reynolds only gave her an awkward shrug as he said, "It's all right. We'll just take over from here, okay?"

Jorja nodded and she turned to face Ryan, who had already begun to walk back to the Jeep. She moved slowly, wondering how she might mend what had just happened. Ryan walked around to the passenger side of the Jeep as Jorja got into the driver's side, but before she shut the door she heard Fritz yell from the driver's side of Bailey's car, "Reynolds! Take a look at this!"

She watched as Reynolds carefully opened the passenger door to peek inside. She then saw Fritz hold an item up for Reynolds to see. Her blood turned cold as she focused on the item Fritz found. It was a hammer and even from where she sat in the Jeep, she saw what appeared to be blood on the head as well as the handle.

CHAPTER 31

Jorja and Ryan entered the bookstore as they argued about what had just happened at the store parking lot.

"You really ticked him off. Did you really think you'd get away with just taking something from Bailey's car without telling Fritz? And now, if they actually found the weapon used on the Chief , she's in a world of hurt and they might still try to charge you with some sort of tampering charge."

Ryan held the door open as Jorja walked inside and removed her coat. She huffed slightly. "I *know*, Ryan. But how was I supposed to know they'd be searching the car? I wasn't even thinking of that possibility when she asked me to get the tape from the car."

Taylor moved toward them, completely curious about their conversation. "Hey, what happened? Who did you tick off?"

Jorja hung her coat on the coat rack and then walked around the register to the other side of the counter where she placed her bag. "Fritz, that's who. He happened to show up just as we were getting ready to jump start Bailey's car and after I had removed a tape cassette from the car that might help prove what Bailey is saying about her husband."

Taylor leaned against the counter as she folded her arms over her chest. "Oh. Why would he be mad at you?"

Jorja pursed her lips slightly as she thought about how to answer. Finally, she said, "Because I tried to hide it from him so he wouldn't take it from me. I wanted to get it to Bailey so she could use it in her defense."

Taylor snorted when she attempted not to laugh. "Oh man. If Fritz was mad about your work before, his attitude is going to be much worse now. Why were they there anyway?"

Ryan spoke up when he saw Jorja's face redden at Taylor's response. "They had a search warrant and planned to search and seize the car. They actually found something right before we left that won't help Bailey with her case at all."

Taylor looked at Jorja and then back at Ryan. "What? What did they find?"

"It was a hammer and it looked like it had blood on it." Ryan said as Jorja moved to the couch to sit down. She plopped herself down on the couch before she leaned back to lay her head on the cushion.

Taylor sat beside Jorja and asked, "Are you serious? You think it's what was used to hit the Chief on the head?"

Jorja closed her eyes as she muttered, "We're assuming that might be the case."

Taylor patted Jorja's leg. "I'm sorry. I know you wanted to help Bailey, but if she had anything to do with the assault on the Chief , there's really nothing you can do. By the way, I hate to give you more bad news, but Brian from the Timely Independent called earlier."

Jorja opened her eyes. "Yeah? What did he say?"

"He said that he spoke to his dad and did a little checking on that reporter for you, but that it looks like the reporter died a few years back. He said to say he's sorry he couldn't help you."

Jorja sighed. "Great. Well, I guess it probably doesn't matter. I'm now more concerned about Bailey anyway. I really can't believe she had anything to do with the assault." She suddenly sat up. "I'm going to try to talk to her again. There has to be an explanation."

Taylor nodded as she quickly glanced at Ryan. Ryan only frowned at Jorja. Taylor turned back to Jorja. "Maybe you're right. Maybe there is an explanation. If there's anything I can do to help, just tell me, okay?"

Jorja smiled at Taylor, but as she caught Ryan's stare, she lost her smile. "What? Come on, Ryan. You don't really believe Bailey actually had anything to do with assaulting the Chief, do you?"

Ryan sighed heavily as he replied, "I don't know Bailey well enough to make any sort of judgment, but I know you shouldn't hang your hat on the assumption that she's telling you the truth. She's been accused of assaulting her own husband, kidnapping her son and now might be accused of assaulting the Chief. How can all those accusations not add up to the possibility that she's not what she wants you to believe?"

Jorja shook her head stubbornly. "No, I won't assume she's telling me the whole truth, but I will continue to help her until the truth comes out. I told her I would help her and I intend to do what I can."

Ryan threw his hands in the air. "Whatever. Just be ready for the fact that the accusations against her might actually be the truth."

The bell chimed as the door opened and three women entered the store. Jorja quickly stood up to greet them as Taylor moved to the espresso stand where one of the three women was already headed. Jorja gave Ryan a brief wave goodbye when he mouthed to her that he was heading home. After he left the store, she tried to ignore the doubtful naggings he had planted in her mind about

Bailey and what acts Bailey might really be capable of committing.

CHAPTER 32

Jorja was thankful for the blue skies and sunshine as she drove to the bookstore to open up for the day. She told Taylor she would open because she had made arrangements to meet with Michael Stafford after he called to request a meeting to further discuss his case. She was curious what he wished to say to her now that he hadn't thought of a few days ago at his house. As she parked her Jeep near the side of the store, she couldn't brush away the pestering thoughts about Bailey and the fact that a possible weapon had been found in her vehicle. Jorja shook her head in an attempt to focus on Michael's case instead. She still wondered about the discussion she overheard between Michael and Gail, but unless Michael wished to tell her about it, she couldn't bring it up to him and admit she had been eavesdropping.

"Come on, Piper, let's get to work," Jorja said as she jumped out of the Jeep and waited for Piper to follow her. Piper was always happy when she was able to tag along with Jorja rather than remain at home. Jorja looked forward to what might be a decent day and the fact that she would be able to take Piper for a nice afternoon walk.

She latched the leash onto Piper's collar and then grabbed her bag before closing the driver's side door. As she walked toward the alley behind the building, she felt shivers run down her spine. Again, she felt as if she was being watched and her anxiety shifted into overdrive when Piper stopped short just before they reached the rear entrance to the store. Piper's growl was low, but a growl nonetheless combined with the hairs standing straight up on the nape of her neck. Jorja quickly scanned the alley and then the sidewalk and street behind her. She saw no one. Looking down at Piper, she whispered, "What is it, girl?"

Piper only lowered her gaze to the back door of the bookstore. Jorja stood where she was as she held onto Piper's leash and listened for any noise or movement. Still seeing no one in the alley and hearing nothing at all, she finally took a step forward and used her key to unlock the door. She opened the door and pulled on Piper's leash, anxious to get inside and away from the insecurity she felt in the alley. After she entered the store, she quickly shut and locked the door before unlatching Piper's leash from her collar. Rather than run to her normal spot to lie down, Piper remained right by Jorja's leg.

"It's okay, girl. We're safe in here. You can go lay down." Jorja tried to hide her panic while she spoke to Piper, but she knew she wasn't doing a good job when her voice cracked.

She shook off her coat and hung it on the coat rack before she entered the break room to make herself a cup of tea. She thought tea might help calm her nerves, but she had to wonder why she felt so jumpy.

Piper followed Jorja into the break room and sat down by the fridge, watching every movement she made. Jorja smiled as she looked down at Piper's big brown eyes staring back at her. "You're going to keep me company, huh girl? You're such a good girl." She reached down to pat Piper on the head before digging out a mug and tea bag. She filled the mug with hot water from the water cooler and then dropped the tea bag into the water. As she was searching for the honey, she jumped when Piper let out a quick bark at the sound of banging coming from the back door. Jorja held a hand over her chest as she peeked around the corner and then she felt silly when she heard Taylor yell, "Come on, Jorja. Open up, my arms are full!"

Jorja quickly unlocked the door and opened it to let Taylor inside. Taylor's arms were full with boxes of cupcakes and cookies from Dylan's bakery.

"Thanks. I'm glad you were nearby and could hear me because I didn't want to set these on the ground. These are some samples of the Valentine's Day cupcakes and cookies Dylan will be selling this weekend."

Jorja peeked at the top box and saw an assortment of heart-shaped cookies and pink and red decorated cupcakes. "They look really cute. Here, do you want me to take some?"

Taylor shook her head. "No, I've got them. I know you're meeting with Stafford this morning so I'm going to run up and get a check for Dylan. I forgot to take the checkbook with me so that I could pay him and I want to have it ready when he stops by later this morning."

"Okay. I'm just making some tea. I don't expect Michael for about another half hour anyway."

Jorja went back to making her tea as Taylor went out to the lobby to place the cupcakes and cookies near the espresso machine. She heard Taylor run up the stairs to the office and it was only a few seconds later when she heard Taylor yell, "Jorja! Come up here!"

Leaving her mug on the counter, Jorja ran out of the break room to the stairs. She ran up the stairs with Piper right on her heels and as she neared the top of the staircase, she saw Taylor peeking at her over the railing. Jorja's heart rate quickened at the shocked look on Taylor's face. She reached the top of the staircase and when she saw her office, she stopped short. The look of shock on Taylor's face was now mirrored on her own as she saw that her office was a complete mess. The drawers to the file cabinet were open, the desk drawers were open and papers were everywhere.

"What the hell? Who would do this?" Jorja muttered as she scanned the room. She couldn't immediately tell if anything had been taken, but she was relieved to see her computer and printer were where they should be. She rushed to her desk to see whether her camera was still in its place and she breathed a sigh of relief to see it hadn't been removed.

"What do you think they were looking for?" Taylor asked, as she too scanned the room.

"I have no idea. Piper must have sensed that someone had been in the store because she was acting up even before I opened the back door. Now I know why." Jorja shook her head as she pulled her camera from the desk drawer. "Well, I guess I better take some photos because I doubt the police will do much."

"You're going to call them, aren't you?" Taylor asked.

"I guess we better, even though Fritz might not be in the mood to help."

Taylor was quick to say, "Oh, Jorja, don't say that. It's his job and if he thought you were in some sort of trouble, he'd care. You know that. Do you want me to call?"

Jorja took a few more shots with her camera before she replied, "Sure, if you don't mind. I'll make sure I get enough photographs and then I'll come downstairs and wait for them with you."

As Taylor went downstairs to make the phone call, Jorja focused on taking photographs. She also took the time to prepare herself for whatever attitude Fritz might have with her when he and Reynolds finally responded to the call.

~ ~ ~

Jorja decided she wouldn't be able to resist the urge to clean up the office as long as she remained in the loft so she knew it was best to go downstairs once she was satisfied with the number of photos she had taken. She glanced at the wall clock near the cash register and realized customers might be arriving anytime with the expectation of receiving their regular morning coffee. As she wondered what to do about whether or not to open the store, she heard a knock on the window of the front door as Brad called out, "Hey Jorja, what's up with your door?"

Jorja turned to glance at the door, but the shade was still drawn over the glass. She walked to the door and pulled up the shade, revealing Brad on the other side. She was getting used to him visiting a couple of times a week to grab a coffee when she opened the store or when he could take a break between classes. She was also used to his easy and affectionate grin when he would greet her as he said hello. Jorja immediately realized that his grin was not in place today.

"What the hell happened to your door? Did you have a break in?" Brad asked as he tore his gaze from hers to stare at the door.

Jorja finally looked at the glass near the door handle and realized that a piece of glass was missing, about the size of both her fists. She immediately looked down at her feet, but didn't see any broken glass on the floor.

"Hey, are you okay? Open up and let me in." Brad said with concern when she didn't answer him.

Finally she looked up, only to shake her head to clear the frustration she was feeling. Someone had actually broken into her store in the middle of the night and ransacked her office. But why? What were they looking for? She shivered involuntarily as she wrapped her arms around herself.

Finally, she said, "I probably shouldn't touch this door. Why don't you go around to the alley and I'll let you in the back door."

Brad needed no further instruction as he turned from her to sprint around the building. He was already waiting for her when she unlocked and opened the back door.

Brad quickly stepped inside and shut the door. "You want to tell me what's going on? Did you have a break in? Have you called the cops? Are you okay?"

Jorja opened her mouth to speak, but she suddenly felt overwhelmed with the idea that someone had violated her space. Memories flashed back from when Officer Cooper broke into her house and she had unwittingly interrupted his search for a necklace that could tie him to the murder of Kat's mother. Jorja knew the break in of her office was probably nothing more than a kid getting his kicks, but she was suddenly fearful of whether it was more than that.

When Jorja couldn't speak for fear of completely losing it, she nodded to Brad in an attempt to let him know she was okay. Brad eyed her skeptically. "You're not okay. You're shaking and you're white as a ghost."

Brad moved to wrap his arms around her. The comforting touch was enough to break the dam and Jorja found herself shedding tears she could no longer hold back. Brad rubbed her back as she laid her head against his chest and cried.

After a few minutes, she felt embarrassed and pulled back slightly to wipe her cheeks with her hand. Brad looked down at her as he asked, "Feel better now? You don't have to pretend with me, Jorja. I know you're tough, but anyone would be scared after something like this, especially with what you've already been through."

She nodded. "Thanks. I feel better now."

"Jorja? Uh, Fritz and Reynolds are here."

She was startled to hear Taylor's voice close behind her and she jumped back slightly from Brad, who did not willingly relinquish his hold on her. She placed her hands against his chest and gently pushed back so that he finally released her. As she turned to look at Taylor, she felt the color return to her cheeks when she also saw Fritz standing not too far behind.

She turned to face both Taylor and Fritz as she stood to Brad's side. She tried to ignore the mix of concern and resentment on Fritz's face as he made eye contact with both her and Brad.

Jorja moved past Taylor toward Fritz. "Hi, Fritz. Did you get a chance to look upstairs? Did you see the front door?"

Fritz looked down at her and nodded. "Yes, I did. Do you have any idea what they were looking for?"

Shaking her head she said, "No idea at all. It doesn't appear anything is missing, but I really won't be able to say for sure until I can actually begin to clean up the mess."

Fritz turned from her to head back to the lobby of the book store. Jorja quickly glanced back at Taylor and Brad before turning to follow him. Both only eyed her with concern.

As she followed Fritz into the lobby, she saw Reynolds kneeling near the now open front door as he inspected the damage. Reynolds saw her and stood up. "Hey, Jorja. How are you holding up?"

She swallowed hard when she saw the concern in his eyes. "I'm fine. Do you think you'll be able to find any prints?"

Reynolds tore his gaze from hers and he glanced at Fritz briefly before looking back at the door. "No, not likely. I mean, there are prints on the door, but I found some fabric stuck in the glass that may belong to a glove.

If the person wore gloves, his or her prints won't be here for us to find."

Feeling deflated by that fact, Jorja moved over to sit on the couch.

Reynolds watched her sit down and then eyed Fritz, who only stood where he was. When Reynolds realized Fritz wasn't going to move, he moved to sit beside her on the couch. "I know it's not what you'd like to hear, Jorja. But if you find out what might be missing, it could give us a better understanding of who broke into the store. If not, then we'll keep the case open because there's no doubt someone out there knows something. Eventually we might get a break and we'll be able to give you some answers."

Jorja looked at Reynolds. "And maybe you won't."

Reynolds shrugged. "True, we might not. You know how it goes. But we'll do the best we can."

Ready for a fight now that she was beginning to feel herself again, she turned to glare at Fritz. "I can only hope you'll do the best you can."

Fritz caught Jorja's glare and he narrowed his eyes at her as he frowned rather than offer a reply.

Reynolds was quick in his attempt to put out the fire. "Jorja, you know we'll do our best. It's not only our job, but we also care about what happens to friends within our community. There's no reason to doubt us."

She tore her gaze from Fritz, feeling guilty for looping Reynolds' professionalism in with Fritz's. "I'm sorry, I know you will. Thanks. Do you need me right now? I need to make a phone call."

Reynolds nodded. "Go ahead. I'll let you know if we need anything. We'll be here for a bit longer."

Jorja stood up as she smiled with appreciation at Reynolds. When she turned to walk around the couch, she glanced at Fritz to discover he was staring at her. She couldn't read his expression, but the look in his eyes unnerved her. When she couldn't hold his gaze any longer, she took a deep breath, straightened her shoulders and moved past him with an air of indifference she had to admit to herself she had real difficulty portraying.

CHAPTER 33

The morning moved slowly as Fritz and Reynolds finished up the investigation before leaving to return to the police station to type up their reports. Brad called the school to request someone sub in for him so that he could board up the front door window and help clean up. When Dylan arrived he also pitched in, after first voicing all his concerns about Jorja and Taylor ever being in the store alone again.

"You just can't be too safe these days. You need an alarm, Jorja. You also need to add a lock to the upper part of your front door. They'd have to bust in the whole window to be able to climb inside and that might deter someone. Maybe it would be best not to have a window on the door. How about a solid wood door instead?"

Jorja nodded at Dylan's ideas. She was only half listening to him as she continued to run the morning through her head. She was no longer full of anxiety at the thought of someone violating her space; instead, she was angry. Angry and disheartened that yet again she was dealing with what might be a potentially dangerous situation. She hated the thought, but she was less inclined to believe the break in was caused by a teenager. Whoever broke in was looking for something specific. If the item they were searching for was not located, what would they do to continue their search? She knew she had to figure out what the person may have been looking for if she was going to protect herself from any future incidents.

"Jorja? What do you think?"

Realizing Dylan was still speaking, she returned her thoughts to the present and gave him a sheepish grin. "Sorry, just running my own thoughts through my head."

Dylan looked frustrated as he glanced at Taylor, who grabbed his hand and smiled. "All your ideas are good ones, babe. I'm sure Jorja will take them into consideration."

"Yes, Dylan, I will. I promise," Jorja said. She then glanced at Taylor. "Michael decided he'd prefer to meet later this week rather than reschedule for this afternoon so I thought I'd go get something to eat at the deli. Do you want something? Dylan? Are you hungry?"

Taylor nodded. "Sure. How about a turkey club? I'll just share mine with Dylan." She leaned affectionately against Dylan before asking Jorja, "Are you sure you want to go? I can get lunch if you'd rather stay here."

Jorja shook her head. "No, I need to get some fresh air and Piper probably needs to take a walk. I'll be back soon."

Jorja put on her jacket and scarf before she and Piper left by the front door where Brad was finishing with the repairs. When she saw the door from the outside she was dismayed at how it looked with plywood covering the window. She hoped she could get the door fixed soon.

While she stared at the door, Brad stood back to critically survey his work before turning to gaze at her expectantly. Not wanting to give Brad the impression she was displeased with his work, she put on the best smile she could. "It looks good. I really appreciate your help. I'm going to grab something to eat. Would you like something?"

Brad's critical look turned to one of worry as his brows creased and he frowned. "No, I'm okay, but do you want some company? I have someone covering my classes until I get back so it wouldn't be a problem."

Jorja shook her head. "It's okay, you should go back to your class and not worry about me. I'll just see you later, okay?"

She could tell Brad wanted to argue with her, but he finally nodded in agreement. "Sure, okay. I'll check in with you later."

Rather than argue with him about his need to check up on her, she had to admit to herself that his protective attitude was sweet. She gave him a wave as she and Piper walked down the sidewalk in the direction of the deli. During the walk, Jorja took deep breaths of the cool air. The fresh air felt good to her lungs, but it was chilly. She quickly wrapped her scarf more tightly around her neck and placed her hood over her head. The walk to the deli was only a few blocks, but it still felt good to get a brisk walk in after the events of the morning.

Tying Piper's leash to a post outside the deli, Jorja went inside to place her order. As she waited for the food, she grabbed a week-old local paper from the counter and flipped through it with mild interest. Her interest perked up when she saw an article about Gabe Carter. It was a piece about his work at the school and how the district planned to hire him on full time. She immediately felt tingles at the thought that he might remain in town.

As long as he wasn't fired for becoming a suspect in the Chief's assault, she thought.

If he really was her father, she needed to figure out how to approach him with the subject. How the heck do you tell a stranger you think he's your long lost father? She wondered if these were the feelings Ryan had when he tracked her down and had to tell her he was her long lost twin presumed to be dead.

"Hello, Jorja, how are you?"

When she looked up from the paper at her unexpected company, she choked on the breath she sucked in and began to cough. After a few quick sips from the water the waitress offered her, she was able to stop coughing and finally respond.

"Hi, Gabe. Nice bumping into you here." She took another sip from her glass.

"You too. Sorry to startle you. Are you here for lunch?"

Nodding, Jorja said, "I'm picking up lunch for Taylor and myself. Are you on a lunch break?"

"Yes, the kids are on their lunch break so I thought I'd grab something here rather than at the school cafeteria." Gabe grimaced as he continued, "I get tired of cafeteria food so something from the deli is a nice change."

She smiled. "You want to sit down here? You can have my table when I get my food. Until then, we can visit."

Smiling in return as he pulled back a chair and sat down, he replied, "Sure. Thanks."

Jorja took another sip of water. She was uncertain where to start a conversation when the only one running through her head had to do with proving paternity.

He beat her to the punch by asking, "So I spoke to my attorney and he said his schedule is pretty open tomorrow afternoon, if you have some free time after I get done with my last class."

Jorja bit her lip, uncertain how to delay the meeting without revealing what she knew about Bailey now becoming a suspect. "Well, tomorrow's a pretty busy day for me. Can I get back to you with how my schedule looks later this week?"

Gabe hesitated before she replied, "Sure, we can schedule it later in the week if that works better for you."

They sat in silence for a moment before Jorja finally asked, "Uh, so are you still enjoying your teaching job? I was just reading here that the school plans to hire you on full time. That's great if it's what you were hoping for."

The waitress stopped to take Gabe's order and when she walked away, he turned to Jorja. "Yes, I'm happy with my job and I'm thrilled to take it on full time. I guess the teacher I substituted for decided to retire. It'll be nice to settle in here after I've traveled so much for most of my life. It'll also be nice if I can mend my relationship with my uncle. That may take some time, but if I'm here for good, time is all we'll have."

She was relieved and pleased he planned to stay, especially if he hoped to mend fences with the Chief . "So you traveled most of your life? Did you like it?"

"Yes and no. I loved seeing new places, meeting new people. Thankfully I had the Air Force because at least I had someplace to belong. Even if I didn't have a real home, I had a family of sorts. But after twenty-five years, I decided it was time to retire. For over five years I tried to make a home in some of my favorite places, but I've always felt drawn to return here. I'm sure one reason is because I never liked how my uncle and I ended our relationship."

Nodding, she said, "Maybe it was something more than that."

"Oh? Like what?"

Jorja grimaced as she looked at her water. Sometimes she had to learn to hold her tongue. "Well, you mentioned leaving without saying good-bye to Gloria. Maybe that bothered you as well."

234 | P . J . H o w e l l

Leaning back in his chair, Gabe gazed over Jorja's head as he seemed to recall years past. "Yes, I do regret that. I regret leaving her. I regret never saying goodbye to her. I regret never following up when Coop told me she was sent to the hospital after she supposedly went insane or some such nonsense."

Jorja's head snapped up. "Coop?" She felt she already knew the answer when she asked, "Who was that?"

When the waitress brought a bag containing her lunch, she barely gave it her attention as she waited for Gabe's reply.

"Oh, he was a friend of mine from school. Jim Cooper. About six months after I left, I made contact with him just before I was shipped out to spend a year in Japan and he told me she was in a psychiatric ward. I was sick with the thought that I wasn't there for her, but I knew there probably wasn't anything I could do. Coop told me she had some sort of breakdown, but he didn't know why."

She tried to ignore the anger she felt at the mention of Jim Cooper. He had caused enough pain and yet it would appear his presence would never quite find an exit from her life.

Gabe watched her with concern before he asked, "Are you okay? Is this upsetting to you?"

Jorja quickly nodded before looking away. "Yes, I'm fine."

"I'm really sorry. I'm not being very sensitive to the fact that Gloria was your aunt. It must not have been easy. Did you form any sort of relationship with her when she was released from the hospital?"

Jorja hung her head slightly as she thought about how much to tell him. How could she really have this conversation here? He was unaware of the incident between her and Cooper. He was unaware of Gloria's condition when he left town. He was unaware of the fact that he could be speaking to his own daughter.

She coughed slightly as she attempted to speak. She picked up her glass to take a sip before she tried again. "You know, I really need to get this lunch back to Taylor. I would like to talk with you some more though, if that's okay. Would you like to come over to my house for dinner next week?"

Eyeing her warily, Gabe took a moment before responding, "Uh, sure, that would be nice. Will your brother be there as well?"

It took her a moment before she realized what he was thinking about the dinner invitation. "Of course he'll be there. This isn't a dinner *date*, believe me. I'm not into older men." Jorja smiled sheepishly. "It's just that there's something I'd really like to discuss with you, but it would be better at another time. Would that be okay?"

With a look of relief, Gabe let out a breath before he awkwardly smiled in return. "Well, then, I'd be happy to come by for dinner. Just let me know when."

Grabbing the lunch bag as she stood up, she said, "Great. I'll check with Ryan's schedule and let you know. Have a great day and I'll talk to you later."

Jorja left the restaurant as quickly as she could while resisting the urge to sprint out the door. She felt her heart rate quicken as she fought the feelings of both anxiety and anticipation at the thought of explaining to Gabe Carter the truth about what happened to Gloria.

CHAPTER 34

It was Valentine's Day so Jorja distracted herself with tidying up the book displays and decorations Taylor used to add some Valentine's Day charm to the store. Jorja had always enjoyed the books offered for children around Valentine's Day, even if they were filled with fun and innocence about the one holiday she would have rather ignored.

She was in the process of straightening a few books when a piercing scream made her jump, causing her to lose her grip on the books so that they fell to the floor. She quickly turned to run to the main part of the lobby to find the source of the sound.

"Oh, I love you, I love you, I *love* you!" She heard Taylor exclaim before she rounded the corner from the children's section and saw Taylor sitting on the couch with Dylan. Jorja quickly glanced around and was relieved to see no customers in sight.

"Taylor? What's going on? You scared the hell out of me!" She instantly knew all was well when she saw Dylan's grin before Taylor turned to her with a smile and tears in her eyes.

"Oh, Jorja, look. Isn't it beautiful?" Taylor stretched out her arm so that Jorja could get a look at the ring on her finger. "Dylan just gave me my engagement ring and it turned out even better than I thought was possible."

Jorja gingerly grabbed Taylor's hand to get a better look at the ring. She had to admit, it was spectacular. When Dylan said he could use Taylor's grandmother's diamond and sapphire brooch to make an engagement ring, she wasn't sure what she expected, but she was certain she could not envision anything as beautiful as what she was now holding.

"It's very beautiful." Jorja looked at Taylor and then at Dylan. "It turned out perfectly, Dylan. I'm really happy for you both."

Jorja released Taylor's hand and sat down on the couch.

"Someday you'll have a ring this beautiful on your hand, Jorja," Taylor said as she held her hand out in front of her, gazing at the ring adoringly.

"Maybe." Jorja leaned over to peek at Dylan where he sat on the other side of Taylor. "So if this is the engagement ring, where's the rest of it?"

Dylan's smile only widened. "Taylor won't get to see that until a week before the wedding. I agreed to let her tell me what she wanted, but I want to keep the final look a complete surprise. For now, she'll have to do with just the engagement ring."

"Oh, I'll do just fine with this ring, don't worry." Taylor suddenly leaned over to give Dylan a hug.

Feeling like a third wheel, Jorja stood up to find more work to do. "Taylor, you can take off anytime you want if you and Dylan have plans for the evening. I'll be fine closing up."

Dylan shook his head. "No, we agreed you two shouldn't be here alone, didn't we? Since Kat isn't going to be here, I already spoke to Ryan and he said he'll come by in awhile to take over for Taylor so we can go out. We can wait until then. Where is Kat tonight, anyway?"

"She has a Valentine's Day dance at the school she's going to with Bruce. I'm hoping she'll stop by to show us her dress before they go out to dinner."

The door suddenly opened, startling the three of them. Jorja expected a customer and was surprised to see Lydia instead. She was holding a vase full of roses. And she was frowning.

Jorja was immediately curious about the sight before her. "Hello, Lydia. What brings you here?"

Lydia moved into the store and stopped next to one of the tables by the espresso stand. She set the vase of roses down on the table, let her arms fall to her sides and after taking a deep breath, she finally looked at Jorja. "These are for you."

Jorja's eyes widened. "Me? Who are they from? And why are you dropping them off?"

Taylor squealed as she sprinted across the lobby to stand next to Jorja. She smiled in delight as she waited for Lydia to reply.

Lydia clamped her mouth shut, taking a moment to respond. Jorja would have guessed Lydia was sucking on a lemon if she hadn't known otherwise.

Lydia finally replied, "Who they're from is on the card. I'm delivering them because I'm working part time at the flower shop for Courtney."

Taylor was quick to ask, "You're working at Courtney's Courtyard? Why? Are you no longer cutting hair?"

Lydia smirked. "Of course I'm still cutting hair. I have too many customers who rely on me. Courtney needed help and I agreed to work at the flower shop part time, that's all."

Jorja barely heard Lydia's explanation. She was more curious about who sent the flowers, but she hesitated to grab the card to read the sentiment and who authored it.

Taylor could no longer contain herself as she clapped her hands excitedly with pure pleasure and asked, "Well, aren't you going to read the card?"

Jorja glanced at Lydia, who quickly turned away before she said, "I have to go. I have other deliveries to make."

Once Lydia was outside the store, Taylor snatched the card from the flowers and placed it in Jorja's hand. "Come on, open it to see who they're from."

"I think I already know who they're from." Jorja glanced at the envelope and finally pulled out the card. She smiled as she read the card.

Jorja, I didn't want you to forget how much you mean to me and that I'm always here if you need me. Happy Valentine's Day, Brad.

"Can I see?" Taylor asked as she tried to read the card in Jorja's hand.

Jorja held the card out to Taylor, who instantly grabbed it. "Oh, how sweet is that? Not sure what this means about your relationship, but at least it's something, huh?"

"I told you, we're just friends. It's sweet he sent the flowers, but it's nothing more than that."

Taylor pouted. "You're taking the fun out of it. He sent you *roses*. He's more than just a friend." She quickly turned to Dylan. "Right, babe? Don't you think he wants to be more than friends?"

Dylan raised his hands in defense. "Hey, don't put me in the middle of this. I don't know what Brad is thinking and I won't pretend to know. Just let her enjoy the flowers."

Taylor hesitated, ready to argue, before she finally decided to let the matter drop. "Well, I think the flowers are beautiful and you certainly deserve them."

Jorja smiled. "Thanks. Well, I'll take these up to the office and maybe get some paperwork done." As she headed up the stairs she said, "Let me know when Ryan gets here, will you?"

Once Jorja was in the office she made room on her desk for the vase and then moved the roses around to fix the bouquet. When she stepped back to admire her handiwork, she couldn't deny it was a beautiful bouquet. She had to remember to call Brad to thank him.

When the intercom buzzed, Jorja heard Taylor ask, "Hey, can you come down for a minute?"

"Sure, is Ryan here already?"

"Uh, not yet. Someone else is here to see you."

Curious, Jorja hung up the phone and moved to peek over the railing. She quickly spotted Reynolds but...not Fritz.

Reynolds was making small talk with both Taylor and Dylan while Jorja took her time walking down the staircase and scanning the rest of the bookstore for Fritz.

Still no sight of him.

Reynolds finally spotted her and he gave her a smile. "Hey, Jorja. I just thought I'd stop by to say hi." He gave her a wink as he continued, "And I have a surprise for you."

Jorja raised a single brow. "Oh? What kind of surprise?" She glanced at Taylor, who only returned her own curious look.

Reynolds extended his arm to point at the front of the store. "You have to go outside for your surprise."

Taylor was already headed toward the door and she grabbed Jorja's hand on the way. "Come on, let's go see what it is."

Taylor tugged on her hand and the two of them moved to the front door with Dylan and Reynolds right behind them. Jorja opened the front door to peek outside. Seeing nothing out of the ordinary, she and Taylor stepped through the doorway and out onto the sidewalk. There, standing beside the patrol car, she saw Fritz holding a door.

Jorja stared at the door in wonder. It was a beautiful dark-stained solid wood door carved to give it an old-world charm and touting a beautiful brass door knob and hinges.

"What…what's this for?" Jorja hesitantly moved closer to the door and couldn't resist placing her hand on the solid wood. It was incredibly smooth to the touch. She looked up to see Fritz watching her with keen interest. Embarrassed, she took a step back as she turned to look at Reynolds. "Reynolds, what's this for?"

Jorja turned back to Fritz when he spoke before Reynolds could reply. "We wanted to help you replace your door. No window means no easy entry. The door is solid and it would take a lot of effort to kick in. We also got you extra locks for the top and the bottom of the door, just in case. If someone wants to break in, they'll have to take out the whole front window and that'll be no easy task when anyone driving down main street is going to see them."

Jorja held his gaze as a wealth of emotions flooded through her. She finally broke eye contact to look at Taylor, who couldn't stop grinning in delight. When Taylor finally realized Jorja had a lump in her throat and might not be able to speak without getting emotional, she stepped in on Jorja's behalf. "This is just the most wonderful gift! The door is beautiful, just beautiful. Isn't it Jorja?"

Jorja swallowed as she made an attempt to speak. "It – it's beautiful, yes. You two didn't have to do this, but I really appreciate it."

Fritz readjusted his footing. "Hey, Reynolds, you want to help me with this? It's starting to get heavy."

Reynolds quickly rushed over to help Fritz with the door just as Dylan also moved to lend a hand. The three of them carried the door inside the store and leaned it against the wall.

"Is it okay if we leave it here until we can come back to install it?" Reynolds asked.

"Sure, that'd be fine." Jorja responded. "Do either of you want a cup of coffee before you leave?"

Reynolds shook his head. "No, I'm good for now. Fritz? You want a coffee?"

Fritz finished covering the door with a blanket he'd been carrying so that the door wouldn't scrape the wall. He looked up at Reynolds' question. "I'm okay. Thanks anyway, Jorja."

Fritz moved to stand near Reynolds and as the two of them looked at her, Jorja tried to find the right words. "Thank you so much for the new door. I'd say again you didn't have to but it will be nice to have the old door replaced with something I know is sturdy. Is there any way I can repay you? There's no reason you two have to put out the money for that type of expense."

Reynolds quickly held up his hand to stop her. "No, Jorja. Don't worry about it. You need the door, we found the perfect one and we have the means to help you out."

Fritz nodded in agreement, but did not respond any further. Jorja thought she saw a hint of color on his cheeks and instantly wondered why he'd be embarrassed.

"Well, okay. It means a lot to me. I can't even begin to really say how much."

Fritz quickly elbowed Reynolds as he said, "We need to get going. Jorja, we'll be back later to help install the door. Right now we need to get back out on the road. See you soon."

Jorja said goodbye and watched as Fritz quickly left the store. She turned to look at Reynolds, who gave her a grin.

When he didn't say anything, she finally asked, "What? Why are you grinning at me?"

He shook his head. "Oh, I'm not grinning at you. I'm grinning about my friend. Do you like your surprise? Do you think it was a nice gift?"

She nodded her head. "Yes, I think it was a very nice gift."

"Well then, I hope you have a happy Valentine's Day. I hope you know he scoured the nearby cities for that door. He had his mind set on the type of door you should have and nothing less would do."

Jorja felt Taylor move closer in her attempt to better hear the conversation. She ignored Taylor as she tried to focus on what Reynolds was saying. "What do you mean he scoured the cities? Is this door from him or from both of you?"

Reynolds winked as his smile broadened. "As far as you know, it's from both of us, but if you can keep a little secret, I'll admit it was his decision, the door was his choice and it was certainly his idea to give you the gift on Valentine's Day, not mine."

Taylor giggled, but just as quickly she tried to hold her hand over her mouth to drown out the sound. Jorja barely glanced at Taylor as she took in what Reynolds said. "Well...I'll accept the gift from both of you and I appreciate it very much, whether it's Valentine's Day or not."

"You're welcome, Jorja." Reynolds winked again as he gave her a nod and walked out the door.

Taylor could no longer contain herself. "Do you believe that? Fritz gave you a door for Valentine's Day! On any other day I'd say it's one of the oddest gifts I've ever seen, but the fact that he took the time to pick out the door he thought would be the best when it comes to your protection? Nothing can beat that...nothing." Taylor quickly glanced down at her hand and the new engagement ring. "Well, almost nothing." She looked up at Dylan to give him a smile.

Dylan shook his head and grinned. "I'm glad you think the ring is more special than a door, Taylor. Well, I have to get back to work. I'll be back soon to pick you up once I get everything cleaned up." Dylan gave Taylor a kiss goodbye before saying goodbye to Jorja and leaving the store.

Taylor turned to Jorja. "So what do you think about your Valentine's Day now? Do you think it's still a holiday you can just ignore?" Taylor winked before walking away to let Jorja gather her mixed up emotions.

CHAPTER 35

"Hello, Jorja. How are you today?" Betsy asked as Jorja entered the lobby of the police station and walked up to the reception counter.

"I'm doing well. You?"

Betsy grinned. "I'm doing great. I actually have a belated Valentine's Day date this evening."

"Oh? Anyone I know?" Jorja enjoyed the sparkle she saw in Betsy's eyes.

With a wink, Betsy leaned forward and whispered, "The Chief ."

Jorja leaned back in surprise. So he finally realized what he had right in front of him. She was thrilled. "Oh, that's terrific. I'm so happy for you. Where are the two of you going?"

Before Betsy could answer, the side door opened, startling both of them. Chief Douglas entered the room with a seriousness about him that made Jorja wonder if he was putting on an act to cover up his newly discovered interest in Betsy. "Hello, Chief ."

He nodded. "Jorja. Thanks for coming." He then turned to Betsy. "Will you let Fritz know we're ready."

Betsy smiled. "Sure thing."

Jorja watched to see if he would smile in return, but he remained solid in his serious attitude. She turned to look at him when he said, "Jorja? Care to follow me?"

She gave a quick wave goodbye to Betsy, who gave her a wink, before she followed the Chief through the doorway and into the hall. They walked down the hallway to the same room she had met Bailey in during her first visit.

"You wait here while we get Bailey. I'll be right back."

Jorja sat down as she placed her bag on the floor. She was more curious now about why he asked her to come by to meet with Bailey. She wondered what had transpired in the last few days to prompt the get-together.

The door across from the table finally opened and Bailey walked through with Fritz right behind her. Bailey smiled widely when she saw Jorja and as she sat down, she said, "I'm so glad you're here. Do you know what's going on?"

Shaking her head, Jorja said, "Not a clue. I think the Chief should be here any moment though to fill us in." She glanced up at Fritz to find him watching her, but when he caught her gaze, he quickly looked away. She wondered if he was embarrassed about the Valentine's Day gift.

When the door finally opened and the Chief entered the room, Jorja tensed up slightly with nervous anxiety at not knowing the reason for the meeting. She was glad to finally get on with it when the Chief sat down and said, "I'm sure you're curious about the reason for this meeting."

Bailey and Jorja both nodded. Bailey's voice shook as she asked, "Has something happened with my case?"

The Chief looked up at Fritz before meeting Bailey's gaze. "You could say that."

When Bailey glanced at Jorja, she could see the panic in Bailey's eyes and the rush of heat to Bailey's face as her cheeks turned red.

"What happened? What did you find out?" Bailey finally asked.

"Well...there has been a slight change in circumstances surrounding your case. A piece of evidence was seized from your vehicle." The Chief glanced at Fritz before he gave Jorja a knowing look. She inwardly cringed as she wondered what Fritz told him about what happened at Bailey's car. The Chief continued, "That evidence was very telling about your relationship with your husband in that it depicted a side of him I'm sure he hoped no one would ever see."

"You mean you watched the video tape?" Bailey asked as her cheeks flushed even more. Tears suddenly formed in her eyes and she looked down at her handcuffed hands. "The whole thing?"

"Yes, the whole thing. It's my job. Now, I will say I'm very sympathetic to what you went through with that man if that video is a true depiction of what he put you through during your brief marriage to him."

Bailey lifted her head to stare at the Chief as tears streaked down her face. "Has anyone else seen it?"

"Not yet. I'm sure you realize it's a piece of evidence, but we'll treat it as delicately as we can. Believe me, I don't wish to embarrass you with this. I just want you to understand I'm here to help you."

Jorja's head jerked as she turned her gaze from Bailey's tear-streaked face to the Chief's sympathetic one. He gave her a quick glance before he nodded slightly and again met Bailey's gaze.

"I have to say I believe you when you said you did what you had to do to get away from him. I also believe you when you say you did not assault your husband. You did remove your son from his residence and across state lines without his permission, but what I saw on that video is nothing a woman should ever go through. That wasn't only assault, Bailey, it was also rape. What I saw is enough to make me wonder how much your husband really wants to force the issue of your alleged kidnapping and so-called assault."

Jorja listened intently and Bailey quickly wiped away tears with the backs of her hands. Bailey's eyes still glistened with tears, but also with newfound hope as she waited for the Chief to continue.

"I want to ask you something. Do you want your husband prosecuted for the acts he committed which you have on videotape? This would mean returning to your home state, making a statement against your husband and possibly having to testify in court against him."

"But it also means a jury might have to view the tape, correct?"

The Chief nodded. "You are correct. They would see the evidence because it's the only thing you have to back up your claims against him."

Bailey shook her head. "No, I don't want to go back there. I just want to live my own life with Justin and I don't want any more contact with my husband at all."

"I thought you might say that. I did a little digging and it would appear your husband's reach is quite long when it comes to the police and prosecutors in his home town. I'm honestly worried that if I send this videotape to them, it might very well disappear if it gets into the wrong hands. I hate saying this about my fellow officers, but I don't want to risk losing the only piece of evidence you have. I can make a copy, but we'd be back at square one trying to get it into the right hands in order to move this case along. So, because I worry the case won't be resolved if your husband uses his influence, I've come up with another idea."

Bailey held her breath, as did Jorja, while they waited for the Chief to explain.

"I had a little chat with the chief in your home town. I don't know where he stands with regard to your husband, but I told him you were claiming to have evidence of a crime committed against you by your husband and that it was all on tape. After he likely spoke to your husband, he called me to say that they would be dropping the case of assault and kidnapping against you if I sent the tape over for their investigation into his actions. I decided to tell him I don't have the tape in my possession yet, but that I'm searching for it based on your claim that it exists. He told me if the tape does exist, his plan would be to charge your husband, but again, because I worry how deep your husband's pockets go, I don't know if he's being truthful or just giving me lip service so that your husband can get that tape to destroy it. That's why I'm asking you how much you care about whether or not he'll be prosecuted. If prosecution is not your main interest, then I'll tell the chief I found the tape, but require that he send proof of the dismissal of charges before I send him the tape."

Jorja listened to the offered reasoning, but it made her sick to think Bailey's husband would get away with committing such a vile act upon Bailey. She would rather see the jerk go to prison, but she knew the reality was that he might not serve much time, if any, and would always have another opportunity to hurt Bailey if he really wanted to. She just hoped he'd never want to hurt Bailey again.

"But what about Justin? I can't send him back there. I won't let him be raised by a monster. If I have to run again, I will." Bailey's face took on a look of hard determination only a mother wanting to save her child could muster.

The Chief smiled slightly. "Well, now, that was where the real surprise came in. When the chief told me they would drop the charges, he also told me your husband would not be requesting the return of his son. He's going to send documents giving you primary care of Justin and he won't force the issue of visitation."

Bailey shook her head in disbelief. "I don't believe him. Why would he give up Justin? He's up to something, Chief . You can't trust him."

Jorja noticed a slight shift in the Chief 's posture and she glanced at him to watch as his demeanor changed from compassion to unease.

"Well, there is a slight catch." The Chief coughed slightly to clear his throat before he continued. "Uh, you're still under investigation here with regard to whoever assaulted me." He quickly held up his hand when he saw Bailey was about to express her innocence. "I know. I understand your position and your claim of innocence. In all honesty, I believed you. However, you are aware that a weapon was found in your vehicle. The lab results aren't back yet, but if the blood on that hammer matches mine, the case against you is not looking well." He again held up his hand. "Now, don't say anything. You need to have your attorney here and I don't want you making any statements about the case to me. Just understand that your husband is willing to let you keep Justin, but if you're convicted of any crime and you end up incarcerated, Justin will be returned to him."

Jorja thought Bailey would begin to cry again, but instead, her face remained passive and she leaned back in her chair as she remained quiet. While Bailey's face did not reveal much, Jorja could tell by the look in her eyes that her mind was in overdrive.

Jorja leaned forward. "Don't worry. We'll work on your case and figure this whole thing out. Don't worry, okay?"

Bailey glanced at Jorja and nodded, but remained silent. Jorja glanced at the Chief and then at Fritz, who again looked away once she caught his gaze.

The Chief suddenly pushed his chair back. "Well, that's it for now. I wanted you to know where you stood on the case with your husband. I'll have Fritz or Reynolds let you know when we get the paperwork. If you're charged with regard to my case, I won't be having any further conversations with you."

Bailey only nodded. Jorja stood up as the Chief stood up. "Fritz will take you back to your cell. Jorja?" The Chief waited as she leaned over to grab her bag. She tried to make eye contact with Bailey before Fritz led her out of the room, but Bailey only kept her eyes down as she walked ahead of Fritz through the door.

Saddened by the quick turn of events, Jorja followed the Chief out into the hall. "Even if you don't believe she did it," she said to his back, "you're making it sound like she might still be charged and convicted."

He turned to her as he reached for the door handle. "No, Jorja, I find it hard to believe she assaulted me, but I can't ignore the fact that the weapon used to strike me may very well have been in her possession. How it got there is the real question, but as it stands now, the hammer in her vehicle may have my blood on it."

Turning the knob, he opened the door to let her enter the lobby. She moved to the reception counter to say goodbye to Betsy as the Chief retreated back into the hall and shut the door.

Jorja felt a heaviness in her chest as she thought about Bailey's predicament, but she tried to wipe away the negativity with thoughts about Betsy finally dating the Chief .

"So, Betsy, do you know where you're going on your date? Is he taking you someplace nice?"

Betsy smiled and Jorja thought she'd never seen Betsy look so happy. "He hasn't said. He just said he'd like to treat me to dinner. He tried to say he wanted to show his appreciation for all I've done for him since he was hurt, but you know him, he's a tough old cuss who has a hard time admitting his feelings. He's just using it as an excuse."

Jorja smiled and nodded in agreement with Betsy's take on the Chief's reasoning. Whatever the reason, Jorja was glad he finally got up the nerve to ask.

When the door behind Betsy opened and Fritz entered the room, Jorja tried to hide her unease when she saw his apparent surprise that she was still in the building. He appeared to be mildly irritated at her presence, if his scowl had anything to say about it.

"Betsy, we need to put these photos in Bailey's file. Can you do that for me when you have a minute?"

Fritz tossed the photos on the corner of Betsy's desk as she replied, "Sure, Fritz. Are you heading out on patrol now?"

The conversation became muted when Jorja caught sight of the man in the photos. She felt a buzz in her head as she leaned forward over the counter in an attempt to get a better look. As she did, she let out a sharp breath when she realized she recognized the man in the photos.

Fritz heard her and turned to look at her in question. "Is something wrong?"

"Uh, who is that? In the photo?" She pointed at a photo on the desk.

Fritz frowned when he saw the look on her face. "Why?"

"Because...because I've seen him before."

"What? When?" Fritz suddenly grabbed the photos and moved closer Jorja. He placed the photos on the counter so that she could get a closer look. "You're sure you've seen *this* man before?" He pointed to the man in one of the photos.

Jorja nodded. She could no longer fight the nervous tension she was feeling. "Yes, he was in my shop not too long ago."

"When? And why?" Fritz was now all business and he quickly looked back at Betsy and whispered to her to get the Chief.

When Fritz turned again to look at Jorja, she was ready to answer. "It was over the past two weeks. I saw him once when he stopped in for a cup of coffee and then another time he asked Taylor for help with finding a book for his son. He said his son really likes alligators and he was hoping to find something he hadn't yet read. Is that Bailey's husband?"

The Chief suddenly entered the room and Fritz turned to him rather than answer her question. "Jorja's seen this man," he pointed at one of the photographs, "in her shop at least twice during the past two weeks."

When the Chief looked up from the photo at Jorja, she saw concern and then anger. "So, he's been here this whole time. I guess the chief over there isn't someone I can trust. Now the question is, why is he here and what's he up to?"

When Jorja looked down at the photograph again, she felt a shiver move up her spine as she too wondered just what the man's intentions were.

CHAPTER 36

Jorja entered the shop with Fritz right on her heels as she argued with him. "I'll be fine, Fritz. I'll have Ryan stay at the shop with Taylor and I and we'll call you if we even get a glimpse of the man."

Shrugging off her jacket, Jorja tried to ward off the curious looks from customers before she realized she and Fritz needed to move to the back of the store. She walked down the hallway as she waved at him to follow her. She saw Taylor crane her neck to watch them and knew it wouldn't be long before Taylor would follow them once she had finished making whatever coffee a customer had ordered.

Jorja hung her jacket on the rack next to the back door before moving into the break room. She opened the fridge to grab a bottle of water and raised it slightly in question at Fritz. He shook his head at the offer. Instead, he continued to chastise her. "Jorja, you don't know what this guy is capable of. I know you didn't see the video of what he did to Bailey, but that man is a monster. I won't let you put yourself in jeopardy again. I'm going to do whatever it takes to make sure you stay safe."

She attempted to glower at him in defiance, but just as quickly she gave up before sitting down at the table. She was irritated, but no longer had the energy to argue. After taking another sip of water, she placed the cap back on, sat the bottle on the table and crossed her arms as she looked up at Fritz. "What are you going to do? Follow me everywhere I go?"

"If I have to, I will. Reynolds and I can take shifts, but either way, you and Taylor will stay protected." He crossed his arms and leaned against the door frame. His expression was determined, but the look in his eyes made her feel funny. She looked down at her water to escape his gaze.

When she heard him shift slightly, she looked up to see his attention had moved to the hallway and she knew Taylor was on her way. She leaned back in her chair and waited. Taylor made only brief eye contact with Fritz before setting her sights on Jorja before asking, "What's going on now? Did something happen at the police department?"

"You could say that."

Taylor sat down next to Jorja. "What happened? Why is Fritz here?"

"Well, it would appear the abusive husband Bailey ran away from followed her here."

"What? How do you know that?" Taylor glanced up at Fritz, but when he didn't reply, she turned back to Jorja.

"I saw a photo of him at the police department and recognized him. Remember that guy who was asking you about a book on alligators for his son?"

Jorja waited while Taylor thought back on the numerous customers she had helped. Finally, she recalled the one. "Yes, I remember him. You mean he's Bailey's husband? Justin's father?"

Nodding, Jorja said, "Yes, and he hasn't made it known to either Bailey or the police that he's here. He was here before she was arrested and if that's the case, you'd have to wonder why he never turned her in since she was wanted for assault and kidnapping." She glanced up at Fritz before speaking to Taylor again. "Do you know what

I think? I think he came here to get out of trouble himself by getting Bailey into trouble with no way out. How else could he get his son back when he knew Bailey had a video of what he was capable of? He hoped to have her arrested for a crime and he hoped to find that videotape before heading back home with Justin right alongside him."

Fritz was looking at her with intense interest, but he refused to take part in Jorja's speculation. "There's no way we can prove what you're thinking."

Taylor looked curiously at Fritz, then at Jorja. "Prove what? What are you thinking?"

Jorja delayed her answer by taking another sip from her water bottle. Finally, she said, "I think Bailey's husband is the one who attacked the Chief . I think he's the one who called in an anonymous tip which got her arrested when I tried to speak to her here. I've felt as if I've been watched for some time now and if he knew Bailey had been coming here and speaking to me, now I know why. I also think he knew the tape might have been in her car, but maybe he didn't have time to search it when he quickly placed the incriminating hammer inside her car. If it is her hammer, I'm betting he knew Bailey probably had an extra key hidden under the car and that's how he got in. If he has been watching me, he probably also saw when Ryan and I made an attempt to jump start her car and he may have assumed we took the videotape from the car. Why else would he search my office?" Jorja glanced up at Fritz. "That's what makes sense, you know. He was searching my office hoping that I had the videotape and was keeping it here. He's the one who assaulted the Chief in an attempt to set up Bailey so he could get his son back without a fight."

Taylor leaned back in shock at what Jorja described. "He seemed so nice, too. Good looking even. I was actually wondering if he might be someone I could set up with one of the girls at the salon."

Fritz finally spoke up again. "You never know just by looking at someone. All I know is that the guy is dangerous and I don't want to take any chances he might come back here when you're not protected."

Jorja shot him a look. "Well how the heck are we going to catch him in the act if we have you glued to us twenty-four seven?"

Placing his hands on his hips, Fritz stared down at Jorja as he asked, "What do you mean, *catch him in the act*? In the act of doing what?"

"Trying to steal the videotape, of course." Jorja glanced at Taylor for support before she continued. "He doesn't know the Chief has the tape, correct? He already thinks I must have taken the tape from the car which is why he ransacked my office. I'm surprised he hasn't broken into my house yet, but maybe that's because Ryan and Nicholas are home so much during the day. If we can somehow let him believe I have the tape, he'll come looking for it because if the tape is gone, there's nothing for him to worry about. He believes Bailey is going to be charged with the Chief's assault once the lab results on the hammer come back, and I'm sure he plans to get Justin and leave as soon as possible."

Taylor's eyes widened as she listened to Jorja. She shook her head before saying, "We can't let that man have Justin. If he's capable of what Bailey's says, he's not the one who should be raising a son."

"Oh? And what if his mother is capable of assault as well? Should she be raising him?" Fritz argued.

Jorja shook her head as she sighed heavily. "Come on, Fritz. Do you really believe Bailey's capable of what happened to the Chief ? Really?"

"All I know is that she was there before it happened and the weapon was found in her car."

"It's just all so black and white to you, isn't it? And, if her husband has been following her, then he saw her leave the Chief's house and saw his opportunity to set her up for a crime. He knew what she drove and he was able to use that to his advantage as well. This guy had it all planned out and you're just sucking it all in."

Fritz threw his hands up in irritation. "Okay, maybe. But again, this guy is capable of dangerous things. You can't be messing with that, Jorja."

Standing in an attempt to make her point, Jorja held Fritz's stare. "If Bailey is innocent of what she's been accused of, then I plan to help her all I can. You can either help me or you can get out of my way."

She walked past Taylor and then brushed past Fritz as she left the break room to head back into the lobby of the store. Taylor quickly ran after her to calm her down, but Jorja barely listened. She was already formulating a plan to finally set Bailey free.

CHAPTER 37

"Aunt Jorja, can I take Piper for a walk?" Nicholas asked as he rounded the corner into the kitchen and came to a sudden halt before slamming into her legs. He turned his face up to stare at her with his big brown eyes, pleading with her to say yes. Piper, who had been following Nicholas, sat on her haunches and also stared up at Jorja as if she too hoped Jorja would agree.

"You know I can't let you take a walk by yourself, Nicholas. Can you wait until I finish making a few phone calls?" She fluffed the top of his hair and moved around him to the phone on the counter.

Nicholas pouted. "I won't be walking alone. I'll be with Piper."

Jorja grabbed the phone as she shook her head. "You know what I mean. You need either me or your dad with you. Just give me ten minutes, okay?"

Letting out an exasperated sigh, Nicholas kicked at the table leg in frustration before he said, "Okay."

Jorja watched with a smile as Nicholas hung his head and slowly left the kitchen. Turning to the phone again, she looked at a notepad nearby as she prepared to dial out, but before she could hit the button for a dial tone, the phone rang, startling her slightly.

She picked up the receiver. "Hello?"

"Is this Jorja?"

"Yes."

"Hi, it's Michael. I was wondering if we could set up a time to meet tomorrow. I'm sorry about not being able to reschedule last weekend, but maybe it was better that you focused on taking care of what was going on at the bookstore. Did you figure out who broke in?"

She hesitated, knowing it was best not to tell anyone else the truth about what she suspected. "No, not yet. Probably just some kids getting their kicks."

"Well, I'm really sorry about that, especially if they caused damage. Anyway, I'd really like to meet with you. There's something I need to talk to you about."

"Sure, we can meet tomorrow. What time would be good for you?"

"How about eleven o'clock? I could swing by the bookstore if that's where you'll be."

"Okay, that works with my schedule. I'll see you then."

"Thanks. I'll see you tomorrow."

Jorja hung up the phone, wondering what he wanted to discuss with her and completely forgetting the phone call she planned to make to her mother. Instead, she thought it might be a good time to take a walk with Piper and Nicholas. She needed to prepare herself for the visit she would soon have with Gabe, who would be arriving for dinner in a few hours.

"Okay, Nicholas, let's take Piper on that walk now." Jorja left the kitchen by the hall near the staircase and was amused by the sight of Nicholas and Piper near the front door. Nicholas was wearing his jacket and holding Piper's leash, which was already attached to Piper's collar as she sat obediently beside Nicholas.

Nicholas gave her a lopsided grin while he placed a stocking cap on his head. "Come on, Aunt Jorja, it's getting dark out already."

"Okay, okay. I'm right behind you." She laughed as she grabbed her jacket and followed Nicholas and Piper out the front door. Not for the first time, she marveled at how often she laughed now that Nicholas and Ryan were a part of her life.

Sprinting to catch up with Nicholas, who let Piper take the lead as he walked briskly while holding onto the leash, Jorja walked behind them and let Nicholas have control for awhile before she knew she'd finally have to take over. After a few blocks, she could tell Nicholas was having a difficult time keeping up with Piper's quick gait so she moved ahead at a faster pace to catch up with them.

Nicholas turned down a side street toward the park they usually stopped at so he could play. Just as Nicholas began to run to the park, Jorja noticed a vehicle parked nearby. It was a dark, nondescript vehicle and did not immediately raise any concern when she looked at it until a flash of light caught her eye.

She narrowed her eyes as she stared at the vehicle. Dusk was beginning to fall and the vehicle wasn't parked under any light so she couldn't tell if it was empty. She then saw the light again and suddenly realized it was the lit end of a cigarette. As she attempted to focus on the inside of the car, she finally saw the outline of what appeared to be a man.

A man watching both her and Nicholas.

The hairs on the back of her neck instantly tingled and Jorja quickened her pace. "Nicholas, wait up!"

Nicholas attempted to slow down, but when he tried to pull on Piper's leash to slow her down, she would have none of it. Jorja finally caught up to Nicholas, grabbed the leash and said, "Piper, heal!"

Piper stopped her quick gait to stand next to Jorja. When Jorja then reached down to grab Nicholas' hand, she said, "We're not going to the park. We need to get home."

"Aw, why not? Can't I play on the toys for a little bit?"

"No, Nicholas. We need to go home. I need to get dinner ready because we have a guest coming over." Jorja snuck a peek at the car and was immediately alarmed when she saw the car door open. When the man stepped out of the car, her anxiety grew. While normal reasoning caused her to think she was being silly, she couldn't deny the instant apprehension she felt when she saw the outline of the man. She was farther away from the vehicle now and it was growing steadily darker so that she couldn't make out the details of his face, but she had a terrible suspicion the man was Bailey's husband. She believed he had most likely been the one to ransack her office. Was he now hoping to do the same to her house? She realized how terrified she was of that thought with the potential danger both Nicholas and Ryan might be put in.

"Come on, Nicholas, let's walk faster so we can get home. You can help me make dinner, okay?"

The offer raised Nicholas' spirits. "Really? Okay. What do I get to do? Can I cut stuff up?"

"We'll see." Jorja jumped when she heard the sound of a vehicle behind them as they neared the end of the block. She dared herself not to turn and make eye contact. She further dared herself not to pick up Nicholas and run like her pants were on fire.

As the car got closer, she could hear it slow down and still she had to tell herself not to turn and make eye contact. Instead, she watched out of the corner of her eye as the car slowly rolled past them and she held her breath when she saw that it was the vehicle belonging to the man with the cigarette. When the car continued to drive down the street, she let out a loud breath. She decided to cut down one of the side streets earlier than usual in order to get out of the driver's sight. Pulling Nicholas' hand as she turned the corner at the intersection she said, "Let's go down this street and then we'll head home."

Jorja held Nicholas' hand while they continued to walk as briskly as his small legs would allow. When they finally neared the house, Nicholas pulled his hand from hers' and he sprinted ahead as he yelled, "I have to go to the bathroom!"

She watched him go inside the house as she let Piper make one last ditch effort at a potty break before tugging on the leash to coax her inside. She tried her best not to give in to the urge to run for the front door when she thought of Bailey's husband driving by to get a look at her and the house she entered. *That's if he doesn't already know where I live*, she thought.

Jorja entered the house, unhooked Piper's leash and tossed her jacket on the hall bench. After she locked the front door, she headed to the kitchen where she could hear pots and pans being moved around.

"Well, there you are. Why didn't you tell me you took Nicholas and went for a walk? I was talking to you from upstairs for about ten minutes before I realized you weren't answering me…what the heck happened to you? You look white as a ghost." Ryan approached her and grabbed her arms with his hands. He stared at her as he waited for her to respond.

"I'm okay. I just got creeped out when I saw a guy sitting in his car watching me and Nicholas."

"Watching you? Are you sure? Did you get his plate number?"

Jorja shook her head and mentally admonished herself for not doing so. "No, it was dusk and he wasn't parked under a light. Actually, I'm not certain, but I think it was Bailey's husband."

Ryan let go of her arms and he took a step back in shock. "What? Why do you think that?"

She shrugged. "I'm not sure. I couldn't see him that well, but the outline, the shape of his head or maybe the shape of his upper body just seemed familiar to me. But there was something about him that gave me a bad feeling. Like he was up to no good."

"Are you going to call Fritz or Reynolds about this?"

"And tell them what? There was some guy sitting in his car, smoking a cigarette and I was spooked by it?"

Ryan rolled his eyes. "Come on, Jorja. You know they'll take it more seriously than that. You're not the kind to get easily frightened and they know that. If it is Bailey's husband, then he must be following you or trying to figure out where you live or worse, hoping to catch you alone. We can't take any chances. I'm going to call them myself." Ryan moved to the phone and was ready to dial when she grabbed it from his hand.

"No, don't call them yet. If we're going to come up with a plan to get that jerk to prove he's the one who attacked the Chief , I don't want him to know that I'm on to him."

Ryan narrowed his eyes as he listened. He slowly shook his head. "I don't like it. I don't think you should mess with this guy. You know he's dangerous and I won't put you or Nicholas in danger by ignoring the potential problem."

Jorja sighed. She knew he was right only because she also couldn't put Nicholas in any danger. "Okay, we'll tell them. But not right now. I don't want them coming here and ruining the evening with Gabe. We need to talk to him, Ryan. We need to let him know who he is and who we are. After that, you can call Fritz or Reynolds and sic them on Bailey's husband."

Ryan reluctantly agreed, but Jorja knew it was only because he also wanted to have the long overdue conversation with the man they believed to be their biological father.

CHAPTER 38

When the doorbell chimed, Nicholas was the first to run for the door, but Jorja quickly called out to him to ask who it was before opening the door. She heard Nicholas' small voice as he said, "Who is it?"

When Nicholas heard a response from the other side of the door, he yelled, "He said his name is Gabe!"

"Okay, you can open the door." Jorja said as she walked down the hall, wiping her hands on a towel. Her heart rate began to quicken as she thought about how the evening would proceed.

Nicholas opened the door to reveal Gabe, standing awkwardly outside the screen door with a bottle of wine in one hand and a bouquet of flowers in the other. Jorja reached over Nicholas' head to push open the screen door and Gabe moved back to get out of the way before stepping inside the house.

Handing the flowers to Jorja he said, "I thought these might look nice on your table. And this, I thought might be nice after dinner, if you and your brother both like wine."

She smiled at Gabe as she took the flowers and handed them down to Nicholas. "Here, go ask your dad if he can find us a vase."

Nicholas grabbed the flowers and ran down the hall as she took the wine from Gabe so he could remove his coat.

"Thanks for the flowers and the wine. That was nice of you."

Gabe found a hook for his coat on the coat rack. "You're welcome. I've learned never to come to dinner empty handed. Many people find it extremely rude behavior."

"Well, I wouldn't have thought any differently of you if you had come empty handed, but it's nice just the same. Come into the kitchen and say hello." She moved toward the kitchen with Gabe behind her.

Ryan looked up from the table where he and Nicholas were placing a vase with the flowers on the table. "Hi, Gabe. Hope you're hungry because we have plenty to eat."

"It smells great and yes, I'm hungry. Thanks again for the invitation." Gabe stood near the counter, seemingly waiting to be told where to sit. Jorja finally moved to the table. "Here, Gabe, you sit here. Nicholas? Do you want to sit by Gabe?"

Nicholas eyed Gabe warily before slowly nodding his head. He then climbed into his chair and waited as Jorja finished placing glasses on the table and she and Ryan finally sat down.

While they ate dinner and made small talk, Jorja did her best not to appear nervous. She let Ryan take the reins with the conversation, adding only a few words here and there, all the while thinking about how she was going to begin the conversation with Gabe that was long overdue.

Finally, when everyone was through with their meal, Jorja stood to take her plate to the sink. When Ryan stood to do the same, Nicholas jumped off his seat before making an attempt to run from the room.

"Not so fast, young man. Take your plate and your cup over to Aunt Jorja." Ryan held his own plate and waited for Nicholas to return to the table.

Nicholas stopped in mid-run and turned to face his father. He then dropped his head slightly and began to walk to the table. Jorja watched with amusement, expecting Nicholas to come up with some reason why he shouldn't have to comply, but he grabbed his plate and glass without complaint before moving around Gabe to the kitchen area. When Nicholas was standing beside her, he finally raised his head when he raised his plate and glass toward the counter.

"I've got them," she said with a smile. "You go play with your Lego's."

That's all it took. Nicholas let go of his dishes, gave her a grin and turned to run quickly out of the kitchen. She heard his feet as he ran down the hallway, up the stairs and to his bedroom with Piper right behind him.

Gabe stood up from the table and also placed his dishes on the counter. "Thanks so much for dinner. That was very nice."

"How about some coffee and a piece of pie? I realize you brought wine, but we have pumpkin pie, if you like it, and it won't take long to get the coffee going." Ryan said as Jorja placed the dishes in the dishwasher.

"Sure, that sounds great." Gabe sat on a bar stool at the counter as he watched Jorja and Ryan in the kitchen. "Is there anything I can do to help?"

Jorja shook her head. "This will only take a minute and once we get the coffee going, we can move into the living room to chat."

She finished loading the dishwasher while Ryan put on a pot of coffee and they made small talk with Gabe. As she closed the dishwasher she said, "Let's go sit down in the living room while we wait for the coffee." Jorja tried to suppress the anxiety as it began to rush over her. How was she going to bring up the subject of parentage with someone who was basically a complete stranger? She quickly wiped her hands on her jeans and realized it wasn't dish water, but sweat. She was more nervous than she had been in some time.

Ryan sat on the couch while Jorja sat at the other end and Gabe chose the recliner. She now wished she already had a cup of coffee to hold so she had something to do with her hands. She quickly ran through her head how she could start the conversation. But when she opened her mouth to speak, she quickly closed it again. She glanced at Ryan, who was patiently waiting for her to start and she could have kicked him for allowing her take the lead. He knew she wanted to take the lead anyway, but she could have kicked him just the same.

Finally, Gabe leaned forward and gave her a hard stare. He glanced at Ryan, held his stare and then narrowed his eyes before returning his gaze to Jorja. "Okay, I give. You two seem to have something you want to talk to me about. I enjoyed dinner and I enjoyed the invitation, but I'm beginning to think there's more to it than just inviting me over for a meal. Care to share what's on your mind?"

CHAPTER 39

Jorja and Ryan gave each other a sideways glance, each giving the other a chance to begin the conversation.

When neither said anything right away, Gabe asked, "Does this have to do with my uncle? Or about his case? I heard they might have another person of interest in custody and that they may have found the weapon. It looks like I might not need your help any further in that regard, but I certainly appreciate what you did do."

Jorja took a deep breath, shaking her head. "No, it doesn't have to do with the Chief...or his case. Well, in a way I guess it does because he had a part to play in all this but, well, no. It's not about him."

Gabe tilted his head in curiosity as he asked, "A part to play in what? What did he do?"

Glancing at Ryan, who only gave her a slight nod to tell her to go on, she turned back to Gabe. "It has to do with Aunt Gloria."

Gabe blinked a few times and then slowly leaned back in his chair. "Oh? What about her?"

"Well...it has to do with you and your relationship with her."

Gabe's forehead creased. "Which was a very long time ago. What about our relationship do you want to talk about?"

Clearing her throat, Jorja did her best to find the words. "I understand it was a long time ago, but something happened to my aunt that I think you should know about. I, or I mean we, feel it's very important for you to know about it."

"Okay. What's so important?"

"Uh, well…" Jorja coughed and felt her neck heat up when she thought about what Gabe's reaction might be.

Ryan reached over to grab her hand. He gave it a squeeze and nodded again in encouragement. Jorja held his gaze for a few seconds before taking another deep breath. She continued to hold Ryan's hand as the two of them turned to look at Gabe. Finally, she said, "When you left town for good, my aunt was in a very serious condition. She wasn't put in the hospital because she just lost it for no reason. She was put in the hospital because when you left, she was also pregnant and something in her snapped when she gave birth."

Gabe suddenly sat up straighter as a guilty look crossed his face. Jorja thought he would be surprised upon hearing Gloria had been pregnant, but instead he asked, "What do you mean, 'she snapped'? What happened?"

Jorja suddenly stood and began to pace. "I don't know if anyone knows, really. She was intent on doing a terrible thing. She had her mind made up and it was only my grandparents' intervention which saved my life and the life of my brother."

"What was she going to do? How do…wait. The life of you and your brother? What are you saying?"

Jorja stopped pacing. She looked down at Gabe and held his gaze. "Yes, me and my brother. We're actually Gloria's children."

Gabe stared at her. He then turned to look at Ryan. Jorja couldn't tell what he was thinking, but she knew his mind must be racing with thoughts as he pieced together what she was saying.

Gabe looked at her again. "You're saying Gloria tried to harm you and Ryan after you were born?"

Jorja nodded.

Gabe leaned back in his chair again. His face looked crushed at the thought of Gloria committing such an act.

"And she was sent away to the hospital after that? Was it ever determined why she would do something like that?"

Ryan piped in when she couldn't find the words. "We don't believe anyone ever discovered what really happened or why she did it. From what Jorja's parents have told her...this would be her aunt and uncle who actually raised her, Gloria might not have known she was pregnant until after you left and then she had difficulty dealing with you being gone and also being pregnant."

Gabe grimaced as he looked down at his fingers, which were laced together in a tight grip. He looked up, seemingly intent on saying something, but instead he clamped his mouth shut as he swallowed hard. Jorja stared at him curiously as she watched his reactions. When she was about to chime in with a question, a thought struck Gabe as he turned to Ryan and asked, "What do you mean, raised 'her'?" Who raised you?"

"I was raised by someone else. Jorja and I only recently met each other for the first time." Ryan glanced at Jorja. "But that's a story we can save for another day."

Gabe frowned. "Well, this is all very overwhelming." Running a hand over his face, he said, "Are you actually telling me that you believe I'm your biological father?"

Jorja and Ryan looked at each other before turning to him and nodding at the same time.

Jorja frowned when she heard Gabe whisper to himself, "My God. All this time. They've been here all this time and I never knew."

She glanced at Ryan, who returned her frown with one of his own. The two of them waited until Gabe looked up at them again. When he finally did, his eyes were rimmed with tears.

"I'm so sorry. I'm sorry for what Gloria did, or attempted to do. I'm sorry I wasn't there for you. I can only hope that the two of you grew up in happy homes with parents who loved you."

Jorja and Ryan both nodded as they listened to him. Jorja said, "We were both brought up by people who loved us. We're fortunate in that regard." She paused for a moment as she eyed him curiously. "I have to say, I'm curious about something."

Gabe returned her stare as he shifted uncomfortably in his chair. "Oh? About what?"

"Well, you already knew Gloria was hospitalized because Cooper told you years ago." She saw Ryan give her a sideways glance and realized she'd forgotten to tell him that little tidbit. She ignored his look and continued, "We told you Gloria was hospitalized after her attempt to harm us was discovered and you do appear genuinely distressed by that fact. You're obviously shocked to hear you're very likely our biological father. However, I don't get the impression at all that you're in the least bit shocked that Gloria was pregnant when you left town." Jorja glanced quickly at Ryan before she looked at Gabe again and asked, "Did you know?"

She and Ryan both held their breath as they waited for Gabe to respond. Gabe looked at both of them, his face riddled with guilt. He closed his eyes, sighed very heavily and then opened his eyes as he slowly nodded his head.

Jorja and Ryan remained silent; waiting. Finally, Gabe spoke. "I haven't told anyone this before and I don't know how you'll feel once I tell you, but I guess I should set the record straight."

Taking a deep breath, he continued, "You'll think very poorly of me, I imagine, but just remember that I was a young man at the time and I was scared out of my wits about what was in store for me and my future."

Gabe paused, but neither Jorja nor Ryan said a word for fear of discouraging him. He finally continued, "I graduated from high school, turned eighteen that summer and had plans to attend college to gain a degree in criminal justice before joining the police academy. My aunt and uncle gave me a car as a gift for graduation, for my birthday and because I'd be moving to attend college and needed a reliable vehicle. But then something unexpected happened. I had plans to leave for college in September, but those plans changed drastically when Gloria told me she had something to tell me."

Gabe leaned forward in his chair. "She told me she was pregnant."

Jorja sucked in a quick breath and Ryan shook his head, his eyes full of disappointment.

"Now, wait," Gabe pleaded. "Let me tell you what happened. She told me she was pregnant. I'll admit, I was petrified at the thought of being a father, but I was even more petrified at the thought of having to tell my uncle. This meant his plans for me would change and I knew he'd be upset because he had already warned me about letting a relationship come between me and my future as a cop. Not that I still couldn't become a cop, but I couldn't afford to go to school when I'd have to take care of Gloria and a baby. I knew damn well my uncle wouldn't help me out in that regard so I figured school would have to be put on hold. I told Gloria I would figure out what to do, but I asked her to keep our secret until after I'd been able to speak to my aunt and uncle."

Gabe leaned back in his chair, sighing heavily. "You can't imagine how scared I was about telling my uncle."

Jorja glanced at Ryan with a slight smirk. She could guess how scared Gabe might have been of the Chief , who she could imagine might have been just as prickly in his younger years.

When she turned to look at Gabe again, he said, "So instead of telling my uncle, I decided to tell my aunt first. I figured she could help me break the news to him. Actually, I was hoping she'd tell him so I wouldn't have to. It was a beautiful day and I asked her if she'd like to go for a drive in my car to a nearby park where we could walk around the lake. I thought it would be better not to break the news to her at the house and it's a decision I've regretted for the rest of my life."

Gabe's voice broke and he leaned forward to rest his head in his hands. Jorja and Ryan remained silent, waiting for him to go on. Jorja wasn't sure how she felt about his story, but she wanted to hear what he said before passing judgment on him.

When Gabe raised his head, his eyes were red and glistening with unshed tears. "My aunt agreed to go for a drive to the park and during the drive, I told her I had something really important to speak to her about. I know now I should never have taken that drive when I was under the stress of having to break that kind of news to her. I was nervous. So nervous I drove much faster than I should have in my attempt to get to the park where we could talk. As I rounded a sharp corner, I came upon a doe and her two fawns in the road and I instinctively tried to avoid hitting them when they remained standing in the middle of the road. I hit the brakes, skidded, lost control and…well, Jorja, you know the rest."

Gabe stopped talking as Ryan gave Jorja a questioning look. She faced Ryan. "The car hit a tree and his aunt was instantly killed. The Chief showed up shortly after the accident and discovered what happened to his wife." She turned to Gabe. "But what happened when you spoke to the Chief after the fact? You told me he threatened to have you arrested for vehicular homicide and he told you to leave. Didn't you tell him about Gloria?"

Biting his lip, Gabe didn't immediately respond. He finally said, "I planned to tell him. Really, I did. But when he told me I could go to prison for vehicular assault since I was an adult, he made an offhanded comment that only scared me even further."

Jorja's brows creased with confusion. "What kind of comment? What could he have said to prevent you from telling him you were going to be a father?"

Gabe swallowed hard, his Adam's apple bouncing up and down in the effort. "Not only did he tell me he could have me arrested for vehicular homicide, he made an offhand remark about the fact that he was glad I hadn't been stupid enough to get anyone pregnant. He told me to leave and go make my life elsewhere because he never wanted to see me again. I knew I should tell him about Gloria, but I was petrified. I couldn't get the words out, especially when he told me I had to leave or I'd be arrested. How was I going to take care of Gloria when he was telling me I'd be arrested unless I left town? I couldn't take Gloria with me, that much I knew. I'll be honest, I didn't think very clearly, but I decided to leave as my uncle ordered and my plan was to find a place, get a job and come back for Gloria."

"Well, your plan obviously didn't work out. What happened?" Jorja asked.

Gabe shook his head. "No, my plan most definitely did not work out. I left town, the state, actually, and found a place in Arizona. It was too expensive to live on my own and the job I found hardly paid the rent, much less anything else. I sold my car to get money and I did what I could to make the place ready when I could ask Gloria to join me."

"But you never told her why you left and where you went?"

With a heavy sigh, Gabe said, "I didn't tell her and I regret that to this day. My young, immature and experienced way of thinking had me believing I could easily find a place to live and a job that could support both of us. I thought I'd be gone no more than a few weeks, but before I knew it, months had passed by. When I finally tried to reach out to Gloria, I knew I couldn't just call her parents so I called my friend, Jim Cooper, instead."

Ryan's head jerked up and he turned to give Jorja a stunned look. She frowned as she nodded slightly and shrugged in acknowledgment.

Gabe quietly but curiously watched the exchange. When both turned to him again, he continued, "Coop told me Gloria was gone. He didn't know where she was except that she was staying with family or friends someplace else. I had decided to join the Air Force and a few months later I called Coop again just before I left for Japan where I remained stationed for a few years. At that time he told me she'd been admitted to a mental institution and he didn't know why. He said he didn't even know what hospital she was in but that it appeared she'd be gone for awhile. I knew I had let Gloria down. I assumed the baby had been born and possibly adopted out, which I thought was for the best." He grimaced. "I'm sorry, but that's how I felt at the time."

"So you never had contact with Gloria after that?"

"Well, no. I didn't know where she was and I couldn't bring myself to ask her parents what had happened. Coop told me he'd let me know if he found out anything, but after moving to Japan, I lost touch with him. When I moved back to the States I never planned to even step foot in Washington State, but when I retired from the Air Force, I began teaching and eventually, decided to go against my uncle's wishes to move back here after I learned about the job opening. My plan had been to somehow mend my relationship with him. I certainly didn't expect to receive news that I left behind a son and daughter when I left Gloria." Gabe frowned. "I let Gloria down and I let the two of you down. You have no idea how much I regret what I've done."

Jorja wasn't sure what to say, so she remained silent.

Ryan glanced at her before he looked at Gabe. "I don't plan to judge you based on what you did as a teenager. I don't agree with the way you dealt with your responsibilities, but I guess I can understand the fear your uncle put you in if you actually thought you had to leave to avoid being arrested." Ryan turned to Jorja and he held her gaze. "Jorja and I only recently found each other," he said. "And we've had to move on with the knowledge that both our mother and even the father who raised me committed acts which greatly affected others."

He turned back to Gabe. "But we can't live in the past. If you're willing, I'd like to get to know you, not as a father, but as a friend."

Gabe listened to Ryan, but did not immediately respond. Instead, he looked at Jorja and waited to see what she had to say. She returned his gaze, but said nothing. Conflicting emotions were churning inside her. She knew Ryan was right...they couldn't live in the past, but after having to accept the fact that her biological mother was intent on taking their lives, she had actually looked forward to finding her biological father who she believed would be thrilled to learn of their existence. Instead, she discovered he knew about the pregnancy and left anyway. Regardless of the circumstances, he left Gloria in the most vulnerable state with no one else to turn to. Jorja shook her head in an attempt to release the negative thoughts bombarding her mind.

She focused her eyes on Gabe, who was watching her intently. He appeared to be holding his breath as he waited for her to say something. She turned to look at Ryan, who gave her a reassuring smile as he gave her a slight nod. She knew he knew what she was thinking. Her thoughts were most likely similar to his, but he was quicker to move past them than she was. Still...she knew he was right. She couldn't move forward if she kept a critical attitude toward Gabe for actions he committed as a young man.

Jorja took a breath as she rubbed her forehead and temples to massage away an oncoming headache. Finally, she said, "Ryan's right. We can't live in the past so I hope we can spend some time together to get to know each other as friends."

Gabe smiled, relief evident on his face. "Thank you. I would like that very much."

Jorja sneaked a peak at Ryan. He gave her an awkward grin, understanding her longing to finally close all the loopholes in their family tree.

She turned back when Gabe asked, "What happened with you two once Gloria was placed in the hospital? Were you treated well by the parents who raised you?"

She nodded. So did Ryan. Jorja said, "I was raised by Gloria's sister and brother-in-law, who I have always known as my parents. Ryan was raised by a doctor. We both had good relationships with our parents and were raised in loving homes."

"They probably gave you better homes than I ever could at that age. But still, I can't imagine what Gloria must have been thinking. She must have thought I abandoned her! And she lived the rest of her life believing that about me. I wish I could take it all back."

Gloria believed it because you did abandon her. Jorja tried to push aside the negative thought.

"But you can't. I've tried to get past the thought of what could have happened or what should have happened, but we can only deal with what did happen. I'm glad you decided to move here and that Ryan and I can get to know you. I'm sure if Gloria were looking down on us, she'd feel content with the belief that she finally brought us together." As she finished speaking, she thought she was going to choke up. She stood suddenly and moved to the kitchen. "I think the coffee is way past ready now."

In the kitchen Jorja grabbed coffee mugs out of the cupboard with one hand while she used her other hand to wipe at a few stray tears. She hadn't known what to expect, but her pent up emotions were beginning to weigh her down. She was thankful for the fact that her future wouldn't hold any more mystery parents she'd have to identify or get to know.

"Jorja? Are you okay?" Ryan said as he rounded the corner into the dining area off the kitchen.

She glanced at him as she poured coffee into the mugs. In frustration, she used her hand to wipe at a few more tears she felt sliding down her cheeks.

Ryan walked up beside her and put his arm around her. "Hey, it's okay. He'll understand if you shed a few tears."

"I know. But I don't know him well enough to cry in front of him. Just help me get the pie so I can compose myself." She placed the mugs on a tray along with spoons and creamer she removed from the fridge.

Ryan took the pie out of the fridge and cut a few pieces before placing them on small plates Jorja had stacked on the counter. He placed the plates on the tray and then picked up the tray.

"Come on. Let's go start a new conversation with Gabe over pie and coffee so we can get to know each other." Ryan gave her a wink and moved to the living room. Jorja patted her cheeks to make sure they were dry, she took one more deep breath and then she followed her brother into the other room to start a relationship that was long overdue.

CHAPTER 40

Jorja finished updating the bookstore blog just before Kat came bouncing up the stairs to say hello.

"Hi, Jorja." Kat quickly sat down on one of the extra chairs across from the desk and looked instantly comfortable in her black leggings and a red shirt sporting the Tenino High School logo in support of the basketball team.

"Hi. Is that a new school shirt you're wearing? I don't remember seeing it before."

Kat looked down at the shirt. "Yeah, the booster club is selling them to make extra money for the team. They're using some of the money to help pay for what they bought for senior night tonight." Kat leaned forward in her chair. "I'm sorry to ask at the last minute, but I didn't realize I was scheduled to work the same night as senior night. Would it be okay if I left early so I don't miss it? Bruce will be one of the seniors receiving his senior gift plus an award and I told him I'd try to make it."

Jorja smiled. "Of course you should be there. I'll talk to Taylor and we'll make it work."

Kat sprang out of the chair. "Thanks! I'll go down to see what Taylor wants me to do while I'm here." Kat turned to head down the stairs when a thought struck her and she turned back to look at Jorja. "Sorry, I guess I could ask you the same. Do you need anything?"

Jorja shook her head. "No, I'm fine. I'm coming down in a few anyway."

"Okay, see you downstairs."

After Kat left the office, Jorja gathered some paperwork, placed it in a folder and straightened up the piles on her desk just enough to make it look like she was organized. She'd already made the decision to take a break between projects so she stood up, stretched her arms over her head and leaned first to the right and then to the left to stretch her back. Feeling a little better as she straightened her back and lowered her arms, she finally went downstairs to find Taylor.

She immediately spotted Kat at the cash register helping a customer, but Taylor was not in sight. She wandered around the store before she finally found Taylor straightening books in the children's section.

When Taylor saw Jorja walking toward her, she smiled and stood from her crouched position. "Hey, how's the blog post going?"

"Okay," Jorja said. "I published the post and updated our calendar. We have a few more people who have signed up to receive our e-mails and there are a few things to do before the book club meeting next week, but I think we've narrowed down the book we'll be reading next month. I'd like to try to get some more book club members, even if they can only participate on-line, so I hope our blog gains some more interest."

"Don't worry, we'll get more interest. We just have to be patient. That reminds me, I was going to ask you what you thought if some of my posts were about the wedding preparations. I know it's not about books or reading, but I can share my experiences and maybe give others some advice based on what I've learned. What do you think?"

Jorja grinned at Taylor. "I think it's a great idea. You know what you could do? Since you'll be referring to some of the books we have here, you can talk about the books you like and use and maybe it'll generate some additional sales. I'm sure many who read our blog would also love to read about your wedding preparations. It'll make us and the store more personal to them."

Taylor's eyes lit up. "I'm glad you like the idea. I was thinking it would also be a great way to help promote some of the local businesses. I'll use Courtney's Courtyard for the flowers, Dylan will be making our cake so I'd love to showcase his baking talents and if everything goes well and we're able to hold the wedding at the local ranch for a country barn wedding, I'm sure they'd enjoy a nice write up too."

Taylor paused to take a breath and Jorja grinned. She doubted she could deter Taylor from her line of thinking…it was obvious she had already expected to take on this task and probably wouldn't take no for an answer even if Jorja bothered to try.

"I think it's a great idea, Taylor. I bet people will love to read about your wedding and you're right, the local businesses will enjoy the promotion. So we'll still stick with two posts a week, right? I do Fridays and you get Tuesdays? Does that still work for you?"

Taylor nodded. "Yeah, that way I can come up with ideas over the weekend before I type up a draft on Monday. I promise I won't make all my posts about the wedding. I'll try to mix it up with other topics."

"Don't worry, I won't hold it against you if you don't." Jorja knew it might be difficult for Taylor to focus on anything *but* the wedding the closer they got to the date. "Before I start my next project, I wanted to run something by you."

Taylor raised a brow. "Oh?"

"Well…when I met with Bailey in the jail that first time, I had a conversation with her that was completely unexpected." Jorja paused and Taylor now raised both brows in question. Jorja continued, "I told her I'd help her and when she said she couldn't pay me, I told her she didn't have to. That she could pay me back by working here."

Taylor frowned slightly. "You promised her a job?"

Nodding, Jorja said, "I did. I really didn't think about it beforehand. It just slipped out. I'm really hoping it all works out so she's not taken back to Colorado if we can prove she's not responsible for the attack on the Chief . I just thought she'd do well working here. Just part time since I hope she'll still have a job at the grocery store. I don't plan to tell her she owes me very much for what I've done, but I'll let her work here to pay that off and then, if you're okay with it, I'd like to actually offer her a paid job."

Jorja stopped just long enough to see Taylor still had some doubt. "We have to think ahead, Taylor. If Kat goes to college, she won't be here to help us. We'll need someone to replace her and this will give us time to train Bailey and see if she's going to work out."

Jorja knew she struck a nerve as she watched Taylor's face before her friend finally said, "I guess you have a good point. I just want to know we're hiring someone we can trust and I won't feel I can trust her unless I truly believe she didn't do what she's been accused of."

Spying a few more orphaned books on a nearby shelf, Taylor's attention was suddenly drawn to them and she reached over to pick them up. She then carefully placed them between other books on the shelves where they belonged. Once she was pleased the books were in order, Taylor turned to Jorja again. "I'm sorry. I understand where you're coming from and I know you only want to help Bailey. I'll try to keep an open mind. You know I trust you and I know if you believe Bailey's innocent, then it's probably true. I just wish we knew already because if she didn't do it, then the jerk who did is still out there."

Jorja nodded in agreement as she thought about Bailey's husband and the fact that he may have assaulted the Chief and was still on the loose. The trick was figuring out how to draw him out so that she could prove it.

CHAPTER 41

"Hello, Michael, how are you?" Jorja said as she greeted him in the lobby of the bookstore.

"I'm doing okay." Michael quickly glanced around at Taylor and the few patrons sitting at nearby tables. "Do you mind if we go upstairs to talk in private?"

Jorja nodded as she gave Taylor eye contact and a quick nod of the head to indicate she was going upstairs. "Sure, follow me."

Once in the office, Jorja sat at her desk while Michael remained standing as he paced in front of the desk.

"So what did you want to talk about? Has something happened with the case?"

Michael stopped pacing and he stared at her without speaking. Jorja waited as she watched him. When she was certain she'd have to break eye contact with him to avoid dry eyes, he finally gave her a curt nod before he fell into one of the guest chairs.

"You could say something has changed. I've decided to take a plea bargain."

Jorja's eyes widened in surprise. "For killing your wife? I thought you said you didn't do it."

Grimacing, Michael fidgeted in his seat. He averted eye contact with her as he scanned the room. He finally looked at her. "I didn't."

"So why take a plea for something you didn't do?"

He sighed heavily. "The prosecutor charged me with Second Degree Murder, but they'll amend the charge to include first degree as an alternative charge if I take it to trial. The evidence is a bit overwhelming and my attorney said it's possible a jury might convict me of Murder in the First Degree if they believe I planned it like the cops said I did. Even if they decide it wasn't premeditated, but still believe I did it, they could convict me of Murder in the Second. Either way, worst case would be twenty-five years and best case might be around fifteen years. I've decided not to take that risk with the new offer the prosecutor gave me."

She leaned forward, resting her elbows on the desk. "What new offer?"

"The prosecutor has agreed to let me plead to a Manslaughter charge. I might serve about five years. Believe me, this is no easy decision to make, but I don't want to risk going to trial and losing to a murder charge. I can't spend twenty years in prison."

Jorja shook her head as she thought about what Michael just told her. She replayed in her mind the conversation she heard between him and Gail. Would he really plead to a murder he didn't commit to avoid others learning the information Gail was holding over him?

"So is this a done deal then? You've already set it up between your attorney and the prosecutor?"

Michael shrugged slightly and replied, "Well, I told my attorney I'd take it and now he'll talk to the prosecutor so they can agree on a date when I can change my plea. We'll set the sentencing out a bit so I can get my affairs in order and make arrangements for Tabitha. I've already had a long talk with Gail and she will have guardianship over Tabitha while I'm gone. We're going to tell Tabitha that I had to move away to another country on business and Gail is going to home school her for awhile to keep her away from prying eyes and loud mouths."

Jorja frowned. She hesitated before asking the question burning within her, but finally gave in and asked, "You're going to risk your daughter learning you've gone to prison for killing her mother. Doesn't that worry you?"

"Hell yeah, it worries me. I don't want her to believe I did something like that. But if I go to prison for fifteen or twenty years, I'll never have a relationship with her. At least if there's a chance I'll be gone only a handful of years, there might be some hope that she'll still be young enough to form some sort of relationship with me."

Michael suddenly stood up. "Well, I need to go. I have a lot to do. Thanks for all your help, Jorja. I know this isn't the end result you were expecting, but I just can't risk going to trial. I hope you can understand."

She gave a quick wave of dismissal with her hand. "No, don't worry about it. This is your decision to make and I'm not about to tell you otherwise. If anything changes or you need anything else, let me know, okay?"

Giving her a half smile that barely touched his eyes, Michael curtly nodded. "Thanks, I'll do that. Take care of yourself."

Michael then turned and left the loft. Jorja listened as he moved down the staircase at a quick pace and it wasn't long before she heard the bell chime when the door opened and closed. Staring at the sand castle figurine she'd bought as a souvenir from Long Beach a few years before, she felt a sudden surge of sadness at what the conversation with Michael actually meant. She knew if the bits and pieces of what she heard between Gail and Michael were true, then he was taking the path to prison he knew wouldn't shed a more vile light on his character. Murder was horrific, yes. But what could be worse than murder? There was only one act even other prisoners agreed was the worst crime of all and she believed he hoped to avoid such a stigma if he were going to prison either way.

Sighing heavily, Jorja leaned back in her chair. Her eyes threatened to tear up when she thought about what life must have been like for Liz before she died. She'd been a young girl living with a father who took advantage of her in the worst possible way and a mother who couldn't put a stop to it. It was a heartbreaking way for a child to live. Even more so when the choices Liz made to gain some control of her life actually cost her life instead.

CHAPTER 42

"Well, I'm done working on Michael's case." Jorja said to Taylor, who was working the espresso stand.

Taylor looked up from the batch of cookies she was trying to arrange into a more inviting pile. "Why? Did he fire you?"

"No, he didn't fire me." Jorja sat on a stool and picked out a snicker doodle to nibble on, leaving the pile uneven. She opened the plastic around the cookie and broke off a piece before putting it into her mouth. "Mm, this is tasty. Can you make me a latte to go with the cookie?"

"Sure. Cinnamon spice?" Jorja nodded and Taylor continued, "So, spill the beans already. Why aren't you working for him anymore?"

Jorja watched as Taylor expertly worked with the espresso machine. She placed the cookie on a napkin to save it until she had the latte in her hand. Jorja had to speak over the noise of the machine. "He's going to take a plea bargain."

The machine came to an abrupt halt as Taylor's head jerked up. "What? He said he did it?" Taylor then quickly refocused on what she was doing so she could finish making the latte.

Jorja waited until Taylor finished the drink. As she reached across the counter to take the cup she shook her head. "Not exactly. He's not saying he did it. Just that he's worried a jury could convict him if he goes to trial because some of the evidence might be overwhelming when the prosecutor tries to prove premeditation."

Jorja had a hard time with the knowledge she had about Liz. She knew she could tell Taylor anything, but did she really want to share this type of information with her? She thought it better not to.

Taylor moved around the counter to sit on another stool. "Wow. So he's actually going to go to prison? For a crime he says he didn't commit? Do you think he actually did it?"

Sipping her latte thoughtfully as she broke off another piece of cookie, Jorja took her time responding as she swallowed her drink before eating the small bite of cookie.

When she looked up to see Taylor watching her with narrowed eyes, she knew she had to deflect her friend's curiosity. She knew Taylor would quickly determine if she was hiding anything and then do whatever was necessary to obtain that information.

"No, I don't think he did it. He's just concerned with how a jury will look at the case and he knows if they think he did it, that's all that will matter. Based on some of the evidence, it might be possible the State could put together a case a jury would fall for...hook, line and sinker. He's just decided not to take that chance."

Taylor eyed her skeptically as Jorja attempted to keep her face immobile and free from guilt at keeping secrets. When Taylor finally pulled her gaze away when the doorbell chimed, Jorja did her best to reduce the amount of air she expelled as she let out a sigh of relief.

"Hey, girls, how's the day going?" Brad said as he casually entered the lobby.

Taylor and Jorja both said hello as Brad leaned up against the counter. Jorja could tell by looking at him that he'd just finished his weight lifting class and she was impressed with the fact that he'd been able to stay fit. She figured he felt the need to give the athletes a good example and she knew it was exactly why he was such a good teacher and coach.

"So what are you up to? You're not into buying a new book, are you?" Jorja asked.

"Oh, just taking a walk after class. It gets hot in that weight room with all the boys and I have to get some fresh air afterwards. I would have been here sooner, but I ran into a fella on the way here who needed some help. He looked familiar but I couldn't place him and when I saw the plates on his car, I figured I must be wrong to think I'd seen him before. He had out-of-state plates. He also had a flat tire."

Jorja tried to hide her concern. "Oh?"

"Yeah. Anyway, seemed like an odd sort to be hanging out here. He wasn't too forthcoming with who he was or why he was here. Have you two seen any strange out-of-towners lately?"

Taylor and Jorja both glanced at each other, unsure how to answer. Jorja realized she had completely forgotten to call Fritz and Reynolds to tell them about the man skulking around her neighborhood last night when she was taking a walk with Nicholas and Piper. The evening with Gabe went long while she and Ryan spent time trying to catch up with him. She wondered if Ryan remembered to call them himself and made a mental note to call him soon to check in with him.

When the doorbell chimed again, all three turned to watch as Chief Douglas entered the store. He let the door shut behind him while he quickly scanned the area before resting his eyes on Jorja. She felt a tingle as the truth about their relationship struck her. She wondered when Gabe would actually be able to tell him.

The Chief held her gaze as he moved toward her. Jorja watched as he briskly took a few long strides before stopping a few feet away from her. His gray eyes were even more piercing than usual. "Jorja, I need to speak with you."

She raised a brow in question as she nervously glanced at Taylor and Brad. Both returned her look with curious stares.

"Uh, okay. In private? We can go back to the break room if you want."

Jorja slid off the stool, grabbed her latte and the rest of her cookie and walked to the break room with the Chief only steps behind her.

When she entered the small room, she leaned against the counter rather than sit at the table. She wanted to feel like she was in control and when he stood over her as he spoke, which he might likely do, she felt anything but in control.

He surprised her by sitting down in the first chair he came to as he asked, "Do you have any water?"

She suddenly realized he looked tired and she felt a stirring of sympathy. She realized his stern expression was probably just an act to cover the pain he must be feeling as he recovered while he tried to work.

She left her latte and cookie on the counter before getting a bottle of water out of the fridge. When she handed him the bottle, he immediately opened it to take a drink. After a few gulps, he sat the bottle on the table and looked up at her. He then waved a hand across the table. "Sit. I need to talk to you."

Her heart began to flutter. She did as he instructed and moved to sit in a chair, completely forgetting her latte and cookie.

She remained silent as she stared at him, waiting. She wiped her hands on her jeans and realized they were sweaty.

Finally, in a gruff tone he said, "I had a plan all mapped out. I'd call the chief in Colorado and tell them that Bailey was completely refusing to tell me where she hid the video tape. I'd let it slip that she had apparently left it in the possession of her newfound friend...a local book store owner."

She remained quiet as he spoke; nodding her head while trying to hide her confusion.

"I knew the chief would either get word to Bailey's husband or, if the chief in Colorado wasn't the leak, then another officer at the station would get word to the husband who would likely come looking for you. Once he made an attempt to get that video from you, we'd be prepared. You'd be the bait, but we'd be ready and we'd get him before he could cause you any harm."

She continued to nod.

"But, that whole idea went to hell as of last night."

She stopped nodding.

"Why?"

He narrowed his eyes as he stared at her. As his attention remained focused on her, she began to fidget in her seat under his scrutiny.

He finally gave her a break when he leaned back to take another drink from his water bottle.

"Why? Because I had a visit from Gabe late last night after he apparently left your house. The boy woke me out of a deep sleep and wouldn't leave the house until I heard what he had to say. He told me a story I still find hard to believe. He told me he actually got your aunt pregnant before he left town. He told me your aunt is really your biological mother. He told me he's your father and I'm your great uncle. It was quite a lot to take in during the middle of the night." He lifted his hand to rub his head. "If I didn't know any better I'd say this crack on my head is giving me hallucinations."

Jorja was stunned. This wasn't how she imagined her first conversation with him would be once he learned the truth, but then, she really wasn't sure what she had expected.

"He told you last night? So…are the two of you on speaking terms now?" She wasn't sure how much she could ask him about his relationship with Gabe, but she figured she would try.

"You could call it that, I guess. He spoke. I listened. I'm still trying to take in the news he decided to hoist on me in the middle of the night. But that's not why I stopped by."

Her eyes narrowed in question. What else could there be?

"I stopped by because I needed to speak to you about Bailey's husband. Last night before I left the station I *did* call the chief over in Colorado. I *did* tell him that Bailey wouldn't tell me where the tape was and that it *was* most likely in your possession. The cat, as they say, is out of the bag. That man will attempt to find that tape, one way or another."

Leaning back in her chair, Jorja gave a nervous chuckle. "Well, that's good then, right? What's wrong with your idea? You said it went to hell last night? Why?"

He gave her a stern look as he shook his head. She felt he was giving her his disapproval for not understanding what he was trying to say. Rather than put any words in his mouth, she waited.

Finally, he gruffly said, "Why do you think? Before, you weren't my great niece. Before, I wasn't leading a dangerous man to the home of my great niece and nephew and that of my great, great nephew. Before, I didn't have a personal stake in the case. Now, I do."

She felt a few extra flutters from her chest when her heart rate quickened. "Oh," was all she could say.

He seemed embarrassed at expressing so much. His cheeks reddened and his lips remained pursed. She thought he was trying to force his mouth to remain shut, rather than risk exposing himself any further.

When he suddenly stood up, Jorja was startled at first, but then quickly stood to follow him when he left the room and quickly moved down the hall.

She had to move fast to keep up with his gait. "Wait, you don't have to change anything. Let's just go with your idea. I think Bailey's husband has already scoped out my house anyway because I'm sure I saw him last night."

Bam!

Jorja slammed into the Chief's chest when he suddenly stopped and turned to face her. She quickly moved away to look at him, only to cringe slightly at the heat from his glare. "*What* did you say? Are you saying he was near your place last night? When?"

"Ah, well, shortly before Gabe arrived for dinner. Nicholas and I took Piper for a walk and he was in a car parked on one of the nearby streets."

"When did you plan to tell me about this? Or Fritz? Or Reynolds? Are you trying to put yourself in danger by keeping that sort of information from us?"

Backing away from him and his anger she replied, "Well, no, I'm not trying to put myself in danger. It's just that Gabe stayed late and then Ryan and I stayed up talking after that and this morning I had a meeting and I just completely forgot about telling you about the man I saw in the car."

The Chief turned from her to walk to the lobby. "You can't forget something like that, Jorja. I need to talk to the boys. If he's already seen where you live, it's not going to be long before he comes back again." He quickly turned back to face her again, pointing his finger at her. "You stay here. Don't go anywhere and don't go home until one of us returns to let you know what we're going to do about this. Is that understood?"

Jorja's instinct was to immediately refuse to be told what to do by someone who was pointing their finger at her, but she quickly decided she had no other choice. She may have had her own stubborn streak, but she knew the Chief's stubbornness would prevail and he would not take no for an answer.

CHAPTER 43

After the Chief left the bookstore, both Taylor and Brad turned to look at Jorja with curious looks on their faces. Taylor finally asked, "What the heck was that all about? What did you do to irritate him this time?"

Jorja gave Taylor a sheepish look while she considered how to answer. Brad wasn't privy to her newfound family and she wasn't sure she wanted to share the news with anyone else yet.

Finally, she said, "He's upset because I didn't tell him about the guy I saw hanging out in my neighborhood while Nicholas and I were on our walk. I told him I thought it was Bailey's husband and he pretty much flipped out, especially since he set something in motion that might have made the guy come looking for me."

Taylor looked stunned. "Why would he do that without telling you to prepare you?"

Jorja glanced quickly at Brad before she returned her gaze to Taylor. "I don't think he thought Bailey's husband would react so quickly."

Brad's posture had changed from relaxed to alert while he listened to their conversation. "What's going on here, Jorja? Who is Bailey's husband and why would he be looking for you? Are you in some sort of trouble?"

"Not really."

Brad gave her a hard stare as he waited for more. Jorja finally relented with a heavy sigh. "Okay, maybe a little, but just because this guy believes I have possession of something he wants."

"And the Chief's plan is what? To use you as bait? What the hell is he thinking?" Brad began to pace in front of the coffee stand. "He can't do that. What if something happens?"

Jorja reached out to touch his arm in an attempt to calm him down. Brad stopped pacing at her touch and his brows furrowed as he listened to her. "Don't worry. The Chief did set something in motion, but nothing has happened and nothing will happen. He's going to speak to Fritz and Reynolds and he'll be back to let me know what he wants me to do. If Bailey's husband makes any sort of move, they'll be there to help me."

When she finished, he shook his head in frustration. "I *don't* like it. What if he doesn't make his move today, or tomorrow, or the next day? Are they going to watch you twenty-four seven? Does Ryan know about this?"

"Well, he knows I saw the guy while I was out on my walk. He doesn't know yet about the rest. I guess I should call him now to let him know what the Chief told me."

When Jorja turned to the register to use the phone, Taylor suddenly exclaimed, "Wait! Brad, you said you helped a guy with a flat tire on your way here? Someone from out of town?" She glanced at Jorja before asking, "What did he look like?"

Brad raised a hand to slap his forehead. "I *knew* there was something off about that guy!"

Jorja realized now where Taylor was going with her question. "What did he look like? What kind of car was he driving?"

"The car was just a mid-size, dark-colored sedan. He was wearing boots and jeans, but I don't know what type of shirt because he was wearing a rain coat. He was wearing a brimmed hat and from what I could see, he had dark hair."

Jorja looked at Taylor and couldn't hide the fear in her eyes. Taylor's stare only mirrored her own.

"Is that the guy? Is that who I helped this morning? Someone who might try to hurt you?"

Jorja nodded reluctantly. "I think so."

Brad made a fist and struck the palm of his other hand. *"Damn!"*

"It's okay, you didn't know. I guess I'm glad you did walk over, otherwise I wouldn't know he's probably waiting for me to leave the store."

"So he's probably the one who broke into your office, right? I'm going to call the Chief to let him know I saw the guy." Brad moved with purpose toward the phone and quickly dialed the police department.

While Brad spoke on the phone with Betsy about what he wanted her to pass on to the Chief, Jorja moved closer to Taylor to whisper, "The Chief actually came to talk to me about something else."

Taylor moved even closer to whisper, "What?"

"I guess Gabe stopped by to see him after he left the house last night and told him that he's my great uncle."

"Oh, wow. How is he taking it?"

"I don't know how he's taking it, but he pretty much admitted this new information gave him a different take on setting the scene with me and Bailey's husband."

Taylor frowned. "What, if he didn't know you were his niece he wouldn't mind serving you up to some psycho?"

"Well, no, that's not it. He just seems to feel more protective or something. I don't know...I doubt I'll ever figure the man out."

They both jumped when Brad slammed the phone onto the cradle. "Okay, I've told Betsy and she'll pass on the message to the Chief . Now I'm going to call the school and have someone cover the rest of my day for me."

"Why?"

Brad's voice was firm as he replied, "What do you mean, why? I'm staying here, that's why. Until Ryan, Fritz, Reynolds or the Chief takes over, I'm staying put. You can't kick me out, Jorja. Don't even try."

Taylor grinned. "Brad to the rescue."

Jorja shot her a frustrated look. Brad didn't give Jorja time to respond as he picked up the phone again to call the school. She watched with some irritation bubbling to the surface, but she knew she wouldn't be able to change Brad's mind. Shrugging to herself, she decided to make the best of it.

When Brad hung up the phone again, Jorja said, "Since you're going to hang out for awhile, do you mind doing some heavy lifting?"

Brad grinned, flexing his arms. "For you, I'll lift whatever you need. Just point the way."

Taylor giggled behind her as Jorja could only return Brad's grin with one of her own. She could tell this was going to be a very long day.

~ ~ ~

Ryan, Brad, Taylor and Jorja were sitting in the lobby of the bookstore making small talk while they waited for Fritz and Reynolds to arrive. The Chief had called shortly beforehand to say they were on the way.

Jorja began to feel nervous about the upcoming evening. As brave as she wanted to be, she did not wish to venture into another confrontation with a man who was up to no good. Officer Cooper still gave her nightmares and while she did her best to keep those nightmares a secret from everyone, she knew eventually the wear and tear of sleepless nights would be difficult to hide from them.

Jorja realized Ryan was speaking to her and she shook her head to clear the fog of thoughts taking over her. "What?"

Ryan gave her a concerned look. "Are you okay?"

"Oh, yeah. Just thinking."

She could tell Ryan didn't buy her answer, but he wasn't going to question her in front of the others. While she had told him about the nightmares she'd been having before, and she felt guilty when he told her he'd had his own nightmares for a time after being shot, she hadn't been honest with him about the fact that the nightmares were still ongoing.

"What do you think about what Brad offered?"

Jorja's quizzical look let the others know she had no clue what Brad had offered. She looked at Brad. "I'm sorry, what did you offer?"

"Well, I think it would be good if I stay at the house. We'll have safety in numbers and I'd rather be with you guys than at home worrying about you."

Jorja began to shake her head with every intention of telling him he didn't have to stay at the house. Before she could form the words, Ryan said, "It's a good idea, Jorja. You and Taylor can stay in the third floor bedroom with Nicholas while Brad and I will watch over the rest of the house. Until we know what Bailey's husband is up to, I'd rather have someone else there to help keep watch."

Jorja began to feel panic set in as the reason for the conversation struck her. They were all likely in some sort of danger from a man because of an item he thought was in her possession. The very reason Officer Cooper targeted her was because she had possession of a locket that could tie him to the murder of Kat's mother. She felt her heart skip a beat when she thought about going through another incident like before. The loss of control left her feeling breathless and she suddenly stood, now in dire need for a breath of fresh air.

"What makes you think he'll come to the house when we're all home?" She struggled to stop herself from running outside to get air while she paced. "He'd be stupid to do that. He's more likely to stop by when no one is there...like right now."

Ryan nodded. "Which is exactly why I left a note on the front door."

Jorja stopped pacing. "What note?"

Ryan smiled. "A note to our housekeeper telling her to just do a light cleaning today and not to bother with cleaning this weekend because we'll all be out of town for a book fair we're taking part in up in Seattle."

"We don't have a housekeeper."

Ryan's smiled widened. "Exactly, but he doesn't know that. Before I left the house I spoke to Fritz and we came up with the idea to leave a note taped to the door where anyone can read it if they're curious enough to get close to the front door."

Jorja sat back down on the couch. She realized Ryan's plan might work. "I don't want Nicholas to be at the house this weekend. I'm going to call Ruth to see if he can stay with her. He'll have fun hanging out with Justin, I think."

Ryan nodded in agreement. "Sure, I think that's a good idea. I'll pack him a bag so that he can just go home with her and Justin after school. If that's okay with her."

"I'm sure it'll be fine." Jorja stood to use the phone to call Ruth. She immediately felt some relief with the knowledge that she could keep Nicholas from harm by letting him stay someplace else.

When she hung up the phone after making arrangements with Ruth, she turned to Ryan. "She said she'll take Nicholas home with her if you can bring him a change of clothes and a sleeping bag."

"Great. I'll head home in a little bit."

The doorbell chimed when the door opened and Fritz and Reynolds walked inside. Jorja felt an instant flush when she saw the stern look on Fritz's face. She wished she could figure out exactly what his expressions meant. She couldn't tell if he was irritated with her or concerned for her or both. Reynolds she had no problem figuring out. He approached her with a concerned expression. "We're all set. Don't worry, Jorja. We talked to the Chief and we're going to get this guy."

She could only nod as she gave an appreciative smile.

"Did you leave the note like we discussed, Ryan?" Fritz asked.

"Yep, it's there and it's very visible. If he's hanging around the neighborhood, I don't doubt he'll see it."

Curious, Jorja asked, "You're okay with this? What are we going to do? Stay someplace else or sleep at the house and just wait for him to break in?"

"I'd rather you stay someplace else, but if you don't, we'll be close by and I'm giving Ryan a radio so he can call us the minute he thinks there might be trouble."

Jorja bit her lip as she thought about whether she should let anyone force her from her home. Stubbornly she shook her head, "No, I'll stay home. We'll stay on the third floor like Ryan suggested, but you better be close by because I don't want anything to happen to Ryan or Brad."

Fritz's eyes narrowed. "Brad?" He turned to look at Brad as he asked, "Why would Brad be there?"

Brad raised an eyebrow at Fritz. "Why wouldn't I be there? I'm going to stay to help Ryan and be there for the girls when this freak decides to do what he's expected to do. You're fast, Fritz, but you're not that fast. I'll be there to help Ryan so we can take him down until you get there to take over."

Fritz returned Brad's stare and Jorja was worried Fritz might try to use his status to take charge of what Brad could or could not do. Finally, he seemed to relent to the idea. "Fine. Just watch yourself and don't do anything stupid. You don't know what this guy's capable of and we don't need anyone getting hurt."

Brad only nodded in response, but he quickly gave Jorja a boyish grin, as if he knew he had won a battle.

Jorja shook her head. *Men*, was all she could think.

Ryan stood. "So we're all set. Nicholas is going to stay with Ruth and Pete for the weekend. I'll make an appearance as I throw a few bags in my car for our pretend getaway and we'll take the car to the Chief's for the weekend. Brad will meet us there and then drive us back and park a few blocks from the house so we can all sneak back to the house through the back yard after dark tonight. I'll keep the radio with me and I'll let you know the second we hear or see anything suspicious."

Fritz stood with his arms crossed and he nodded while Ryan described the plan. He then turned to look at Jorja. He held her gaze, but said nothing. As she stared up at him, she had fleeting thoughts of how much he and Reynolds had helped her ever since the night with Officer Cooper. When she began to feel self-conscious about his stare, she broke eye contact as she fidgeted on the couch.

She heard Brad cough slightly before he said, "I think we're good. You guys get back to whatever you were doing and we'll call you when we need you."

Fritz finally tore his gaze from Jorja and she looked up again to see him shoot a look at Brad before responding, "You make sure you do."

Reynolds, who had merely watched the whole display, finally spoke up. "Jorja...Taylor... remember, we won't be too far away. Don't worry, we'll get this guy."

Taylor responded with, "Thanks, we know you will," but Jorja could only give Reynolds the best smile she could muster while her nerves threatened to take over.

When Fritz and Reynolds left the store, the four of them sat in silence as they each thought about the situation they might soon take part in. Brad finally broke the silence when he stood and said, "I think I'll run over to the café to grab some lunch for us before Ryan has to take off. Turkey clubs sound good with everyone?"

Jorja doubted she could eat, but she nodded her head anyway. She then stood as she realized she had to keep busy or the thoughts running through her mind would completely take over. She had to remind herself that this time would be different than the night with Officer Cooper. She had been alone then and when Ryan did show up, he was not prepared to meet an intruder who had no qualms about shooting him. This time she had friends and family who would be with her and who would be prepared. But as much as safety in numbers should relieve her, she couldn't quiet the anxiety she felt as she thought about putting those she cared for in any danger at all.

CHAPTER 44

Jorja tried to relax with a book, but after reading three paragraphs she realized she couldn't remember what she'd just read. She tried to look through a magazine, but the articles held no interest and the photographs didn't give her any pleasure. She threw the magazine to the floor and quickly got off the bed she'd been sitting on.

"What's wrong?" Taylor asked from the Yoga pose she was positioned in.

"How can you do Yoga right now? I can't focus on anything. This is going to drive me crazy as we wait and wonder when or if Bailey's husband will even attempt to break into the house."

"I know how you feel. It's just easier for me to focus on holding a pose rather than sit around waiting."

Jorja walked toward the door. "I'm not sure I can eat right now, but I'm going to go grab my leftover sandwich from earlier. Do you want anything?"

Taylor moved into another pose before responding, "No, I'm good for now. Maybe just grab me some more water, would you?"

Jorja nodded. "Okay, be right back."

She almost tripped over Bella, who wanted to follow her downstairs to the kitchen. "No, Bella, you stay here." Jorja gently nudged the cat back into the room as she shut the bedroom door. She had already decided it would be better if Bella stay locked up with them on the third floor so Ryan and Brad weren't tricked into thinking any noise made by the cat was made by an intruder. Piper was not as easy to hide since she might bark at any noise she heard so Jorja had decided to ask Ruth to board her overnight. While she would have preferred to keep Piper home for protection, she knew to keep it real they had to leave Piper with a friend or at a kennel, which they would have done if they had really gone away for the weekend.

Jorja moved down both flights of stairs and at the bottom landing she immediately spotted Ryan and Brad sitting in the dimly lit living room off the eat-in kitchen.

"What are you doing down here?" Ryan asked.

"I just want to get the rest of my sandwich and some water for Taylor. I'll only be a minute."

"Okay, but don't leave the fridge open long and don't turn on the light. Even with the blinds shut I worry any light we use might shine through them."

She sighed in resignation. "Don't worry, I won't."

When she moved through the living room into the kitchen, Brad reached out to grab her hand. "Jorja? You doing okay?"

She looked down at him and even in the dim light she saw the concern in his eyes. "I'm okay. Just restless and I can't wait till we don't have to worry about this guy."

Brad nodded. "We'll get him. But you need to stay upstairs. I can't think straight if I know you're down here in harm's way."

She pulled her hand away from his. "Okay, I'm going."

Jorja walked to the fridge, opened the door just enough so she could reach inside to grab her sandwich and a bottle of water and then shut the door. She pulled a paper towel from the roll on the counter and moved through the kitchen to the stairway. Her stomach growled and she realized she was actually hungry. She'd been going all day on only half a sandwich and as she moved up the staircase to the second floor, she now looked forward to finishing her meal.

But as she reached the landing on the second floor, she heard a noise. It sounded like the creaking made by the hinges of the screen door.

Jorja stopped on the landing, holding her breath. She waited to see if Ryan or Brad had also heard the noise and when she peeked over the railing, she saw Ryan crouched near the door frame of the living room, looking up at her.

The few raps on the front door made her jump, causing her to lose her grip on both the sandwich and the water bottle. She cringed as the box dropped to the floor and she did her best to cling to the water bottle, fearing the noise it could make if it rolled down the staircase. After a moment she was able to grasp the bottle and she glanced down at Ryan as she let out a sigh of relief. Even in the dim light, Jorja was certain Ryan rolled his eyes at her as he also let out a breath of relief.

She waited for any more noise and soon heard the screen door shut. Her furrow creased in confusion and she wondered whether the visitor was Bailey's husband or someone else. When she saw movement, she looked at Ryan and realized he was waving at her to go back upstairs. She hesitated, which only made him wave more forcibly at her to get moving.

Reluctantly, Jorja quickly picked her sandwich box container up off the floor and made her way back to the third-floor bedroom where Taylor was waiting for her.

When she entered the bedroom, she shut the door and leaned against it. Taylor was holding another Yoga pose, but was turned away from the door as she said, "How are the boys doing?"

When Jorja didn't respond, Taylor tried to peek at her from the position she was in. "Jorja? Is everything okay?"

"I think he might be here."

Jorja didn't think Taylor's body could tighten any more than it already was, but her frame appeared to tighten in alarm just before she released her pose to look squarely at Jorja. "You think he's already here?"

Jorja nodded. "I heard the screen door open as I was going up the stairs and then someone knocked on the door. I think he's just making sure no one's here."

Taylor swallowed hard. "Did Ryan and Brad hear it too?"

Again, Jorja nodded.

Taylor sat down on the side of the bed. "Okay, so now what do we do? Just wait?"

Finally, Jorja moved away from the door to sit by Taylor. "That's all we can do. We'll just get in the way and I don't want Ryan or Brad distracted if they have to worry about us any more than they already do."

This time, Taylor nodded. "Yeah, I know you're right, but I hate sitting up here, just waiting. What if something happens?"

"We can't think like that. Ryan has the radio and I'm sure he's already contacted Fritz and Reynolds. We have to believe that-"

Crash!

Both of them immediately jumped from the bed.

"What the heck was that?" Taylor asked as Jorja ran for the door.

Jorja opened the door a few inches and she looked back at Taylor as she tried to listen for any further noises. When they both heard yelling, Jorja opened the door the rest of the way and flew through the frame toward the staircase with Taylor right on her heels.

They ran down the second floor staircase and stopped on the landing, hesitant to run down the first flight right away. Jorja listened and could hear what sounded like muffled struggling and then someone yelled, "*Get the hell off me!*"

Jorja and Taylor glanced at each other before they both ran down the staircase and then into the living room. Seeing no one, they heard noises to their right and ran into the dining room.

"Ow!" Jorja yelled as her shin struck a hard object and she grabbed the nearby counter to stop herself from falling to the floor. Too late, she realized she had run into a dining room chair which was on its side.

"Jorja? You okay?" She heard someone yell from outside.

It took her a moment to understand why she was hearing anyone speak to her from outside. When she was able to right herself, she lifted the chair to an upright position before reaching over to turn on the dining room light, only to be shocked by the fact that her sliding glass door was gone. It was broken out and lying in pieces on the patio outside where, she could finally see, Ryan and Brad were sitting.

Jorja moved to the door frame and when she turned on the outside light, she saw Ryan and Brad sitting on top of their intruder. They were also breathing heavily and bleeding from various cuts on their faces and arms.

Jorja was quickly concerned with their injuries. "Are you two okay?"

She and Taylor both jumped slightly when the intruder suddenly moved in a futile attempt to get both men off of him. He quickly gave up and was soon breathing heavily as he whispered under his breath, "You people have no idea who you're messing with!"

Brad looked down. "No buddy, you have no idea who *you're* messing with. Stay put or I'm going to clock you good."

Ryan looked at Jorja. "We'll be fine. Just some cuts from the glass when we went through it. I don't think I have any deep cuts, do you Brad?"

Brad shook his head. "I don't think so, but even if I did, the adrenaline won't let me feel it just yet." He looked at Jorja. "Sorry about your slider. When I tackled this perp, I didn't realize we'd be flying right through the glass door. Fritz and Reynolds should be here any time. You want to make sure they can get in the front door?"

"It's okay. I don't care about the glass. I'm just glad the two of you are okay." Jorja backed away from the slider and her legs suddenly felt weak as it hit her that the danger was over.

Taylor reached over to grab her hand and gave her a reassuring smile. "It's over and everyone's safe. Come on, let's go wait for Fritz and Reynolds."

Jorja smiled in return and squeezed Taylor's hand. When the sound of a siren in the distance alerted them to the arrival of the police, they both walked toward the front of the house to meet them.

CHAPTER 45

"Daddy, how long will you look like that?" Nicholas asked.

"Like what?" Ryan responded.

"You're all scratched up. You look like Bella attacked you." Nicholas said as he stared intently at Ryan's injuries from his fall through the sliding glass door.

Jorja listened to Nicholas' question with the knowledge that Ryan wasn't going to reveal the real cause behind his injuries. Ryan had decided it best not to let Nicholas hear about someone breaking into the house and Jorja heartily agreed. Nicholas had been provided only limited information after Ryan had been shot by Officer Cooper and neither one of them wanted Nicholas to feel their home wasn't safe. Jorja was thankful both Ryan and Brad's injuries were mainly superficial and it didn't appear any of the cuts should leave lasting scars.

"Well, it was Bella I tripped over before falling into the sliding glass door, but I don't hold it against her. She was just chasing a toy mouse and having fun."

"I bet she's sorry, huh dad?"

Ryan chuckled. "I'm sure she is."

Jorja jumped when someone tapped her on the shoulder. "Miss?"

She turned to find the contractor she had hired to replace the sliding glass door staring at her with an apologetic smile. "Sorry, didn't mean to startle you. I'm done with the job. Here's a statement for the final cost of the repairs."

Jorja reached out to take the piece of paper he was holding. She quickly glanced at it to see it was exactly what he had quoted before she reached into her bag on the counter for her checkbook. As she wrote out a check she said, "I appreciate you taking care of this so soon and I really appreciate the fact that you didn't mind doing the job on a Sunday." She ripped the check from the checkbook and handed it to him.

"Not a problem. It worked out for me and I'm glad to be of help. You enjoy the rest of your day." The contractor folded the check, placed it in his upper front pocket and waved a farewell to Ryan and Nicholas as he moved toward the front door.

Jorja followed him and was surprised when the contractor opened the door, only to take a step back into the house rather than head straight outside. She then heard him say, "Ma'am," before he touched the brim of his baseball hat and walked through the door frame onto the front porch.

When Jorja caught sight of who the contractor spoke to, she was surprised to see Gail standing on the front porch still holding the screen door open.

"Hi, Gail. What can I do for you?"

Gail watched the contractor leave and then looked at Jorja. She appeared hesitant before she said, "Hi, I'm sorry to stop by unannounced, but do you have a minute?"

Jorja immediately noticed Gail had lost her cool, composed demeanor. Gail made eye contact for only a moment before finding another object to focus on as she bit her lip. Jorja's curiosity heightened a notch and she stepped back. "Sure, come inside."

Once Gail was inside the house, she immediately spotted Ryan lying on the couch in the living room. Jorja watched Gail hesitate from taking another step when she glanced from Ryan to Jorja.

"Have you met my brother, Ryan? And this is my nephew, Nicholas." Jorja said as Nicholas walked between them to the staircase. "Nicholas, can you say hello?"

Nicholas stopped, turned to look at them and broke into a grin. "Hi. Do you want to see my Lego collection? I can show you how to make a pirate ship, if you want."

Gail relaxed enough to laugh lightly as she smiled. "Thank you, Nicholas, but I need to speak to your aunt about something right now. Maybe another time?"

"Okay," he said. Then he turned his head and yelled, "Piper! Come upstairs with me!" As he ran up the stairs, it only took a moment for Piper to come charging around the corner from the kitchen, but when she spotted the new visitor, she stopped briefly to give a quick bark before sniffing Gail's shoes. Jorja heard Piper take a few sniffs before she turned to run up the stairs to catch up with Nicholas.

Gail's smile widened. "Piper reacted like she understood what Nicholas just said."

Jorja nodded. "In a way, she did. She doesn't usually go upstairs unless it's with one of us and she's gotten used to Nicholas saying when he's going up to his room. Just like the word 'walk' she also likes the word 'upstairs'."

"Well, it seems Piper is a good playmate for your nephew." Gail suddenly lost her smile. She quickly glanced at Ryan before asking, "Is there someplace we can speak in private?"

"Sure, follow me back to the formal dining room." Jorja led the way down the hall to the formal dining. Once they entered the room, she pulled out a chair and motioned for Gail to take a seat.

Gail hesitated a moment, but finally relented and sat down. She placed her purse on the floor and then intertwined her fingers before placing her hands in her lap.

Jorja waited for Gail to speak first, uncertain of the purpose for the visit. Gail returned Jorja's gaze with uncertainty of her own. Finally, Gail reached down, grabbed her purse and placed it in her lap. She opened the bag and pulled out an envelope.

"I'm not sure if I should be doing this. I know you worked for Michael and his attorney so maybe you won't believe me or you won't want to hear it, but I gave this a lot of thought and I believe you need to know the truth."

Jorja leaned forward in her chair. "The truth about what?"

Gail coughed to clear her throat. She opened the envelope and pulled out a piece of paper. "The truth about why my sister did what she did."

Jorja leaned back in her chair. "What do you mean, 'what she did'?" Are you saying you know what happened to her?"

Gail sighed heavily as she nodded. "Yes, I know."

"What happened? Are you saying she killed herself?"

"Yes."

"And that she set Michael up to be arrested for murder?"

"Yes."

"Why? Why would she take her own life and leave her remaining daughter motherless?"

Gail's chin quivered and her eyes began to tear up. "Because she didn't want Tabitha to go through what Liz went through. She was at the end of her rope. She didn't get help from the court and she knew if Michael was granted custody of Tabitha, it would be the end of that innocent sweet girl."

"What happened to Liz?" Jorja held her breath, waiting to see whether Gail would actually accuse Michael of the only crime she thought worse than murder.

Gail placed a hand over her mouth as tears rolled down her cheeks. She shut her eyes, took a deep breath and then looked at Jorja again. "He...molested Liz, that's what he did."

Jorja's chest tightened, knowing what Gail said was probably true. "How do you know that's true?"

Gail opened the paper she was holding and placed it on the table. As she used her hands to smooth out the creases she said, "Because I saw Liz's journal. I took a chance and found where Michael hid the journal in his bedroom. Liz didn't write about what happened verbatim and I wouldn't have known she was talking about her own father had I not also received a note from Cynthia. It was a note hidden in some items I received after her death. And then one day..." Gail stopped suddenly and swallowed hard before continuing, "One day I was talking to Tabitha and she actually told me that her daddy didn't love her as much as he loved Liz. When I asked her why, she told me her daddy doesn't cuddle with her at night like he did with Liz."

Gail quickly wiped at the tears running down her cheeks before continuing. "I knew it could be a long shot to prove what he did, especially since Liz and Cynthia are gone, but I decided to give him a choice and based on the choice he made, I know what my sister claims is true."

Gail pushed the paper across the table to Jorja. "Here, you can read what Cynthia wrote."

Jorja hesitated to pick up the letter. She wasn't sure she really wanted to know the truth behind why a man would willingly plead guilty to a crime he didn't commit. But she couldn't deny she needed to know now that the answer had been offered to her. She reached for the letter and silently read what had likely been the last thing Cynthia wrote before the day she died:

My dearest Gail,

I'm sorry we haven't been as close as sisters should be but please forgive me for that. It was due to my insecurities and had nothing to do with you. There is much about my life I wished to share with you but could not bear admitting to you. I hope someday you will understand. If you receive this letter, it's because the custody case did not go well today. If that happens, then you will already be grieving for me. Please don't hate me. You may not understand but believe me when I say that a mother will do anything to protect her child. You might think this to be extreme but please try to understand my reasoning. My plan is that Michael will be held accountable for my death. You will then gain custody of Tabitha and raise her as your own. Keep her safe. But if something goes wrong and my death doesn't send Michael to prison, where he should rot for the rest of his life, I need you to do what I wasn't able to do. I was never able to prove Michael hurt Liz in the most vile way possible. It's true, he defiled her. Liz never told me but she acted out in her attempt to show me something was wrong. I was just too naive to notice. After she passed away, I found her diary. Oh God, you can't imagine my horror when I realized she was speaking about her own father! My mistake was in confronting Michael myself to tell him that I had the diary. He took the diary, stole it from me, so that I had no proof against him. If I lose in court today, I have no choice. I can't let him be allowed to groom Tabitha to take the place of Liz! Please, Gail, I beg of you to help me if Michael doesn't go to jail for my death. I am betting my life, in the worst way possible, that he kept Liz's diary. He is a sick man and I can only imagine he enjoys reading it. You must find that journal and use it

320 | P . J .   H o w e l l

against him. If you can't find it, lie to him and tell him you've found other evidence. Make him take a deal and go to prison for my death or risk being labeled and imprisoned as a child molester. Either way, <u>don't</u> let him have Tabitha. Do whatever you must. Please, I'm begging you from the grave.

With all my love, Cynthia

Jorja placed the letter on the table. She felt a lump in her throat when she thought about the decision Gail made on behalf of her sister. "So you gave him a choice? What did you say to him?"

"I told him to either plead guilty to my sister's death or take the risk that his real secret be revealed which would mean going to prison as a child rapist."

Jorja's mind raced with the knowledge about why Michael had decided to take a plea bargain for a crime he didn't commit. She was now concerned with having proof of that knowledge and what she was supposed to do with it.

"Gail, you do realize, don't you, that you've blackmailed Michael into pleading to a *murder* he never committed? Do you understand this might bring trouble to you for your part in this? What am I supposed to do with this information? I don't want to be a part of your blackmail scheme. I *can't* be a part of it."

Gail frowned as she listened to Jorja. She reached over to grab the letter, but Jorja grabbed it first. "Why are you telling me this? What is it you want from me?"

Leaning back in her chair, Gail's look turned cold. "What do I want from you? I want you to know the kind of person you're working for. I want you to know the type of blood money you're accepting when you take on cases like this. I want you to know that he's *guilty* and I don't care what he pleads guilty to but he *has* to go to prison."

Jorja shook her head, saddened by the anger seeping from Gail's words. "But this isn't the way to do it. You can't blackmail him into taking a plea to a crime he didn't commit."

Gail shrugged. "I gave him an option and it was his decision to make. He'd prefer people, even his own daughter, believe he's a murderer rather than a child molester. That's his choice."

"I can't let him do that. You should know I just can't sit on this information."

Gail pushed her chair back, grabbed her bag and stood up. "You do what you must. You can speak to him about it, but you can tell him if I hear he isn't taking the deal, he will never see Tabitha again. Whether I gain custody or not, if I hear he's backed out of our deal, Tabitha and I will disappear. For good."

Jorja was speechless. She was also unprepared when Gail reached over, grabbed the letter in one swift movement and then spun on her heels before walking out of the room. Jorja got out of her chair in an attempt to catch up to Gail, but she heard the front door slam shut just as she made her way to the hallway. She stared at the door for a moment, considering her options. She was brought out of her thoughts when Ryan poked his head around the door frame and asked, "Everything okay? She seemed to fly out of here pretty quickly."

Shaking her head, Jorja said, "No, I would say things are not okay and I'm not exactly sure what to do about it."

CHAPTER 46

Jorja was still weighing her options about what to do with the information Gail dumped on her when Taylor came home later that afternoon.

"Hey, the new slider looks great. Glad the contractor was able to get here to do it, especially since it's going to get pretty cold again tonight."

Jorja absently nodded. "Um-hmm."

"I got caught up with most of the new inventory and I've left some instructions for Kat when she comes in after school tomorrow."

"Um-hmm."

Taylor looked more closely at Jorja. "And I thought it would be a great idea to invite Lydia over for dinner to talk about old times."

Jorja only mumbled, "Sounds good."

Taylor waved a hand in front of Jorja's face. "Hello, are you in there? Have you heard a word I've said?"

Jorja was startled and leaned away from the intrusion. "Huh? Oh, hi. When did you get here?"

"What do you mean when did I get here? I've been talking to you this whole time and I thought you were talking back. What's wrong with you?"

In an attempt to focus her thoughts, Jorja quickly shook her head. "Nothing. I just had an odd conversation with Michael Stafford's sister-in-law and I'm trying to figure a few things out."

"Well, I'd offer to help you figure it out, but you need to focus on something else for awhile. Fritz and Reynolds are on the way over to talk about Bailey. They stopped by the store and when I told them I was heading home, they said they'd follow me. Are you ready for some company?"

Jorja perked up at the idea that she might learn more about the status of Bailey's case and the man Ryan and Brad tackled in the dining room. "Sure, I'm ready. Ryan's upstairs so I'll go tell him to come downstairs."

By the time she returned downstairs with Ryan, Fritz and Reynolds had already arrived and were waiting in the family room with Taylor.

When Jorja entered the room, Fritz looked at her from where he was standing, but it was Reynolds who spoke to her from where he was seated next to Taylor. "Hello Jorja…Ryan. We wanted to come by to give you an update regarding Bailey and her husband. Ryan, how are you feeling?"

Ryan sat down on a chair while Jorja remained standing. "Oh, I'm fine. Just a few cuts and scrapes, but nothing compared to a bullet wound."

Jorja cringed. Even with the danger now gone, she hadn't been able to get Ryan to open up about how he was faring after two physical confrontations in the course of only a few months.

She could feel Fritz staring at her so she turned to catch his gaze. Rather than look away, he smiled at her and she smiled back. She turned back to Reynolds when he spoke again.

"So the man who broke into your house was definitely Bailey's husband, Scott Wheeler, and we've figured out what we have against him to make our case. It might not be the strongest case, but it's a case nonetheless. Remember when you had the break-in at your store, Jorja?"

She nodded in response.

"Remember the piece of material we found in the glass from what we assumed might be from the glove of whoever broke in?"

Again, she nodded.

"Well, what we didn't tell you was that some material was also found at the Chief's home on the night he was attacked. At the time, we didn't know what the material came from and when your break-in occurred over a week later, no one realized at the time that the same person might have been responsible for both crimes."

Jorja glanced at Fritz, recalling her own prediction that Bailey's husband was trying to set Bailey up for the Chief's assault.

Fritz finally spoke, "And when we took Bailey's husband into custody the other night, he was wearing a pair of gloves that matched the material taken from the scene at the Chief's and also from the break-in at your store."

Jorja finally decided she wanted to sit down. "But is that enough to prove he assaulted the Chief and not Bailey? Is Bailey going to be released and will she be allowed to stay here with Justin? Is she still wanted in Colorado?"

"It's enough to make him realize we have proof he was at both crime scenes so that we can attempt to negotiate with him." Reynolds said. "We also know he had access to Bailey's car because Bailey said he knew she always kept a hidden key after locking herself out of her vehicle more than a few times. We believe he gained access to the car to retrieve the hammer and then he used it to attack the Chief before placing it back in the car to frame Bailey."

Reynolds gave Jorja a sideways glance and she swore she saw a glint of humor in his eyes as he continued, "The day we met you and Ryan at Bailey's car, we were able to obtain video from the grocery store. We lucked out because there is footage of a man who looks like Wheeler who appears to retrieve the key from the hidden location before opening the drivers' door. What he did in the car is only an assumption since we can't clearly tell from the video, but he knows what he did so his guilt should help move things along."

Jorja wondered if the interaction between her and Fritz with the tampon box was clearly seen on that footage. She thought it might be what was now tickling Reynolds' funny bone.

Fritz added, "What we can see from the footage along with the material from the gloves found at both scenes give us plenty to work with to make him believe our case is pretty strong. And we need him to believe it, especially when Bailey is adamant she won't go back to Colorado to make him face any charges related to what was on the video tape. If the prosecutor agrees to a deal minus the charges involving Bailey, we may be able to work out a plea bargain everyone's happy with. I don't think the guy wants to go to trial. He has no friends here like he believes he does in Colorado."

Jorja was quiet while she thought about the fact that Bailey's husband would not be taking responsibility for the crimes he had committed against his own wife. She thought it was ironic that Scott Wheeler might get an offer to avoid admitting what he put his wife through when Michael Stafford was taking a plea offer for a crime against his wife he never committed.

"Does Bailey know yet?" Taylor asked.

Reynolds responded by saying, "I went to see her today to fill her in. She's very happy, as you can imagine, and she said she owes a lot to you, Jorja, and can't wait to begin working at the store for you. Did you offer her a job?"

All eyes were on her as she said, "Yes, I did. I told her she could work at the store to pay me back for any time I put into her case and then she can work for a wage once we're even." She waited, expecting Fritz to make a negative comment about the idea.

Instead, Fritz said, "She's lucky to have you in her corner." When Jorja turned to acknowledge the compliment, he suddenly looked uncomfortable. He turned from her to look at Ryan and Taylor as he continued, "She's lucky to have all of you to help her."

Jorja grinned. She knew the compliment made him uncomfortable, but she was pleased with him for saying it. Maybe now he finally understood how important her job as an investigator could be and he might cut her some slack, especially when she was certain to irritate him again the next time she worked a case he didn't approve of.

CHAPTER 47

Monday morning at the bookstore Jorja caught up on paperwork and spent some overdue time with her mom on the phone to catch her parents up on what had occurred over the weekend. She felt terrible for not having told them the news about Gabe only to have to add the fact that someone had broken into her home again. She knew her dad would be upset with her for not filling them in beforehand. She wondered if her dad might feel threatened by Gabe, but quickly shook off the notion. There wasn't anyone who could replace her dad...even her biological father. She did her best to smooth things over and ended the conversation with a promise to her parents that she would drive up to visit the following weekend.

Once the long conversation with her mom was over, Jorja hung up the phone and rubbed her ear, now stinging from having the receiver against it for so long. She had to make another call so when she picked up the receiver she had to place it against the opposite ear.

The phone rang twice before a receptionist answered, "Bates, Rather and Brown, how may I direct your call?"

"Is Eric Rather available? This is Jorja Matthews."

"I believe he is, hold please."

Jorja waited as music played over the phone. Elevator music...never been her favorite.

"Hello, Jorja. How are you?" Eric finally said over the phone.

"I'm okay, but I need to speak to you about Michael's case. An issue has come up that I believe you should be aware of. Can I come by your office later today to talk?"

There was silence on the other end and Jorja thought she had lost the call.

"Eric? Are you there?"

"I'm here. And I believe I know why you're calling."

"You do? And you're okay with it?"

"Uh...I can't say I'm okay with it, but there's really nothing I can do about it."

Shaking her head in confusion, she asked, "Well, you can refuse to let him take the offer, that's what you can do about it."

Again, silence.

"Eric?"

She heard him cough over the phone before he said, "Exactly what are you talking about?"

Leaning back in her chair, she bit her lip as she wondered whether they were actually on the same page. "I'm talking about Michael's sister-in-law, Gail. What are you talking about?"

"Oh, so she called you too? Did she tell you where he went?"

Jorja sat up. "What do you mean, where he went? He left? Where did he go?"

"I don't know. He's just gone. Fled the country is what she told me. Apparently he came by to say goodbye to her and Tabitha yesterday and told Gail he wouldn't be returning. Why she didn't call the police is what I'm wondering, especially if she knew he was fleeing to avoid taking the plea offer or going to trial. But he's gone and there's nothing I can do about it at this point because he made it clear to Gail that he was going to a country where he couldn't be extradited."

Now Jorja was silent as she took in what the attorney was telling her. She knew Gail would have been glad to hear Michael had decided to leave the country if it meant he'd never have contact with Tabitha again.

When she remained silent, Eric finally asked, "Was there something else you wanted to tell me?"

"Huh? Oh…no, I guess it doesn't matter now anyway. So what happens if he ever comes back?"

"Well, he hasn't been convicted of any crime yet. He'll remain a wanted person with regard to his wife's death and should he ever return they could continue with the case against him, but if he's been planning this since the charges were filed, he may have been able to send enough money out of the country to live on for quite awhile. If I owe you any money, send me a bill, but for now you can close out your file."

Jorja wasn't sure what to think about this unexpected news. She said goodbye to the attorney and it occurred to her that this turn of events was probably the best outcome for all involved. Not only was Michael avoiding prison time for a crime he didn't commit, she knew Tabitha could remain free from harm by her own flesh and blood. Jorja wasn't sure she liked Gail's tactics, but she knew at this point Gail wouldn't care in the least what she thought.

CHAPTER 48

"I think the book club went pretty well tonight, don't you?" Taylor asked as she and Jorja finished picking up around the bookstore.

"Yeah, it went well enough. I like the fact that our group is growing and everyone really seems to enjoy themselves. Even Lydia appears to be having fun." Jorja said, throwing some paper cups in the nearby waste basket.

"Hey, Jorja, we're just about done putting the extra chairs away. Is there anything else you need? Kat and Bruce are cleaning up the kitchen for you and I think all the leftover food has been boxed up." Brad said as he and Dylan stood near the hallway.

Shaking her head she replied, "No, I think that's it. You guys are good to go. Thanks for helping tonight, both of you."

Jorja stood where she was and looked around the bookstore. Taylor tossed some wet wipes she'd been using into the garbage before kicking off her shoes and tucking her feet under her as she sat on the couch. Dylan approached Taylor from behind the couch and he leaned over to give her an upside-down kiss. Jorja smiled as she watched them, feeling extreme happiness for both of them. She saw Kat and Bruce walk down the hallway toward the lobby and she was instantly mesmerized by their youth and all the years they still had before them to map out their future. She looked at Brad, who had found Nicholas wandering out of the children's section with a book under his arm. Brad said something to Nicholas who pulled the book from under his arm and offered it up to Brad. The two of them moved to an overstuffed chair where they sat together and where Jorja heard Nicholas share the news with Brad about the wolf he had adopted at Wolf Haven. Brad smiled at Jorja to show her how much he liked the idea and then he began to read the book to Nicholas. Jorja considered the fact that Brad was not only good with teenagers, but with all ages of children and she realized she hadn't really thought of him that way before. She shook her head slightly to remove such thoughts.

She then heard a noise behind her when both Ryan and Gabe entered the store. The two had decided to forego the book club meeting in order to have a beer together at a nearby tavern. Brad and Dylan had willingly stayed behind to help Jorja and Taylor with the meeting so that Ryan and Gabe could have some quality time together. Jorja was fighting off some jealously at the thought, but she knew she would also be spending more time with Gabe in order to work on their newfound relationship as father and daughter.

"Hey, Jorja, how'd the meeting go?" Ryan asked.

"It went fine. How about you two? Did you enjoy yourselves?"

Gabe nodded, smiling. "We had a great time. Sorry we didn't stay for the meeting, but I promise to attend next time. I want to be involved with whatever you have an interest in. I really want to make up for lost time and hopefully I'll get my uncle to be more involved too, if that's okay with you two."

Jorja smiled. "It's okay with me, but I know he might need more time to adjust his way of thinking."

Gabe laughed. "You could say that. He's the most stubborn person I know."

Jorja inwardly acknowledged to herself that she could now pinpoint where her stubborn streak probably came from. "If you two are hungry, there might be some leftover sandwiches in the kitchen if you want to look."

Ryan rubbed his hands together. "That sounds good. I wasn't tempted to try any of the food at the bar because it all looked like it was an inch thick in grease. No thank you..."

When Ryan and Gabe moved together down the hall to the kitchen, Jorja decided it was finally time to sit down. She moved to the couch and sat on the end opposite Taylor. Once Nicholas saw her, he quickly jumped from his place by Brad and scrambled onto the couch next to her.

"Aunt Jorja, do you want to read me a story?" Nicholas asked, his big brown eyes staring up at her pleadingly.

"What am I? Chopped liver?" Brad asked.

Nicholas turned to look at Brad, his brows furrowed in thought. "Why do you want to be liver? Yuck! You should be something more fun...like chicken nuggets."

Jorja smiled and ruffled his hair. "He means why do you want me to read to you instead of him?"

Nicholas looked at her. "Because I like it when you read to me, Aunt Jorja."

She looked over Nicholas' head at Brad, who grinned at her. "You can't argue with that logic, Aunt Jorja. Here..." Brad reached over to hand Jorja the book, "You can read to him."

Jorja grabbed the book and leaned back on the couch. Nicholas instantly molded his body alongside hers as he leaned his head on her shoulder.

She opened the book and imagined that with her and Ryan as role models, Nicholas would never lose his love for books. With Nicholas cuddled next to her and her friends and family around her, Jorja realized she felt completely content.

She should have known it wouldn't last long.

The bell chimed as the door suddenly burst open. When Jorja looked over the book she was holding, she was surprised to see Fritz and Reynolds. Her first thought was to joke with them for arriving late for the book club meeting, but then she saw the anxious looks on their faces and an intense stare not only from Fritz, but from Reynolds as well.

It was bad enough to see that look on Fritz.

It was worse to see the same from both.

Jorja handed the book to Nicholas as she slowly stood from the couch. Fritz didn't lose eye contact with her while he moved toward her.

She made an effort to speak, but she was suddenly afraid to know what had brought them to the store.

Brad also stood and moved to stand beside her. He was the first to ask, "What's wrong? Why are the two of you here?"

Fritz glanced at Brad before looking at Jorja again. He held her gaze as he said, "I'm afraid we have some news. It's about Cooper..."

Jorja's head began to buzz as fear weaved its way through her. A shiver also ran up her spine and she crossed her arms in an attempt to bring some warmth to her core. She found it difficult to speak, but was finally able to ask, "What about him?"

Fritz and Reynolds made eye contact briefly before Fritz turned to her with a regretful look, causing her to wish he didn't have to reveal whatever he came to say. Finally, he said, "I'm sorry Jorja. I hate to have to tell you this, but we just learned some upsetting news about Cooper. We don't have all the details yet, but somehow...Cooper has managed to escape."

And with those five words, Jorja's world once again turned upside down.

To be continued...

ABOUT THE AUTHOR

P.J. Howell grew up in a small town in Washington State and has always called the Evergreen State her home. She continues to reside in the Pacific Northwest with her husband and two sons, as well as a mix of spoiled dogs and cats. While writing has always been a passion, P.J.'s desire to write books transpired after years of working in a law firm as a legal assistant and then as a criminal defense investigator when she opened her own private investigative agency. P.J.'s interests in criminal law, investigations and mysteries, combined with her desire to bring characters and stories to life, inspired her to put the stories on paper and share them with others.

No Mother of Mine and *Best Kept Secrets* are the first two books in the Jorja Matthews Mystery Series. The novels introduce readers to life in a small town, characters anyone can relate to and what it takes to unravel the mysteries of life and crime. While P.J. chose to use her nickname for this book series, she also uses her given name in other forums. For updates, upcoming events and information relating to current and future titles, please visit her blog at www.paulajhowell.blogspot.com.